NOT JUST A GAME

ALSO BY DOUG ZIPES

Nonfiction

Into Africa

Taking Ban on Ephedra

Fiction

Stolen Hearts (short story with Joan Zipes)

The Black Widows (a novel)

Ripples in Opperman's Pond (a novel)

Medical Textbooks (coeditor, coauthor)

Comprehensive Cardiac Care (seven editions)

The Slow Inward Current and Cardiac Arrhythmias

Cardiac Electrophysiology and Arrhythmias

Nonpharmacologic Therapy of Tachyarrhythmias

Cardiac Electrophysiology: From Cell to Bedside (six editions)

Treatment of Heart Diseases

Catheter Ablation of Cardiac Arrhythmias

Antiarrhythmic Therapy: A Pathophysiologic Approach

Arrhythmias and Sudden Death in Athletes

Heart Disease: A Textbook of Cardiovascular Medicine (six editions)

Electrophysiology of the Thoracic Veins

Sudden Death: A Handbook for Clinical Practice

Clinical Arrhythmology and Electrophysiology (two editions)

Electrocardiography of Arrhythmias

Medical Articles

More than 850 authored/coauthored

NOT JUST A GAME

DOUG ZIPES

NOT JUST A GAME

iUniverse books may be ordered through booksellers or by contacting:

iUniverse
1663 Liberty Drive
Bloomington, IN 47403
www.iuniverse.com
1-800-Authors (1-800-288-4677)

ISBN: 978-1-4917-9025-0 (sc)
ISBN: 978-1-4917-9026-7 (hc)
ISBN: 978-1-4917-9027-4 (e)

Library of Congress Control Number: 2016904487

Print information available on the last page.

iUniverse rev. date: 4/26/2016

I dedicate this book to the many athletes who have given their lives to their sport—literally and figuratively—especially to the Munich Eleven and to the families and friends who have supported them. I want to recognize the role of Ankiee Spitzer, whose courageous fight may have finally gotten the IOC to do what is right.

The time you won your town the race,
We chaired you through the market place;
Man and boy stood cheering by,
And home we brought you shoulder-high.
Today, the road all runners come,
Shoulder-high we bring you home,
And set you at your threshold down,
Townsmen of a stiller town.

—A. E. Housman, "To an Athlete Dying Young"

Young bones heal
Minds not so well;
Crippled by lies
Their fathers tell.

—Peter Jacobus

ACKNOWLEDGMENTS

I am indebted to Amy Orlando, competitive USFA A-rated épée fencer, member of the US Summer National Gold Medal Team, NCAA Fencing Championship Team, and the World University Team and winner of many titles. Amy taught me all I know about épée fencing and made major suggestions for the fencing bouts Kirsten fought. Any mistakes are mine.

My usual brain trust read drafts, picked up errors, and made great suggestions: Clair Lamb, Michael Rosen, Peter Jacobus, Patrick Perry, Marilynn Wallace, and my children—Debra, Jeffrey, and David. As always, my wife, Joan, did the yeoman's work, at home and for the novel.

CONTENTS

Chapter 1 1
Chapter 2 5
Chapter 3 12
Chapter 4 16
Chapter 5 20
Chapter 6 28
Chapter 7 36
Chapter 8 42
Chapter 9 50
Chapter 10 52
Chapter 11 63
Chapter 12 71
Chapter 13 77
Chapter 14 82
Chapter 15 91
Chapter 16 99
Chapter 17 110
Chapter 18 113
Chapter 19 116
Chapter 20 125
Chapter 21 132

Chapter 22 138
Chapter 23 142
Chapter 24 149
Chapter 25 153
Chapter 26 159
Chapter 27 162
Chapter 28 165
Chapter 29 172
Chapter 30 182
Chapter 31 188
Chapter 32 197
Chapter 33 203
Chapter 34 209
Chapter 35 215
Chapter 36 221
Chapter 37 225
Chapter 38 237
Chapter 39 245
Chapter 40 252
Chapter 41 259
Chapter 42 264
Chapter 43 268
Chapter 44 273
Chapter 45 280
Chapter 46 284
Chapter 47 288
Chapter 48 291
Chapter 49 296
Chapter 50 299

CHAPTER 1

TEL AVIV, JUNE 1989

"IT'S A GIRL! TEN TINY FINGERS AND TOES AND a beautiful face," Adam told his mother as he drove her from the assisted-living community to the Ichilov Hospital in central Tel Aviv. "Your new granddaughter has your smile, complete with dimples, Dannie's blonde hair, and my blue eyes." Adam thought for a moment. "Her hair's more red than blonde. She's the prettiest baby ever."

Traffic was light. He glanced at his mother. She had lost more weight in the past month. Or was it two months since he had seen her? Not remembering triggered guilt pangs, but his law practice was so busy. He'd taken her to the best heart doctors in Israel, but he thought maybe he should take her to the States. Visit Mayo or Hopkins? He owed her so much. How could he ever repay it? A granddaughter was a start, and that made him feel good.

Gretchen laughed, a happy sound. "So says every father. But finally I get to hold my grandchild," she said, rocking her folded arms back and forth, fingers twitching. "I've been waiting for this a long time."

Adam smiled. "It's never too late."

"Seemed you took forever," Gretchen said.

He nodded. No need to explain the difficulties of a middle-aged man trying to have a baby with a young wife.

"And what will you name her?" Gretchen asked, getting out of the car with Adam's assistance.

"We haven't decided yet."

Almost eighty, Gretchen was frail, her heart failing since the second heart attack. Her cheekbones, always prominent, now seemed like angular bumps in a fragile, sunken face. When Adam had asked if she was getting enough to eat, she laughed. "You know the story about the Jewish mother waiting for her son to call?" He shook his head. "She lost weight because she stopped eating so she wouldn't have a mouthful of food when the phone rang."

Adam had moved her to a residential complex two years earlier so she could receive around-the-clock attention. Though she dressed with care, clothes once a perfect fit now hung from her bony frame.

Adam had a curbside wheelchair ready. He eased Gretchen in and pushed her to the maternity wing. Broad shouldered and trim from daily workouts, Adam moved with an athlete's grace, maneuvering the chair along a crowded hallway. His cobalt blue eyes and thick, dark hair still turned heads as young nurses walked by.

At Dannie's room, Gretchen insisted on standing. Adam helped her out of the chair, holding it steady with one hand, the other cupped under her elbow. She walked slowly to the bed where Dannie cradled her daughter at her breast. The baby was a tiny pink bundle, only her silky reddish-blonde hair showing. Dannie's cherub face, rounded from the pregnancy, showed exhaustion from the twelve-hour labor.

When Adam had left this morning to get his mother, Dannie's blonde hair had been soaked with sweat, hanging in wet strands clinging to her forehead. He had passed two nurses as they entered her room with fresh towels, washcloths, and a change of bedclothes. Dannie now looked beauty-parlor fresh with pink lipstick and rosy cheeks, wearing a soft white robe. She glowed with a new mother's look of love and patted a place beside her for Gretchen to sit.

"We were expecting a boy, so we're not quite prepared for this," Dannie said. "We already painted her room blue." Dannie moved over to make room on the bed. The baby lost her nipple and squirmed, grunting until she found it again.

Gretchen sat on the edge of the bed and caught her breath. Her dress hiked up, showing knobby knees and varicose veins. She quickly rearranged it to cover them. After a moment, she leaned over and stroked soft cheeks busy puckering and relaxing at Dannie's breast.

She turned to her son. "How about Kirsten, after your grandmother?"

Adam looked to Dannie for a response.

"Wonderful idea." Dannie smiled and nodded. "This hungry little bundle," she said, caressing the baby's downy crown in the midst of slurping and suckling noises, "will be Kirsten."

"I like that name," Adam said, pulling up a chair beside the bed.

"What was your grandmother like?" Dannie asked Adam.

Adam shrugged and looked at his mother. "I don't remember much. Mom?"

"She was Austrian and lived in some small town near the German border. But I don't know for sure," Gretchen said. "I know she went crazy before she died and was buried near her home. It was in the early 1930s, before the war." She turned to Adam. "Your dad was training for the '36 Olympics at the time. Dietrich didn't talk much about the funeral when he came home. There was no inheritance, so he buried her, and that was it. We never talked about her again."

"What about your grandfather?" Dannie asked.

Adam again looked at his mother.

"I only know he left your grandmother while she was still pregnant, before your father was even born. Just disappeared and never returned."

"A one-night stand?" Dannie asked.

"I guess something like that. She never married. That I know."

"But Grandmother Kirsten was Jewish, yes?" Adam knew the mother's religion determined the child's. One could always be certain who the mother was.

"Of course, which is why both you and your dad were circumcised," Gretchen said. "And your father being an Olympian was more important to the Germans than the fact we were Jews, so we were protected during the war."

Gretchen shook her head, as if to clear it of these memories. "Enough with the past. This little bundle"—she patted the baby's freshly diapered bottom—"is all about the future."

"I agree. In fact …" Adam let the sentence hang and sat on the edge of his chair, watching Dannie cradling Kirsten, now fast asleep.

"What?" Dannie and Gretchen asked.

Adam tried to hide a grin. He stood and walked about the small room. He picked up the picture of his new daughter cradled by Dannie, already printed by the hospital photographer and set in a silver frame on the small night table. A beautiful touch, he thought, especially if it were a free perk. He had his doubts.

Looking at the picture, he said, almost to himself, "Suppose—just suppose—this little bundle became an Olympic athlete."

Dannie knew where her husband was going. She smiled. "A fencer?"

"I don't understand. You two are moving too fast for me to keep up," Gretchen said.

Adam set the picture down, went over to his mother, and put his hand on her shoulder. "The Olympics, Mom. Wouldn't it be wonderful if Kirsten grew up to become an Olympian? For the Munich athletes and for my father—her grandfather Dietrich." He pointed at his new daughter. "Maybe a fencer, to celebrate Levi Frankel's life, or a runner, for Father." He knew it was far-fetched, planning an Olympic career for a daughter not even a day old, but he couldn't help dreaming. Maybe it would help lessen his pain, his guilt.

"Do you suppose Sharon would teach her?" Dannie asked.

A big smile lit Gretchen's face as the enormity of his vision sank in. "Dare we even think about it? Dream about it? Your father would've liked that, Adam. Fencer or track star, it doesn't matter. An Olympian medal winner, that's what Dietrich would've wanted, what would've mattered to him. Gold, silver, or bronze. Any medal would liberate that man's tortured soul."

Gretchen bowed her head, her forehead touching the pink blanket that swaddled her granddaughter. Softly, she said, "Please, dear God, let this little bundle of joy accomplish that. Touch Kirsten with your special love so she can redeem her grandfather's reputation and make her father proud."

"Amen," Adam and Dannie said together.

CHAPTER 2

BERLIN, SPRING/SUMMER, 1936

DIETRICH'S BREATH WAS RAGGED, BURNING, AND the pain in his legs excruciating, like hot metal boiling beneath his skin. It started in his instep, each time his track shoes hit the street surface, and traveled up his calves and shins, into his thighs. Those bulky muscles, two inches bigger than they'd been three years before, screamed for relief, for oxygen and more blood, but he wouldn't stop, couldn't stop. He imagined others around the globe doing the same, training as hard for the gold. He drove himself through the wall of agony, knowing if he kept running, the pain would lessen.

"Go, Dietrich, run—don't stop. You can do it," Lutz urged, running alongside. "Another kilometer, and we can rest for water before we start the sprints."

"Don't know if I can make it," Dietrich panted, glancing at Lutz barely breathing hard. He gritted his teeth and concentrated on the rhythm of his feet pounding the road. The thud was like his heartbeat: *lub-dub, lub-dub, left-right, left-right.*

His thoughts went to Jesse Owens, as they did so often now that the Olympics were approaching. Jesse was his major competitor, and Dietrich tried to copy him. He had read an article about the track star. "From the air, fast down, and from the ground, fast up," Owens had said, focused on his feet spending as little ground time as possible. "Like running on hot coals."

But that had been easier to do five years ago, and still easier five years before that. Then, at age twenty, Dietrich could run all day, outpace dogs and even horses for short distances. He lost only twice in almost one

blond hair and blue eyes, a ready smile, and a sense of fairness. A tough competitor, he displayed maturity beyond his years.

Lutz had become Dietrich's best friend, but the two had argued more than once over the importance of the Olympics. They did so again at the beginning of their run today.

"Dietrich, yes you have to train hard, but after all, it's just a game," Lutz said. "Remember—that's why they're called Olympic *games*. Keep it in perspective."

"Easy for you to say. You're going to be a lawyer. If I don't win—" He left the sentence unfinished.

The discussion had ended when they began their run. But a banner hanging from a streetlamp as they approached Pariser Plaz an hour later reminded Dietrich of their conversation. Dietrich used it as an excuse to stop and rest.

Both were breathing hard and dancing on their toes to keep muscles warm and loose. After a moment, Dietrich controlled his breathing enough to speak.

"Look around you, Lutz," he said, pointing to the black and red swastikas hanging from every flagpole and the banners shouting Deutschland Über Alles and Alles für Deutschland in every storefront window.

"Hitler guaranteed the world we will dominate the competition. These aren't just games, Lutz; these are battles in a different kind of war. Can you imagine if that American Negro, Owens, beat us?"

Lutz stopped running in place and listened to his friend.

"I read that in his country, Owens can't eat at the same restaurants as his teammates or sleep in the same hotels," Dietrich said. "Hitler didn't want them to compete at all—no Jews or blacks in the races."

"True, and the United States threatened to boycott the Olympics if he did. Dietrich, you don't really believe any of that bullshit, do you? Between us, I know why you say those things."

"You do?"

"Yes. I also know why Hitler says those things," Lutz said. "Propaganda, so he can unite all Germans behind him. Hitler isn't even German. He's

Austrian. And I've heard rumors he has Jewish blood—a grandmother or grandfather. His blue eyes are about the only Aryan thing he's got. And that stupid little mustache. Like he glued a broken comb to his lip. I bet he doesn't believe those dumb signs any more than we do."

Dietrich clamped his hand over Lutz's lips and pressed down, his eyes fearful, scanning the neighborhood. "Are you crazy, Lutz? Are you absolutely mad, saying those things in public? Do you want to get us arrested? My God, man."

They both stiffened as they heard the distant synchronous hammering of jackboots on pavement. Down the road, Dietrich could make out the rigid, goose-stepping march of a group of brown-shirted storm troopers turning from Friedrichstrasse onto Unter den Linden, where they stood. At least thirty marched as one—stiff-legged, right arms swinging to the same height, rifles on left shoulders, eyes straight ahead, and kepi caps pulled low over foreheads. Heels nailed the street in unison, almost shaking the buildings.

"Oh, shit, not now," Dietrich murmured, his face blanching. "Just let them pass." He took his friend by the arm and spun him away from the street, facing the pedestrian mall.

"Hey, you two. Over here," the captain of the storm troopers ordered, halting his troops.

They didn't move.

"Now!"

"Do what he says, Lutz. We don't want any trouble," Dietrich whispered, still holding Lutz's arm.

"What kind of trouble? We haven't done anything wrong." Lutz pulled loose.

"Maybe the guy heard what you just said."

"Impossible. They were still around the corner," Lutz said. He turned and shouted back, "What do you want?"

The captain stood hands on hips, studying first one, then the other. He pointed with a short brown leather riding crop. "What are you doing? Get over here."

"It'll be okay, Dietrich," Lutz muttered, putting his hand on his friend's shoulder to guide him. "Just act natural." Louder—"We're coming."

They walked to the captain and stopped in front of him. The captain stared at Lutz for several moments, then at Dietrich, slapping the crop into his open-gloved hand. Brow creased, he turned back to Lutz.

"I know you," he said, pointing the crop at Lutz and jabbing him lightly in his chest. "You're the track star, aren't you? Your picture was just in Der Stürmer for winning the German long jump."

Lutz reached across the crop and held out his hand. "I'm Lutz Long, Captain." He nodded at Dietrich. "This is my friend Dietrich Becker. We're both training for the Olympics in August, me in the long jump, and Dietrich in the sprints."

"To win for the Fatherland," Dietrich added, bobbing his head up and down. His face had regained color, but his fingers trembled as he shook the captain's hand. If the captain noticed, he didn't comment.

"Okay, then," the captain said. "I wondered why you weren't in the army or marching here with us." He swept his hand toward his troops. "But training for the Olympics is acceptable." He smiled. "We'll win our war; you win yours."

"Thank you, Captain," Dietrich said. "Maybe after the Olympics we will join you." He prayed that would not happen. He'd rather die. Just their presence gave him chills. He walked blocks out of his way to avoid crossing paths with any Brownshirts.

"I hope so. I wish you good luck in your competition." His look became stern. "Show them German superiority."

"We'll do our best, Captain, I promise you," Lutz said.

"Heil Hitler," the captain said, saluting with a stiff right arm and clicking his heels. Both men followed suit and let their arms drift downward as the captain abruptly turned away and marched off with his men.

Dietrich collapsed on the curb. "My heart's pounding like I just ran the two hundred meter. Christ, that was close."

"Close for what, Dietrich? He was just making conversation."

"Maybe so, but I don't like those storm troopers. They scare me."

"Why?"

"Lutz, Germany scares me now that Hitler's chancellor. About him being Austrian or part Jewish? None of that matters anymore. If he says he's Aryan, then he is. No Jewish blood, it becomes a fact. If he says we're superior, then we are, and we have to behave that way." Dietrich pulled his shoulders back, inhaled, and stood tall. Lutz punched him playfully in the gut, and Dietrich exhaled with a *whoosh.*

"So, what do you think will happen if you lose the sprints to Owens?" Lutz asked.

They walked to the park and sat on a wooden bench. Gentle breezes stirred the leaves and cooled their sweaty bodies. A warm afternoon May sun breathed life into the green grass and bright yellow daffodils.

Dietrich ran his fingers through his thinning hair and massaged his scalp. "I don't know, and I don't want to think about it. Not yet. August is still two and a half months away. But that's why I train so hard. It's easy for you. You're seven years younger, like Owens. That makes a huge difference. I don't know why they picked me to run. There're so many younger guys."

"They picked you because you were a superstar and will become one again. The age thing is in your head. You're the same guy who never lost a race in university."

"Not true. I lost twice," Dietrich said.

"I never told you this, but you were my idol growing up. I had a scrapbook with all the newspaper stories about you, and I tried to be like you. You think we just happened to start running together? I *asked* the training center to team us up."

Dietrich grinned. "Show me that scrapbook."

"After you beat Jesse Owens, I'll *give* it to you. You can keep it alongside the gold medal you're going to win. Frame them both."

They chatted until the urge to run sprints evaporated with their sweat. They walked back to the training center together to clean up and change. Dietrich waited until Lutz finished showering. He walked through the training center, checking the rooms. When he was sure he was alone, he undressed and took his shower.

shaking hands and returning the smile. “Who’s your friend?” he asked, nodding at Dietrich.

“Dietrich Becker. You’ll race against him tomorrow.”

Lutz waved Dietrich to come over and join them, but Dietrich didn’t move.

Jesse said to Lutz, “That was an incredible jump you pulled off to qualify. Must’ve been close to an Olympic record.”

“Yes,” said Lutz, grinning. “It *was* a new record, but it won’t matter if I don’t beat you.”

“One more foul, and I’ll be gone. Then you won’t have to worry.”

“That’s what I came to talk to you about. I don’t want you to foul out. I want to compete against you so when I win, I will have beaten the best. Will you let me make you a slight suggestion?”

Jesse’s eyebrows rose.

“It’s okay, really. You can trust me. And if you don’t want to take my advice, you don’t have to,” Lutz said.

“What suggestion?” Jesse asked, his voice tentative.

“The judges are calling fouls very close against non-Germans.”

“Tell me,” Jesse said. “Especially the fat German guy. My first run wasn’t even a jump attempt.”

“I know. I saw it. But then you did fault on the second. That was a fair call,” Lutz said. “Maybe I can help you.”

Lutz looked over at Dietrich, who was shaking his head. Lutz ignored him.

“Like what?” Jesse asked again.

“Maybe jump a few inches *before* the takeoff marker? Your jumps are so long, you will still qualify. That way you will not foul.” Lutz saw Jesse’s eyes squint, suspicion in his face.

“Thanks, Lutz. I’ll think about it.”

The two men shook hands and parted. Jesse walked off a few yards to ready himself for his last qualifying jump. He looked back at Lutz talking with Dietrich, surrounded by autograph seekers.

Shaking off the feeling the German was setting him up, Jesse ran several ten-yard sprints to loosen his leg muscles, completed a few deep-knee bends and jumps in place, stretched his hamstrings and gastrocs, and thought about what he'd do.

When the official called his name for his final qualifying attempt, he still hadn't decided.

CHAPTER 4

JESSE OWENS WALKED TO THE LONG JUMP RUNWAY and paced off the distance from the beginning of his run to the foul line. Twenty-two strides at peak acceleration would bring him to the eight-inch-wide wooden board that marked the end of the runway. Stepping past it left a mark on the puttylike material after the board and would finish him. The crowd, sensing the American sensation might be eliminated, was on its feet, yelling, "Go home, American. Go home." Jesse tried to dial them out, but the booing penetrated. *Not like home*, he thought. He couldn't eat at the same restaurant with white folks, but at least he wasn't booed.

His mind whirred with Lutz's suggestion. Should he do it? The jump, no matter where he started it, was measured from the board to wherever he landed. He figured he had to jump at least twenty-three feet to make the cut—longer to be certain, and still longer if he jumped before the runway's end. And the jump would be harder because he would be pushing off from a flat surface and not the board.

His heart pounded. The noise from the huge crowd, the uncertainty of what to do and possibly being eliminated, and the stress of his first Olympics were all taking a toll. He was sweating, and he hadn't even started his run.

He heard the official call his name. He saw that Lutz and Dietrich were standing off to the side, watching. He tried to read their expressions to figure out if they were hoping he'd fail or succeed, but their faces revealed nothing discernible.

Jesse paused at the top of the runway, balancing on his toes, his mind in turmoil. *What should I do?* The official waved to him to begin. Still unsure, he started his twenty-two steps.

"Feet fast down, fast up," he said to himself, as he pounded down the runway and accelerated to maximum speed. He could see the foul line approaching—should he or shouldn't he? He concentrated on his last two strides, the penultimate being the longest before he lowered his center of gravity, and his dominant right leg pushed off the shorter, final step.

But where should I put that one? From the board or inches before? he agonized.

His mind constricted, focused, as athletic instinct honed over hours and hours of practice took control. The crowd disappeared, and there was nothing but the runway.

His feet decided, *fast down, fast up* as his right track shoe hit three inches short of the wooden board.

He launched at a perfect twenty-degree angle, kicking off and swinging both arms forward to increase his forward momentum, churning his feet in midair. As he landed, he fell forward so his heel prints, not his body falling backward, marked the first break in the smooth sand.

Jesse rolled over, stood, and brushed sand from his body. He heard the roar of the crowd once again. They were on their feet, screaming. The official measuring the jump smiled. "Twenty-three feet, six inches. Nice work, American. You're in."

Jesse threw his arms skyward, exultant and relieved. Lutz left Dietrich standing on the sidelines and rushed over. He crushed Jesse in a giant bear hug and lifted him in the air. A big grin lit up his face as he danced in a circle holding Jesse.

This was a first for Jesse. Never had another athlete hugged him or danced with him, especially a white athlete.

"Congratulations, my new American friend. Now let's see what you have left for the finals."

The two slugged it out that hot afternoon. The rest of the jumpers knew they were only competing for bronze. Jesse and Lutz broke Olympic records five times as the lead shifted back and forth. Finally, Jesse jumped twenty-five feet, ten inches and flashed Lutz a triumphant look. But Lutz matched the jump, dusted himself off, and flipped Jesse a quick smile and mock salute.

"So, American, I gave you some good advice to qualify, but you'll have to do better to beat me for the gold."

"Not to worry. Gold is going home with me."

Lutz's next three jumps all fell short of twenty-six feet.

Jesse liked the German, but it was time to end the competition. "This is it, Lutz. You'd better be happy with silver, because the only gold you'll get is if you pick my pocket."

Pumped with surging adrenalin, Jesse tore down the runway for his final jump. Again the crowd disappeared, and there was nothing but runway. Fists clenched, he pummeled the air as he charged, a boxer raining body blows. His eyes were pinpoint in concentration, brow furrowed, and lips compressed. His neck veins bulged with the strain, engorged almost to bursting.

Counting his steps carefully, Jesse hit the board at full stride. His legs churned the air, and his wiry body strained forward, aerodynamically perfect. A gentle cross breeze blew, neither helping nor hurting, but Jesse didn't feel it. His seamless liftoff carried him twenty-six feet, five and a half inches, a new Olympic world record that would remain unbroken for the next quarter century.

As Jesse stood and brushed off the sand, he saw Lutz watching from the sidelines. Lutz shook his head, a resigned look on his face. But he came running over, the first to congratulate him, and they walked off arm in arm to ear-shattering cheers from the crowd.

Hitler rose from his seat and waited until most spectators were looking at him. He turned his back on the black and blond twosome and stormed out of the stadium with his entourage, leaving the viewing box empty.

The press mobbed the pair before they reached the dressing room, capturing them in a tight circle.

"What do you think, American?" a reporter asked. "You set a new world's record and beat Germany's best jumper."

Jesse grinned at Lutz and faced the reporter. "You can melt down all the medals and cups I have, and they wouldn't be a plating on the twenty-four-carat friendship I feel for this man I met only hours ago." He wrapped his arm around Lutz's shoulder and reached for his hand. Lutz wiped a tear from his cheek, shook Jesse's hand, and smiled.

"Anything you want to say?" the reporter asked Lutz.

"Our jumps said it all. Thank you very much."

Later that day, standing on the winner's podium to receive his gold medal, Jesse saluted the American flag while the band played "The Star-Spangled Banner." Lutz, a silver medal hanging from his neck, raised the Nazi stiff arm to Hitler's vacant box. As he looked at the flag, Jesse remembered the prejudices he endured in the United States. Maybe a gold medal would change all that. But deep down, he didn't think it would.

CHAPTER 5

"LUTZ, WHAT WILL YOU DO NOW?" DIETRICH asked, sipping his coffee.

Lutz bit into his lamb chop and chewed for a moment before answering.

"Do? I'll keep competing, Dietrich. I've got a few good years left. Right now, though, I just want to finish dinner, drink my beer, and go to bed. It's been a long day."

Dietrich persisted. "If you didn't give Owens the tip, he might've fouled out, and you'd be sitting here with the gold." Dietrich looked petulant, his brow wrinkled and lips pursed. "Maybe he would've felt so bad he would've gone home."

Lutz shook his head and put down his fork. "You'd like that, wouldn't you, so you wouldn't have to race him tomorrow. The reality is he would've pulled himself together and qualified with his last jump without my help. He knew what he had to do without me telling him. What I did was the right thing. I told you before, Dietrich, it's a game—never forget that. A friendship's worth more than the medal. Besides, silver in the Olympics is pretty respectable. It's not like I was a disgrace to Germany."

Dietrich dismissed the remarks with a hand flip. "No, not true. Gold, that's what the führer said, Lutz. Gold. This is a war, like I told you. We're just fighting without guns or killing people." He toyed with a napkin, folding and unfolding, distracted. "Did the führer shake your hand?"

"No, he only congratulated German gold winners. He didn't shake Owens's hand either," Lutz said.

"I wouldn't expect him to shake the hand of a Negro, but if silver's so respectable, Hitler should have shaken your hand. He didn't so much as give you a nod."

Lutz didn't respond.

"He didn't, Lutz, because silver's not so good—it's not acceptable." Dietrich shook his head to emphasize his point. "One of my friends said Hitler was angry at you. Someone told him you and Owens were pals, and that's when he left the stadium."

Lutz spread his hands, palms upright. "Not much I can do about that. Jesse and I are friends, and I'm proud of that. Hitler probably saw me talking with him and didn't like me talking to a Negro."

Dietrich, contemplative, brought his fist to his mouth and chewed on a knuckle. "He's good, isn't he?"

"Owens? The best. He moves with a dancer's grace. Nothing's forced. When I see him jump, I think of a cheetah chasing an antelope. It's that beautiful."

Lutz watched Dietrich play with his food. Still hungry, he speared the remaining lamb chop from Dietrich's plate. Dietrich didn't even look up.

"Nervous about tomorrow? Jesse's pretty good in the sprints."

"I really needed to hear that. Thanks a lot, Lutz."

"Just joking. Relax. You're pretty good too, you know."

Dietrich pushed his plate aside and stared off into the distance. The sun was setting, and a sliver of moon competed with the bright orb disappearing over the horizon.

"Yes, I'm nervous. I need to win. Silver won't do."

"A game, Dietrich. Remember it's *just a game*."

Dietrich grimaced. "Not for me. It's so much more. Not just what the führer said or expects, but it's three years of my life. Three years of somebody in the training center supporting my family and me. I don't even know who it was, but I can't let him down. Even worse, I don't know what I'll do if I lose."

"You go back to your regular life, same as before."

"Ha, right. An accountant—if they take me back. You at least will be a lawyer. No, if I lose to that black man, nothing for me will ever be the same again. Nothing."

Dietrich felt nauseated. He'd slept barely four hours, was up by six o'clock, and tried to swallow bacon and eggs at the German athletes' training table. The greasy food went down—and came up an hour later. He knew he had to remain hydrated, but his stomach accepted nothing, not even water. He went outside for a walk in the warm morning sun to calm his nerves. He stretched and practiced bolting from starting blocks in response to an imaginary starter's pistol. He wanted to run short-distance sprints to loosen up, but the bathroom called him back before he had a chance.

Finally, feeling drained, he walked to the Olympiastadion. His heart pounded as soon as he saw Jesse Owens running short spurts on the track. Lutz, who had been watching Jesse, trotted over to Dietrich.

"So, my friend, how was your night?"

"Awful, Lutz. Yours?"

"Slept like a baby with my silver medal tucked under my pillow. But I'm not running against Jesse Owens today."

"Whose friend are you, anyway?"

"Yours, of course. Come on, pal. I'm trying to lighten up your mood a little. I'm here to cheer you on to your victory for the führer." Lutz pointed at the booth. "He's watching, you know."

Dietrich blocked the sun with his hand, looked up, and saw Hitler staring down at him—or at least he seemed to be. "You think he's really looking at me?"

"He's sure not looking at me. After all, I only won silver. Why don't you give him a salute and see if he returns it."

Dietrich frowned at Lutz. "Are you serious?"

"Of course. Try it and see. What've you got to lose?"

Dietrich faced Hitler's box, stood at attention, clicked his heels, and gave Hitler the Nazi salute. Hitler half-raised his right hand, the wrist limp, and appeared to nod at Dietrich.

"Oh, my God. Did you see that, Lutz? He *was* looking at me. He responded."

Lutz smiled. "I bet he's confident you're going to beat Owens, even if I couldn't."

"Just what I need, a little more pressure."

"Is Gretchen here?" Lutz asked.

"No. She couldn't find anyone to watch Adam."

"Sorry about that."

"Maybe it's just as well," Dietrich said, his face clouding. He really had wanted her to come and was angry she hadn't found a babysitter.

The starter's voice interrupted their conversation. "Participants in the hundred-meter race, please take your positions."

Dietrich felt the blood drain from his face and go white with panic.

"Relax, my friend," Lutz said, putting his arm around Dietrich. "You've been racing almost your entire life. This is just one more."

"Yeah, right, Lutz. Just another race. Like I said last night, if I lose, everything changes. I'll probably have no job, but worse, I'll have let the Reich down."

Lutz shrugged. "Then don't lose."

Dietrich walked to the track. The hundred-meter race was run on the home stretch of the four-hundred-meter oval, with the start set back on a short extension so the race could be run in a straight line. Dietrich took his time walking over, making the other runners wait for him and think about their start. The runners milled around nervously, bouncing on the balls of their feet, adrenaline practically oozing from their pores. Dietrich nodded at Jesse Owens as he passed by but didn't greet him by name.

"Take your marks," the starter said.

The eight runners moved to assigned lanes, stepped into their starting blocks, and put their hands down on the starting line. Dietrich was in lane two, next to Owens in lane one. He glanced at the black man. *How can I beat this American?* he thought. *I must fight with every fiber in me.*

"Get set," came the command. They all crouched into launch positions—no movements allowed at this point, not even a head nod or twitch until the gun went off.

Dietrich bolted forward. The gun boomed a fraction of a second after he left the starting blocks.

"False start," yelled the official, jabbing his finger at Dietrich and waving his hands in the air, signaling no race. "One more, and you're disqualified."

"*Scheisse*!" Dietrich said. Shit! He faced Jesse. "Sorry." Jesse returned a grim smile, then stood, jogged in place a couple of seconds, and leaned forward to stretch his back.

After a brief pause, the starter repeated, "Get set." The runners resumed their crouches, hands on the line, feet in the starting blocks.

Bang!

Jesse flew off his blocks, surging forward so fast Dietrich could feel the wind he generated. Dietrich followed, a step behind already. He tried to elbow Jesse as he passed, but he was out of reach.

Dietrich ran as hard as he could, *feet fast down, fast up*, as Jesse was doing. Ahead of him, he could see Jesse's perfectly formed calf muscles tense and relax with each stride that took him farther into the lead. From the corner of his eye, Dietrich saw the field surge past him. He stifled a cry, lowered his head, and dug into the track with every ounce of his being. But after the first five seconds, he realized it was hopeless.

The runners sprinted madly to the finish line. No strategies, just all-out running. Jesse reached a top speed exceeding twenty-five miles per hour. The race was over almost before it began. It left the crowd gasping.

The starter's pistol had triggered a huge photoelectric stopwatch mounted near the Marathon Gate so all could see the results instantly.

Jesse had set a new world record at 10.3 seconds. He was officially the world's fastest human.

Dietrich finished sixth. Crossing the finish line, he fell to his knees, head in his hands. Bile-tasting saliva poured into his mouth, and he struggled not to vomit. Dietrich didn't have the courage to look into the stands at Hitler's booth. He could almost feel the heat of the führer's fury. When a hand touched his shoulder, Dietrich startled and stared into Lutz's face.

"Not your best shot, Dietrich. I'm sorry. You didn't have it today. Maybe the bad night?"

Dietrich sobbed as he fought to catch his breath. "Goddamnit, Lutz. Goddamn that black guy. He's lightning. Even on a good day, there's no way—"

"I know. Too bad your false start didn't rattle him."

Dietrich jumped to his feet and grabbed Lutz's shoulders, jaw thrust forward. "What're you saying? That's an ugly accusation."

"C'mon, Dietrich. You're talking to your best friend." He gently pried Dietrich's hands from his shirt. "I know you. You hoped it would make Owens more cautious, make him wait an extra fraction of a second to be sure he heard the starting gun before running. But that didn't work. Nor did your elbow."

Dietrich shrugged, knowing his face gave him away. "He was too quick. I did the best I could."

"Yes, you did. And I'm proud of you for that. You see, I am your friend." Lutz paused a moment and said, "What about the two hundred meter tomorrow? Will you race?"

Dietrich's shoulders sagged, any remaining signs of bravado melting away. "I'm scheduled to, but I don't know. Owens is sure to run away with it. And there's a second American black runner who's pretty good also. Robin somebody—has a younger brother who's supposed to be a pretty good athlete too."

Lutz nodded. "Mack Robinson. I think his kid brother's name is Jackie."

Dietrich had no choice. He had to redeem himself, or all was lost. His life would change. He had two races left, the two hundred meter and the 4 × 100 sprint relay. Owens was not one of the four American runners scheduled for the relay, and Dietrich hoped that might be his chance to win gold. At this point, he'd take silver—or even bronze. Anything.

The two-hundred-meter race went as Dietrich predicted. Jesse Owens won gold and set another world record at 20.7 seconds. Mack Robinson took silver, barely losing by a half step. Dietrich didn't try any tricks and finished fifth. He was still depressed, but advancing to fifth cheered him a bit. He was also starting to feel better physically, his sleeping and eating returning to normal.

His hopes were high for redemption as the anchor for the German team in the relay race. He pictured standing on the winner's podium, gold dangling from his neck—or even silver—and Gretchen and Adam in the audience. She'd be sure to come if he won a medal, and she would bring his son. Adam was only six, but he would know enough to be proud of his dad. "That's my daddy," Adam would say. "He won the Olympics."

At dinner the night before the relay race, Lutz asked, "Did you hear about the substitutions for tomorrow?"

Dietrich's hand stopped halfway between his plate and his mouth. He sat still as a statue, his face ghostly pale in the dim light. Then his hands began to tremble, tree branches in a hard wind. He stared at Lutz. "What're you talking about?"

"Hitler complained to the IOC about the two Jewish sprinters on the American team, Glickman and Stoller. He told the committee if they competed, he would withdraw Germans from the race and the rest of the Olympics. The IOC folded, ran chicken. Avery Brundage, head of the US Olympic Committee, leaned on the American coaches to replace the two Jews. Guess who's running."

Dietrich's shaking hands flew to his mouth. His eyes got big. "Not Owens. Please don't say Owens."

Lutz nodded. "And Metcalf."

"Metcalf finished second to Owens in the hundred meter," Dietrich said in a voice so soft the words barely got past his lips.

"Lost to Jesse by a tenth of a second and took silver. So the Americans still have a powerful finishing duo," Lutz said. "Maybe even better than before."

Dietrich dropped the fork onto his plate and ran both hands through his hair. His face was white, and his lips pressed into a thin line. He shook his head. "*Scheisse! Scheisse! Scheisse!* I can't get rid of Owens. I'm having nightmares about him."

"At least you're racing. Think of those poor Americans, how disappointed they must be. They trained hard, qualified for the race, came all this way, then got pulled because they're Jews. That's terrible. Brundage was wrong."

"Well, maybe they deserve it. After all, we are the superior—"

Lutz slapped the tabletop with his hand. The sound reverberated in the room like a gunshot. His beer glass tilted, swayed, then toppled. Fellow diners looked over, and Lutz, red-faced, lowered his voice to a whisper.

"Stop with that bullshit, Dietrich. It's an act. I know you too well. You and I both know you don't really believe what you're saying. You're just afraid of the Nazis."

Dietrich sat, unmoving, his expression confirming the accusation.

"And besides, you weren't so superior in the one hundred and two hundred meters. If you felt that superior, you'd be looking forward to the relays to show Hitler he's right, instead of being scared stiff of losing. Stop with the Aryan crap," Lutz said in an undertone. "Be you. You're good without it, a fine athlete and track star."

Lutz took a deep breath. "It's just a shame about the IOC and that guy Brundage. They should've told him to go to hell. Shows how corrupt Olympic politics can be. Anyone who thinks the IOC makes decisions for the benefit of athletes has his head up his ass. It's not just a game to them." Lutz took his napkin and Dietrich's and mopped up the spilled beer.

Dietrich gazed out the window into the darkness. Nausea replaced appetite, and he pushed his plate away. He saw his life slipping out of control.

CHAPTER 6

SLEEP WOULD NOT COME. THE ROOM WAS HOT AND stuffy. Every creak, footsteps across the hall, a cough in a distant room pounded in his ears. Light creeping under the door seemed to shine in his eyes no matter how he twisted and turned. His stomach ached, and he trotted to the bathroom hourly. It was almost four in the morning before he managed to doze a bit.

Dietrich rose to sip some water. The dreary room had become claustrophobic, and he had to escape.

He walked outside and sat on a low stone wall that surrounded the complex. The stones were cool, and he lay down on his back on top of them. He let his arms fall to his sides, and the black night settled around him like a protective coat. In the distance, as if anticipating sunrise, lights from the Olympiastadion lit up the horizon. If only he could sit here forever. No Hitler. No races. No worries. He tilted his head and looked up into the sky. Not many stars out, a few flickering pinpricks. Maybe rain on the way. He rubbed his eyes, gritty from lack of sleep. Tears welled and eased the scratchy feeling. He massaged his left knee that was beginning to ache, tender around the scar. Probably not too many races left before that knee called it quits.

What could he do? To race was to lose to that black man for the third time. Not to race would be equally humiliating. After the Olympics were over, what would he do? The checks would stop. He'd have to find a job—a new one since he had already spoken with the accounting firm, and they weren't hiring. Gretchen would be nagging about quitting teaching and wanting an addition to their family. Adam needed a little brother or sister, she insisted, before he got any older.

They'd fought, he and Gretchen, on his last night home—the babysitter thing and just in general. "I have something to tell you," she had said. "What?" he answered in a tone indicating he really didn't want to know. The upcoming games were consuming him. "Never mind. Good luck at the Olympics."

Dietrich shook his head. Life seemed so simple before that phone call. Now, after dedicating three years to the Fatherland, what would be his reward? Humiliation, probably—certainly no gold medals, or even silver. He should have known he was too old to compete with the best athletes in the world. But the person at the training center was so certain, so convincing, and so supportive. Who was that, he wondered, who made those decisions and sent the checks?

That black guy. My God, was he good. Der Stürmer quoted Hitler in the morning edition saying blacks had more primitive bodies that had not evolved to the higher planes as Germans, and that gave them the advantage of raw strength to win in such competition. However, they would be inferior when it came to culture and intellect. That would be the true measure of their different races. The article provided body measurements from blacks, Aryans, and Jews, testifying to the superior anatomy of the uncontaminated Aryan man.

He knew if he were to stand any chance against the Americans, he had to get some rest. He returned to his room, lay down on his bed, and covered his eyes with the pillow. He thought of Gretchen and how their life might have been without this madness, just living a simple German existence. He blocked out the Olympics.

It seemed he had just fallen asleep when a knock on his door woke him. Groggy, he reached for the light. Damn, it was eight thirty! He'd slept more than four hours and was due to race at ten o'clock. An Olympic official wearing a tight-fitting tan uniform over a bulging belly was standing at the door. He held out an envelope.

"For me?"

"Are you Dietrich Becker?" the man asked.

Dietrich nodded.

The man handed him the letter, turned on a heel, and left.

Dietrich closed the door and sat on the edge of his bed. He stared at the envelope and checked that it was addressed to him. No stamp or postmark, hand delivered. He turned it over for a return address but saw none. He held it to the light of the bedside lamp, but the thick, high-quality paper prevented him from seeing through.

Who would write him, especially here, and especially now? All his senses were bad. He didn't want this letter. He didn't want to open it. He wanted to tear it into a thousand pieces and flush the remnants down the toilet.

But he knew he had to read it.

Heart hammering against his chest wall, he slipped a shaking finger under the seal and slowly peeled it open. He glanced at the signature at the bottom, and his heart jumped an extra beat, swelled in his chest to bursting, and almost stopped. He fell back onto the bed, faint, not wanting to read further. But he had no choice, no escape. Slowly he sat up and read the letter.

Dear Dietrich:

Your performance has been disappointing to your führer. We have supported your training for three years, and your level of achievement at the Olympics has not been acceptable. We are certain you will do better in the relay race, your last chance. We have eliminated Jewish trash from racing, which will elevate the field. The führer plans to present you personally with the gold medal after you win the race. Be sure you do.

I wish you a speedy and successful victory that will affirm your role in the New Order of the Third Reich when

the Olympics are over. Do not let the führer down. The consequences will not be pleasant if you do.

On behalf of the chancellor of the German people, Adolf Hitler, I am sincerely yours,

OFFICIAL

Heinrich Himmler
Chief of the German Police
Reich Ministry of the Interior

My God! What could he do? Run, perhaps, but where? In the race or just away?

A moment later, he ran to the toilet to vomit.

It was a quarter after nine, and Lutz was concerned. Dietrich should have been at the track warming up. Perhaps he'd overslept, though it was more likely he hadn't slept at all. Lutz would give him another fifteen minutes and then call him.

At nine thirty, after getting no answer, Lutz walked to the apartment building housing the German athletes. It was a simple redbrick building at the edge of the Olympiastadion. Dietrich was in room 5A on the second floor. Lutz rang the bell and got no response. He knocked on the door but was greeted with silence. He knocked louder. Still nothing.

Lutz tried the door, but it was locked. He put his shoulder to the wood, but it wouldn't budge.

Panic slowly built. Could Dietrich have left, unwilling to compete in the final race? Such a desertion would be disastrous to his career as well as to him personally. Better to race and lose than turn tail. Lutz had to find him quickly. Dietrich would need warm-up time, and the race would be starting soon.

Lutz ran to find the building superintendent.

Ten minutes later, the superintendent unlocked the door and let him into the apartment.

"Dietrich, are you here? Dietrich?" Lutz shouted. No answer.

"Dietrich, answer me!" Louder this time.

Still no answer.

Lutz looked around. The bed was unmade, and Dietrich's clothes were scattered about. He saw an envelope addressed to Dietrich on the bedside table, but it was empty. The closet door was open, but the door next to it, presumably the bathroom, was closed.

Lutz knocked on the door, not wanting to embarrass Dietrich. He knew what the Olympic pressure did to Dietrich's bowels. Again no response. Lutz twisted the knob and opened the door.

Oh, dear God.

Dietrich was hanging by his neck. His track shoelaces were wrapped around the overhead light fixture, a toppled chair beneath his feet. His right hand, an eerie white, gripped a letter crushed in a death spasm.

"Help me get him down!" Lutz shouted to the superintendent. "Lift him."

The superintendent seized Dietrich's legs and elevated the body while Lutz stood on the chair to undo the laces from his neck. Gently they laid him on the floor. Lutz felt for a pulse but found none in his friend's cold, lifeless body. Still, he shouted at the superintendent, "Go find a doctor." He knew it was too late.

Lutz pried the letter from Dietrich's hands and smoothed the wrinkles to read it. On the bottom, Dietrich had scrawled, "Lutz: I can't take the pressure anymore. Please take care of Gretchen and Adam."

Lutz notified the German authorities. Their only response was to find a replacement for Dietrich in the relay. The officials delayed the race an hour until they recruited an alternate runner.

It didn't matter.

On August 9, 1936, Jesse Owens, Frank Wykoff, Foy Draper, and Ralph Metcalf stunned the world with a record time of 39.8 seconds in the 4 × 100 relay. Jesse Owens earned his fourth gold medal, an achievement never accomplished before.

Lutz left the Olympiastadion to find Gretchen. He needed to tell her in person but had no idea what to say. How did you tell a wife her husband just hung himself?

He knocked at the door of her flat. Gretchen answered wearing a red-and-white striped apron; she had been in the middle of making dinner. She had on no makeup, and her hair, streaked with early gray, was piled in a bun on top of her head. Loose strands dangled down her neck. Adam was sitting at the kitchen table drawing a picture.

"Look, it's Uncle Lutz," Adam shouted, jumping up from the table. He ran to Lutz and threw his arms around his waist. Lutz bent down and picked him up. He hugged Adam to him, looking at Gretchen over the boy's shoulder.

Gretchen's warm smile faded as she took one look at Lutz's face. She said, "Adam, you need to go to your room."

"I want to stay with Uncle Lutz."

"Please do as I say, Adam. Now. We'll have dinner soon, and I'll call you then," Gretchen said, her voice sharp.

The boy shook his head and hung onto Lutz. "No, I don't want to go."

"We'll play in a minute, Adam. Do what your mother says first," Lutz said, setting him down.

The boy stomped out of the kitchen, bumping into the table as he left. They heard the door to his room slam shut.

"What happened?" she asked, collapsing into a chair at the kitchen table. Her brows furrowed, tears forming. She buried her face in her hands, looking at Lutz between the fingers.

"Was he hurt in the race?" she asked.

Lutz shook his head. He broke the news gently.

"No, I don't believe it," she said. "He would never do that to me—to us," and shook her head in denial. "No, that couldn't have happened. You are mistaken, Lutz. How could you tell me such a cruel thing?" She stood and paced about the kitchen, groping like a person seeing it for the first time.

She moaned. "Why?" she asked, hands gripping her belly. Eyes closed, she slowly shook her head, hair falling onto her forehead. "Why, why would he do that?"

Lutz told her about the letter from Himmler, then handed it to her.

She read it silently. She shook her head several times to clear the tears so she could make out the print.

"I knew Dietrich was under pressure, but I didn't know how much," she said. "What will happen now? I don't know where to go or what to do," she said, sobbing.

Lutz rose and guided her to a chair. He put his hands on her shoulders and sat down next to her. "I am so, so sorry. He was my best friend. I should have sensed how bad it was for him and done something." He took Gretchen in his arms. She buried her head in his shoulder and sobbed. After a while, he asked, "Do you have family?"

She shook her head. "Only my mother. My father was killed in the First World War. She's a widow and lives on a small pension."

"Where?"

"Düsseldorf."

"Would you move there?"

Before she could answer, she saw Adam standing in front of her. "I heard you crying," he said. "Did Uncle Lutz make you cry?" He looked at Lutz.

She sat still, a vacant look on her face. She tried to smile for the boy. "No, child. Uncle Lutz didn't make me cry. Daddy had an accident, and Uncle Lutz came to tell us."

"Will he be okay?" Adam asked.

She didn't know what to say and looked at Lutz. "He's very sick, Adam," Lutz said. "He may not come home."

"Then I will visit him," Adam said.

"Maybe tomorrow, son, maybe tomorrow," Lutz said.

The room fell quiet.

Finally, Gretchen broke the silence. "Lutz, I'm pregnant again." Her hands relaxed, and she patted her belly. "I found out a few days ago and didn't tell Dietrich. I wanted to wait until the Olympics were over. He had enough on his mind without adding this. My mother can't take in two of us and a third on the way. Her flat is one bedroom with a tiny kitchen."

"I understand. Now is not the time for decisions. But at some point you will have to decide what to do. Let me know, and I will help any way I can."

The vacant look returned. After a while, she said, "I don't know. They won't let me teach at school once the baby begins to show. And then, after the baby, I'll have to take some time off to care for it." She cried.

He handed her his handkerchief and reached out to stroke her arm. "Maybe the government can provide some support. After all, Dietrich died while representing the German Reich at the Olympics. I'll check into it."

She dabbed at her eyes. "Do you think they will?" Her voice held a hopeful note.

"I'll do my best to persuade them," he promised.

Lutz convinced the government to support Gretchen and her son. Worries about a second child sadly disappeared when Gretchen began spotting in her fifth month and lost the baby soon after. She returned to teaching and generated a small income to sustain them. Adam helped doing odd jobs.

Lutz kept in close touch and did what he could until 1939, when he was drafted into the German army. After that, he wrote monthly, depending on where he was stationed. His letters stopped abruptly on July 14, 1943, when he was killed carrying a wounded comrade to safety during the Allied invasion of Sicily.

The checks stopped in May 1945, when the war ended.

CHAPTER 7

RIO DE JANEIRO, SUMMER, 2016

IT WAS HER FIRST OLYMPICS, AND KIRSTEN WAS nervous as she and Sharon boarded the plane at the Ben Gurion International Airport in Tel Aviv. The day was windy and blew her red curls, always untamed, into her face. When the sun hit, she looked on fire. She brushed the longest behind an ear as she walked up the mobile stairway from the tarmac to the plane.

"You'll do fine," Sharon reassured her on the long flight. "You've peaked your skills just right. I've said so often, fencing is different from other sports. Strength's important, but mental preparation means more. Fencing's like playing chess at high speed. Always think one step ahead of your opponent, two if you can. Keep the opponent off guard."

They flew Iberia Airlines with two other Israeli athletes. The coach section was full, and they were sardine-cramped for hours. Sharon had an aisle seat and was up and down to the restroom multiple times. Two movies and a TV clip helped pass some of the time. A stopover at the Madrid-Barajas Airport provided a three-hour layover to walk, stretch, and eat some decent food.

They arrived in Rio ten days before the Olympic Village opened, planning to rent a car for sightseeing and acclimate to the time change. They leased a Brazilian *pousada*, a nineteenth-century colonial house converted to a bed-and-breakfast hotel in the Santa Teresa district of southwest Rio de Janeiro. Similar old mansions transformed into tourist pousadas dotted narrow streets and alleys that meandered around the Santa Teresa Hill overlooking the city.

Kirsten grunted as she practiced her footwork in the tiny makeshift basement gym of the pousada. She was tired, and sweat poured off. Sharon, in her late sixties, sat on a wooden chair critiquing her workout. Kirsten loved the spirit still sparkling in Sharon's hazel eyes, undimmed by the gray hair and a face aged by years of challenges. Her competitive feeling was contagious.

"Remember your *T*s: toughness, tactics, and technique," Sharon said. "Twenty-seven years old is the perfect intersection of all three. You have the energy and stamina of youth, tempered by the strategy and mental maturity of age—and the perfect physique. Being tall with long arms is a fencer's dream. Combine all that with the three *T*s, and you're going to win gold."

"I know, Sharon. I *know*. You've told me and told me. I'll cross all the *T*s. I promise."

Kirsten wiped sweat from her brow and looked wistfully out the window at the beautiful Sugarloaf Mountain, inspiration for countless artists living in the area. How that mountain resembled a loaf of sugar was beyond her.

"Sharon, let's break and visit some of the art studios and galleries in the neighborhood. Maybe go for a coffee." Santa Teresa was a favorite tourist draw. Kirsten was ready to quit training for the day. "This place is magical. I want to see some of it—all of it."

Sharon appeared not to hear. "And don't ever forget, you have that inborn gift coaches call 'fencing surprise.' You can spot your opponent's weaknesses and strengths and *predict* the next move. Only the great fencers have that killer instinct. Combine that with *sentiment du fer*, 'feelings through the blade,' and you will not lose."

Kirsten had heard it all many times. She gave up and changed the subject. "Israel's never won an Olympic medal in fencing."

"True. You're going to be our first—"

"From your lips to God's ears," Kirsten interrupted.

"—since Olympic fencing started."

Kirsten's iPhone rang. She ran to her coat, slung over a chair, and pulled the phone from an inside pocket. She plunked down on the chair next to Sharon.

"Hi, Mom."

"My darling, did everything go okay?" Dannie asked.

"Yes, we arrived safely yesterday—a very long flight but no problems. Everything was on time." She looked at her watch. "It's 5:00 p.m. here—I guess 11:00 p.m. in Tel Aviv? Isn't it time for you two to be asleep?"

"Soon. We wanted to hear your voice and make sure you arrived safe and sound," Dannie said. "Where are you staying?"

"In a lovely bed-and-breakfast with a nice basement, so I'm practicing with Sharon."

"Did she do okay?" Dannie asked.

"Yes, she's fine." Kirsten looked at Sharon. "Tired but fine. It was smart to come early so we could adjust and see the country."

"Have you met any other Olympians?"

"Not yet, but I would guess other athletes have done the same thing. Two Israelis were on the plane with us. We're going to quit for the day and visit some of the art galleries around here—maybe bump into some other Olympians then."

She looked at Sharon again, with a hopeful smile. "Aren't we, Sharon?" Sharon raised an eyebrow and creased her lips downward but returned the smile. Kirsten pumped the air with her fist and mouthed, "Thank you."

"How's Dad?" Adam was eighty-six and couldn't travel. Dannie stayed home to care for him.

"Doing fine. He sends his love."

"Great, Mom. Give him mine."

"Here are my three taps—*tap, tap, tap,*" Dannie said. She dispensed this bit of family superstition, usually on the shoulder, before any major event to ensure victory. "Good luck, darling."

"Thanks, Mom. I'll do my best. You know that."

"I know you will. This means a lot to all of us. We miss you."

"I miss you too."

"Go for gold," Dannie said.

"Okay, just for you and Dad," Kirsten said. Sharon smiled.

"We love you."

"I love you too. And say hi to Dad. Bye for now. I'll call in a few days."

She jumped up from the chair. "Now can we go, Sharon?"

"Okay, but put on a jacket first. You're sweaty, and I don't want you to catch a cold."

They strolled arm in arm through the serpentine streets of the old section where the Santa Teresa Carmelite nuns lived, secluded behind the high stone walls of their convent. The streets were crowded with tourists, and Kirsten saw a few athletes wearing the Olympic jackets of their country. She was glad Sharon suggested she wear hers. They passed the splendid residence of a former arts patron, his house now a museum with Picassos and Monets.

"Want to go in?" Sharon asked, admiring the grounds.

"Maybe tomorrow. Let's just walk now. I want to soak it all in."

Artists had transformed sections of the once upper-class residential neighborhood into their own outdoor art studios. They lined the sidewalks and hung paintings from easels, walls, and tree branches. Hawkers called to passing tourists to sit for a sketch—only ten dollars American, fifteen for two people, and twenty framed.

They stopped at an outdoor café whose bright red-and-white tablecloths and climbing purple bougainvillea caught Sharon's eye.

"How're you feeling, Sharon?" Kirsten asked after they finished a Brazilian coffee and a Danish.

"Fine, why?"

"Rested?"

"Enough to chaperone you. What're you getting at?" Sharon asked.

"Are you up for a twenty-minute walk to the Lapa Steps?"

"Sure, I guess. What are they? Where are they?"

Kirsten took the guidebook from her purse and pointed to a picture. "According to this, it's a tiled stairway of 215 steps that connects Santa Teresa, where we are, to the Lapa."

"Which is?"

"Near the center of the city, an old aqueduct or something, with lots of activity, restaurants, and stuff. This Chilean artist, Escadaria Selarón, covered the old steps with over two thousand blue, green, and yellow tiles, the colors of the Brazilian flag."

"Why?"

"Just for fun, I guess. Maybe to make the neighborhood pretty? It says here," she pointed to a paragraph she had circled, "that he hand-painted three hundred tiles with the picture of a pregnant African woman that he explained was a personal problem from his past. Might be fun to go see."

"I'm game," Sharon said.

They were unprepared for the burst of vibrant colors from the shiny tiles that created a mosaic of rainbows in the setting sun. Street vendors grilling meats and vegetables over small fires filled the air with delicious smells. "My mouth is watering," said Kirsten, "and my stomach's talking to me."

"Oh, look at the tiles," said Sharon. "They're beautiful. I'm so glad you got us here." She took out her iPhone. "Stand on the top step, Kirsten. I'll send this picture to your parents."

They descended the stairs slowly, pausing every few minutes to look back and take another picture. People jostled, traveling in both directions.

"Hold tight to your purse," Sharon said, clutching hers to her chest. "The guidebook warned about muggings, even in broad daylight and with other people around."

Kirsten gave her purse a squeeze. "I am. I left the little jewelry I brought in the room safe, along with my passport. I just have a copy with me," she said.

When they reached the bottom step, Sharon turned for one last picture, waited until the throng thinned, and snapped.

"That's the best one," she said, holding the iPhone for Kirsten. "This'll go to Adam and Dannie."

Kirsten looked over her shoulder. "Lovely."

"Now where to? I'm getting hungry." Shadows were growing longer as daylight faded.

"To the Lapa Arches. Brazilians call it the Arcos da Lapa. We can find a restaurant there for a Portuguese dinner. I've got a couple of recommendations written down. According to the map, we just follow this street into the Rua Riachuelo, and then we're there. A few minutes' walk."

They strode at a quick pace—the guidebook also advised tourists to walk purposefully, as if they knew where they were going—but Sharon and Kirsten, busy chatting, failed to notice the wrong turn and were walking alone on a sundown-darkened street.

CHAPTER 8

THEY DIDN'T SEE THE *BANDIDO* BOLT FROM THE shadows of a dilapidated building hidden behind shrubs. A black wool cap pulled low over his face and a turned-up ragged shirt collar concealed most of his dark features. His bare feet made no sound as he approached them from behind.

He snatched Sharon's purse and tried to run back into the building. The strap was looped over her shoulder, and she curled her arm to resist the tug. The man dragged her onto the pavement, skinning her knees, but she wouldn't let go.

Kirsten was frightened. She'd never experienced a personal attack unrelated to fencing and froze—but for only a moment. Recovering, she jumped at him, flailing at his head with her purse. She knocked his hat off, and he backed away, out of range.

He looked around, took in the deserted street, and reached into his pocket. With a click, the knife blade sprang open. He flipped the weapon back and forth between his hands while staring Kirsten in the face. Slowly he let his eyes slide down her body, smiling all the while.

Kirsten read the taunt in his eyes but stood still, balanced on the balls of her feet. Her mind whirled with possibilities. She glanced at Sharon, still on the ground. She could easily outrace him, but not with Sharon.

"*Puta suja*!" he shouted. You dirty slut! He charged, knife blade held in his right fist and extended toward her, arm stiff.

A simple attack with a foil, her brain telegraphed. *Parry and riposte* was the automatic response, and she blocked his arm in a fencing move, pushing the knife aside. She was untouched as his momentum carried him past her.

But this wasn't a refereed game to be won by scoring a "touch" with a saber's tip. This was a fight against an angry man who wanted to steal a purse—and now wanted more.

The man whirled, grabbed her coat with his free hand, and brandished the knife with the other. Sharon, still down, screamed—a shrill, loud, continuous clamor for help that burst from her lungs.

Kirsten fought free, but he came back at her, raking the air with wild swipes of his knife blade. The *Sarbo Tactical Wheel to Defeat Specific Fencing Actions* was no longer helpful. Totally unpredictable moves made logical defense impossible, and they grappled at close quarters. Though Kirsten was almost six feet tall and strong, he was much heavier and street tough. Kirsten fought for her life, trying to avoid his knife hand.

Sharon got up and struggled to interfere, but he easily pushed her down again. She fell hard on the road, twisting her ankle. She shrieked again, "Someone, anyone—help! *Help!*"

The man grabbed Kirsten by the front of her Olympic jacket, pulled her close, and attempted to slash her face with a quick blade thrust. She held up her arm to block the knife. It gashed her right forearm—*her fencing arm.* Her blood seeped through the shredded leather sleeve. She tried to push him away and hit at his face with her left fist. Her right arm hung uselessly at her side.

He hauled her to him and in one continuous move flipped her over his hip. She landed on her back with a thud, and her head hit the pavement. Thick curls cushioned the impact. As she fought to remain conscious, he sat on top of her, held the knife to her throat, and pulled up her skirt. He hooked his thumb under the waistband of her panties and began pulling the lace down over her hips. His grin broadened as a look of terror exploded in her eyes.

Kirsten shrieked and hit at his face. "No, dear God, no! Not that. Please. You can have our purses, all our money, anything, just—"

Wham!

The bandido went flying off Kirsten into the ditch alongside the road. The impact made him drop the knife. A tall young man wearing an Olympic jacket displaying France's flag of blue, white, and red was on him in an instant, pummeling his face with blows. The bandido held up his hands to ward off the barrage of fists, but they proved useless against the fury of the Frenchman's attack. The bandido lost consciousness, and his hands fell to his side.

The Frenchman studied the man's bloodied face. When he saw no signs of movement, he stood. He ran to Sharon, who was holding Kirsten against her body.

Kirsten sagged against Sharon, sobbing, pressing her bleeding right arm against her chest. "My fencing arm, Sharon, my fencing arm! What will I do?"

"It's okay, Kirsten. You'll be okay. Easy, honey, easy." Sharon didn't notice her own left ankle, swollen to balloon size, black and blue.

The Frenchman untied a sweater knotted around his waist and wrapped it around Kirsten's right forearm to stem the bleeding.

"Do you have a phone?" Sharon asked in English.

He pulled one from his pants pocket.

"Dial 190," Sharon said. "Rio emergency number. I looked it up before we left the hotel."

A police van arrived in minutes, already in the area assisting other tourists. They piled into the back of the van and sped to the hospital, not bothering to arrest the bandido still lying in the ditch.

Hospital Copa D'or in Copacabana was six minutes away and staffed by well-trained, English-speaking physicians. Emergency personnel immediately took Kirsten into surgery, and Sharon for x-rays, leaving the Frenchman alone in a clean and well-lit waiting room. The hospital staff assured him they had the finest surgeons and equipment in Rio, comparable to the best in the United States or Europe.

"Not to worry," the nurse said. "The ladies will be fine."

Sharon returned an hour later on crutches, with her ankle in a white cast. "A bad sprain and minor fracture of an ankle bone," she said. "They told me which bone, but I forget. Plaster cast and crutches for three weeks and then a walking cast."

"Sorry for that," the Frenchman said.

"Could've been worse." Sharon dropped on a chair next to the Frenchman. He retrieved another and helped her raise her ankle onto its seat.

The police took a full report, first from Sharon and then from the Frenchman, filled out a lot of papers, and left. They promised to go back and look for the bandido.

"My God," Sharon said, once the tremors subsided and she could hold a cup of black coffee without spilling. The sedative was taking effect. "I thought he was going to kill us." She shuddered again, and coffee dribbled over the side of the cup. "Thank you for saving our lives. I'm Sharon Frankel. Who are you?" She held out her hand.

The Frenchman sat with long legs stretched in front of him, sipping a Diet Coke. "Stefan Pasteur," he said, shaking her hand. "No relation to the scientist," he said. "I'm on the French Olympic fencing team and was jogging close by when I heard your screams."

"Thank God you did. I don't know what would've happened if—" She shivered.

"I recognized your friend's Olympic jacket. With her lying on the ground and that guy on top of her, I went crazy. No way was some local hood going to hurt a fellow Olympian. I don't know her, but we're all family here in Rio as far as I'm concerned."

Sharon studied this young man. He was tall, more than six feet, well muscled, with a chiseled face: square jaw, prominent cheekbones and forehead, and a straight nose. Brown hair and eyebrows capped hazel eyes that seemed soft despite the solid face.

She leaned toward him and gently kissed his cheek. "Thank you again."

He blushed.

"Where do you live?" she asked.

"Paris. I came down early to do some touring and acclimate before the games start."

"Yes, so did we. Kirsten's on the Israeli fencing team—or was. I don't know whether she'll be able to compete now. She had such high hopes for a medal."

Stefan smiled and patted Sharon's knee. "We all do, Sharon. That's why we're here."

"I know, but there's so much history behind this. For us, at least."

"And not for the rest of us? We've all got stories to tell. The events that got us here, the things we've sacrificed, and the people who've helped—or hindered. All of us are competing for gold but would happily settle for silver or even bronze."

"I suppose," Sharon said, convinced their quest was different. She checked her watch. "It's been over two hours. Don't you think they—"

The door marked Private/Sterile—Do Not Enter swung open. A man in green scrubs with a blue OR hat askew on his head and a white paper mask dangling on a hairy chest emerged. His thick sideburns and goatee were dark, sprinkled with gray. His attire and in-charge attitude left no doubt who he was. He walked over and stood in front of Sharon.

"You are the mother?"

"No, her trainer—for the Israeli fencing team."

"I'm Dr. Rubén Shemberg, chief surgeon." He looked at her cast. "Broken?"

"Sprain and a hairline fracture. I'll be fine."

He nodded. "Bones are more brittle in older people." He turned to Stefan. "Husband or boyfriend?"

"Neither. We just met."

The surgeon shrugged and turned back to Sharon. "She was fortunate to have her injury while I was in the hospital."

"I'm so glad. How is she?"

"She'll do very well. Her leather jacket took the brunt of the knife slash, and she has only superficial skin injuries. There's no damage to underlying nerves or tendons, and her muscle strength should be good."

"Thank God," Sharon murmured. "Thank you so much."

"It was my pleasure to help."

"Yes, well ..."

He saw her look. "You have a question? We'll keep her overnight if that's what—"

"No. I'm ashamed to ask—but since she'll be okay, I will." Sharon wore a worried look. "Do you think she can compete in ten days?"

Shemberg smiled. "Exactly her question as soon as the anesthesia began to wear off."

He paused, considering. "I sewed the wound well—it took over sixty sutures—so it should no longer bleed, and, as I said, she was lucky with just the skin cut. I cleaned it thoroughly. But I don't know. If she were hit in the arm, the pain would be very great, and it could start bleeding again. I don't think the wound would open, but it could if the sutures ripped. Maybe give her a day or two of rest, then see how she feels."

"Can I see her now?"

"In a few minutes. The nurses are moving her from the OR to a private room, so—"

A nurse came over and said she was already there. He nodded.

"These ladies," he made a sweeping gesture, "are far too efficient for me to keep up with. Follow Luiza," he tipped his head at one nurse, "and she'll take you to your friend. I'll say good-bye now." They shook hands, and he turned and strode back through the private door.

Stefan turned to Sharon. "Do you mind if I come along?"

"Surely you joke. You saved her life. Of course I want you to come."

They trailed the nurse to room 326. Sharon moved slowly on crutches. "These hurt under my arms," she said.

"We can get a wheelchair if you'd rather," said the nurse.

"No, I'll be fine. Just go slowly."

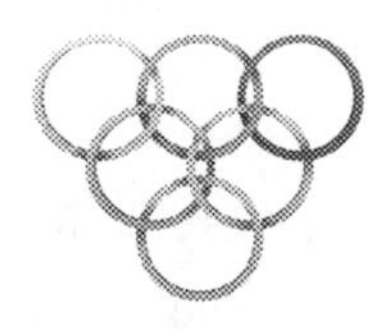

Kirsten fought through the fuzziness of anesthesia's lingering effects. She looked around the hospital room, trying to remember details of the fight. "I hope I see that bastard again," she thought, "and have a saber in my hands when I do." Pain from her forearm brought a reality check. "If I can still fence," she said, holding her arm up.

She heard a light knock on the door. "Come in."

The nurse opened the door a crack, peeked in, and then held the door wide so Sharon and Stefan could enter.

Kirsten lay in bed in a green hospital gown, a white dressing on the back of her head, and her bandaged arm suspended in a blue cloth sling that hung from her neck.

Sharon gently cradled her in her arms and kissed her forehead. "Are you okay? How awful."

Kirsten bit her lip not to cry. "I'm okay, Sharon, I guess." She held up her bandaged arm. "I just hope I can fence."

"The doctor said it might be possible but to wait a few days and see how you feel."

Kirsten saw the crutches. "What happened to you?"

Sharon told her.

"I'm so sorry, Sharon. I'm to blame. I got us lost."

"Nonsense. Just a fluke—wrong place and wrong time."

Kirsten looked up and locked eyes with Stefan, who had come a few steps closer. They held each other's gaze for a long time—instant, unspoken communication. Finally, he smiled at her and went to the bedside. He bent and took her hand.

"Hi. I'm Stefan."

"I'm Kirsten."

"I know. We met in the street. You were resting on your back. Maybe getting some Brazilian sun?"

She barely suppressed a smile. "I have a friend who owns an auto body repair shop in Tel Aviv."

He looked at her and raised an eyebrow. "So?"

"The company's slogan is 'We meet by accident.'"

He laughed. "We did, and I'm glad." He paused. "Not the accident part but that we did meet."

"My parents met by accident, also—a car accident."

His eyebrows rose.

Sharon, leaning on her crutches, watched the exchange. "You guys are amazing," she said.

"Why?" Kirsten and Stefan asked at the same time.

"Kirsten, not two hours ago you were almost robbed and raped at knifepoint on a deserted street. And Stefan, you were jogging alone, minding your own business. Now you two are flirting, and Kirsten's worried whether she can fence. The resilience of youth," Sharon said. "Thank God for that. I guess it's not entirely wasted on the young."

Kirsten and Stefan were looking into each other's eyes. "Didn't hear a word you said, Sharon," Kirsten said.

CHAPTER 9

SEATED AT THE SMALL COPA CAFÉ ACROSS THE street from the Copacabana Beach on the Avenida Atlántica, Max Jaeger let out a long, contented sigh as he sipped his second espresso.

The trip from Germany, hard enough for a man eighty-seven years old, was made more difficult by a canceled flight and missed connection. Traveling first class helped but didn't shorten the lines through passport and customs checkpoints—he had to stand in the queue with the rest of the riffraff—or prevent an unplanned overnight stay in a three-star airport hotel. Going home, he vowed to hire a private jet regardless of the cost.

When he finally arrived in Rio, Max checked into the luxurious Belmond Copacabana Palace Hotel. He had a steak dinner, half a bottle of an excellent red Bordeaux Supérieur, and a good night's sleep. Now it was time to activate plans years in the making.

He stretched his legs, relishing the bright, warm sunshine a moment longer. He took in his lovely surroundings: the beautiful white sands of the Copacabana Beach across the street and the blue Atlantic Ocean beyond, sparkling in the sun. He was so thankful to be where he was, who he was, especially considering the paths he'd traveled.

He shook his head in wonder, amazed he could still remember it all. The humiliation of living in the same building with those Jews, the Beckers, and all the track races he lost to Adam were as fresh as yesterday. The worst had been when Adam beat him to qualify for the 1948 Olympics. It didn't matter in the end, but it still was painful. The wonderful revenge that followed was his favorite memory. It always put a smile on his face. He could hear the chant about Becker's pecker in his ears right now.

He knew the Beckers had immigrated to Israel but had lost track of them after that. Max himself had prospered as an industrialist rebuilding Germany's economy and restoring its proper place among nations. Wherever Adam was, if still alive, Max could buy and sell him. Yet the old grudge festered.

It was interesting, Max reflected with the clarity of age. The "painful paradox," he called it. The psychological traumas of youth scarred permanently while physical mishaps readily healed. In old age, the reverse was true. Recovery from physical injury was challenging, but psychological insults rolled off Teflon-coated nerve endings.

Max hated Adam and the Jews now as much as he did seventy years ago, maybe more. Emotional debts were harder to collect than financial.

His cell phone rang. "Jaeger here." He walked away from the café to avoid eavesdroppers.

"Everything is in place, Herr Jaeger. Shall I pick you up?"

"Not necessary, Gordo. I can stroll and be there in fifteen or twenty minutes."

"Thank you, sir. I shall alert everyone to be ready."

Max returned to the table, left money, picked up his cane, and walked away. A tall man and elegant dresser, Max attracted stares as he strode along the beachfront. His full head of gray hair, Roman nose, and deep-set eyes gave the appearance of retired gentry. His thoughts were anything but that.

CHAPTER 10

BERLIN, 1948

ADAM HAD TRAINED HARD TO BECOME AN OLYMPIC track star like his father. He compared himself with pictures of Dietrich many times. Adam was taller and his face a softer version. The same straight nose but not as sharp, the lips more full. Dark hair covered the prominent forehead, but the same heavy eyebrows arched over the same blue eyes.

Postwar Germany was in shambles. Everything was in short supply, from food to clothes to equipment. Adam worked after school to help his mother make ends meet, but that interfered with practice time. Training was far more difficult than it had been for his father, Dietrich. Adam was driven to win, like Dietrich, but for a very different reason.

Adam had grown up with The Lie.

Many families live with lies but camouflage them or sink them with the weight of other truths. Some families distance themselves from the lie by moving away. Some stifle those who would expose the lie, and others simply ignore the lie.

"Your father was a hero of the Berlin Olympics," Gretchen often told Adam after his father's death in 1936, "but that black man was always a half step faster. Your papa died during his last race, running for Germany. He probably would've won, too, if someone hadn't tripped him and made him hit his head. I think maybe Otto did it."

Asleep or awake, Adam dreamt about his father's last race. He knew his father would explode from the baton handoff to take an early lead on the legendary Jesse Owens. Hearing the fans cheering him on, his father's face would become radiant, ignited by the anticipated win.

He'd be a step from the finish line when Otto Jaeger, a half meter behind, would trip him. Dietrich would go down, hit his head on the metal edge bordering the cinder track, fall unconscious, and never stir again. Der Stürmer would proclaim him Germany's greatest Olympic hero, the athlete who died defending Germany's honor.

Adam tried to believe the lie, but his schoolmates knew otherwise. They wasted no time telling him. Play period in the yard outside the elementary school was brutal, with no end to the bullying of a six-year-old.

"Adam, Adam has no father and isn't even worth the bother.

All the racers beat his stride, so his father committed suicide."

They'd form a circle around him and chant. Adam would run at whoever yelled the loudest, but that boy—sometimes a girl—would be swallowed by his crowd of friends, and someone on the opposite side of the circle would take up the chant. Adam would run from one to another and finally break down and cry. His sobs or the school bell ended the bullying.

At age fourteen, it all changed. *"Adam, Adam has no father—"* Adam flew at the kid, a boy his own size, with his fists flailing. Adam knocked him down with a punch to the chin and locked his arms around the boy's head, squeezing as hard as he could. The boy screamed for his buddies to help. They did, kicking Adam off their pal and pinning him to the dirt until a teacher came and broke up the fight. That ended the bullying, except for one boy.

Max Jaeger. The Jaegers had moved into the same apartment building as the Beckers right after the war. It was one of the few structures still inhabitable on Berlinerstrasse in Berlin. Bombs had destroyed the top two floors of the six-story building, but the remaining floors were intact, though with fractured glass windows or nailed-over wood replacements.

The Jaegers lived on the fourth floor, and Adam and Gretchen lived on the third. Otto Jaeger, Max's father, had gone to high school and university with Dietrich, and both had been on the same track team. As Jesse Owens was always a step faster than Dietrich, so Dietrich was a half step faster than Otto. In all their races, Otto never won—and Otto hated Dietrich for it. In fact, he despised him. After Dietrich's death, Gretchen told Adam the whole story, blaming Otto for tripping Dietrich during the last race.

Gretchen told him whenever Dietrich and Otto competed, Dietrich knew to avoid the lane next to Otto. There would always be an elbow, knee, or leg in his way. In the straightaway, Dietrich would stay as far from Otto as possible. When Otto was running directly behind him, Dietrich would zigzag to avoid Otto stepping on his heel. Gretchen said it was Otto who made up the suicide jingle and taught it to his son, Max, who shared it with his schoolmates.

Max and Adam both ran track. As with his father, Adam was a half step faster than Max, though not invincibly so.

As they grew, Max, almost a year older, twenty-five pounds heavier and an inch taller, would wait for Adam after school and pounce. "Give me your money, you dirty Jew, or I'll rip up your books, and then what will you do? No more As in class." Adam was no match for the bigger boy but still took him on and ended up with a bloody nose or black eye after each encounter.

Adam got even on the cinder track and ran his heart out to beat Max. He once won running with a hairline fracture of his thighbone. After the race, Adam collapsed in pain.

The rare times Max won triggered days of depression. Adam barricaded himself in his room. His mother would leave a food tray outside his door.

"Adam, come out," she pleaded. "You have to keep up your strength. I made you a nice pot roast dinner with boiled potatoes. Come and eat." Most often, the food went untouched.

In his room, no longer believing the lie, Adam would think about the demons that had driven his father to suicide. He contemplated his own. His world was unfair. Max's tormenting and the loss of so many friends and relatives in the war were heavy burdens.

In the year leading to the 1948 London Olympics, Max and Adam trained hard to qualify and represent Germany in track competition. The 1940 Summer Olympics, scheduled for Tokyo, Japan, had been moved to Helsinki, Finland, and then canceled because of World War II. The 1944 London Games were postponed four years. Athletes around the world, hopes for medals suspended twelve years, flocked to the 1948 London Summer Olympics, the Games of the XIV Olympiad. The press called them the Austerity Games.

Adam wore his father's running shoes, shirts, and shorts. Nutritious food was nonexistent. The school's indoor track had been converted to classrooms, so athletes trained outdoors regardless of the weather. They returned to the school to shower and change in the boys' locker room.

Competition for the Olympic slots began in April, before the races started in late July. The track choice came down to a tie between Adam and Max. The selection committee decided the winner of a final two-hundred-meter race would represent Germany in the London games.

"I want this so bad, Mama," Adam said at dinner the night before the race. "I want to prove to everyone that we Beckers are not quitters. That we'll fight to the end to win and that we can win."

"Then go out and do it. You can beat that horrible boy." Gretchen tapped him three times on his shoulder. "Now you are sure to win."

It was a sunny spring Berlin day, with trees greening and birds nesting. The entire student body turned out to watch, most cheering for Max. Eight athletes were racing, but only two mattered.

Adam's heart dropped when he drew the lane next to Max. But he was prepared.

At the gun, Adam moved to the furthest side of his lane. Max's elbow came first. Adam ran through, pushing it aside. When Max stuck his leg out, Adam jumped over it. Max tried to grab Adam's shirt, but Adam pulled away. As they approached the straightaway, Adam was a step ahead. He could hear Max breathing hard right behind him. Two meters before the finish line, Adam sharply veered to one side, barely avoiding Max's lunge for his heels.

Adam won the race by 0.1 second.

He danced in the air, arms overhead. The ultimate victory, at last! He hoped his father was watching. He'd win an Olympic medal for him.

Adam had never been out of Berlin, and now he was going to London to race in the Olympics. He shouted at the top of his voice:

"No racer ever beat my stride.

You can all commit suicide!"

Max stood there, fists clenched, glaring at Adam. "I'll get you, you bastard," he yelled. "You'd better watch your back." Adam laughed, turned on a heel, and walked away.

After the race, the athletes returned to the boys' locker room. Max threw his shoes into his locker and slammed the tin door. He picked up a metal chair and hurled it against the wall. The metal clattered against the concrete, echoes reverberating. Other boys coming in from the race stood still and watched.

"You son of a bitch," Max yelled at Adam. "I'm sick and tired of you. Why don't you and your family leave Germany? Go somewhere else."

"Fuck off, Max. I beat you for Germany's Olympic spot, and you can go to hell."

Adam waited until Max and the others showered before he undressed. As he was lathering, a faint noise made him whirl around, hands covering himself. Seeing no one, he went back to washing.

Strong arms wrapped him in a tight bear hug and lifted him off the tiles. Adam struggled but was helpless in Max's iron grip. Holding him, Max spun Adam around to present to five classmates gathered in the shower room.

"Look! I told you something was strange with our friend Adam, more than just his father committing suicide. Look at that pecker. He's circumcised! This boy's a Jew!"

Bedlam followed. Adam, soapy, slipped from Max's grasp. Someone else tackled him while others attacked with snapping wet towels. A bucket of soapy water stung his eyes, blinding him.

Adam fell to the tiles, regained his footing, and threw wild punches at his attackers. As his eyes burned, years of taunting echoed in his mind. A boy ran close enough for Adam to grab, and Adam wrestled him down to the tiles. But then they all jumped on him so the boy could get free.

The torment continued for ten minutes until the boys tired. Adam was exhausted. He crawled into a corner, soaking wet, shivering, with his hands over his groin.

"This isn't fun anymore," said Max. "I have an idea. Let's tie him in a chair and set him outside for all to see."

The boys yelled in enthusiastic agreement.

Three of the bigger guys tackled Adam and pinned him down while Max went into the locker room to find a chair. He brought it back into the shower, and they forced Adam onto it. Using towels, they bound one foot to each chair leg and his arms behind the chair back. They tied one towel across his chest, securing it around the back of the chair.

"Max, don't do this. You lost the Olympic slot in a fair race. Untie me, you son of a bitch. Let me go."

"Too late, Jew." Max waved a hand to halt the three guys about to pick up the chair. "You made it through the war, but at least everyone will know you're a Jew now." He turned to his friends. "Outside, guys, into the hallway with him."

Adam screamed, "No! No! Stop!" They stuffed a towel in his mouth and stifled his voice. But his mind raced on. "They're just joking," he told himself. "No way would they do this. I hate that bastard, but even Max wouldn't stoop to this."

The three big guys flipped the chair feet up so Adam was on his back. They carried the chair out of the locker room into the hallway.

The bell to change classes had just rung, and the hallway was crowded with students rushing to their next class. They placed the chair in the middle of the hallway so everyone had to detour around it.

Immediately a crowd gathered. "No, dear God, no," Adam said to himself, seeing his classmates stop and gawk. He bucked and heaved at the bindings, but it was no use. Finally, he shut his eyes, hoping no one would see the tears.

"Oh my God!"

"Can you believe this?"

"Goddamn!"

"Jesus Christ!"

The girls stared as hard as the guys. "That's what a circumcised penis looks like?" one petite blonde asked, moving in for a closer look. "Pretty shrunken." She giggled.

"I guess," said her brunette friend, examining Adam inches away. "I've never seen *any* kind before, never mind a circumcised one, so I wouldn't know a shrunken one from a—" She groped for a word, couldn't find it, and left the sentence hanging.

Adam, muscles straining, fought and pulled even harder against the towels, and finally overturned the chair with a clatter. He tried to shout through the towel in his mouth, but only grunts emerged. Max righted the chair and yelled, "Anyone wants to see a Jewish prick, come close and have a look. It's free. Come see Becker's pecker."

Max's friends took up the chant, and the school hall echoed, "*Becker's pecker, Becker's pecker. Come and see Becker's pecker.*"

Finally, the noise brought a teacher to investigate. Boris Swartz had a reputation in the school as a former German SS officer. He was now a world history teacher and one of many Nazis who had escaped postwar detection. Skinny and bald, Swartz had a pointy nose in a pinched face. He stood owl-like, staring, hands on hips. "Yes, that's what they look like," he pronounced. "I saw a lot of them during the war. Shriveled up little peckers—just like the Jews."

Behind him walked another teacher with a different reputation. Twenty-six-year-old Oskar Weingarten had added almost one hundred pounds to his six-foot frame since his liberation from Auschwitz three years before. Darkly handsome and intriguing with a scar from a bullet that creased his forehead and parted his hair, he had been a German resistance fighter caught in early October 1944 and sent to the concentration camp. As a strapping youth, he was spared the gas chamber and put to work on a railroad line but was near starvation when the Russians liberated the camp in January 1945. He proudly wore number C12,745 tattooed on the inside of his left forearm.

"Shriveled up little peckers, you say? Not this Jew," Oskar yelled. He swung a roundhouse left fist that smashed into Boris's right ear. The former SS officer collapsed, barely twitching.

Oskar untied Adam, beginning with the towel around his chest, which he used to cover the boy's lap. Max and his friends stood there, grinning. Oskar removed the rest of the bindings. When the last one came off, Adam ran to the locker room, trying unsuccessfully to hold back the sobs. He plowed blindly through the crowded hallway, one hand pushing people out of the way, the other holding a towel around his waist.

"Who did this?" Oskar bellowed. No one said anything. "I said, who did this? Who is responsible for this disgusting act?" Oskar's face was red with rage. He whirled around at the crowd, muscled arms swinging in a wide circle. The students began melting away.

The responsible boys just lounged there, grinning, poking at each other.

Oskar knew Max from his science class. "You think this is funny, Max?"

"I do, Herr Weingarten. I think it was very funny." Max and his friends kept laughing. The crowd around them tittered.

Oskar walked over to Max and stood in front of him. Although Max was tall, he had a runner's wiry build. Oskar was a tank, wide and powerful.

"Will you still laugh after I take off your pants and expose you tied on that very same chair?" Oskar pointed.

"You wouldn't dare."

The teacher made a move toward Max. He backed away as Oskar came closer. "You're not laughing anymore, Max. No longer funny?"

"You wouldn't dare," Max repeated. He collided with the wall and couldn't back up any farther. His friends stopped laughing and stood still, observing. Students stared, holding their breath.

"Oh, no? Watch me, Max." Oskar lunged at Max, tackling him around the waist. The two rolled to the floor. Weingarten leveraged his weight and flipped Max onto his back. He straddled him. With one broad left hand pinning Max around the throat, Oskar used his right to unbuckle Max's belt. He tugged the belt from Max's pants. His thumb and forefinger worked the top pants button and began to pull Max's pants down when—

"Stop! What's the meaning of this?" The harsh command stopped both of them. The school director, Herr Johann Schmidt, stood ramrod straight over them. Thick black eyebrows, lips compressed to a reedy line, a florid face, and full black mustache was a face all the students feared.

Oskar released Max, and they both stood, facing Schmidt. Without a belt, Max's pants started to slide. He grabbed the waistband to hold them up.

"Both of you, follow me," Schmidt ordered, spinning on his heels and marching off to his office. Students parted to let them through.

Once in his office, Schmidt faced them and said, "Fighting in the halls is forbidden. In fact, fighting anywhere in the school is forbidden. What's the meaning of this?"

Silence. Oskar stared at Max and was fighting to maintain self-control. He wanted to kill Max with his bare hands. He could feel his fingers closing Max's windpipe, hear the kid gasping for breath, begging to live as so many of his friends did in Auschwitz.

"Max, you first."

Max froze.

"Well?" Schmidt said. "Nothing to say?"

Max, pale, remained silent, one hand gripping his pants.

"Herr Weingarten?"

Oskar spoke up. "I'm not too sure how it began or what caused it, Herr Director. But Max and his friends tied Adam Becker naked to a chair they placed in the middle of the school hallway."

"True, Max?"

Max regained his composure, and his color returned. He shifted from one foot to the other, his face alternating a look of superiority with one of bemusement. Finally, he blurted, "Adam is a Jew."

The room was quiet as the director looked from one to the other. "Is this true?"

Oskar nodded. "Apparently. I didn't know this before."

"He's a *Jew*," Max repeated, lips pursed and brow wrinkled. He spat out the word.

"Max, this is 1948. The war is over. Jews are welcome back in Germany," the director said.

"Adam and his family never left," Max said.

"Oh, really?" The director paused, weighing that information. He nodded slowly, realization dawning. "Yes, I guess that must be true. His father raced in the 1936 Olympics, and Adam was in school here during the war." Schmidt smoothed his black eyebrows with a forefinger. "I'm as surprised as you, but that's neither here nor there, Max. The fact is Adam is a student attending the school of which I am the director. And as long as I'm the director, this behavior of yours is not acceptable and is not to happen again. Do you understand?"

"Yes, Herr Director," Max said, head bobbing. "I understand."

"Make sure you do." He gave a nod of dismissal and pointed to the door. "You may go."

Max covered his face with one hand to hide his smile. He left the office with a swagger, keeping hold of his pants with his other hand.

Weingarten stared at the director, eyes wide and mouth half-open, straining to contain his anger. His neck veins ballooned with the effort. "That's it? You're done with him? He ties a boy to a chair naked for public display in your school, and you just tell him not to do it again? That's his punishment? How can this be?" Oskar paced back and forth, his teeth clenched so tight his cheek muscles quivered.

"Herr Weingarten, stand still," Schmidt ordered. Oskar stopped pacing and took a few deep breaths. "You are a young man in your first teaching assignment, and lucky to have it. Do not dare presume to tell me how to run my school. I am finished with the situation. I have handled it to my satisfaction. It is done.

"*Fertig.* Finished. You may leave also. Now." Once again he pointed to the door.

Weingarten shook his head. He balled and unballed his fists. It took him several attempts to get the words out. "This is postwar Germany, and—"

"It is what it is, Herr Weingarten. Some things will never change. This discussion is over, finished. Leave if you intend to continue teaching science here—or would you like to find a new job in a different school? Maybe you could find one in a district that would punish a boy like Max, but I doubt such a place exists in postwar Germany. At least not the Germany I know."

Oskar stared at Schmidt a moment longer, long enough to register his disgust without getting fired. Then he turned, shoulders squared, and strode out of the director's office.

The notice came in the mail a week later. "Dear Adam: Although you have qualified to represent Germany in the Olympic Games, Germany, along with Japan, is not being invited to participate in the 1948 London Olympics. We are sorry. Thank you for your efforts."

CHAPTER 11

RIO DE JANEIRO, AUGUST 2016

LEANING SLIGHTLY ON THE IVORY-HEADED CANE, Max walked four blocks to a rundown warehouse set back from the main street in a poor neighborhood. Surrounding buildings were in similar states of disrepair. All windows were boarded shut, and the thick slab of wood used for the front door had no knob. Two muscled young men, one blond and the other dark-haired, guarded the secluded back door. Max whispered something, and they let him in.

Inside, the building had been transformed into the domed Great Hall envisioned by Hitler's architect, Albert Speer, from a sketch Adolf made in 1925. Nazi flags in all shapes and sizes hung from white Carrera marble walls. The black swastika set in a white circle against a red background was the most prominent decoration. Other flag displays included the eagle atop the swastika, SS lightning bolts, and the death's head insignia of concentration camp officers.

Male servers, dressed as Brownshirts of the storm troopers, in the lighter brown color of Hitler Youth, and in black SS uniforms, stood at attention. Female servers sported uniforms of the Bund Deutscher Mädel, the League of German Girls, the female equivalent of Hitler Youth. All servers wore Nazi armbands and signed "Heil Hitler" when someone took drink or food from their tray.

A bronze statue of Hitler's hero, Frederick the Great, the Soldier King of Prussia, stood near the center of the room, alongside a bigger-than-life statue of Hitler addressing his troops. A copy of *Mein Kampf*, protected by a glass covering, was showcased on a large, round mahogany table next to the statue. It bore number five of the original limited edition of only five hundred. During the Third Reich, it had become the best-selling German book of all time.

As Max strolled through the hall using the cane as a walking stick, crowds of people parted for him, raising the Nazi salute. He returned it with smiles to his friends, some of whom he had known for more than fifty years. They stood around chatting, sipping champagne from fluted glasses, and sampling tiny sandwiches and canapés.

After an hour, a butler rang a xylophone of muted chimes, and the crowd filed into the large auditorium. At least a thousand sat in red velvet chairs in various dress, from suits and long dresses—generally the older people—to jeans and shorts for the teens and thirty-somethings. All rose respectfully as Max walked on stage sans cane and approached the podium. A large Nazi banner prominently mounted on the wall behind him was a fitting backdrop. All stood until he told them to be seated.

Max had instructed the organizers to provide a bottle of water and a stool to sit on if he became tired. But the dinner and restful night had restored a feeling of vigor, and the size of the crowd, less than 10 percent of his total followers, buoyed him still further. He cleared his throat, thanked everyone for coming, and began.

"Many of you know the story I'm about to tell. You've heard it before, and some of you have actually lived parts of it. But there are so many young people here—whom I am thrilled to see—that I think the reason we are all assembled is worth repeating. You old-timers, bear with me," he said with a smile. "You young people can Google Fact Checker to be sure what I say is true."

There were titters in the audience. No one was about to do that.

"And if you have any questions, just raise your hand or shout it out. As much as possible, I want to talk *with* you, not *at* you.

"The date is Monday, April 30, 1945, and it's about 1:00 a.m. The place is Berlin, Germany, and Hitler's Third Reich knows the end is near—at least for the moment. World War II is essentially lost. Berlin is in shambles, total rubble. Fires are raging out of control on almost every block from the constant shelling by Russian artillery. Russian troops are only a half kilometer outside Berlin and are preparing to storm the city that morning.

"Adolf Hitler married Eva Braun, his longtime companion, the day before, on Sunday, and the two are burrowed in the Führerbunker, a warren of thirty rooms protected by almost fifteen feet of concrete, about thirty feet beneath the garden of the Reich Chancellery at 77 Wilhelmstrasse. This subterranean bunker complex has been their home since they moved in on January 16 and has become the operations center for running the war."

Max rested a moment and sipped water.

"Hitler realizes he faces three options," he continued. "Be captured—unthinkable. Commit suicide—contemplated. Flee—to where, and how? He seeks a fourth, to become the German Lazarus. To rise from the ashes and lead a new Germany."

Max paused again, this time for effect. He took another sip and adjusted the glasses on his nose. He scanned the audience, recognized some old friends, and smiled at them. "But how can he do this? How can he become a Lazarus?

"The standard history books tell us Adolf Hitler and Eva Braun committed suicide sometime between two and three o'clock on the afternoon of April 30, 1945—she by swallowing cyanide, and he by a self-inflicted gunshot wound to the head.

"Hitler's body and Eva's were brought out of the bunker into the chancellery's garden, doused with two hundred liters of very scarce petrol, and burned beyond recognition.

"Events after that become cloudy. The Russians, as many of you know, were the first non-Germans on the scene. Their archives indicate initial internment of the charred remains in an unmarked grave in a forest west of Berlin. Why there? I don't know. Then, again for unknown reasons, they were moved to a plot in Magdeburg, Germany, and finally in 1970, exhumed a second time, totally cremated, and the ashes scattered in complete secrecy. Strange proceedings, I'm sure you will agree."

A hand rose. Max nodded at the young man, who stood. He was wearing jeans and an open shirt, certainly one of the thirty-somethings,

Max thought. "Wasn't there some talk years ago about finding Hitler's bone fragments?"

"Good for you. Yes. Hitler's skull and jawbone were said to have survived intact. How that happened—*if* it happened—is not clear, but that's the ridiculous claim. We now know that American scientists performed DNA testing on the skull in 2009 and concluded it belonged to a woman less than forty years old, who was not Eva Braun. These are the facts, as history tells us."

"So there's no body and no definite proof of death," the man said and then sat down.

"That's absolutely correct. In fact, at a press conference June 9, 1945, Marshal Zhukov, head of the Soviet army, said they had not identified the body of Hitler and could say nothing definite about his fate. Zhukov was willing to consider the possibility that Hitler had escaped. Stalin agreed.

"Even General Dwight D. Eisenhower, probably the most respected and liked leader in the West, said there was 'not a bit of conclusive proof' Hitler was dead. To this day, no tangible evidence of Hitler's death exists."

A pretty blonde jumped up in the front row. Max noticed her full chest and narrow waist. *To be young again*, he thought. *She'd be mine in an instant.*

"How is this possible?" she asked. "How could the world's most-wanted human evade discovery?"

Max looked into the faces of the audience. They sat captivated. No one stirred or made a noise after her question. The blonde looked around, embarrassed, and sat down.

"I need to remind you, particularly younger people in the audience, that the European world was in complete chaos at that time. Adolf Eichmann and Josef Mengele, almost as recognizable as Adolf Hitler and nearly as wanted by the Allies, managed to escape undetected to Argentina. So did Martin Bormann, private secretary to Hitler, along with thousands of other Nazis—some of whom are probably your parents or grandparents." The audience came alive with nods of agreement.

"As you remember, General Juan Perón, eventual dictator of Argentina and a friend to Germans, opened his country to fleeing Nazis. Records show he sold ten thousand blank Argentine passports to the Germans. 'Fill in a name and come on down,' he said. Perón wanted their scientists and wealth."

The blonde was persistent and bounced back up. "After all this time, wouldn't there be proof one way or another?"

Max smiled at her. "Excellent question. Is it crazy to not know definitively whether Adolf Hitler escaped after all this time? Not really. Those who remember the assassination of the American president John F. Kennedy know that now, more than fifty years later, doubt persists whether Lee Harvey Oswald acted alone. The world *wanted* to believe Hitler was dead, just as it *wanted* to believe Oswald was alone.

"People do not like uncertainty. Hitler understood this. He said, 'Make the lie big, make it simple, and keep saying it; eventually they will believe it.' Joseph Goebbels, Hitler's minister of propaganda, was expert at doing just that. He knew it didn't matter what something *was*—only what people *thought* it was."

Max sipped his water.

"Perhaps the story of Adolf Hitler's death needs to be rewritten. I recommend a book to you called *Grey Wolf: The Escape of Adolf Hitler* by a historian and journalist. It tells a different story. In this history, Adolf Hitler and Eva Braun escaped to live a fine life in Argentina and Brazil. Hitler shaved his mustache, had a little plastic surgery, and lived until February 13, 1962, when he died peacefully at age seventy-two."

A hand shot up, another thirty-something man. "If that's the real story, how did it happen? How could they have possibly escaped?"

"Thank you for that question," Max said. "It brings me to the next part of my story.

"On Saturday, April 28, 1945—the day Benito Mussolini was captured and executed by Italian partisans—Adolf and Eva, led by Gestapo Chief Heinrich Müller, left the bunker by a hidden tunnel. They were transported a kilometer to the Hohenzollerndamm, a broad boulevard running through central Berlin. Several thousand meters had been cleared of vehicles and rubble, and bomb craters filled in, for an improvised runway. Aunt Judy—*Tante Ju*—a Junkers-52 that was Hitler's personal plane, waited for them. Captain Peter Baumgart of the Luftwaffe was at the controls. As soon the führer and Eva were buckled in, Baumgart took off and headed north.

"The escape route was circuitous, with several stops to avoid Allied detection. In Spain, General Franco provided them a new plane to the Canary Islands, which was a secret Nazi submarine base during the war. A submarine waited, courtesy of Admiral Karl Dönitz, U-boat mastermind and commander in chief of the German navy. He promised 'an impregnable fortress for the führer in paradise.'

"The ten-thousand-kilometer voyage to Argentina took two months. They landed at Necochea, a port city on the Argentine coast, five hundred kilometers southwest of the lovely city of Buenos Aires."

Someone shouted, "Heil Hitler!" And the entire audience clapped and cheered for two full minutes.

Max continued.

"Bormann planned to make Hitler's escape foolproof. He and Müller had secretly recruited Hitler and Braun lookalikes—they had used them as stand-ins for parades and such when Hitler didn't want to attend. The man's name was Gustav Weber, but the woman's name is lost to history. Both deserve medals for sacrificing themselves for the Third Reich.

"As Adolf and Eva fled on the twenty-eighth, Weber and his partner entered the bunker. They got 'married' the following day, Sunday the twenty-ninth. Once Müller was certain Hitler had escaped safely, on Monday, April 30, he drugged the pair and dressed them in Adolf and Eva's clothes. Müller forced a cyanide pill down the woman's throat and shot the man in the head at close range to look self-inflicted. The bodies, faces covered, were carried into the garden for immediate burning. No one suspected a thing.

"Some of you may have read the novel *The Odessa Files* by Frederick Forsyth. The real ODESSA is an acronym for the Organization of Former SS Members. Heinrich Himmler established ODESSA to create secret escape routes for SS officers hunted after World War II. At least ten thousand

Nazis escaped to South America, mostly Argentina but also to Brazil, Chile, Paraguay, and Uruguay. Some went to the Middle East. And some, showing real courage, returned to Germany and lived right under the noses of the very people hunting them. As you know, today we have tens of thousands of friends and followers in all these countries."

The audience broke into applause again, this time lasting even longer than before. Max had to quiet them. He did so with some reluctance. The overwhelming support of his efforts was a fulfillment of his life's dreams.

"Hitler established himself initially in Patagonia to lay a foundation for the Fourth Reich, which in turn would be the bedrock of the Thousand-Year Reich. He recruited as many Nazi escapees as possible. That included many of you old-timers, or the parents or grandparents of the younger folk here. Hitler had a vision back in the 1930s, shortly after he became chancellor of Germany, to create a foreign Fatherland for Germans to settle the world. He liked watching American Wild West movies and imagined Nazis colonizing South America as Americans did the old Wild West.

"The first attempt he named Guayana-Projekt, headed by Joseph Greiner. Greiner founded a Nazi camp deep in the Brazilian Amazon. Sadly, he died of malaria in 1936, and the project faltered."

Max was getting tired. His speech slowed, and his voice became hoarse. He stopped, put his hand up, sat on the stool, and took a drink of water. An attendant came on stage with a wet cloth to wipe his face and neck. He massaged Max's back and shoulders. The audience sat expectantly, patiently, whispering to each other until their leader regained his strength.

After almost ten minutes, Max rose again. The audience applauded. "We have pictures of Greiner's grave site in the Amazon, marked by a large wooden headstone carved with his name, date of birth and death, and a Nazi swastika. Another fifty or so crosses with carved swastikas mark other Nazi graves. You can find it on the Internet. Greiner's history is detailed right here in the National Museum in Rio. If you have time, go visit.

"Greiner's site was supposed to be the first of multiple Nazi settlements across the region. But back in the 1930s, they didn't have the knowledge or means to cope with malaria, yellow fever, poisonous snakes, and so on. Our European brothers died easily.

"Hitler made another attempt. He ordered Otto Skorzeny, a colonel in the SS, and Reinhard Gehlen, his chief intelligence officer, to start Die Spinne in 1944, when he saw the possible fall of the Third Reich. The Spider had the backing of several wealthy German industrialists, many friends of mine, and started its own kind of brain drain out of Germany.

"The US recruited people like Albert Einstein, Wernher von Braun, and other brilliant German scientists, along with more than a thousand ex-Nazis as spies against the Soviet Union. Many of these intelligent men were openly Nazis, but the Americans rewrote their personal histories so they could emigrate to the United States. They even paid social security benefits to so-called war criminals and former SS guards who came to the United States and then left for Europe.

"The Spider did the same to lay the foundation for the Fourth Reich. And that brings me to today and why we are all here."

CHAPTER 12

STEFAN ARRIVED AT THE HOSPITAL COPA D'OR BY eight the next morning to take Kirsten back to her pousada. He knocked on the door of her hospital room, and Sharon opened it. He felt his face go slack in disappointment.

"I spent the night," Sharon explained, pointing to a pullout bed. "Don't worry. Once we're back at the pousada, you two can go off by yourselves." Her voice grew more serious. "But, fair warning, my new friend," she said softly. "This young woman," she tipped her head toward Kirsten, "is in my charge and is my life. Respect that."

Stefan said, "I understand. How's the ankle?"

"Hurts. They gave me pain meds, and I fell asleep. Supposed to keep it elevated."

He turned to Kirsten. "How are you this morning? Arm hurt?"

Sitting on the side of the bed, she waved it around. "Actually, it feels pretty good. A couple of twinges during the night and when I bumped it dressing this morning, but it's okay now. I should definitely be able to fence in nine days."

"Not so fast," said Dr. Shemberg, walking into the room. "Good morning, all. Let's take a look before we make predictions." He pulled up a tray table next to Kirsten and placed her arm on it. Gently, with the nurse's assistance, he unwrapped the bandage. Sharon and Stefan looked over his shoulder.

A four-inch gash held together by interweaving black stitches ran almost the length of her inner forearm. A healing crust had begun to form.

Shemberg inspected his work. "Quite nice," he pronounced it. "Because of my superior surgical skills, you probably *will* be able to fence in nine days."

"Yes!" said Kirsten, pumping the air with her other fist. "Thank you *so* much, Dr. Shemberg. You've given me back my life."

He smiled. "A bit of an exaggeration, my dear. From what I heard, this young man did that." He nodded at Stefan. "But I'm happy to accept the compliment." Shemberg backed away to let the nurse rebandage the arm. When she was done, he inspected the binding and nodded his approval.

"Ordinarily, I'd take stitches out in seven to ten days," he said, "but in this case, I think it best to leave them in until your fencing is over as insurance against the laceration reopening. Just be sure to keep it clean. We don't want that wound to get infected."

"What about bathing?"

"No problem after the first twenty-four hours. Just dry it thoroughly when you finish. I'll leave a supply of sterile bandages and antibiotic ointment. Before you return home—" He stopped, looking at Sharon.

"In ten or twelve days," Sharon said. "Earlier if we lose."

"Before you go home, in *no earlier than ten days*," Shemberg said, laughing, "come see me, and I'll take out the stitches."

"Yes, Doctor," Kirsten said. "Can I leave now?" She looked at Stefan.

"You're all set. No swordplay for two days. Then you should be okay. Start slowly. Good luck in your matches. I hope you win a medal."

"Thanks. I'll do my best."

Stefan and Kirsten went for lunch at the Restaurante Aprazivel, not far from Kirsten's pousada in Santa Teresa. She picked it because it advertised authentic Brazilian dishes.

They sat at the outdoor patio, a deck covered by a straw roof with thick green vegetation growing all around them. Chairs and tables were made from tree limbs and trunks, or bamboo. The panoramic view of Guanabara

Bay and downtown Rio was so extraordinary they refused to go inside, even though the air was cool and the day cloudy.

"I'll bet sunset here is spectacular," Kirsten said.

"We'll have to come back and see it," said Stefan.

"You know it is. You've already seen it—with me," said a voice behind them.

Both turned in the direction of the sound. A slender brunette, medium height increased by three-inch heels, had just pushed back her chair and was standing to leave with a young man. Kirsten noted the black halter top that emphasized her chest and exposed her midriff. A gold loop dangled from her belly button. Tight white leggings outlined shapely legs.

She walked over, leading the man by the hand. He followed, a reluctant step behind.

"Hi, Stefan," she said. "Are you going to introduce me to your friend?"

Stefan stood, hands rubbing his pants leg. "Kirsten, this is Monique Cloutier, a fencer with the French Olympic team."

"Hello," said Kirsten, extending her hand. "I know your name, so it's nice to meet you in person."

"Likewise," said Monique brusquely. "And this is my friend Luigi Antinori, a discus thrower with the Italian team."

They all shook hands. Silence settled uneasily around them like a rain cloud. Finally, Monique said, "I hope you enjoy the lunch with Stefan as much as we enjoyed dinner together here two nights ago. The sunset was gorgeous, wasn't it, Stefan?"

Monique blew Stefan a kiss, turned, and led Luigi away. Before leaving the patio, she said over her shoulder, "See you in the fencing arena, Kirsten. I'm the number-one seed, in case you didn't know. Perhaps we'll match up—if you make it that far."

That was interesting, Kirsten thought. She disliked labeling someone a bitch before getting to know her, but that woman qualified. She stared at Stefan after Monique left and waited until he spoke.

"We dated a long time, almost two years. She moved in with me last year. But I broke it off several months ago."

"Why?"

"The relationship was going nowhere, and we started fighting a lot. I wanted out, to meet new people. So I ended it. Monique insisted we have one final dinner together here. We did, and that's it."

Kirsten was silent. She didn't know what to say.

"I don't know why I feel compelled to justify it to you, but I do. Monique and I had a relationship that ran its course. It is over." He reached for Kirsten's hand.

"You're right. You don't need to justify anything to me," Kirsten said. "Your life is your own."

He nodded. "But I want you to know there are no other women. I have no commitments."

She gave his hand a squeeze. They sat, sharing the exhilaration and awkwardness of a new relationship. Kirsten played with her napkin. The cool, moist air frizzled her red curls, and she kept pushing errant red ringlets behind her ear. Stefan put on a pair of glasses and fiddled with his iPhone. Then he placed the glasses on top of his head where they sat like a crown. Finally Kirsten spoke.

"I don't know anything about you, except you saved my life."

"That's not enough?" He smiled.

She laughed. "Not nearly."

He put the glasses on the table and ran a hand through his hair. "What else do you want to know?"

"Start with your family."

"You're sure? Not very pleasant."

She nodded. "Tell me all the sordid details."

"Not sordid but not pleasant. I'm an only child. My parents divorced when I was young, and I was sent to boarding school. I only lived summers at home."

"What are your parents like?"

He looked over her shoulder at Guanabara Bay before answering. "My father left soon after the divorce. I only saw my mother two months a year when I was not in school."

"How awful."

He shrugged. "Actually, not so bad. I got along great with my friends at school, and the teachers were nice. They didn't fight and scream at each other all the time."

"Not fun at home?" *I can't believe I'm being so nosy on the first date*, she thought. But he was intriguing. And so good-looking. Her heart did a little flip-flop thinking where this might go.

"Not fun." The corners of his mouth turned down. "Terrible, actually. My mother is French, and my father's German. They met in Paris, married—Lord only knows why, perhaps she was pregnant, but she's never said—and moved to Germany. My mother grew to hate all things German, especially during the Cold War. Berlin's drudgery didn't compare with Paris's beauty. The language was too guttural, the food too coarse, and ultimately, so was my father. Also, he was older and didn't want to do the things she did."

"Like what?" She wanted to know more.

"Like going out at night and socializing. Going to the opera or concerts. She's a party person, loves music and art. He liked sports and beer. After the divorce—I was young but old enough to remember the squabbling—she resumed her maiden name, Pasteur, and we moved back to Paris. We spoke only French or English. My father had a fit and stopped sending any support, so she had to get a job. I haven't seen him since."

She wondered about boys growing up without fathers. But he wasn't a momma's boy. And certainly had proved his bravery.

"How did you get involved with the Olympics?"

"I ran track in school and was pretty good. I also had a decent coach who encouraged me to compete."

"But you're a fencer," said Kirsten.

Stefan blushed. "It'll sound very silly."

"That's okay. I want to hear."

"When I was about fourteen years old—an impressionable age—I was assigned to write a critique of *The Three Musketeers* by Dumas."

"*Les Trois Mousquetaires*," Kirsten said.

"*Mais oui*," he said and smiled.

"And after I read about d'Artagnan and *'tous pour un, un pour tous'*—all for one, one for all—I researched Dumas himself. He was a practicing fencer. It seemed romantic and noble. The movie version sealed my fate. I fell in love with its spirit and, of course, the sport. So here I am, a fencer with the French team."

She shook her head. "I think that's neat, but there's got to be more. First of all, you're past university age, aren't you?"

"I am. I'm in medical school, still running track to stay in shape but fencing all the time I'm not in class. Getting my medical degree at Montpellier Medical College in Paris. I graduate next year."

"So"—she took a guess—"you're, umm, twenty-four." She hoped they were close in age.

"Twenty-six. I took time off from school to train for these Olympics."

"I'm twenty-seven."

He grinned. "I've always been attracted to older women. Especially after I've saved their lives."

Kirsten laughed.

"Your turn," he said, taking her hand and casually stroking the back of it. "Tell me about you." Her heart did another flip.

The waiter interrupted with lunch. *Good timing*, she thought, as the mood lightened a bit. This relationship was going very fast.

Over a dish of *bobó de camarão*, shrimp in a puree of manioc meal and flavored palm oil, Kirsten said, "My family's boring compared to yours. My father married my mother late in life. He wanted me to be an Olympic athlete. He almost was in '48. I started training with Sharon when I could barely walk. She's been a second mother. She taught me everything I know about fencing. I've never had another coach."

"What do you mean your father was *almost* an Olympian?"

"Long story," she said. "Maybe over a glass of wine sometime. He's become an Olympian through me. My winning a medal would be the closest thing to him winning one."

"He was never in the Olympics?"

"Not as a racer, but he was at the 1972 Olympics …"

CHAPTER 13

MUNICH, AUGUST 1972

MUNICH WAS THE HOME OF THE 1972 SUMMER Olympics, the Games of the XX Olympiad. Adam was part of the Israeli delegation.

Gretchen and Adam had immigrated to Israel soon after graduation. He couldn't wait to leave Berlin. His humiliation was so great that every day back at school was painful. He couldn't look anyone in the eye without imagining that person saw him naked, strapped to the chair. Only a handful did, but the story was on everyone's lips and repeated so often, many who were not there felt they were. They could cite the conversations of Max and Oskar verbatim. Max and his friends achieved hero status with many classmates. Others—a minority—now despised them.

Settling in Tel Aviv, near the Ramat Aviv neighborhood, Adam enrolled in Tel Aviv University. He became captain of the track and field team as a sophomore. In his senior year, he had forty-eight track wins and three losses, a new record for TAU. Tel Aviv U won the All Israel track competition.

After graduation, the Israeli Olympic Committee invited Adam to join. He agreed, but Tel Aviv School of Law took up much of his time. To do both, Adam rose at five in the morning and ran five miles before school. Weekends, he trained with the Olympic team.

Law school exacted its toll and began to add fractions of a second to his running times in the hundred- and two-hundred-meter races. Editing the *Law Review* journal demanded even more effort, as did participating in the law school moot court team. Adam faced a difficult choice. He decided his future was law, not track, but he would stay involved with the Olympic team as a legal advisor.

After finishing law school, Adam turned down several offers to join prestigious law firms, preferring to start his own. Clients came slowly, but he was happy with his small office and part-time paralegal secretary. He continued his legal work for the Olympic team.

A young fencer caught Adam's eye. Levi Frankel was a Dutch-born émigré who had settled in Israel as a teenager when his father was recruited as a civil engineer. Levi and his family survived WWII hidden in a house with a false basement on the same Amsterdam canal where Anne Frank and her family hid. After the war, fencing became Levi's obsession. His dream was to win the first-ever Olympic medal for Israel. Adam liked Levi for his open friendliness and joyful demeanor. Each fencing match was a happy challenge, win or lose. Levi just loved the sport.

Levi and Adam often stopped for a beer after a training session. At the Shaffa Bar in Old Jaffa one night, Levi said, "Adam, I have to make a tough decision. You've already made yours, so I thought maybe you could help."

Adam set his beer on the table. "Because I'm a few years older, Levi, doesn't make me smarter."

"Maybe, but listen." Levi scratched his chin, sipped, and watched the bartender clean glasses. "I'm a good fencer," he said.

"You are."

"But not good enough to win Israel an Olympic medal," Levi said.

"Not true, you—"

"Wait," Levi said. "Let me finish. I've thought a lot about this."

Levi sipped his beer again, struggling with a decision. "I appreciate your support, but *I* know I'm not that good, and my opinion's the only one that matters."

Adam nodded, waited.

"But I love fencing more than anything. My question is how you handled giving up running."

"It was easy for me," Adam said. "I had the law. She's a powerful and demanding mistress."

"Regrets?" Levi asked.

Adam shook his head. "None."

"My whole life's fencing," Levi said. "I'd be lost without it."

Adam was hesitant. "Don't be insulted, but you know that phrase, 'Those that can, do; those that can't, teach.' You could coach. Become a teacher."

Levi nodded. "I was offered a teaching job back in Holland," he said, "at the National Fencing Academy in the Hague. I'll come back to help the Olympic team if they want, but this way they can replace me with an up-and-coming superstar."

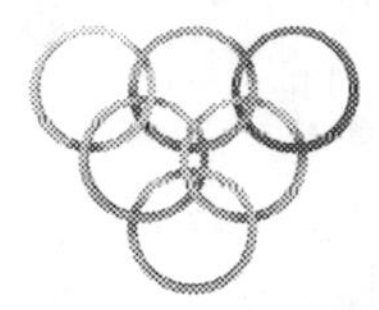

Three years later, Levi returned to Israel with a pregnant wife named Sharon. Levi was the new coach of the Israeli fencing team. He joined them just in time to go to Munich along with Adam, who was the assistant head of the Israeli Olympic delegation. Still unmarried, Adam devoted much of his spare time to the Olympic team. His one-person law firm had prospered and had room for a second lawyer, but he preferred working alone.

"I'm very concerned about the lax security," Shmuel Lalkin complained to the German authorities a month before the start of the games. "As head of the Israeli Olympic delegation," Shmuel said, "I'm responsible for housing and safety, and I don't like what I'm seeing. I just toured Olympic Village, and I found at least a dozen areas that need tighter security. If you won't place more guards around our living area, at least grant my assistant and me a permit to carry guns."

"No guns," came the official German response. "When we hosted our last Olympics in Berlin, Hitler wanted to show the world our military strength before the war. All that has changed. Now we want to display the new Germany as calm and serene, with understated security, not bristling with armed guards at every corner. The world must see the transformed, peaceful Germany, with tolerance for all people."

"But you're housing the Israeli delegation in remote ground-floor dormitories on 31 Connollystrasse," Adam said.

"So?"

"Have you not seen the area?" Adam asked. "The building sits right next to gate 25A, which means easy access. That's not safe. At least place an armed guard there."

"I don't think one is needed," replied the head of security, Gerhard Gobbles. "We don't expect any problems."

"You're being naïve," Lalkin retorted. "From what happened in Mexico, we're very concerned. Some group might be politically motivated to disrupt these Olympics. I've talked it over with my assistant, and he agrees with me." Shmuel turned to Adam. "Tell them."

Adam cleared his throat. "Maybe you remember the Mexico City Summer Olympics just four years ago?" Adam asked. When no one responded, he continued. "The American black runners Tommie Smith and John Carlo won gold and bronze medals. During the 'Star-Spangled Banner,' they raised black-gloved fists for black America. Avery Brundage, now the president of the International Olympic Committee, expelled them from the games."

Gobbles shrugged. "As I remember, there was no violence, was there?"

"No, but it drew worldwide attention," said Shmuel. "And showed how easily fanatics can subvert the Olympics for their political goals."

Gobbles fluttered his hands. "Mr. Becker and Mr. Lalkin, rest assured we are well prepared. The matter is finished."

The Germans did not tell Shmuel and Adam that three weeks earlier they had dismissed as not credible a rumor that Palestinians were planning an incident.

Shmuel and Adam took their security fears to the Israeli government, but they were similarly complacent and nonresponsive.

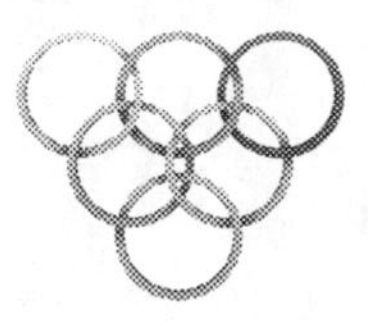

The 1972 Olympic games began auspiciously for Jews competing in Germany. Many were wary about returning to the country that had annihilated six million of their brethren less than thirty years before. Mark Spitz showed no reluctance and set swimming records while winning seven gold medals.

But on the day following Spitz's last win, events took a turn for the worse—much worse. Spitz left for the United States on the next available flight.

CHAPTER 14

IT WAS MONDAY EVENING, SEPTEMBER 4, 1972. Lalkin, Becker, and most of the Israeli contingent of twenty-five athletes, coaches, and managers had journeyed into the city to enjoy a German production of *Fiddler on the Roof.* Afterward, they dined with the play's star, Israeli actor Shmuel Rodensky.

A ten-minute walk from the theater, eight Palestinians assembled and ate dinner in a private room at the Munich Central Railway Station. They'd just finished six weeks of intensive training at a top-secret desert camp concealed deep in Libya, where they had evolved into a cohesive band. Jordanian passports and a West German entry visa forged in Beirut had gotten them into Germany. These Black September Palestinians were prepared to die for their cause.

Luttif Afif, codename Issa—Jesus in Arabic—became their leader because of his fluent German. He'd been working in the Olympic Village for several months as an engineer. He knew the layout as well as he knew his own home.

"Here's your assignment," Issa said, handing each a detailed map of the Olympic Village. "And your weapons." He beckoned to a Black September commander standing off to the side who distributed firearms to the terrorists.

"We have your parents to thank," Issa said, nodding to the youngest member of the group. "They showed much courage."

A middle-aged Palestinian couple, traveling as husband and wife, had deposited four identical pieces of luggage in lockers at the Munich Central Railway Station. These suitcases contained eight AK-47 assault rifles, eight TT-30 Tokarev pistols, multiple magazines loaded with hundreds of 7.62 mm bullets, and ten grenades. A customs agent had stopped the couple at the German border. The neo-Nazi just "happened" to inspect the only suitcase that held clothes and passed the couple through.

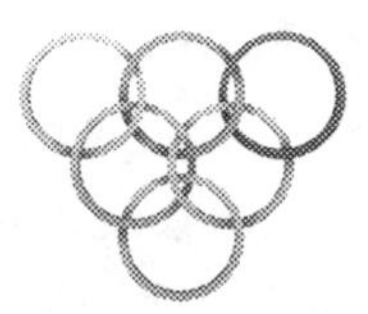

The Israelis returned on a team bus to their five apartments on 31 Connollystrasse around half past midnight on September 5.

"Okay, guys," Adam said to the group as they exited the bus, tired and sleepy. "You all know your room assignments. Have a good night, and I'll see you in the morning. Wake-up call is 7:00 a.m., but the training table opens at 6:00 for those who can't sleep. Remember—no pancakes with syrup. Stick to proteins and avoid the carbs. Eat steak with your eggs. Good night, all, and pleasant dreams."

They dispersed among the five apartments in the building. No one checked to see if the main door was locked. It opened into a large foyer where apartment 1 was located. A stairwell on one side led up to the other apartments and down to an underground car park.

At 4:10 a.m., the eight Palestinians wearing Olympic sweat suits assembled near gate 25A. The early morning hours were cool but clear. September rains had blown over, leaving dense clouds that obscured the moonlight. Grass underfoot was still moist.

"All of you, just act natural and keep your mouths shut," Issa instructed.

"We'll look like the other athletes sneaking back to their rooms after curfew."

As they were about to climb the border fence, four drunken Americans stumbled along and joined their group.

"Hey, guys, how you doing?" said one American, slapping an arm across Issa's shoulders. "Gimme a hand, will you?" He tried to climb the six-foot chain-link fence, lurched into it, and fell.

Issa propped him up. With the other terrorists, he helped the tottering American athletes scale the enclosure and followed them into the compound, all laughing and mingling together. Six German postal workers reported the break-in, but no one took action.

The Palestinians said good-bye to the Americans and split. Once inside the foyer of the building, each removed an AK-47 from a shouldered Olympic duffel bag, fingered a round into the chamber, and plugged the thirty-bullet cartridge in place. They crammed the Tokarev pistols and grenades into the sweat suit side pockets, pulled on ski masks, and converged outside the door of the first apartment where seven coaches and referees slept.

"Everybody ready?" whispered Issa. All nodded. He held up a key. "To the first apartment," he said. "Be quiet." He put a finger to his lips.

The counterfeit key wasn't a perfect fit, and the jiggling lock woke Yossef Gutfreund, a wrestling referee. He rose from his bed, went to the door, and put an ear against the wood. The door suddenly opened against him. Yossef, almost three hundred pounds of muscle, spotted rifles and ski masks and managed to heave the door closed for a few precious seconds.

"Jesus Christ!" he screamed. "Wake up and run! We're under attack!"

He couldn't hold the door long. But it was long enough for Tuvia Skolsky, a Holocaust survivor whose entire family was murdered during the war, to wake and hurtle through a plate glass window. He escaped into the street with slashes from the shards, bleeding as he ran.

The rest were not as quick. The terrorists crowbarred the door open using a Kalashnikov gun barrel and crashed into the room. Yossef fell back onto the floor.

Moshe Weinberg, the weight lifting coach, had just sneaked back into the building after a night out in Munich. He wasn't as sleepy as the others. Springing from his bed, he yelled, "You motherfuckers," and attacked Issa, knocking the gun from his hands. As Issa fell, a terrorist standing behind him shot Weinberg in the face. Moshe went down, bleeding profusely from his mouth shredded by the bullet. Miraculously, the bullet tore through his cheek and missed everything else.

"Anybody else move, you will be shot like this guy," Issa yelled, getting up from the floor. The terrorists trained automatics on the rest of the athletes in the room, and no one stirred.

"Tie them up, except this guy," Issa ordered. "You," he pointed his gun at Moshe, "are going to show us to the other apartments."

The terrorists removed ropes from Olympic bags and bound all the Israelis together, sitting them on a bed side by side. They forced Moshe at gunpoint to lead them to the other apartments housing Israeli athletes.

Holding a scarf to his bleeding cheek, Moshe stumbled into the stairwell and up the stairs. He passed by the door to apartment 2.

Issa grabbed him by the shoulder and spun him around. "Who's in there?" he demanded.

"Don't know," Moshe mumbled through the scarf. "None of us," he said, walking past the door.

"You'd better not be lying to me," Issa threatened and poked the gun barrel in his ribs. Moshe ignored the jab and led them to apartment 3, where the weight lifters and wrestlers slept. He knew who was in apartment 2 and hoped the big guys in apartment 3 would be able to overpower the terrorists.

Not a chance.

The terrorists burst in on the sleeping athletes, screaming and waving automatics. "Don't anybody move," shouted Issa, "or you're dead." In seconds, before the Israelis could even get out of bed, the terrorists took all six as prisoners.

Issa decided to keep all hostages in the same room. "Everybody back to apartment 1," he ordered. He lined up the men and herded them at gunpoint back to the first apartment.

Gad Tsabari, the light-flyweight freestyle wrestler, was at the front of the line going down the stairs. Under his breath, he hissed, "Moshe, I can't take this. I'm going to make a break for it."

"You'll get shot," Moshe mumbled.

"And if I stay? Same thing."

Moshe nodded. "Go for it. I'll do what I can."

In the foyer, when one of the terrorists prodded him in the ribs with his gun to enter apartment 1, Gad slapped the barrel aside and leapt down the stairwell. A hail of bullets followed, ricocheting off the walls. He raced around the curving stairwell and sprinted to the safety of the underground car park.

When Gad made his move, Moshe grabbed the gun of the man closest to him, knocked him unconscious with the barrel, and slashed another with a knife snatched from a table. A burst of bullets ripped his chest to shreds, killing him instantly. Later the terrorists threw his body into the street.

Yossef Romano, a wrestler on crutches because of a torn knee ligament, saw his friend Moshe get murdered.

"Sons of whores!" he screamed. "No way!" He threw his crutch to the side and lunged at the terrorist who had killed Moshe. He dragged the man to the floor and had his hands around the terrorist's throat when a bullet in the back ended his life. The terrorists left Yossef's bleeding body at the feet of the bound hostages.

The gunshots and shouting woke Adam Becker in apartment 2. Quietly he roused his colleagues. "What's going on?" they asked.

"I don't know, but I heard gunshots from the first apartment," Adam said. "Not good."

Shaul Ladany, the Israeli race-walking champion, had survived Bergen-Belsen concentration camp. He said softly, "I'm not going to die here. Not after all I've lived through." He rushed to a rear window and hurdled from the second-floor balcony onto the street. Shaul ran off to warn authorities what was happening. The rest barricaded the door and gathered to attack anyone who tried to get in.

Through the window of apartment 1, one of the terrorists saw Ladany run away and concluded apartment 2 was now empty.

At 5:08 a.m., the Black September terrorists made their demands known. Issa threw two sheets of paper from the second-floor balcony listing the names of 234 Palestinian prisoners held in Israeli jails and two imprisoned German guerrillas they wanted freed in return for releasing their hostages.

"I'll kill one hostage every hour if all prisoners are not freed by 9:00 a.m. and transported to Egypt," Issa shouted to the crowd gathering below.

"What in hell am I going to do?" Gobbles said when he heard the demands.

They waited, motionless, on both sides of the door to apartment 2, each holding a leg from a dismantled chair, ready to attack any intruder. They propped a second chair under the door handle as a barricade.

After ten minutes, Adam whispered, "They must not know we're here. Otherwise they would've broken in by now."

"Who do you think they are?" said Kadir Altschuler, the fitness coach.

"Terrorists. Security's nonexistent," Adam said.

"What should we do?" Kadir asked, setting his chair leg down on the floor to flex the cramp in his hand.

"Maybe they've left the building," said Adam.

"Or could be waiting to attack us as we leave," said the coach.

Adam nodded. "Stay here. I'm going to find out," he said. "Lock the door behind me."

Adam gripped the door handle, his heart beating so loud he was sure the terrorists could hear it. He opened the door millimeters at a time and peered out. The hallway appeared deserted. He took one step, scanned right and left, then took another, and inched into the hall. Sweat poured off his face. His hand clutching the chair leg shook, while the other steadied him along the wall.

Down the dark hall to his left, Adam saw light from the door to apartment 3. He held the chair leg with both hands overhead, crept to the open door, and peeked in. The room seemed empty, but he had to be sure.

With a racing heart, he entered, holding the chair leg aloft, and looked around. No signs of a struggle. He checked closets, under the bed, the bathroom. All empty. Were they captured or did they escape? Adam wondered. No way to tell.

He turned, went back into the hall, and stopped at the door to apartment 2. He knocked softly. Kadir opened it a crack. "Empty," whispered Adam. "I'm going to check the other apartment."

He made his way to the top of the stairs. Voices from apartment 1 stopped him.

Adam stepped down one step … a second … and a third. The wooden stair creaked underfoot, and he cringed.

The voices halted, and so did he.

He barely breathed and stood statue still. The stair groaned as he shifted his weight.

The voices resumed, this time shouting, and he rapidly descended three more steps to the landing. From there, he peered around the wall to look at apartment 1. The door was closed.

More shouting and noises from the apartment—a thumping against a wall—covered him as he bolted back up the stairs.

"They're in the first apartment," Adam told the others when he returned. "They must have our guys there. What do you want to do?"

"What do you think?" Kadir asked.

"Fight or flight?" asked Adam.

"Flight," Kadir said.

"And leave Gutfreund, Weinberg, and the others?" asked Adam. "All our friends."

"We don't know where they are or if they're still alive. And the terrorists have guns. All we've got are busted chair legs." He held his up and waved it in the air.

"What do the rest of you think?" Adam asked. "If we creep down the stairwell, past the apartment door to the underground car park, we're out of here and safe. Or we can break into the apartment and try to free our guys."

"Adam, I admire your loyalty, but be sensible. We are four unarmed men against we don't know how many armed terrorists—but a lot, since they captured ten or eleven of our guys. I say we get out if we can. Maybe try to help the police free them afterward," said Kadir.

Adam looked at the others. They both nodded.

How could he leave his men? He was responsible for their safety. If only he and Shmuel had been more insistent with the Germans, made them provide more security. If only he had a gun—*if*, *if*, the world was filled with *if*s.

And where was Shmuel? Adam hoped he wasn't captured with the others.

Adam stared into each face, watched their eyes. These were honest men, outstanding Israeli athletes who cared about their friends. But they were right. It would be suicide.

"Okay, we try to escape. We'll be spotted if we use the window like Shaul. Out the door, quickly and quietly, down the stairs to the car park. Take your chair leg, just in case. I'll bring up the rear."

The fitness coach was first out the door, trailed closely by the other two. Adam hung back, guarding the rear. At the head of the stairs, they paused when they heard noises coming from apartment 1 and looked at Adam. He nodded, and they descended the stairs.

The thought occurred to Adam that he had forgotten to warn about the creaky third step. No need. Voices from apartment 1 drowned out the squeak.

Until the next-to-last man.

Apartment 1 became silent just as his foot hit the step. The harsh sound reverberated in the hall. To Adam, the screech bounced off walls with a hundred echoes.

"Down the rest of the stairs, quick," Adam ordered. "Get the hell into the car park."

Now, heedless of the racket, the men bounded down the stairs two and three at a time and disappeared below as the door to apartment 1 flew open.

A terrorist emerged and pointed his automatic at Adam.

"Shit," was all Adam had time to say.

Empty clicks sounded. The gun magazine had jammed.

"*Ebn el sharmoota*," the terrorist shouted. Son of a bitch. He charged Adam, waving the gun over his head like a club.

Adam sidestepped, parried the gun barrel with his chair leg, and whacked the back of the terrorist's head as he flew by. The man stumbled and went down on his knees, dazed. Adam debated a killing head strike, but another terrorist stormed through the door and changed his mind. Adam leaped down the stairs to the car park. Bullets careened off the walls.

"What happened?" Kadir asked as Adam ran out of the stairwell.

"Smacked one of them with my chair leg." Adam held it up, pointing to the bloody end.

"Enough. Out of here, now," Adam ordered, and they ran out the exit to the street.

CHAPTER 15

"HOW DID IT HAPPEN?" GOBBLES ASKED ADAM after he and the others made their way to the security office.

"They caught us sleeping," said Adam, his voice cracking with the effort to remain calm. He wanted to shout, "You stupid bastard. You're to blame. Why didn't you provide more security or let us have guns?"

"I've seen their demands," Gobbles said. "I have no control over the prisoners in Israel, but I put in a call to your prime minister. I'll talk with her, then with the Black September leader, this man they call Issa. We'll get them freed. Don't worry."

Gobbles met with Issa, but he had neither a plan nor the negotiating skills to end the standoff. The terrorists refused to change their demands, and Golda Meir would not bend to blackmail.

"I begged Meir to free the prisoners," he told Adam. "I did everything I could. Her response was, 'No, absolutely not. If I did, no Jew would be safe anywhere in the world.'"

"Tough lady," Adam said. "She wasn't elected to be a pussycat."

"She offered to airlift a team of Israeli commandos to rescue the hostages."

"Great. Those Mossad guys are fantastic. When do they arrive?" Adam asked.

"I told her no, we could deal with it," Gobbles said. "She offered a hostage negotiating team."

"Let me take a wild guess. You said no."

Gobbles nodded, sarcasm lost. "I told her I'd handle my end if she'd handle hers." He shook his head in dismay and frowned. "Then she said the Federal Republic of Germany was now in charge and she'd hold me personally responsible if the athletes got hurt." He shrugged. "Can you imagine that? Like it was my fault that all this happened."

Gobbles had no antiterror unit. Even if he had, it could not act without local approval for any action. Munich was a province of Bavaria, and only Bavarian authorities could make decisions, adding hours to any response.

Adam was furious when he heard. "That's ridiculous. Declare a state of emergency so federal power supersedes."

"Good idea," Gobbles said. "You're a good lawyer." He made the declaration and commandeered the rescue plans.

After meeting with his police chief, Gobbles decided to send in a small police force disguised as Olympians. The police were to walk across the shale roof of the building and crawl down the ventilator shafts into the apartment. At the code word "sunshine," they were to storm the terrorists.

Burdened by heavy gear beneath their Olympic sweat suits, the police gingerly crawled along the slippery roof. Twice, one of them stumbled and almost plunged to the ground twenty feet below. The effort was valiant but futile. TV camera crews filmed the rescue operations from the building across the alley. They broadcast the entire event live on TV.

"Look at this," one of the terrorists called to Issa, pointing at the TV screen in apartment 1. "The cops are on the roof over our heads. They're unscrewing one of the ventilator shafts right now."

"Stupid bastards," Issa said, dialing the hotline number.

"Are you crazy, Gobbles?" he shouted into the phone. "You think I'm a fool? Call off the cops or I'll kill two hostages immediately. You can watch me do it on TV."

"Okay, okay." Gobbles gave the order, and the police retreated.

He tried another approach. "Issa, we'll pay whatever you want. Name your price and let the hostages go."

"Not a chance. Free the prisoners first."

"We're working on that. But it takes time. Let me substitute for the Israelis. Hold me hostage in their place."

"Stop this bullshit," Issa screamed into the phone. "You heard my demands. Nothing less. Do it or I will kill Israelis. You don't have much time left."

The Munich Olympic organizing committee voted to cancel the rest of the Olympics. Avery Brundage, veteran of the 1936 Games, overruled the decision. Three thousand fans watched Japan beat West Germany in volleyball while the nine Israeli athletes remained captive minutes away, hands and feet bound, denied food, drink, or the bathroom.

Gobbles convinced Issa to extend his deadline multiple times. By five in the evening, Issa reached the end of his patience. He paced up and down on the second-floor balcony, waving the Kalashnikov automatic over his head.

"Enough with delays," he yelled to the crowd below. "I'm going to kill the hostages, one every hour, starting right now." He let loose a barrage of bullets that made everyone jump for protective doorways.

Gobbles called Issa on the phone. "We're doing all we can. The Israelis aren't budging. Meir's being unreasonable."

"She's a bitch," he screamed into the phone. "I'm changing my plans. Fly all of us to Cairo. We'll exchange hostages for prisoners there."

"Okay, anything you want. Give me time to get a plane." Gobbles conferred with his advisors. They agreed but wanted to be sure the hostages were unhurt.

An hour later, Gobbles called Issa. "We want to know the hostages are all okay first."

"Watch the building," Issa said. "One of them will tell you."

Issa put his gun to the back of the fencing coach, Levi Frankel, and stood him at a second-floor open window on live TV. Frankel, newly married and the father of a one-month-old baby girl, wore a white tank top, with his hands bound by a thick rope in front of him. He looked nervous, brows creased and lips tight. Issa had told him what to say.

"We're all okay," Frankel started, "except for—"

"Jesus Christ," Adam said, staring at the balcony. "That's Levi."

Before Levi could finish telling them the body of Yossef Romano lay at their feet, Issa gun-butted him in the back of the head and dragged him away.

The TV cameras captured it all live.

"My poor friend," said Adam. "We've got to save him—all of them."

"We will," said Gobbles.

Issa allowed Gobbles and the police chief to visit the hostages. Afterward, Gobbles described the calm dignity of the athletes, despite the horror of their situation. He said they were all bound together, sitting on the edge of a bed, with Romano's body lying in a pool of congealed blood at their feet. They could smell blood in the air.

Logistics to meet Issa's new demands proved challenging. Gobbles sought Adam's input. They were able to locate two Bell UH-1 military helicopters that would transport the group from the Olympic Village to the Fürstenfeldbruck airfield and a waiting 727 airplane. Adam suggested they walk to the helicopters through the underground garage where he and his colleagues had escaped.

"That's where we'll ambush them," Gobbles said. "Station police behind parked cars in the garage."

"Do it carefully," Adam warned. "Those guys will be looking for traps."

The police hid behind cars as ordered. But Issa insisted on a walk through alone before bringing the hostages. Shadows flitting in the dimly lit garage caught his eye, and he spotted the concealed officers.

Issa turned on Gobbles, and the police chief had to jump between them. "You're playing with Israeli lives," Issa shouted. "Another attempt like this, and I'll execute two on live TV like I said before."

"Okay, okay," Gobbles said, trying to calm him down. "Anything you want."

Both sides finally agreed on a bus to take the terrorists and hostages to the helicopters.

Undeterred by Issa's threats, Gobbles planned another ambush at the airport. He would use sharpshooters to pick them off. Remembering five terrorists from his visit to the apartment, he instructed the police chief to supply five sharpshooters.

"Do the police have sharpshooters?" Adam asked, hearing the plan unfold.

"Of course they do," Gobbles said. "Don't you?" he asked the police chief.

"Not really," came the reply. "We've got guys who can shoot a rifle fairly straight, but they've never been trained as marksmen. And they don't have state-of-the-art sniper rifles. We have no telescopic sights or infrared scopes for the dark."

The chief didn't add that the five shooters had been on their feet since early morning, more than twelve hours ago. Also, they had no means of communicating with each other to synchronize their shots. Gobbles had been mistaken about the number of terrorists too; there were eight, all heavily armed, not five.

Gobbles planned on armored vehicles to support the police during their attack at the airport, but those vehicles got stuck in city traffic and were delayed for hours.

If the sharpshooters failed to kill the terrorists when the helicopters landed, Gobbles had a backup plan. He ordered thirteen police officers from a special task command force to board the 727 dressed as flight attendants. They would surprise the terrorists as they entered. However, the police officers decided their mission was suicidal. They walked off the plane without telling anyone before the terrorists arrived.

Preparations deteriorated further. The helicopters landed at 10:36 p.m. but faced the wrong direction for the snipers to visualize and shoot their targets. The terrorists were able to use the helicopters as shields from the shooters.

When the helicopters landed, Issa jumped from one and grabbed his assistant, Tony, as he jumped from the other.

"We need to check out the plane first." They ran to the Lufthansa Boeing 727 waiting on the tarmac. The plane was deserted. "That son of a bitch, Gobbles. This is another one of his tricks. Out, quickly, before it explodes." They ran back to the helicopters.

Gobbles was enraged. "Where are your police?" he yelled at the chief. "They were supposed to be in the plane to capture these guys."

The police chief looked at him and shrugged. "I don't know what happened."

"I've had enough of this," Gobbles snapped. "Tell your snipers to start shooting. Take out those bastards."

The first sniper, ordered to kill Issa, missed and hit Tony in the thigh. Two others, belatedly ordered to shoot, killed one terrorist. That triggered a firefight that shot out most of the airport lights, making it impossible to distinguish terrorists from police.

Seeing they weren't making much headway, the police chief ordered his men to storm the terrorists. The men refused without armored vehicle backup, which still hadn't arrived. The fight became an hour-and-twenty-minute stalemate of darkness, shadowy movements, and little action.

Around midnight, the droning, deep-throated sound of heavy equipment could be heard approaching. The armored vehicles had arrived at last.

The terrorists heard them also.

"This fight is going to shift quickly, and we may lose the mission," Issa said. "Kill the hostages."

"You sure? Maybe we could—" one of the terrorists began.

"Do it. Now!"

The Israelis were manacled together, four in one helicopter and five in the other. At 12:04 a.m., Issa threw a fragmentation grenade into the first helicopter. The explosion set the fuel tanks on fire, killing all four Israelis.

Seconds later, Tony, limping from his gunshot wound, jumped into the second helicopter and mowed down the remaining five shackled Israelis point-blank with a barrage of over fifty bullets from his AK-47.

Issa tore from the helicopters and ran across the tarmac, shooting at the police as he sprinted. They returned fire, killing him. His body crumpled near the 727.

By one thirty in the morning, it was all over. The police killed five terrorists, including Tony, and captured three. Only then did they put out the flames of the burning helicopter. A later autopsy showed one of the hostages, David Berger, died of smoke inhalation, not from burns, and might have been saved.

A stray bullet killed one German police officer, their only casualty.

Jim McKay, the US announcer of the Olympics, finished fourteen straight hours of broadcasting by stating, "Our worst fears have been realized tonight … They're all gone."

At the next day's news conference, Gobbles dodged reporters' questions with practiced footwork. He blamed the outcome on Golda Meir's refusal to release the prisoners and the outstanding skill of the terrorists. Coming to his aid, the Munich police chief said the terrorists "made no mistakes." Neither the West German nor Bavarian governments ever took responsibility for the tragedy.

Two days later, Israel bombed bases in Syria and Lebanon and raided them with infantry, tanks, and armored personnel carriers. It was too little, too late. Golda Meir promised the grief-stricken families to pursue each and every terrorist involved. "We will chase them to the last," she said.

Shmuel and Adam returned home, beaten and depressed. The mood in Israel matched theirs. Not only had they failed to save eleven of their finest Olympic athletes, but the massacre had happened on German soil with either German complicity or at least German ineptitude. Wounds of the Holocaust reopened and reverberated throughout the country.

Almost two months later, on October 29, Lufthansa flight number 615 from Frankfurt was hijacked in midair. A hijacker named Abu-Ali threatened to blow up the plane with thirteen male passengers aboard, unless the three captured terrorists were freed.

Without informing the Israeli government, the West German government flew the three terrorists to Zagreb, Yugoslavia. Met by Lufthansa 615, passengers and terrorists took off for Libya and landed in Tripoli at about nine at night. The alleged hostages, who had been partying with the terrorists during the flight, were freed and immediately flew back to Germany. Documents that surfaced later suggested the West German government staged the hijacking and even paid $5 million to get rid of the terrorists.

In *Operation Wrath of God*, the Mossad, Israel's national intelligence agency, and the Israel Defense Force eventually killed two of the three terrorists and several collaborators. The master planner, Abu-Daoud, survived five bullet wounds in an assassination attempt and died of kidney failure in 2010. Jamal Al-Gashey, the only terrorist that escaped, later said he was proud of what he did because "it helped the Palestinian cause."

CHAPTER 16

TEL AVIV, DECEMBER 1986

AFTER MUNICH, ADAM TRIED TO REENTER ordinary life. It was hard, like returning from the trauma of war. He often had dreams about Levi reaching out to him for help. Levi would be drowning in the middle of the ocean, tied up in a burning house, or stranded on a cliff. Adam would cry out to Levi but not be able to help. Adam's outburst would wake him, sweating and shaking, filled with remorse. He stopped running and barely ate. He lost twenty-five pounds and looked it.

Over time, the nightmares eased, and his legal practice grew. But he brooded and couldn't escape a sense of failure. He had let his comrades down. They had died because of it.

Could he have worked harder to convince the West German government, or even his own, to improve security? Could he have gotten a gun? What if they hadn't left apartment 2 and stayed to fight the terrorists? Could they have saved them? Even some of them? He tortured himself with imponderables and became depressed and withdrawn.

Adam took refuge in the ordinary and orderly pattern of his life: legal work, an apartment, and Friday-night Shabbat dinner at his mother's. Just the two of them, she'd light Shabbat candles, recite a *baruch* over the wine and bread, and they'd eat. Conversation was one-sided. Only an occasional movie, dinner date, or a rare sleepover with a woman punctuated this routine, despite repeated urgings from his mother.

"Adam, you're still a young man. You need to get out more, be with friends, and socialize. My friend Chava has a daughter who—"

"Mother, no. I'm happy as a bachelor, being a lawyer, and volunteering with our Olympic team. Stop being a matchmaker."

"And if I'm not a matchmaker, when will I ever hold a grandchild? Answer me that, my happy bachelor lawyer." She'd point an accusing finger at him. "And eat your pot roast I made especially for you. It will stick to your ribs. The boiled potatoes will put on some pounds. No girl wants a man so skinny she can count his ribs."

A rare snowstorm blanketed central Israel in December 1986. Two inches shut down Jerusalem and Tel Aviv. Cars slid off the roads and into each other. Windy blizzard conditions closed the major Ayalon Highway and Ben Gurion International Airport; one hundred thousand homes and businesses lost power.

Adam, worried about his mother, set out cautiously from work. After driving bumper to bumper for two hours, he was a block from her apartment when he stopped at a yellow light turning red. The car behind him didn't. The fender bender bounced him against the steering wheel and squeezed out a rare "Fuck!"

Rubbing his bruised chest, Adam parked his car at the curb. He got out and approached the culprit, ready with a tirade about incompetent, tailgating drivers. Through the driver's window, he saw long blonde hair, hands cupped over her ears, and a forehead resting against the steering wheel. Concern replaced his anger, and he knocked on the window. The head didn't move. Worried she was unconscious, Adam banged harder. The head jerked up, and she looked at him glassy-eyed.

"Are you okay?" he yelled through the window. Her face was blank. He repeated the question louder. She still didn't respond. Finally, he gestured a circular motion for her to roll down the window. When she did, he asked, "Are you okay?"

She started to cry. Tears running down her cheeks left dark trails of smudged mascara.

Adam became more concerned. Maybe she was injured. "Are you hurt?"

She shook her head.

"Can I help?"

She shrugged. Her apathy made him fear head trauma, but she had no bruises.

By now, a gaggle of cars had lined up behind her, and horns were blaring. He said, "Scoot over so I can drive." Mechanically, she did, and he slipped in behind the wheel. He drove the car to the curb and parked it behind his.

Adam turned off the motor and looked at her. She was young and quite beautiful, with shoulder-length, wavy blonde hair, brown eyes, and creamy skin. She had high cheekbones, full lips, and a tiny cleft in her chin.

Gradually her crying stopped. He gave her his handkerchief, and she dabbed at her eyes and drippy nose.

"I'm so sorry," she said. "I thought you'd go through the yellow light, but you stopped, and I tried to stop, but I was going too fast, and it was slippery, so when I hit the brakes—"

She started crying again. He took the handkerchief from her hand and brushed away her tears.

"It's okay," he said, patting her shoulder, "it's okay. No injury to us, and minor damage to the cars. Not a big deal. Could've been a lot worse in this weather."

She began to shake. Her teeth chattered, and she hugged herself to get warm. With the motor off, the car's interior had begun to cool.

He slipped out of his coat and wrapped it around her shoulders. "What's your name?"

"Danica. Danica Cohen. Dannie, really."

"I'm Adam Becker. Look, Dannie, my mother's apartment's a block from here. We can walk there, get a cup of coffee or a bowl of soup to warm you up. After that, I'll drive you home, or if you feel okay, you can drive home yourself."

Gretchen beamed a huge smile as Adam led Dannie into her apartment.

Ignoring Adam, she hugged Dannie like an old friend, and then she held her at arm's length.

"Finally, my son the lawyer is bringing me a girlfriend," Gretchen said. "And she's a beautiful young lady. What's your name, darling?"

"Danica Cohen. Everybody calls me Dannie."

"I especially like the Cohen part," Gretchen said. "Come in and sit down." As she helped her out of Adam's coat, Gretchen flashed Adam a smile. "Who are your parents, Dannie?"

"Easy, Mom. Let her drink a cup of tea or a bowl of soup before the inquisition."

"You're right, Adam. Please excuse my rudeness, Dannie. I'm just so happy to have a young woman in my apartment. At last." She pinched her thumb and first two fingers together, kissed the tips, raised her eyes, and spread her fingers to the ceiling, letting the kiss float upward.

Gretchen draped an arm across Dannie's shoulders and guided her into the kitchen. "Come, Dannie, sit down. I have fresh chicken soup, just needs to be heated. It'll take out the chill."

The kitchen was tiny, the walls white, with a small refrigerator, sink, and stove. Adam and Dannie squeezed into chairs at the round kitchen table with a gray Formica top.

Gretchen turned on the gas range and lit a fire under a large covered metal pot. She bustled about the kitchen. She put on a red-checked apron, fussed with her hair to be sure the bun was intact, buried a few loose ends, and set about preparing a meal. Her eyes never left Dannie's face.

Adam watched his mother and knew, despite the domestic activities, she was plotting. There was nothing he could do; he sat there helpless, caught in his mother's web.

As she stirred the soup, she said to Dannie, "It'll take only a few minutes to heat. I'll slice some nice fresh challah. It's wonderful toasted with butter. And with the soup, it will be a meal. What did you say your parents did?"

"Mom, slow down," Adam said, frowning. "We've just come from a car accident and—"

Dannie patted Adam's arm. "It's okay, Adam. I don't mind." Her shivers had stopped, and she began to relax in the warmth of the kitchen.

"My dad's a doctor at Hadassah Medical Center. My mom's a dietician there. I have two younger brothers. And that's my whole family."

"Nice. Very nice," said Gretchen. "And what do you do, if I may ask?"

Adam raised his eyebrows, but Gretchen tossed him a look that said, *I know, I know, but I'm your mother. I have a right to ask.*

Adam squeezed Dannie's arm, but she smiled and said, "I'm a computer programmer at a Microsoft spin-off company just outside Jerusalem."

Gretchen nodded with lips pursed, brow drawn. "Very impressive for a young lady. You like it—doing that hard computer work?" Without waiting for an answer, she said, "Or maybe you're ready to settle down, get married, and have children?"

"Why don't you just propose for me?" Adam said, shaking his head.

"This is only your first date, Adam. Next date I will," Gretchen said.

Six months later, in June, at age fifty-six, happy bachelor lawyer Adam Becker wed thirty-year-old computer programmer Danica Cohen in a ceremony held at the Wailing Wall in Old Jerusalem.

"So when do I get to hold my grandchild?" his mother asked six months later, cornering him alone at Shabbat dinner. "Dannie's young, but you're not."

"Soon, Mother, soon. We're having a little trouble conceiving. Old sperm don't swim uphill as well as young sperm, or something like that, the doctor said. But we're working on it."

Persistence rewarded, a year and a half later they were expecting their first child.

Adam answered the door to their apartment late one Sunday afternoon in June. It was an unusually cool day in Tel Aviv, with overcast skies blocking out the sun. An attractive woman, dark hair pulled into a loose ponytail at the back of her neck, stood at the door. She smiled, but her eyes were not happy.

"Sharon," said Adam. "It's wonderful to see you again. How are you?"

Adam had visited each family after he returned from Munich but had lost touch in the many years since then.

They stood in awkward silence.

Dannie saved him, coming up from behind. "Where're your manners, Adam? Sharon, I'm Dannie," she said, holding out one hand, the other supporting her bulging abdomen.

"Sharon, this is my wife, Dannie," Adam said. He turned to Dannie. "Sharon's husband, Levi, was a star fencer and the Olympic coach—a wonderful, gentle man."

"Please come in and sit down," Dannie said. "Let me bring you some coffee and cake."

Sharon started to protest, but the pressure of Dannie's arm over her shoulders drew her into their apartment. The living room was modest, cream-colored walls with a small dark blue couch flanked by wooden end tables. A round glass-topped coffee table stood in front of the couch on a turquoise rug.

Sharon sat in an easy chair facing a TV screen, and Adam took the corner of the couch closest to her. She wore a sad look, tired, dark lines under her down-turned hazel eyes. For a moment, she rested her head on the chair back, her hands folded in her lap. The only sounds were from the kitchen as Dannie prepared coffee.

"What can I do for you, Sharon?" Adam finally asked.

The question brought tears to her eyes. She fumbled in her purse for a tissue. Dabbing at the drops ruining her mascara, she said, "You're my last hope. The Bavarian authorities refuse to tell me what happened in Munich. They say the records are lost. I have so many questions. I have been searching for answers for almost twenty years." She blew her nose.

"I went into that room—apartment 1—where the men were held captive, on Connollystrasse. I saw where Yossef Romano and Moshe Weinberg were executed, and I felt the terror they must have felt, bound hand and foot, with madmen waving guns and screaming at them." She shuddered. "My Levi wanted nothing more than to participate in the Olympics. That was all he talked about, and to be killed so"—she searched for a word—"so brutally." Sharon sobbed into the tissue. "All these years have passed, and it feels as fresh as when it happened."

"For me too," Adam said softly.

Dannie came into the living room with a tray of cups, cake, and a coffeepot. She poured, sliced the cake, and sat in the other easy chair, not saying a word. She wore a slight smile as she communicated with her kicking baby, hands pressing her abdomen.

Sharon composed herself after a few sips of coffee and continued.

"I have sued the German government to produce whatever information they have about the massacre that took the lives of our eleven athletes. How did it happen? Was it all Black September Palestinian terrorists, or was there collusion with neo-Nazis? I can't get it out of my head that Germany is the same country that wanted to kill every one of us only a generation ago. We need to know all that happened, especially for the families, for my daughter. We want closure. We don't have any money to pay you, but we know you were there in Munich and have done work for the Israeli Olympics. We wondered if—"

"Stop wondering. Of course I'll help. I'll do all I can." He rose, walked to her, and took her hands. "There won't be any charge."

"Bless you." She paused and looked from Dannie to Adam, deciding something. Finally, "One of my other reasons—I've never told anyone this—but I feel responsible for Levi's death."

"How could you?" Dannie asked, and Adam started to say the same thing.

She fluttered her hands to silence them. Adam sat down again.

"I am Dutch. I met Levi while learning to fence at the National Fencing Academy in The Hague. You remember, Adam, Levi was the fencing coach."

"Of course," Adam said.

"We fell in love, married, and moved to Israel. Two weeks before Munich in the summer of 1972, we had a baby girl we named Esther."

"I remember," Adam said.

"I left the baby with my parents in Holland and met Levi in Munich."

She took several deep breaths before continuing.

"We were having a wonderful time before the games started when my brother, a doctor, called to say they had taken Levi's mother to the hospital with chest pains. Levi insisted we check on her, and we left Munich immediately for Holland. We spent two days in the hospital with his mother until the doctors said she was fine. Then I drove Levi to the train station to return to Munich. We were halfway there when he said he wanted to return to the hospital to kiss his mother one more time. He had a sudden premonition she was going to die. I told him he would miss the train, but he insisted. We went back, he kissed her, and he did miss the train." The tears came again.

"But then I drove like crazy to the next train stop, about thirty kilometers away. We got there as the train was pulling out. Levi caught it on a run, forced open one of the doors—and that was the next-to last time I saw him alive."

She was sobbing loudly. "How often I've thought if I had driven just a little slower, or had a flat tire, or more red lights, or took a wrong turn or—I don't know." She shook her head, resigned. "Esther would have a father, and I'd have a husband."

She buried her face in her hands, her body shaking in silent sobs. Dannie went to her, lifted her head, smoothed her hair, and held her close. Sharon's cheek was against her big belly.

Sharon's head bobbed. She stopped crying and smiled. Unembarrassed, she put her arms around Dannie and held her belly to her face.

"Hello, little one," Sharon said softly, stroking Dannie's belly. Her head jumped again as the baby kicked. "I'm glad to meet you too." She blew the baby a kiss.

"Are you hoping for a boy or a girl?" Sharon asked later, over coffee and cake.

"Just a healthy baby. But after we count ten fingers and ten toes, we're hoping for a boy," Dannie said.

"Wouldn't it be great if he became an Olympian?" Sharon asked, a happy note in her voice. "Maybe a fencer? I could teach him."

"Could be. My father was an Olympian," Adam said, "and I almost was."

"Almost?" Sharon asked.

Adam brushed the question aside. "A long story, too long to tell here. But maybe this little one," he pointed to Dannie's belly, "will be what I wasn't. I'd like that. I was a runner, but maybe he could be a fencer." His face wore a wistful look. "Wouldn't that be great? Just thinking about it feels right."

"Levi's mother was okay, Sharon?" Dannie prompted her to finish the story. "Nothing serious after a stay in the hospital?"

Sharon's voice again became heavy. "We brought her home from the hospital, and she was fine. I was staying with my parents, actually sleeping in my childhood bedroom, when they woke me on the morning of September 5. They asked me how many were in the Israeli delegation. I took one look at their faces and raced to the TV in the living room.

"The screen showed the building where Levi and the others were staying, with Moshe Weinberg's body lying outside the door. After that, everything became a haze, mixed with the terrorists' demands, the attempted rescue, and threats of execution. Sometime that afternoon, Golda Meir called and told me they wouldn't give in to the terrorists' demands without risking future kidnappings. 'That might be true,' I told her, 'but that won't help the athletes.'

"Then, later that afternoon, I saw my Levi on the balcony of the building, in his undershirt and without his glasses. He answered a question, and one of the terrorists clubbed him in the back of the head. They dragged him away."

Adam remembered. He felt the guilt build in the pit of his stomach.

"That night, a government spokesman said all the terrorists had been killed and the hostages freed. My family rejoiced, and my father opened a bottle of champagne. But I had a feeling—a bad feeling. I said, 'Wait. We'll know he's okay when he calls me.'

"At 3:20 in the morning, I was still in front of the TV and heard that American announcer Jim McKay say, 'They're all gone.' And it was finished. I turned off the TV, went into my bedroom, closed the door, and just hugged a pillow. I sat on the edge of the bed, rocking, until morning. I didn't think I'd ever finish crying."

Sharon stopped, took a deep breath, and looked from Dannie to Adam. She shrugged and held her hands out, palms up. "What more could I do?" she asked.

There were no answers. The room fell silent.

Sharon finally asked, "You were there, Adam. What can you tell me?"

"Very little more than what you know. But what I can do is help you fight the bureaucracy to uncover the truth."

That afternoon visit triggered lawsuits, countersuits, and appeals as the German government continued to stonewall every attempt to get answers. Adam tried all possible legal avenues, to no avail.

Three years after Sharon's visit, someone heard her plea on a TV program. A month later, Sharon received from an anonymous clerk more than three thousand files, almost a thousand photographs, and dozens of investigative and eyewitness reports that had been hidden for twenty years. The information told a shocking story of neo-Nazis helping the weapons pass through customs, making sure the building at 31 Connollystrasse was unlocked, providing Issa the key to apartment 1, and organizing the fake airplane hijacking. Germany offered to settle the litigation for 3 million euros. Divided among twenty-five plaintiffs, that came to $115,000 per person, nowhere near enough but likely the best the families could get. Most important, the settlement proved Germany's duplicity in the Munich attack. Reluctantly, families settled.

One of Sharon's demands remained unfulfilled—that the IOC commemorates the slaughtered Israelis at the opening ceremony. Olympic officials acknowledged the fairness of her request but told Sharon "their hands were tied" because Arab countries threatened to boycott the games if they made such an announcement.

"My husband's hands were tied," Sharon said. "Not yours."

CHAPTER 17

RIO DE JANEIRO, AUGUST 2016

WAITING FOR DESSERT AT THE RESTAURANTE

Aprazivel gave Kirsten a chance to think about what Stefan had said. He had a crazy family. Did she really want to get involved with him? It didn't take her long to decide. Yes, absolutely yes.

"You're German, not Israeli?" Stefan asked, sipping his coffee. The crème brûlée was untouched.

"No. We're *from* Germany, but we consider ourselves Israelis. I'm a sabra."

"What's that?"

"A Jew born in Israel."

"Your family must've been lucky to escape Hitler."

"Because my grandfather was an Olympian who competed in the 1936 Olympics."

His eyebrows rose. "Wow! The Olympics when Jesse Owens won four gold medals. I read about it. Amazing!"

"My grandfather was killed in his last race against Owens. Stumbled, or was tripped, my father said, and fell. Hit his head and died."

"I'm sorry. What an exciting Olympics, with Owens blowing out the Aryan supremacy myth. Showed Hitler and the damn Nazis a thing or two."

"You know," she said, lowering her voice and looking around at the other diners, "thousands of Nazis escaped to South America after the war, mostly Argentina but Brazil also. They could be all around us."

He nodded. "They probably are. Did you read the theory about Hitler escaping to Patagonia at the end of the war? Pretty far-out story. Hard to believe."

"Yes, and from there to a town called San Carlos de Bariloche," Kirsten said. "I found Bariloche on the Internet. The house he supposedly built was called Estancia Inalco. It looked lovely, right on a freshwater lake with a weird name." She thought about it. "Lake Nahuel Huapí."

"Near here?"

"Argentina. Why? Want to see it?" Kirsten asked, her voice eager.

"Why not," he said. "We have time, and we did come early to see some of the country."

Kirsten's face brightened. "It would be awesome. The house Adolf Hitler and Eva Braun supposedly lived in, almost ten years after the world thought they'd died. And we can explore it," Kirsten said, fork suspended. "All the stories we'll have to tell when we get home. Wouldn't that be great."

"What about your arm?"

She held it up for inspection. "It's fine, really. I can't fence for a few days anyway. I just need to keep it bandaged."

She had worked her fingers squeezing a rubber ball several hours each day to keep her hand and forearm limber. Doctor Shemberg had warned her about scar tissue buildup that could reduce her mobility.

"What about Sharon?" Stefan asked.

Kirsten shook her head. "She won't be able to travel on crutches."

"Will she be disappointed if we leave her?" he asked.

"No—at least I don't think so," Kirsten said. "We can ask her. But wait a minute." She rummaged in her purse. "There's a map in this tourist book. Let's see what this trip would involve."

She unfolded the map. "We're up here in Rio." Her forefinger covered Rio. "And we'd have to fly south to Buenos Aires." She put her thumb on Buenos Aires. "Then rent a car and drive to Necochea." She pointed with her left hand. "From there drive to San Carlos de Bariloche, near the Argentine border with Chile."

"We can't do all that driving," Stefan said, looking at the map. "It'd take forever. And who knows what the roads are like. Or the cars. Why stop in Necochea?"

"That's where they say Hitler landed the summer of '45."

Stefan studied the map. "What we really want to see is his house in Bariloche. Suppose we just fly from here to Buenos Aires," he pointed, "and from there to Bariloche? Cut out the middle steps."

"If there's an airport," Kirsten said.

"Let's check." He pulled out his iPhone.

Two minutes later, he said, "You asked *if* there's an airport? There're *only* seven daily flights from Buenos Aires to Bariloche. Must be a popular tourist spot."

"We have the time." She smiled, thinking, *My God. We've just met, and we're going to travel together?* If her parents only knew, they'd have a fit. A young Israeli woman traveling to Hitler's house with a handsome man, alone. How exciting.

The waiter refilled their coffees. "Didn't like the dessert?"

"We're full. Thanks," Stefan said, still looking at the map. The waiter left with a frown.

"Say we arrive in the afternoon and rent a car," Stefan said. "Stay overnight, and the next morning drive to Hitler's house. Spend a day touring the house and grounds, drive back to Bariloche to sleep, and fly back to Rio the next day. We're gone all of three days, total. No big deal. We can miss that much training, and it gives your arm time to heal."

"How much do you think it'd cost?" Kirsten asked.

"Good question. Maybe a thousand euros between the flights, hotel, and food."

"I'd need to check with Sharon. That's a lot of money," Kirsten said.

"Would you consider a loan? I really want to do this with you. Whether or not Hitler's house is a fairy tale for tourists, it'll still be fun. You game?"

She reached for his hand. "Game? Are you kidding? Count me in!"

CHAPTER 18

"*YOU!*" MAX SAID, POINTING DRAMATICALLY AT the audience, sweeping his arm left to right—first at people sitting in the orchestra section and then in the balconies, "are the salvation of modern Germany.

"*You,*" he repeated the gesture, "are the new Fourth Reich.

"*You* will restore our greatness.

"*You*—" Clapping, cheering, and shouting drowned him out, and he had to stop. The audience stood and stomped their feet, pumped the air with fists, and pounded one another on the back. Many with tears running down their cheeks hugged one another and jumped up and down.

Max sat back on the stool and watched, a satisfied smile on his face. He was glad for the breather. In the pause, he reflected on this vindication of his work. He would have a second helping of revenge, even more satisfying and far-reaching than the first.

The clapping and stomping morphed into a rhythmic cadence that seemed to shake the building, and Max actually feared for the domed structure that cost him eight million euros to build. He stood, raised his hands palms down, and waved them up and down until the crowd quieted.

When all regained their seats, he placed his right hand over his heart. "I cannot express to you what I am feeling at this time, seeing your response to where we've come from, where we are, and where we are going." The cheers started again, but he waved them quiet. "We need to remember this day always and communicate the importance of what it represents to all our comrades, colleagues, and families who could not be with us, who are home in the villages and cities throughout South America—in fact, throughout the world—who believe in what we are trying to accomplish."

Again the cheers from old and young alike, and again he quieted them.

"You and I—we, together—are revolutionaries, as our great leader Adolf Hitler once was. But times have changed, and we cannot start a beer hall putsch to overthrow the Weimar government, as the führer attempted in 1923. We cannot kill the Indians and settle the West, as the Americans did in the 1800s. Or storm the citadel with automatic weapons to wrest control of the régime, as in several Middle Eastern countries recently.

"You all know better than I that the presidential decree of May 15, 1939, officially dissolved the Argentine Nazi Party, but that hasn't stopped us here in Brazil—or even in Argentina, for that matter. Our new Nazi party, Bandera Vecinal, led by our own Alejandro Banding, has now been officially registered in Argentina to legally recognize neo-Nazis. Under the local flag for which it is named, it will offer candidates to compete in elections that will run the country. I know many of you are members. This is a giant step for us. We have reason for great optimism.

"Nevertheless, we must be cautious. To achieve our ends, to achieve Hitler's dream—our dream—of Volksgemeinschaft—the ideal and pure German society—we must be model citizens. We must infiltrate and assimilate, be good neighbors, be voted into political offices around the world, and use social networks like Facebook, Twitter, and LinkedIn. Those sites can be more effective and powerful than a Kalashnikov automatic. All this will take a great deal of funds, but that will be my responsibility and my contribution to our wonderful movement.

"While doing all this, we must never forget our Aryan principles: that we are the superior beings, that Jews and blacks and Hispanics are contemptible, beneath us, and rightfully made our servants, and that laws applying to them do not affect us. That, simply said, is what we are, who we are. But in today's society, we need to be subtler, not as obvious and open as we could be seventy years ago. Regardless, always remember that our great founder, Adolf Hitler, was himself the incarnation of Aryan purity and unshakable principles, and he dedicated his entire life solely to the German people."

He removed the microphone from the lectern and dramatically strode to midstage, letting his eyes wash over the audience. The blue contacts gave him Hitler's eyes, but he didn't like looking out at a tinted world.

"Let us go forward from this day with renewed vigor to accomplish our goals, to spread the word and world of Nazism, to disseminate its ideals around the globe, to free us from the subjugation of Jews and the yoke of inferior races that threaten world domination, and to create the Fourth Reich. From it will blossom Hitler's dream of the Thousand-Year Reich. The universe is rightfully ours to conquer! It is our Lebensraum—our living space. Go forth and take it!"

His voice rose to a ringing crescendo, arms uplifted to the audience, eyes hallucinogenic ovals. He stood solidly on two feet spread apart, a messianic expression on his face mimicking countless Hitler speeches he had studied, only lacking the leader's mustache.

To finish, he stood at clicked-heel attention and shouted into the microphone—"Heil Hitler!"—while thrusting his right arm to the ceiling. The audience rose as one, right arms stiff as flagpoles, screaming at the top of their voices, "Heil Hitler! Heil Hitler! Heil Hitler!"

CHAPTER 19

STEFAN AND KIRSTEN LEFT RIO ON AEROLINEAS Argentinas flight 1269 at six o'clock the next morning. With a two-and-a-half-hour layover in Buenos Aires, they were in San Carlos de Bariloche by four that afternoon. At the airport, they rented a compact car from Hertz.

"It's seen better days," Kirsten said, eyeballing the car in slot 12. "You sure it's ours?"

Stefan pulled out his receipt and checked it against the license plate. "It's ours. It must be at least ten years old. I hope I can see out the windshield." The glass was spidery from trauma.

"Can we get a different one?" Kirsten asked.

"The guy at the counter said it's the last car available, and we're lucky to have it."

"What kind of car is it?"

Stefan shrugged and walked to the back of the car. "It says Nissan, but who knows? Probably a patchwork of several. The bumper's been crushed and hammered out, and it looks like a door has been replaced."

"As long as it runs, I guess we're okay."

Stefan opened the trunk and loaded their luggage. He slammed the lid, but it popped back open. After the fourth attempt and threats under his breath, the latch held.

They got in, sat down, and closed their doors. "Damn," Stefan said as the door handle came off in his hand. He held it up for Kirsten to see.

"You can get along without a door handle," Kirsten said, laughing, "as long as the wheels stay on."

The motor seemed angry at being disturbed and groaned until the engine started with a pop and snort.

Except for a shimmy at speeds exceeding forty miles per hour, the car performed as it was supposed to. They made the short drive to town without a problem.

As they drove, Kirsten thought about where she was and what she was doing. She had a hard time believing it all. She had had to work hard to convince Sharon to let her do this, and she knew her parents wouldn't have approved at all. But, for goodness sake, she was twenty-seven years old and could make her own decisions. She lived with her parents out of convenience, not dependency, and if she wanted to take a trip alone with a male friend, so be it. She stared at Stefan, who was intent on driving the rickety car. *Strong profile*, she thought. *I like his nose. Powerful hands, gripping a saber or ...* She was sure. This was the right decision.

He glanced at her. "What?" he asked.

"Nothing," she said, smiling. "Just hard to believe where we are."

He nodded and reached for her hand.

As they entered Bariloche, Kirsten studied the buildings. "We could be in Europe, not Argentina," she said. "It looks like Switzerland."

"Or Germany," Stefan said, pointing to a half-timbered building with dark beams crisscrossing white plaster in the front and a clock tower alongside. "That's German architecture, straight from Bavaria. Even some of the street names are German."

They booked adjoining rooms in the Grand Hotel Bariloche. The hotel was small, clean, in the middle of downtown, and affordable. They left their bags in their rooms and walked through town toward the lake.

"It's beautiful," said Kirsten, stopping to admire the shimmering waters. "No wonder tourists come here." She looked to her left. "The Andes still have snow on the peaks."

"They probably do all year round, but remember it's August—winter down here."

"Oops, I forgot. The weather's so mild. I was thinking summer, like at home." She linked her arm in his, and he grinned, giving it a squeeze.

"I'm glad you're here with me," he said.

"Me too."

The town had developed along the southern shore of Lake Nahuel Huapí, bordered on the west by the tall, snowcapped Andes Mountains that separated Argentina from Chile, with the Patagonian Desert to the east.

"Hungry?" asked Stefan.

"Soon." She patted her stomach. "Still digesting peanuts from the plane. Let's walk along the lakefront till I get my appetite back. The landing was a bit bouncy."

As they strolled among tourists, Kirsten read from the guidebook. "This whole area started with a single shop by a German immigrant who crossed the Andes. The town drew lots of Europeans, then took on an alpine décor because of the great skiing. It was even called 'Little Switzerland' at one point. Ultimately became a wealthy tourist hangout."

Stefan observed the passing crowds of well-dressed tourists. "I can see that," he said. "But nothing about Hitler or other Nazis?"

"Wait, I'm looking," she said, thumbing pages in the book. Stefan grabbed her arm and guided her around a lamppost she was about to walk into.

She stopped walking, stared in his eyes, and smiled her thanks. Her face was close to his. Would he? she wondered.

He bent his head, and their lips touched. "I guess my role in life is to save yours."

She grinned agreement and then looked around, embarrassed. She quickly turned back to the guidebook. But her heart was tripping too fast to concentrate. It took her a moment to regain her composure.

"Here's a paragraph. It says hundreds of Nazis settled in Bariloche after the war. Not just Hitler but Martin Bormann and Erich Priebke. Bormann escaped Germany with billions, and Priebke was an SS captain who murdered over three hundred Italians during the war. He lived here for fifty years and was even head of a German school in Bariloche. An American news team tracked him down in 1994 and made him go back to Germany for trial. Mengele lived here too. The place was a hotbed of Nazis."

"Was?" Stefan asked.

"You think it still is?"

"Wouldn't surprise me," Stefan said.

"Excuse me," said a gravelly voice behind them. They turned to find a wrinkled old man with a several-day-old beard and unkempt gray hair trailing behind them. He was stooped over and leaning on a gnarled wooden cane. A half-finished cigarette dangled from his lips.

"My legs and back don't work so good no more, but my hearing's excellent. If I was you, I wouldn't be talking so open about Nazis around here," he said in Spanish-accented English, "unless you want trouble. Tourists don't care, but many people living here wouldn't like it, you saying they are Nazis. Even if they are."

Kirsten and Stefan stopped walking, looked at each other, and shrugged. They turned back to the old man.

"Who are you?" Stefan asked, moving in front of Kirsten.

"Name's Pepé, but that don't matter. I've lived in Bariloche most of my life. Grew up here as a kid—even went to that school Priebke ran. He was a tyrannical son of a bitch, but so were the other teachers." Pepé leaned closer, ash falling off the cigarette onto his shirt. "All of them was Nazis. They beat us for anything we did wrong, made us join a youth group, salute the Nazi flag, march in parades wearing Nazi uniforms."

"Where was the school?" Kirsten asked, standing alongside Stefan. She knew where it was and its history but wanted to test this stranger who just materialized out of nowhere.

"Instituto Primo Capraro? Three blocks from here, on Avenida Angel Gallardo, down that way," he said, tipping his head left.

"What were the classes like?" Kirsten asked.

"We started each day with a salute to the führer, standing and facing his picture on the wall, that he should live a long life," Pepé said. "Nazi flags hung all over the school and in the town. Older kids played war games with real guns. They taught us we were the avengers for the Third Reich, that we would lay the foundation for the fourth one."

"Why're you telling us this?" Stefan asked, suspicious.

He pointed to their jackets. "Olympics. You two are athletes. So was I, before these." He held up the cigarette, took a final drag, and flipped the butt into the street where it fell in a shower of sparks. "Not your level maybe, but I played professional football for Argentina years ago—soccer, the Americans call it. That's how my legs and back got messed up. Got a few hits too many. After one win when I scored three goals—a hat-trick—I even met Juan and Eva Perón." He stood straighter. "I don't want you to have no trouble in my town, with the Olympic games starting soon. I plan to go, if these," he smacked the side of one leg, "work okay. Maybe I'll see you in Rio."

He was walking away, but Kirsten called him back. Maybe he was legit and could give some helpful information.

"Wait a minute. Thanks for the warnings," she said, "but I have a question. Did you ever visit Hitler at Estancia Inalco?"

Pepé stared at her, eyes hooded. It took him a moment to decide. He grabbed each by an elbow and walked them to the side of a building on the corner, protected from the path of tourists. He gathered them close, a tight circle of three—a coach with his two athletes. Up close, the stoop disappeared, and Pepé seemed taller and stronger than he first appeared. Perhaps younger also.

"Years ago, when Hitler was still living there," he said in a harsh whisper. "Scariest thing I ever did. Inalco grew most of its own food and was pretty self-sufficient. But once a month, there'd be a batch of stuff from Bariloche that mostly came by ship from Germany. Hitler took a lot of different medicines they had to import—probably twenty or thirty different kinds a day. Mostly pills but some by injection. I helped deliver them one time and rode there with the truck. I was maybe twelve or thirteen. We had to pass checkpoints called *refugios*, like chalets, guarding every mountain pass, every entrance into Adolf Hitler's Valley. That's what the area was called. Guards with guns swarmed all over the place. One refugio was named Berghof, like Hitler's home in the Bavarian Alps. You know?"

They didn't answer.

"Perón skied from there a bunch of times. The Germans also built the Saracen Tower, maybe thirty or forty feet tall, on the shore of the lake. A dozen guys with binoculars slept in the tower and screened air and water approaches all day and all night. I got so frightened by the trip I never went back, all these years. I hope you're not planning to visit."

Stefan looked at Kirsten. She nodded.

"Hitler's dead," she said. "It can't be like when you went. Don't tourists visit?"

"You got to get a special pass from the tourist bureau, and they don't give out many. You need that pass to get through the checkpoints on the road, especially when you get close to Villa la Angostura, the last town before Inalco. The bureau people will tell you they've exceeded the quota for the month and can't give out any more, so come back next month. Of course, no one does."

"Then how do we get one?" Kirsten asked.

"You really want to go, don't you?"

They both nodded.

"There's a guy in the tourist bureau named Jorge. He can get you a pass. Cost you a hundred dollars, American. Tell him Pepé sent you." He looked around, appeared to recognize a face coming toward them in the distance, turned, and walked away quickly. Over his shoulder, he said, "Wouldn't go if I was you. Definitely wouldn't do that."

"Let's find a restaurant on the lake," Stefan said when they were alone. "We can talk about this. Maybe we need to reconsider."

Kirsten pulled out a pamphlet she had pocketed from the hotel lobby. "The Butterfly Restaurant on Avenida Hua Han is ranked number one in Bariloche. Sits right on the lake."

The Butterfly décor was simple with white tablecloths and white dishes, a few pictures on the walls. They sat on the deck overlooking the lake and watched a lovely sunset, with pinks and reds flickering off the rippling water churned up by the westerly wind. Kirsten enjoyed seeing the colors play off Stefan's face. She wondered if he was doing the same.

Against their better judgment, they let the maître d' talk them into the restaurant specialty, a seven-course chef's tasting menu for only 355 Argentine pesos. They declined the wine pairing and drank the local beer, Blest Bock.

The restaurant was crowded. Even though they were sitting on the deck, the noise level made it hard to hear. A table of five women was closest to them, and their shrill laughter and constant chatter were piercing. She and Stefan spoke in hushed undertones, heads close together, not wanting to be overheard.

"Did you believe him?" Stefan asked.

"Not at first, which was why I asked him about Priebke's school. He knew all about it. That convinced me. Do you think Inalco's still as dangerous as he says?"

"If it was, the guidebooks would warn tourists not to go there." In response, Kirsten held up her bandaged forearm. "Yeah, I guess you're right. Caveat emptor or something," Stefan said.

"We've come a long way to turn back now," Kirsten said.

"You're still up for it? Not scared, even after your brush with death?"

"I've got you to save me, don't I?" Kirsten asked, reaching for his hand. "I've nothing to fear but fear itself. Didn't somebody important say that?"

"Some American president—Kennedy? Roosevelt, maybe. Yeah, Roosevelt," Stefan said. "Okay, it's a go. We'll get to the tourist office early tomorrow morning, find that Jorge guy, slip him the money, get our pass, and we're gone."

"Remember—it's in dollars. We'll need to change currency. And one other thing," Kirsten said. "Do we know how to get there? Like, driving directions. No GPS here."

"For a hundred dollars, Jorge better tell us."

The waiter brought the first of their seven dishes, a rabbit tartare, and food trumped more serious talk.

An hour and a half later, they pushed back from the table, stuffed after the seventh dish, a blueberry tart, four beers for him and three for her.

"I have a serious question," Stefan said, draining the last of his beer, speech slightly slurred.

"Uh-oh. We can't have a serious discussion now, after all that food and booze."

"Very serious, and I have to ask it," he said.

She sighed. "Oh well, if you have to ..."

"Where did you get your red hair? Your mother or your father?"

Kirsten burst out laughing. She drew looks from the table of women. "Whew," she let out her breath. "That one I can answer."

"And the freckles. Did they come with the red hair?"

She laughed again. It was so easy being with him, she thought. So natural—like they were meant to be together.

"The last question first. Yes, the freckles came with the hair." She rubbed the base of her nose. "I tried for years to hide them with makeup, but it made me look like I was wearing a clay mask. So I just said, here they are. That's me. Take it or leave it."

"I like them," Stefan said, reaching across to run his finger over her face. "And the red hair?"

She brushed a red ringlet behind an ear. "More difficult. My mother's blonde, so I guess the red came from the same gene on her side of the family. I don't know. Certainly not my father. He's got dark hair."

The waiter interrupted with the bill.

As they read it, they giggled over who could say "Bariloche Blest Brewery" fastest. Stefan refused Kirsten's offer to split the bill, and they staggered out, glad the Bariloche Grand Hotel was within walking distance.

Kirsten leaned against Stefan for support going up the hotel steps, her legs rubbery. He walked her to the door of her room, and they stood there, holding hands and looking into each other's eyes. After a moment's hesitation, he bent down, put his arms around her, and gently kissed her lips, lightly at first but more urgently as her body collapsed into his. She opened the door to her room, backed in, took both of his hands, and said, "Come in and save me again."

And so he did, his promise to Sharon dissolved in the alcoholic haze.

Later that night when Stefan woke from a dream, he saw Kirsten had kicked back the covers and lay partially exposed. As he gently pulled the covers to her chin, he said softly, "Christ, she's beautiful." In the darkness, he didn't notice the brief flicker of her eyelids or her tiny smile.

CHAPTER 20

HE WOKE FIRST, PROPPED ON AN ELBOW, AND looked at her. The sun was rising, its golden rays turning her red hair amber. He tried counting freckles but soon gave up with a chuckle. The noise made her stir.

She opened her eyes to his face hovering over hers. "Morning," Kirsten said. "I like that."

"What?"

"Waking up next to you, seeing your face first thing," she said.

He bent to kiss her, but she covered her mouth. "Morning breath," she said, turning away.

Gently, he moved her hand and brought her face to his. "Not to me," he said, kissing her.

Stefan and Kirsten were at the tourist bureau by eight o'clock and discovered it didn't open until nine. They went for breakfast, exchanged euros for dollars, and returned an hour later.

"We'd like to get a pass to drive to Estancia Inalco," Stefan told the receptionist.

"Sorry, all gone. No more this month. Come back next month," she said, "or maybe the month after that."

"Can I talk to Jorge?" Stefan asked.

She gave him a squinty-eyed look and then disappeared into a back room. Several minutes later, she returned with a man walking behind her. He was short and swarthy, with dark hair and a full black mustache. He wore a food-stained white undershirt that barely covered his hairy chest and arms. “I’m Jorge. Who wants to know?”

“Pepé told us to ask for you,” Stefan said, placing his hands on the counter. “We want to visit Estancia Inalco. He said you could get us a pass.”

“He did, did he? He tell you how much?” Jorge asked, a smug look on his face.

“A hundred US dollars.”

“That was last month. This month it’s one-fifty.”

“If it includes directions,” Kirsten said.

Jorge studied both of them, taking in the leather Olympic jackets, one with a right slashed sleeve poorly repaired.

He shook his head. “Directions cost twenty-five dollars more. Total, one seventy-five American dollars, and for you, special. I won’t charge no tax,” he said without a smile.

Stefan looked at Kirsten and shrugged. *We’ve come this far,* his body language said. He took out his wallet, counted out the dollars, and handed Jorge the money. He worried about showing so much cash, but he had no choice.

Jorge pocketed the dollars, removed a map from a drawer, and spread it out on the countertop. “We are here in Bariloche.” He circled it with a black marker pen. “Take Route 237 northwest out of town about twenty kilometers and then make a right onto 231 for seventy kilometers to Villa la Angostura, over here.” He pointed on the map and drew an arrow to Villa la Angostura. “The highway is paved, so driving will be about one hour. It used to take nine hours when the road was dirt, and before that when Hitler lived there, you could only reach it by boat or plane. You go through three checkpoints. That will slow you down a little, but this paper will get you across.” He waved the pass at Stefan. “From Angostura, you have to go slow, very slow.”

“Why?” Stefan asked.

Jorge paused, looking at the woman for confirmation or permission. Her head nod was almost imperceptible.

"The road to the house is hidden behind a big boulder, and you would drive right past it without knowing. It is an unmarked, one-lane dirt road on the left side, five kilometers after you leave Villa la Angostura, so you have to watch for it careful. You make a left turn just after the boulder, and it looks like you are driving straight into the woods." He showed them on the map.

"After that, you go about a kilometer and pass through a narrow tunnel that allows only one car at a time. An armed guard will be there. Be sure and stay in your car. He does not like visitors to wander around.

"After the tunnel, the trees open up, and the road changes to two lanes. Go about five or six kilometers down that road along the lake, and you will be there. No signs or nothing, but you will see buildings in a clearing in the woods. The biggest, facing the lake, belonged to Hitler. Ten bedrooms. Hitler picked that spot for the beautiful setting but also because it was so hard to find and easy to protect."

"Right on the lakeshore, like the picture in the tourist book?" Kirsten asked.

"Yes, on the last piece of land at the west end of Lake Huapí, called Última Esperanza, or Last Hope in English." He turned to the woman, who rattled off a response in Spanish. "Explorers named it that because they thought it was the last chance to find a water passage from the lake through the Andes to Chile."

"Will anybody be there? Are people living in the houses?" Kirsten asked.

"No tourists. We gave out all the passes last month, and you're the only ones to get them now."

"Why us? Why are we so lucky?"

"Pepé."

Stefan nodded. "Any workers there?" he asked.

"Yes, people to maintain the house and grounds. One of them will take you through the house. You cannot go inside alone; it is locked. So do not try. Also, do not walk around on the grounds around the house. There's a fence in the back so you do not stray into the woods. A tourist did that last year and died. Do not forget, you're at the foothills of the Andes Mountains with many trees, very far away from everything. Animals are in the woods. It would be easy to disappear, and no one would ever find you. The old man built his house there for a reason."

He stared hard at each of them until he got a nod that the warning registered. "And bring food and water. No McDonald's at Estancia Inalco."

The drive was beautiful along the sparkling shores of Lake Nahuel Huapí with the snowcapped Andes Mountains always in the distance. The car behaved, the sun was shining, the sky was blue, and their hearts were filled with each other. Stefan had difficulty keeping his hands on the wheel and his eyes on the road. Kirsten rode with a dreamy smile on her face. He reached for her hand.

"What do you think we'll find there?" Kirsten asked after they made the right turn onto Route 231 and passed through the first checkpoint.

"No idea. Did the guide book say how well it was preserved?" Stefan asked.

"Not really. It just showed the picture taken in the 1950s. The house was beautiful then," she said.

"What are we going to look for?" He glanced at her.

"There can't be much remaining except for the house. When Hitler left in 1955, the Nazis would have taken all the important stuff, papers and whatever."

"Or burned them," Stefan added.

"True. And whatever tourists they've let in since are certain to have picked clean any scraps the Nazis forgot."

"Then why are we going?" he asked.

"First, it's a thrill. A lark. Is it really possible that the most vile, evil man ever to live on the face of this earth walked in that house, slept in it, ate in it? That the history books got it all wrong? Imagine being able to tell our friends he did not commit suicide in 1945, and we were in his home to prove it."

"Or maybe the history books got it right," he said, smiling, "and this is a wild goose chase to make money from tourists like us?"

She reached for his hand and put it to her lips. "A waste of time, you think?"

He grinned and then turned serious. "Kirsten, whatever we find at the house, and whether or not I win a fencing medal—or you do, more likely—these 2016 Olympics will always be the most important events in my entire life, and I hope yours too. Because, you may not have realized this yet—I'm going to marry you."

He stopped talking, an astonished look on his face. "I can't believe what I just heard me say."

Kirsten laughed. "Pull the car over."

"Here? In the middle of the day?"

"No, later, in the middle of the night. Of course, now. The road is deserted, the lake is beautiful, and the sun is shining—and I think I'm in love."

An hour later, they arrived at the second checkpoint. "You are late," the guard said, examining his watch as he read their pass.

Kirsten felt her face flush. "We stopped by the lake to look at the beautiful scenery and eat lunch."

"Too early for lunch," the guard said.

"We were hungry," Stefan said.

"You ate breakfast before you left Bariloche."

"How did you—" Stefan began to ask.

Before he could say anything more, the guard held up his hand and said, "No more stopping, or we will make you turn back to Bariloche." He stamped the pass. "Now, go."

Stefan stepped on the gas and sped away. Stunned to silence, they drove the next few minutes without speaking.

Stefan broke the spell. "Scared?"

"Should I be?" she asked. "I have you."

"I don't know. We're being watched."

"It may not be that sinister."

"It is."

"No. I can explain," she said.

"How?"

"Somebody saw us arrive at the tourist office early, go to breakfast—the restaurant was right next door—and return in an hour for the pass. He had to notify the checkpoint guards to let them know when we were coming and mentioned that part as well. They probably laughed at the stupid tourists coming so early." She took the pass from him and scanned it carefully. "I can't read Spanish, but the time we got the pass is stamped on this. And so is the time we hit the first checkpoint, and now this one."

"Kirsten, you're being too logical."

"We're not important enough for anyone to spy on. And if we are, they got a good porno show at the lake." Smiling, she popped open the second button on her blouse.

He laughed. "How can I be in love with you already? It's too quick."

"Because I'm so adorable?"

"And fearless. You're sure you want to go through with this?"

She straightened her shoulders. "You asked me that before, and I didn't finish my answer.

"If coming here was a lark initially, now it's different. Now I want to walk in Hitler's house to—I don't know how to express it, like spitting on his grave or something. To defile the house and him by my Jewish presence, as he defiled human beings all over Europe and Russia. My being there says, 'I'm here, you evil bastard, despite what you did to millions. My family survived, and so did millions of other Jews. And we will continue to survive, as we have for thousands of years, despite you and others like you.'"

She shuddered. A single tear trickled down her cheek. "I had the same feelings when I visited the concentration camp at Auschwitz," she said. "I felt *compelled* to stand on the very spot Mengele stood, on that concrete platform alongside the train tracks where the Jews disembarked and that … that … I don't have words to describe that monster who decided which poor souls went left to the gas chambers and which went right. It was holy ground for me. In fact, some sort of monument should be built *right on that exact place* and blessed by a rabbi."

"And a priest."

"Yes. And schoolchildren of all denominations should visit and hear the words 'never again' and be reminded of the Holocaust."

She stopped to calm her breathing and brushed the tear away. After a few moments, she continued. "Being in Auschwitz-Birkenau felt like a victory, not just for me and other Jews but for all humanity. Same for my being here. Do you see that?"

"I do. Perhaps not as intensely as you, but I respect what you're saying."

She put her hand on his knee. "More than just respect, Stefan, I want you to *feel* some of this."

He pulled her close with one arm and gave her a quick kiss. "I'll try, I promise."

"The world is so filled with evil people and evil empires," Kirsten went on. "The good guys defeat one regime, and another dictator takes its place. The cycle seems endless."

"I didn't know my future bride was a philosopher," Stefan said.

She watched the glistening snow on the Andes peaks pass by before answering. "Growing up, I considered becoming a rabbi. I feel passionate about things like the Holocaust, and when I do, I tend to preach. My folks thought becoming a rabbi would be a good outlet for my talents."

"What happened?"

"I double-majored at the university," Kirsten said, "in philosophy and religion. That was the closest I got. But this trip has reignited my feelings about the Holocaust and Hitler."

CHAPTER 21

THEY PASSED THROUGH THE THIRD CHECKPOINT at Villa la Angostura with no words from the attendant. Four kilometers later, Stefan slowed, and they both watched for the big boulder on the left. It came up exactly at the 5 km mark, and Stefan turned left onto the hidden dirt road.

"It does look like we're driving into the forest," he said. They came to the stone tunnel dug into the hillside, barely large enough for one car at a time.

"Jorge said there'd be a guard here, but I don't see one," Kirsten said, looking around.

"He's probably hiding in the trees, watching us. If we got out, I'm sure we'd see him."

"Should we test that?" she asked, her hand on the door handle.

"You're not serious, are you?" he said.

She laughed and shook her head. "Just joking. Seeing how brave you are."

He managed a little smile. "Not very."

They drove a bit farther and came to a clearing where the road widened to two lanes.

"My heart's beating so fast," Stefan said. "Yours?"

"Pounding like I've just fenced for ten minutes."

Kirsten's head swiveled side to side, taking in the sparkling lake waters on the right and a wall of towering pines on the left. Stefan slowed so he could look also.

"If this really was Hitler's choice for his wolf's lair, it was perfect,"

Kirsten said. "The scenery's gorgeous, the solitude's wonderful, and if I were worried someone might try to kill me, this would be the ideal place to hide."

She gazed in wonder. "The idea that he was still alive and living in this paradise, after all the death and destruction he caused in Europe and Russia, is too incredible to fathom."

"And if he was here, it wasn't a secret. The whole town knew, and probably all the Nazis in South America," Stefan said.

"They called this Hitler's Valley," Kirsten said. "Whether he was here or not, someone wanted all of Patagonia to know—maybe to recruit followers and plan for rebirth of the Reich. They had to know their leader was alive and well."

"If all these people knew that, surely the Russians and Americans would have heard something about it. And if they did, why didn't they try to capture or kill him, like the Israelis did Eichmann?"

"I don't know," Kirsten said. "Maybe letting him live was part of the agreement with Churchill, Stalin, and Roosevelt to end the war. Or maybe they tried to kill him and failed. The Israelis failed to capture Mengele."

As the road straightened, the house came into view. "There it is," Kirsten said. "It looks just like the picture in the guidebook."

The three-chimney building was a sprawling, multipeaked, two-story structure of gray-brown stone and wood. Picture windows in the front great room opened onto the lake with the Andes Mountains in the distance. A second-floor deck off the master bedroom provided a similar view. Paint was peeling around the windows, and some of the wooden beams were warped. The grass needed mowing, and the garden weeding.

Stefan drove to the house and parked the car on the crest of a hill in a small parking lot. A gray-haired old man shuffled slowly toward them.

"*¿Qué idiomas habla usted?*" the old man asked. Getting no response, he switched to English. "What languages do you speak? I can do several."

"How about Hebrew," Kirsten answered in English.

That brought a loud guffaw, and his eyes crinkled. "In this place? Yes, that would be a good joke. Hitler would come running back from his grave."

"This was his house, then?" Kirsten asked.

"Of course."

He looked to be in his eighties, tall with a big beer gut hanging over his wide brown belt, red-faced with a bulbous nose. He switched his cigarette from his right hand to his left and reached out with tobacco-stained fingers to shake their hands.

"Name's Lobo. Means wolf in Spanish." Then, in the monotone of a speech given countless times, he said, "Did you know Adolf means 'noble wolf'? Hitler liked thinking himself cunning and brave as a wolf. He even liked to be called Mr. Wolf. He named his yacht the *Seewolf*, his airplane the *Fliegende Wolf*, and his field headquarters in East Prussia the Wolfschanze, the Wolf's Lair. Hitler liked my name so much he made me manager of this house in 1950, when I was just twenty."

"You've been here more than sixty years?" Kirsten asked, eyes wide.

He nodded. "I live alone in the caretaker cottage. My wife died ten years ago. I don't plan to stay forever though. I want to retire."

"Why is the house called Estancia Inalco? Nothing about a wolf," Kirsten asked.

"Smart lady. The locals named it, not Hitler. Jorge telephoned me you were coming to see it. He doesn't let many people visit."

Lobo ran a hand over the gray stubble on his chin. "Come with me so I can show you the house and get it over with. I'm the only one here today. I gave the guard several days off because his wife was having a baby, and we didn't expect any more tourists this month."

Stefan and Kirsten started to walk quickly to the house. "Wait, slow down," Lobo called after them. "You walk too fast, and I get chest pains."

Stefan's eyebrows rose, medical education kicking in. "That sounds like angina, from blockages to your heart."

The man stopped, rubbing his chest and left arm. "You a doctor?"

"Almost. Medical student." Stefan tipped his head at the cigarette, now a stub almost burning the old man's fingers. "You should stop."

"After seventy years? Haven't missed a day since I was sixteen. Too late now. Won't happen until they bury me." He flicked the ash onto the grass, ground it into the dirt with his heel, shredded the remaining butt, and rolled the cigarette paper into a tiny ball he put on his tongue and swallowed. "Got to keep the place clean," he explained. After a moment, he said, "Okay, pain's gone. Let's go again—but slower this time."

They walked to the house, pausing on the expansive lawn that ran to the beach to let Lobo catch his breath. The house, evocative of Hitler's Berghof chalet in Berchtesgaden, was nestled in a grove of trees so close and so tall they shadowed the grounds, making it seem like midnight all day long.

Kirsten read the sign over the front door: *Arbeit Macht Frei.* Work makes you free. It was the sign over the entrance to Auschwitz and other concentration camps. She shuddered.

Lobo fumbled with a silver key ring on his belt to open the front door. Then he leaned against it motionless, brow wrinkled and wet.

"Wait just a minute. More chest pains," he said, rubbing his chest again and taking deep breaths.

"Do you have any nitroglycerin?" Stefan asked.

"What's that?"

"Haven't you seen a doctor for this?"

"No. It just started a day ago, and I haven't had a ride out of here." He took out a handkerchief and wiped his forehead. "Hot," he said. "Today, the pain is much worse. Comes on even if I'm not doing anything." He staggered and braced against the wall. "Not feeling so good. Dizzy. I think I'm—"

Lobo's face turned ashen. His eyes rolled back, and he collapsed to the ground. His head glanced off the concrete corner of a step as he went down.

"Oh my God," Kirsten cried, frozen by his inert, bleeding body.

Stefan rushed to Lobo's side. He ripped open Lobo's shirt and put his ear to his chest. "No heart sounds or respiration. Cardiac arrest." He began chest compressions. "Kirsten, call for emergency help."

She attempted to dial. "I have no signal. There's no connection out here."

"Try the door to the house. Maybe it's unlocked, and you can call from a phone inside."

The door wouldn't open.

"See if one of his keys works." She tried, but when she looked up and saw the sign overhead, her hands shook so much she couldn't unlock the door.

Stefan continued CPR. After a minute, Lobo began to stir, and Stefan stopped chest compressions. Lobo looked around, blinking his eyes rapidly. He groaned as he took a deep breath.

"Christ, did you break my ribs?" Lobo gingerly touched his chest and struggled to sit up. "Ugh," he grunted. Stefan gently guided him back down. "And my head. What did you do to me?" Lobo's fingers cautiously explored the gash in his forehead, still bleeding.

"Rest. You're in the middle of a heart attack."

"I can't rest. There's too much to do." Lobo pushed Stefan's hand away, pulled himself up by the side of the house, and stood on rickety legs. "I need to get to my cottage. Help me." He squinted against the blood, mixed with sweat, trickling down his forehead and clouding his vision.

"I think you should lie down until we get emergency help here," Stefan said.

"Stop!" The old man's eyes became fierce gun barrels. "You don't know what in hell you're talking about. You do as I tell you, so just stop. Now!"

The savagery of his response interrupted Stefan's attempt to help. "What do you want me to do?"

"Both of you," he beckoned to Kirsten, "help me to my cottage in the back. No questions! Just do as I say. Now!"

They each took an arm, draped it over their shoulders, and half-carried Lobo off Inalco's veranda. Lobo steered them around the back of the house to a place deep in the woods. There, totally concealed from view, stood a small wooden cottage enveloped by the surrounding forest. The rear of the cottage merged into the hillside, with the grass of the hill carpeting the cottage roof and sides. A chest-high meadow around the log cabin concealed its walls. Not even a worn trail to the front of the house betrayed the camouflage.

Lobo took out the silver key ring, fumbled with a key, and unlocked the front door. They helped him into the front room. It was small, with a single black overstuffed easy chair in front of a wide, eight-feet-tall, stone fireplace that looked as if it had never seen a burning log. A potbellied stove and sink completed the room. To the back was a doorway that opened to the bedroom.

With a great sigh, Lobo collapsed into the chair. Kirsten and Stefan stood back alongside the fireplace. The mantle and relief-carved frieze were ornate rose marble.

Lobo sat quietly for a long time, stroking his chest and taking deep breaths. His face betrayed inner turmoil. Beads of sweat coalesced with the blood still oozing from his head wound, dripping onto his shirt. He made no attempt to wipe it dry. Finally, a determined look on his face, he spoke.

"I'm about to die," he gasped. "I know that, and you, young doctor"—he feebly pointed at Stefan—"know that too." His hand collapsed onto the arm of the chair with the effort of pointing, and he panted to catch his breath.

"Strange, the quirks of fate that decide men's lives. You saved mine." He nodded at Stefan. "In return, I must change yours."

"How?" Stefan asked.

"Maybe for the better," Lobo said. "But probably for the worse."

He stopped, breathing heavily. "Everybody else has died, or moved away, and I'm the last to know—certain things. I can't let these secrets die with me. They're too important." His head fell backward, resting on the chair back for a moment. With an effort, he brought it forward again. "I have no one else to tell. Incredible—fate." He sucked in big mouthfuls of air and continued in a raspy voice. "But I am sorry. Your lives will never be the same."

CHAPTER 22

"HITLER HAD—A JEWISH SON."

Lobo stopped to let his words sink in. Even in his state, he smiled at the expressions on their faces. The room was deathly silent except for his harsh breath sounds. After several moments, his breathing slowed and became less labored.

"I know what you're thinking. How the hell does this old man know that? He's crazy, he's a liar, and he wants the world to remember him after he's dead."

Lobo's confession drew tiny smiles from Kirsten and Stefan.

"I don't blame you. I would think the same. So I'll prove it. First, tell me your names. I need to know who I'm talking to."

"I'm Stefan, and my friend is Kirsten."

"Stefan, move to your left a bit. Stand directly in front of the fireplace."

He did.

"Now, turn and face the fireplace. Place the palms of both hands on the swastika over the mantel. One hand above it and one below. Push."

Nothing happened. "Move your bottom hand a bit to the right and your top hand to the left. Try again."

With a click and a grinding noise, the entire fireplace swung back like a door on hinges. It opened to reveal a dark passage dimly lit from the room.

"The light switch is on your right." Stefan flipped it on. Bright lights flooded a long tunnel. Kirsten gasped.

"The tunnel leads directly into the hill behind the house. The hill's actually a cave in the side of the mountain. Hitler built this cabin to conceal its entrance."

He paused to catch his breath. "You won't find this in any tourist book. Only a handful of people ever knew it existed—the intimate group. The cave extends several hundred meters, with perfect humidity and temperature.

"Martin Bormann stored his art here, everything he stole from European Jews and ransacked museums. Rembrandts, Vermeers, and Monets. Incalculable wealth. All gone now, except one that couldn't be moved. You'll see that in a moment."

He stopped, withdrew a handkerchief from his pocket, and wiped his drippy face. He sank back in the chair and closed his eyes, panting, arms hanging deadweight over the armrests. His head drooped onto his chest, mouth open. Stefan stared hard for chest movement.

"Is he dead?" Kirsten whispered.

Stefan shook his head.

Finally Lobo stirred, opened his eyes, and sat up. He looked around bewildered until he saw the open fireplace and remembered what had happened.

He began to speak again, this time more slowly.

"In 1943, Martin Bormann saw the war was going badly. He wanted to do something to protect the führer. Hermann Göring—head of the Luftwaffe, the German air force—was a morphine addict stealing every European treasure he could lay his hands on. Bormann had to move fast. He called it Aktion Adlerflug—Project Eagle Flight. He smuggled money, jewels, gold, and artwork out of Germany. The plan was to make a safe haven for Hitler in case they lost the war.

"Everyone got into the act. The Peróns took their share. They stole from the Nazis as the Nazis stole from Europe. Estancia Inalco, what do you think it cost? A billion dollars—even more. Argentine vaults are full of Nazi gold, mostly as bribes to let Nazis into the country. Eva Perón took millions from here, right here," he pointed to the cave, "to Swiss banks after the war." He stopped again, huffing. "She left almost nothing.

"But you will see for yourself." He smiled through his pain. "Go back into the cave. The room will speak for itself. Here," he handed Stefan an amber-colored key from his key ring. "This will open the steel door at the end of the tunnel. Once you've gotten over the shock, you will see on a small table in the corner of the room two little boxes I managed to hide when Hitler and his entourage left Inalco. Hitler was sick then and not thinking too clearly. Bring them out. Do it quickly," he panted. "I don't have long."

Stefan and Kirsten hurried along the tunnel. At the steel door, Stefan tried the key Lobo gave him. The amber key slid in easily and opened the lock. He turned the knob and pushed on the door.

The orange-yellow brightness of a thousand suns assaulted their eyes, and they had to shield them from the glare. They stared at the most incredible room they'd ever seen. The walls and ceiling were totally covered in glowing, carved amber. Panels displayed intricate textured mosaics, busts of men and women, cherubs, and shimmering candelabras, interspersed with chiseled mirrors placed strategically to capture and enhance the images. Gold leaf coverings adorned figures studded with precious stones. The diamonds, rubies, sapphires, and emeralds added to the rainbows of reflected light.

Kirsten leaned against Stefan, weak with discovery. "I've never seen anything like this. It's so beautiful it scares me." She turned slowly, taking in the walls of the room. Her eyes glittered like the jewels.

She looked at the ceiling, twenty feet overhead. "Look, Stefan, even the ceiling's covered in amber. And what's that gorgeous painting in the middle? I can barely make out the signature. It looks like—my God, it's a Vermeer!"

"And look down." Stefan tapped his foot. "The floor's inlaid wood. Look at these exquisite patterns made from mother of pearl." He shook his head in disbelief. "So, this is Lobo's secret. Hitler must've stolen it, and someone must still be searching for it."

"Lobo would know," she said.

Stefan walked to the nearest wall and lightly traced the elaborate convolutions with his fingertips. "Unbelievable. The amber's carved like the intricate bas-reliefs in—" He groped for an example.

"Brunelleschi's bronze doors in Florence?" she offered. "Or maybe a Michelangelo statue?"

He nodded and stood even closer. "It must've taken years, with scores of craftsmen. I can't believe it."

"And the jewels, Stefan," she touched the implanted stones, "these must be diamonds and rubies." Together they walked along the four walls, sometimes lightly touching, other times standing back, staring, and absorbing the unreality of what they were seeing. It was like a fantasy movie set.

Finally, Stefan said, "We'd better get back. We've been gone a long time."

She nodded, and they started to leave. "Wait," she said. In one corner stood a small table with two sealed cardboard boxes on top. "I guess these were what he was talking about." She gave a short laugh. "Cardboard seems wrong in this room." She scooped them up, and they left. Stefan locked the steel door with the amber key, and they rushed out the long tunnel back to the cabin.

When they got there, Lobo was dead.

CHAPTER 23

STEFAN LISTENED FOR A HEARTBEAT. HE SHOOK his head. "Nothing more I can do."

"What are we going to do?" she asked, a tremor creeping into her voice.

He went to her and held her in his arms. After a moment, he said, "We have two choices. The first is to leave him and get out as quickly as possible. No one has seen us here."

"True, but the guys at the checkpoints know we came, and probably the guard at the tunnel," she said.

"Okay, but no one has seen us at this cottage—"

"That we know of," Kirsten said.

"I suppose there could be security cameras, but we've got to take that chance."

"What's the second choice?" she asked.

"We try to get in touch with the authorities. That will let everyone know we were here when he died. If we leave now, we can say he showed us the house, and we left. We have no idea what happened after that," said Stefan.

"I don't like either," Kirsten said. "The first makes me feel dishonest, a thief in the night. The second incriminates us."

"We haven't done anything wrong," said Stefan. "The heart attack killed him."

They just stood there, looking from Lobo back to each other.

"We've got to do *something*, Kirsten," Stefan said at last. "We can't just stand here looking at each other."

She stared into his eyes, imploring him to decide. "My mind's a total blank. It's never happened to me before, but I'm numb. I can't think straight." Her voice quivered.

He squeezed her hand. "Don't lose it. We'll be okay. I say we get out of here now. Lobo told us he gave the guard a few days off. When he returns, he'll find the body and do the appropriate things. From what Lobo told us, no one knows about the fireplace. Which reminds me—"

Stefan carefully placed his hands on the fireplace and pulled. The hearth returned to its original position and, with a loud click in the quiet room, locked into place.

"Okay," Kirsten replied, robot-like, and they started to walk out of the cabin. "Wait!" she said. "The cardboard boxes."

"We don't want to be caught with them, Kirsten. Just leave them here on the floor."

"We can't, unless we bring them back to the amber room where we found them," she said.

He shook his head. "No time for that," he said. "Grab them and let's get out. I'm getting bad vibes the longer we stay."

They walked quickly to the car. Kirsten flipped the boxes into the backseat. Though the sun was warm, she shivered, put on her Olympic jacket, and zipped it up before they drove off.

They got into the car, and Stefan turned the key. The car wouldn't start.

He rotated the key in the lock and held it in place. The motor groaned and moaned but wouldn't budge. "I may have flooded it. Wait a minute, and I'll try again." They sat still, heads twisting to be sure no one was coming. Stefan turned the key again, but the motor still balked.

"What can we do?" Kirsten asked. She ran trembling fingers through her hair, fighting back tears. "We can't stay here."

"We're parked on a slight hill. Can you jump-start the car if I give it a push to get it moving?"

"I don't have the foggiest idea what you're talking about," she said.

"Okay, reverse roles. Can you get behind the car and give it a push to get it going down the hill?" She nodded, got out, and walked to the back of the car.

Stefan turned on the ignition, put the car in first gear, and depressed the clutch, with his other foot on the brake.

He rolled down the window and shouted, "Okay, push." He took his foot off the brake, kept the clutch depressed, and Kirsten leaned into the back of the car. It started rolling down the hill. Just before the road flattened, and the car gained full momentum, Stefan let out the clutch. The car coughed, chugged, and the motor caught. He put the gear in neutral and revved the engine to be sure it held. It snorted and sputtered but kept going.

"Good job!" he yelled to Kirsten over the motor noise. "We're golden. Hop in, and we're off to Bariloche."

Stefan kept the speed down, two tourists leaving unhurriedly after visiting Hitler's house. They came to the tunnel and, with no guard in sight, drove on through.

They reached the big boulder and turned right toward Villa la Angostura. When they arrived at the first checkpoint, Stefan handed over the pass. The guard stamped it, and they drove through, onto Route 231.

"Kirsten, take a good look at this pass." He handed her the paper. "Does it list the license plate anywhere?"

She read the paper. "Not that I can see."

He took the paper back. "That means there's no record of us being here. The guy on the boardwalk—what was his name?"

"Pepé."

"He doesn't know our names. Neither does the guy in the tourist office," Stefan said.

"No proof of us ever being here," Kirsten said.

"Correct." He checked his watch. "I can't believe it's only two o'clock."

"Seems later," she said. "We never did get to see inside Hitler's house."

He gave a snort. "True. You didn't get to spit on his grave, but we've heard a lot more damaging stuff than that."

"But I'll never get another chance like this one."

"Maybe not. Does your iPhone work here?"

She dug it out of her purse and clicked it on. "Yes."

"Check for flights back to Rio this afternoon. My gut tells me we should get out of here as fast as we can."

After a few minutes she said, "There's a flight at five thirty."

"See if we can change tickets."

Several minutes later, she said, "Done. Two new tickets for *only* 150 euros, plus a cancellation charge of about a hundred euros."

"Ouch. But that'll give us plenty of time to return to the hotel, check out, and get to the airport."

"Unless we stop for another quickie on the beach," she said, smiling for the first time in almost an hour.

He returned the smile. "How I'd love that. When we get to Rio, and then for the rest of our lives."

"Deal."

"I have an idea, now that your phone works," Stefan said. "Does it have enough juice?"

"Charged it overnight." She checked. "Yes, 85 percent battery life left."

"While we're driving, pull up Google and plug in something like 'amber Hitler' or 'amber room' or 'Nazi WWII thefts' and see what you get."

A moment later, she exclaimed, "Good lord, you're never going to believe this."

"What?"

"I put in 'amber room.' This is an entry from the Smithsonian Institution, in Washington. They call the Amber Room the Eighth Wonder of the World."

"Read it to me."

"Too long. I'll paraphrase. The Amber Room was built between 1701 and 1711 for Frederick I, the first king of Prussia. In 1716, the new king of Prussia, Frederick William I, gave it to Tsar Peter the Great to strengthen their alliance. Czarina Elizabeth moved the room to her Summer Palace, Tsarskoe Selo, just outside St. Petersburg in 1755, and enlarged it with more amber. When the Germans invaded St. Petersburg in 1941, Hitler ordered the Amber Room to be seized, shipped to Königsberg, Germany. When the Allies started bombing in late 1943, Hitler ordered the room moved again—and, somehow, twenty-seven crates of carved amber, gold, and jeweled panels were loaded onto a special freight train and disappeared."

She read slowly, emphasizing each word. "'The original was never seen again, despite intense investigations by art detectives from all over the world. A replica has been built in the Tsarskoe Selo State Museum outside St. Petersburg.'"

"Can you believe that? We're the only ones *in the world* who know where it is," Stefan said, "and, except for Lobo, probably the only ones who've seen it in the last fifty years."

"Incredible," Kirsten said.

"Oh, shit," Stefan said, fumbling in his pocket.

"What?" Kirsten asked.

He pulled out the amber key.

"My God," she said. "You took the key."

"In the rush, I forgot I had it," Stefan said.

"What do we do now?" Kirsten asked.

"We're sure not going back," he said.

"That's scary, Stefan. Now we *have* done something wrong."

They passed through the second checkpoint, turned left onto Route 237, and came to the third checkpoint. The guard halted them so he could examine another car coming through in the opposite direction. Stefan kept the motor revving. As the other driver drove past, he stared hard at Stefan and Kirsten before driving off.

Stefan's face blanched, and he sat unmoving when the guard asked to see his pass. Finally he handed the guard the paper. The guard checked it, stamped it, and waved them through.

"Can we keep the pass?" Kirsten asked, leaning across Stefan's lap to speak out the driver's window. "Tourist souvenir."

The guard shrugged indifference and handed her the pass. They drove off.

"What's the matter?" Kirsten asked, studying Stefan's worried look. "Are you okay?"

Stefan was slowly shaking his head. "I thought I recognized the driver. But that couldn't be." His face regained its color, and he waved his hand. "Forget it. Must be a lookalike. Mistaken identification."

"Whoever it was got Jorge to write another pass," she said.

After a pause, he turned to her, "Good thinking, to ask to keep the pass."

"See," she said. "I'm not all nervous fluff." He laughed.

They drove, each deep in thought. Kirsten broke the stillness. "You know, we've been so fixated on the Amber Room, we've completely forgotten the first thing Lobo told us."

He nodded. "I was just thinking the same thing."

"It got lost in everything else," Kirsten said.

"And Lobo told us he had proof, not some dying man's crackpot lie."

"What kind of proof could he have had?" she asked. "Something etched in amber?"

"Yeah, right. Maybe one of those cherubs was circumcised," he said. She laughed.

They were both silent again. Then, together, "The cardboard boxes!"

Kirsten leaned over the backseat and retrieved them. "They're sealed tight. Do you have a knife?"

"I've been carrying one ever since you were attacked." He pulled a pearl-handled knife from his pants pocket, flicked open the blade, and handed it to her.

She sliced through the bindings of the first cardboard box and opened it. Sitting on top was a messy hairbrush, hairs still clinging to the bristles. Beneath was a small leather book held shut by a silver metal clasp. The pages were gilt-edged. Kirsten clicked it open. "It's handwritten in German," she said.

"Can you read it?" he asked.

"Yes. I can't speak German very well, but I can read it," she said.

"What does it say?" Stefan asked.

She read the first page. "Oh my—this is Eva Braun's diary."

"Really?"

"And this hairbrush has her initials on the handle." Kirsten held it up for Stefan to see. "It must be hers."

"Christ," Stefan said. "This is getting to be too much." He slowed the car and pulled to the side of the road, keeping the motor idling. Kirsten passed him the diary. He turned it over in his hands and riffled the pages. "This is overwhelming. Do you realize what we've got here? Historians—never mind Nazis—would kill for this little book. And the hairbrush! Unbelievable. What's in the second box?"

She slit the binding and opened the box. "A copy of *Mein Kampf*, labeled number three, so I guess it's one of the original printed copies." She flipped open the cover. "Hitler's signed the inside cover to Eva, 'My one and only.' He dated it 1932."

She took the book out of the box. "There's a brush at the bottom—too small for hair, more like a comb." She handed it to him.

"Big enough for a mustache," Stefan said.

"Exactly. Even has hairs still in the bristles," she said.

Stefan pulled out onto the road again. "Reseal both boxes. We're almost in Bariloche."

CHAPTER 24

THEY SAT HUDDLED TOGETHER ON THE FLIGHT back to Rio, heads so close they were touching, her red curls intermingling with his brown strands. Kirsten whispered in Stefan's ear as soon as the plane took off. "I can't wait. I want to read her diary now."

He looked around. The plane was half-empty, no one sitting near them. The old 707's engine noise was deafening. "Okay, but keep the diary covered and just whisper in my ear what you find."

She unzipped her carry-on and took out the diary. She held it on her lap for a moment, stroking the grainy, brown leather cover with her fingers almost reverently. Then she clicked open the clasp. "There could be some powerful stuff in here," she said, taking a deep breath.

"No doubt, but I've been thinking. It's old, Kirsten, historical interest only—even if it contains the secrets to the German invasion of St. Petersburg or the bombing of London with V-2 rockets. Nothing monumental that would affect people today."

"That Hitler had a Jewish son? That's not monumental? Wouldn't that be of great interest even today? Maybe he hated his son, and that's why he hated Jews."

He fell quiet, eyes on the flight attendant as she passed with a tray of drinks. Kirsten took a Diet Coke, and he had a coffee.

"Interesting to some, if the proof's in here, and that's a big if. I guess any Nazi organizations that still exist would be interested to know their founder was a hypocrite."

Kirsten took the airline magazine from the seatback in front of her, spread it open, and cradled the diary in its pages. She pulled up the armrest between their seats, leaned close to Stefan, and hid the diary in the airline magazine snuggled between them. They looked like any couple in love.

She turned the first page, read it slowly, and translated a summary in whispers.

"The first entry's about when she met Hitler. Eva was seventeen, working in the photo shop of someone named Heinrich Hoffman in Munich. She wrote the exact date, October 4, 1929, when Hoffman introduced her to a man he called 'Herr Wolf,' who had come for a photo portrait." Kirsten giggled as she read on and turned the page.

"What?" Stefan asked, grinning at her giggle.

"Typical woman's talk. First, she remembered the exact date. I doubt a man would. Then she says Herr Wolf was 'devouring her with his eyes.' She was standing on a ladder when he came in the shop, and he stared at her legs—remember she was just seventeen."

"How old was Hitler?" Stefan asked.

Kirsten thought. "He had to have been forty or forty-one. Eva says she looked down at him, and he looked up at her, and 'we both liked what we saw.' He offered her a ride home in his Mercedes. But she worried what her parents would say and refused!"

"Little Red Riding Hood meets a horny Wolf?"

Kirsten laughed. "Could be. Hitler left in a bit of a huff, and later, when Hoffman told Eva that Herr Wolf was actually Hitler, she got upset she hadn't recognized him and accepted his offer. Before they finally did go out, Hitler had Bormann check out Eva's family to be sure they were appropriate Aryans with no Jewish blood. Eva says her older sister, Ilse, was having an affair with a Jewish doctor, but Hitler told Bormann to ignore that."

"Selective anti-Semitism," Stefan said.

Kirsten scanned a few more pages and put down the book. "Nothing about a Jewish son, and by this time their relationship was starting to heat up."

"How hot? Was he gay?" Stefan asked. "Some biographies intimated that, since he didn't marry Eva until the end."

"She doesn't say. But she quotes his chief of staff saying he once overheard Hitler tell a visitor he already had a bride, the German people and their fate," Kirsten said.

"Bull," Stefan said. "She said he devoured her with his eyes. That's not a gay wolf married to the people."

Kirsten flipped pages. "Wait, here's the answer. She says he asked her to stay over in his apartment one night to help him with a political question, and that was the start of their 'intimate relationship.' Beginning in 1932, she slept overnight regularly, and her parents threw a fit. Her mother even warned her about becoming pregnant."

"That's more like it," Stefan said. "So, at age forty-three, Hitler, the German people's paragon of virtue, takes a twenty-year-old virgin as his secret mistress. The idea of celibacy and sole devotion to the German cause was a bunch of Nazi propaganda for public consumption."

Kirsten read on. "Uh-oh, here's more," she said, turning pages. "This is what we want. Eva says one night after they had spent 'a great deal of intimate time together experimenting'—she doesn't elaborate—she 'gathered her courage' and asked him about getting married. He gave her his stock answer, that he was married to the German people. She asked if he would be faithful to her without being married. He said probably, 'from now on.'"

Before Kirsten turned the next page, she whispered to Stefan, "Wrong answer."

His eyebrows rose. "Why?"

"Any woman's then going to ask, 'what do you mean *from now on*? What happened *before*?'"

Kirsten flipped the diary page, read on, and snickered. "Sure enough, just like I said. Eva asked him, and Hitler confessed he had been in love with his twenty-three-year-old niece, Geli Raubal, his half sister's daughter."

"His niece? Unbelievable," Stefan said. "That's incest."

"Eva's pretty clear about it," Kirsten said. "She said Hitler told her he had 'an affair with Geli lasting many months. Geli ended it by committing suicide. She shot herself with Hitler's gun, a Walther 6.35-caliber pistol, September 18, 1931.' Eva writes that Hitler said Geli was 'driven by jealousy and guilt of incest,' but there was no suicide note. The police suspected Hitler killed Geli because she was pregnant and was going to tell her mother about him. They couldn't prove it and called it a suicide." Kirsten set down the diary. "This is more exciting than reality TV."

"Incredible that it was all hidden from the public," Stefan said. "I guess it was a time when you could get away with anything, especially if you controlled the press like Goebbels. Nothing to hint Hitler liked the young ones. I wonder what other little girls he had that we won't ever know about. And incest! Could he really have killed Geli? That would make him a murderer years before the war."

Kirsten went back to the book. "That's exactly what Eva asked him, whether he killed Geli. She says his answer was evasive, not really admitting or denying it."

"Doesn't matter at this point," Stefan said. "What's one more murder among millions? It's just that, if he did kill her, it was the first one, before all those millions."

Kirsten read on. "Eva then asked him if he had had a relationship with anyone else besides Geli. Hitler stalled, she says, and only after his third glass of schnapps did he admit it. He told her that when he quit high school at sixteen, he got drunk and 'became intimate twice with a Jewish woman at the inn.' The woman became pregnant and had a son in 1906 that Hitler never acknowledged but later supported."

CHAPTER 25

STEYR, AUSTRIA, APRIL 1905

BUT FOR A QUIRK OF FATE, THE BOY MIGHT HAVE grown up as Schicklgruber.

However, some thirteen years before he was born, the boy's father, Alois Schicklgruber, shed his mother's last name, which he had carried as her bastard son for thirty-nine years. With newfound legitimacy, Alois took his father's surname before his own son was born. It is unlikely the boy could have accomplished what he did, saddled with a family name like Schicklgruber.

"I hate school," the boy said to his mother. "All the teachers are dumb and give me bad grades, except for drawing. I'm good at that. They say I'm bad-tempered. Who wouldn't be with those morons teaching? I'm going to quit when I'm sixteen."

After his last day of school, he was so elated he got roaring, mind-numbing drunk.

At dawn, a young milkmaid found him lying on a country road outside Steyr. She looped the reins of her old mule over a low tree branch, helped him sit up, and brushed off his shirt. "Are you hurt?" she asked, helping him stand.

The boy stood on wobbly legs and shook his head, throbbing like a drum. "Thirsty. You have any water?" He held out his hand. He was thin, almost emaciated, with a pallid complexion but penetrating blue eyes. His unkempt brown hair fit the rest of his disheveled appearance: the torn collar of a coffee-stained shirt and greasy black pants with holes in the knees and ripped pockets.

"Only milk." She went to the rear of the wagon, unscrewed the top of a metal can, and poured some milk into a tin cup. "Here," she said, handing it to him. "Drink it slowly. It's all I can spare."

He downed it in a single gulp and presented the empty cup to her. She pinched her lips together, paused to consider, and poured half a cup more. "Sip it this time," she instructed, her tone more severe.

He watched her movements. Shapely figure, round face pretty enough, and nice legs but too young. Barely past thirteen or fourteen, he guessed, probably still growing breasts. He liked older, experienced women, at least twenty years old.

As he sipped, he asked her, "Have you seen Kubizek?"

"Who?"

"Kubizek. He's my friend. We started out together last night at the Bummerlhaus in Steyr. We were drinking great big steins of cold beer." He spread his hands apart, indicating. She smiled, her mouth open, dimples flashing.

"After we finished with the two women—" He stopped abruptly, eyes fixed on the young girl. He shook his head as if to banish the image, erase it from her mind.

"The last time I saw him was through the first-floor bay window, running across the square. When he reached the street on the other side, he got sick and threw up against a tree. That was very late last night or early this morning—I forget which. Then I drank more beer, and the same woman came back, and we—" Again he stopped abruptly. "Somehow," he looked around, bewildered, "I ended up here. I don't remember much more than that."

"Do you live nearby?" she asked.

He nodded. "I share a room at the Grünmarkt with Kubizek. We attend high school together. Or used to. I am finished!" He jumped in the air and kicked his heels together. When he landed with a jar, he held his head and grimaced.

She laughed a bubbly sound and clapped her hands. "Did you graduate?"

"No, but I am still finished." He threw his hands up at the sky. "The teachers are all idiots and tyrants, and I don't learn anything useful. So I quit. I walked away and quit. I want to become an architect or maybe a painter. Or even a German nationalist."

"I don't know what that is," she said, palms up.

"You're just like Kubizek," he said, shaking his head, the corners of his mouth turned down. "No imagination. He wants to become an upholsterer, like his father in Linz. How boring. Even being an architect or a painter is more exciting."

"That is what you want to do?"

"Only temporary. I want to change the world. I despise the Habsburg monarchy." He raised his right arm, forefinger pointing skyward and eyebrows bunched. "I *will* change the world!" He tried to look fierce.

"How will you live? Are you old enough to get a job?"

"I am sixteen." He stretched as tall as he could—all five feet eight inches—polished the toe of one shoe against the back of his pants leg, then did the other. He smoothed his wrinkled shirtfront and tucked it into his pants. "I will go to Vienna. I want to roam the streets, study the buildings, see the people, and maybe even attend the Vienna Academy of Fine Arts."

"Without a high school diploma?"

"I will take the entrance examination, and when I get a very high score—maybe the highest ever recorded—they will recognize I am a genius. They will have to let me in." The boy thought there was nothing he could not accomplish. If he failed, it was the other person's fault. "One thing I won't do, though, is become a civil servant like my father."

"Why not?" she asked. "It's an honorable profession."

"My father was in the customs service," said the boy. "He retired at fifty-eight and died seven years later from a lung hemorrhage. I was only thirteen. We fought a lot."

"You and your father?"

"He was mean and beat me all the time when I was small. He didn't dare try when I got bigger." The boy stood tall again, remembering the last time his father tried to beat him. He'd punched the man in the face and knocked him down. That made him feel good, very good. "I'd rather die than sit in an office all day filling out paper forms. I don't like to be bossed—by him or anybody else. I will *not* be bossed."

He kicked at a stone in the gutter, emphasizing his point. The rock skipped across the road and bounced off the left front leg of the mule. The animal whinnied, pulled its lips back over yellow teeth in a bizarre grimace that sent its gray hairs quivering, and tugged the rein loose from the branch. The girl ran to the animal and stroked its flank.

"Easy, Trudy, easy," she said in a soothing voice, holding the rein. The mule took a few steps and settled down. "Please be more careful," she admonished the boy.

She looked up at the sun overhead and held out her hand. "I have to deliver this milk before it gets any later, or it will spoil. I wish you good luck in Vienna."

He shook her hand. "Thank you. I will do well, I know. It is my destiny."

He helped her climb onto the wagon seat, brushing against her breasts as she moved past. She looked down at him, taking in his bedraggled appearance. "Maybe we'll meet again. Good luck, world changer. I hope you succeed." She clicked to Trudy, snapped the rein, and went on her way.

He watched her leave and wished he had asked for another glass of milk. Or maybe even gotten her name.

The boy lived with his mother, Klara, who was dying from breast cancer and struggling on a meager income. He did not help financially. Her death in 1908 hit him hard. Years after she died, the young man said he honored his father but loved his mother. He forgot about the beatings.

At nineteen, he moved to Vienna, beginning four years of extreme poverty. He was barely kept alive by charity, slept in flophouses and hostels, and ate leftover morsels in soup kitchens.

"You look cold," said the Hungarian Jew, a secondhand clothes dealer, as the young man entered the dark, dreary hostel for the night.

Shivering, he nodded and hugged himself to warm up. "Hungry too."

"Dinner scraps are gone. Sorry. Here," said the Jew, "there's a few bites left from my dinner." He handed him a tin plate with a clump of white fat, a shiny chicken bone, and a withered bread crust. The boy attacked them eagerly. Strong teeth cracked the bone, and he sucked at the remaining marrow.

The old man rummaged through a pile of clothes beside him. "Here," he said once again. "Take this coat. It's old, but the lining's still good. It'll keep you warm. And this hat too. The brim's got a bite out of it, but the rest is good."

"I have no money to pay for all this." The boy swept an arm over his newfound booty.

The man brushed the protest aside with the back of his hand. "Consider it a gift from a pious Jew. We call it *tzedakah.* Justice or charity. It's part of our religious obligation to do right. You can pay me back after you're successful."

"I will do that, pious Jew. I promise." When he left, the boy thought, *Stupid old man, giving away valuable things. Never give anything away. Always take.* But he knew the man would cheat someone to get something back. Charity was rubbish.

For the next four years, the young man was rarely seen without the black, worn overcoat that hung to his shoe tops like a caftan, its long, frayed sleeves curling over his dirty fingernails. The dented black derby concealed a head of matted dark brown hair that fell over his forehead and drooped over his grimy collar in back. Several days of black stubble always covered his cheeks and chin. Razors were expensive and hard to come by. His appearance did little to attract pretty women, but he managed to get by with the whores in the flophouses.

During those years, the vagabond did not work. A regular job was beneath this tramp. He read—or more accurately, *devoured*—books wherever he could find them. The librarian at the public library greeted him by first name several times a week. She suggested he read *The Foundations of the Nineteenth Century.*

Houston Stewart Chamberlain's depiction of Germany's place in the world held him spellbound. When Chamberlain wrote, "Germanic races belong to the most highly gifted group ... usually termed Aryan ... they are by right ... the lords of the world," and that only Aryans exerted a positive force on European culture, while Jews had a negative impact, the boy knew he had found a voice like his own. He now had a calling. He would restore and preserve European culture, especially German.

Twice the young man applied for admission to the Vienna Academy of Fine Arts. Twice they rejected him. The academy deemed him unfit for painting and recommended he study architecture. He lacked the academic credentials for acceptance, so that was impossible. He was convinced someone at the academy was against him. Probably a Jew.

He painted and occasionally sold watercolors of popular Viennese scenes, usually cribbed from other artists. His paintings were crude and cartoonish, buildings drawn better than people. He eked out an existence sketching advertising posters for shopkeepers to sell products like Teddy's Perspiration Powder: a cartoonish figure of a man sprinkling himself with white powder after a bath.

At twenty-four, he left Vienna for Munich to live the same friendless, penniless, jobless life as before, until the war began.

The Great War reshaped his future—and ultimately the world's. Conscripted in 1914, he was wounded twice and decorated for bravery twice. He received the Iron Cross, First Class, a medal he wore proudly the rest of his life. When Germany surrendered in 1918, he was among those who blamed a conspiracy of traitors at home, the Jewish and Communist "November Criminals" that stabbed Germany in the back and made it lose the war.

It was then that Adolf Hitler decided to enter politics and, as he promised the young milkmaid, change the world.

CHAPTER 26

RIO DE JANEIRO, 2016

THE AIRPLANE ENGINE NOISE BROUGHT THEIR heads even closer together. Stefan buried his nose in Kirsten's hair and inhaled. "I love the way you smell."

She smiled at him. "Is that romantic? How I smell?" she asked.

"It is if it turns me on," Stefan said.

"Does it?"

He nibbled her ear. "If this plane doesn't land soon, I'm going to need an ice-cold shower."

Kirsten laughed and gave him a peck on the lips. "Back to the diary."

"Where were we? I've been distracted," Stefan said, inhaling again.

"Hitler's Jewish son," she said, laughing and pushing him away.

"Right. That must be the proof Lobo was talking about," Stefan said.

"Of course it's not proof," Kirsten said. "It's a 'he said, she said.'"

"True, but you've got the handwritten diary of the woman closest to Hitler saying that's what *he* said to *her*," Stefan said. "How could anyone disprove it?"

"I guess," Kirsten said. "But who was Eva writing this for, anyway? Pretty intimate stuff. Can we believe everything she says?"

"Who knows? She's got no reason to lie. I believe her. What did Eva do?"

"Wait, I'm reading as fast as I can." Kirsten scanned pages. "Oh, wow. I don't know if anyone ever knew this."

His eyes got big. "Knew what?"

"She attempted suicide, just like Geli! She says in August 1932, after she found out about his past, she wrote Hitler a farewell letter, took her father's pistol, and shot herself. Her sister Ilse found her and rushed her to the doctor, who removed a bullet lodged in her neck."

Stefan kissed Kirsten's neck. "Right about there?"

"You'd better stop," she said, gently pushing his head away, "or we'll never get through this diary." He put his hand on her knee. "Stefan," Kirsten said in a low threatening voice, "behave yourself."

"Yes, Mother," he said, removing his hand.

Kirsten continued. "Eva says Hitler canceled a campaign rally in Berlin to join her in the hospital. When the physician told Hitler she had almost died, Hitler promised he would look after her forever so she would never do it again."

"Was it a real attempt or just to scare Hitler?" Stefan asked.

"She doesn't say, but it sounds serious." Kirsten turned pages rapidly, caught up in the drama. Her look was intense. "Oh my goodness."

"What now?" he asked.

"She says Hitler was so remorseful, to regain her trust, he crawled in bed alongside her in the hospital room and whispered the most important secret in his life." She paused, dramatically.

"What could be more important than having a Jewish son?" Stefan asked. When Kirsten didn't respond, he elbowed her and said, "Don't leave me hanging."

"Hitler told her he had Jewish blood from his father, Alois, who was half-Jewish."

"Holy Christ!" Stefan exclaimed so loud the passenger in the seat in front turned around.

They looked at each other, slowly shaking heads in amazement. "He'd be a quarter Jewish," Stefan said. "How did it happen?"

She went back to the diary.

After reading a few pages, she translated, "Apparently, when Hitler's grandmother, Maria Schicklgruber, gave birth to Hitler's father, Alois, Maria was working as a household cook for a Jewish family named Frankenberger. Hitler thinks the family's nineteen-year-old son, Leopold, and not his grandfather, fathered Alois. To avoid public condemnation, both families—Hitler's and the Frankenbergers—went along with the lie. That's why it took thirty-nine years for Hitler's grandfather to legitimize Alois."

"My God! You can't make this stuff up. It could've altered world history and maybe prevented World War II. Think of the lives saved," Stefan said.

"Could've, would've, and should've. But it didn't," Kirsten said. "People suspected, but nobody really knew Hitler was part Jewish."

"Maybe so, but Lobo told the truth. Thanks to him, we have secrets the entire world would love," Stefan said. "Now, what do we do with them?"

"Good question. Lobo said our lives would never be the same," Kirsten said as the wheels of the plane touched down at the International Rio de Janeiro Galeão Airport. "He may be right."

CHAPTER 27

"HOW IMPORTANT DO YOU THINK THESE SECRETS really are in 2016?" Stefan asked as they drove from the Rio airport to Kirsten's pousada late that night. "I think Lobo inflated their impact. I mean, who would care about the Amber Room except for a few art experts?"

Though after midnight, the Rio roads were bustling with traffic. Drivers ignored traffic signals, and Stefan knew intersections could be deadly. Whoever arrived first claimed right-of-way and shot across, regardless of stoplights or signs. Various hand gestures and honking horns greeted interlopers that failed to follow the rule of first in, first out.

Kirsten watched Stefan's eyes flicker in the oncoming headlight glare. "Certainly the art world cares, and historians, and maybe politicians and lawyers if Germany and Russia fought over ownership. All that amber and jewels must be worth millions—even hundreds of millions."

He nodded. "That's only a handful of people, Kirsten. Russia's already built a duplicate, so the original's as exciting as yesterday's newspaper. And who cares whether Hitler had a Jewish son or was part Jewish? Sure, some neo-Nazi groups might, but who else? Lobo was wrong. Knowing this won't change our lives."

She opened her bag and took out the diary. She scanned pages in the flickering lights of passing cars. She knew he was wrong. He had to be. First of all, the Amber Room was original art. Copies never cut it like the original. The jewels and the Vermeer alone skyrocketed the value into hundreds of millions. Add the exquisite amber carvings, and the total was unimaginable. She could picture people lining up for blocks to get inside whatever building housed it.

And the fact that Hitler fathered a Jewish son and was part Jewish was awesome. The son would be 110 years old, but what if he had children? She remembered the movie, *Boys from Brazil*, when they tried to clone Hitler.

"That desire to have Hitler's bloodline leading a new Germany, a Fourth Reich, is not so far-fetched." Kirsten said.

"I suppose not," he conceded.

"And if Hitler had a son, with whom? Who was this Jewish woman at the inn? Where did she and her son live after the boy was born? Did that son grow up? Did he have children? Do the children have children? One hundred and ten years is plenty of time for a third generation or even a fourth. Dozens of Hitler's offspring could be living in Europe or South America right now. Neo-Nazis would love a leader with direct lineage to Hitler. That could promote a resurgence of Nazi power and anti-Semitism."

Stefan glanced in her direction when the road cleared a bit. "Or would the son and progeny being Jewish actually be a big negative and help destroy Nazism?" he asked. "Combine Jewish ancestry with Hitler's philandering, incest, and possible murder, and all of a sudden, Aryan purity is a myth, a fairy tale manufactured by propaganda, probably Goebbels."

She cocked her head, thinking. "I hadn't considered it that way, but you could be right. It might boomerang, although whatever Hitler did personally pales beside what he and his Nazi killers did to Jews and Europe."

"Maybe some of his hatred was because he knew he was Jewish. Would be a good way to deflect suspicion."

"Interesting thought. Still," Kirsten chewed on her lip a moment, "I think the lineage angle is critical. Imagine the potential importance of the rise of a powerful Nazi Fourth Reich led by a descendent of Hitler," Kirsten said. "The world is already having a problem containing Islamic fundamentalism. Add Nazism, and we've got a *real* problem."

"You should've been a lawyer, Kirsten."

She flexed her right arm. "I've enough trouble being an Olympian, now that we're back." She looked at the pousada as Stefan pulled the car to the curb. It was near one in the morning, and all was quiet. "No lights. Sharon must be asleep."

Kirsten leaned against the car door away from Stefan and extended her hand, a smile on her face. "Thank you for a most interesting trip, Dr. Pasteur. I've enjoyed being your traveling companion."

Stefan laughed, brushed Kirsten's hand aside, and pulled her to him. "I'm not leaving without a good-bye kiss."

His lips smothered Kirsten's response.

"Can I see you tomorrow, traveling companion? And every day after that forever?" Stefan asked.

"We do have to start thinking about training. I don't know about you, but I want a medal."

"How about I come by around ten—you can sleep late—and we go for a 10K run?"

Kirsten smiled. "Pretty resourceful. Okay." She opened her car door and started to get out.

"Wait! One more kiss?"

She leaned back in, and they kissed. He held her, not wanting to leave. "Kirsten, these two days have been the most important in my life."

"Mine too."

"I feel like that guy—what's his name in *West Side Story*?"

"Tony?"

"Yeah, like Tony falling in love with Maria and not wanting to leave her on the balcony that first night."

They held each other a moment longer, her head on his shoulder, eyes closed. Finally she stirred. "I have to go."

"I love you, Kirsten."

"And I love you, Stefan."

"See you tomorrow."

She got out of the car and collected her carry-on with its precious cargo from the backseat. She closed the door and blew him a kiss.

Stefan shouted, "I love you," as he drove away with a screech of tires and honk of the horn. Kirsten waved and mouthed the same.

CHAPTER 28

SHARON WAS UP EARLY THE NEXT MORNING making breakfast when Kirsten joined her in the kitchen.

"The smell of your pancakes woke me. I'm starving. We ate a bag of chips for dinner last night on the flight back."

Sharon kissed her good morning. "I'll feed you if you tell me everything, especially why you came back a day early."

"Because I missed your pancakes?"

"Ha. Eat and then we'll talk."

Kirsten sat down at the kitchen table, and Sharon piled her plate high with hot pancakes. Kirsten dabbed a pat of butter on top and in between the four layers. Then she poured golden honey over the mound. She watched the syrup penetrate before she attacked.

"Hmm, delicious, Sharon," Kirsten said, mouth full and honey dripping down her chin. "You're the best."

Sharon sat at the table with a cup of coffee and waited until Kirsten finished. "Ready? Tell me all," Sharon said.

Over the next half hour, Kirsten briefed Sharon about the trip.

Sharon asked, "Weren't you scared when this Lobo character died?"

"Yeah, though there was really nothing threatening. I couldn't think clearly, so much was happening. Stefan seemed unfazed, and we got out of there fast. I did almost lose it when the car wouldn't start, but Stefan got it going somehow. I remembered to take the boxes as we were leaving." She nodded at them, sitting on the chair next to the table. "Eva's diary is the smoking gun."

"Should we be concerned?" Sharon asked. "Is someone going to try to steal them?" She waved a crutch in the air. "I can't fight off another bandido with only one good leg."

Kirsten laughed and shook her head. "No one knows we have them. I think Eva kept her diary in secret. From the intimate details, I doubt even Hitler knew she was writing. Somehow Lobo got hold of it. And he's the only one who could prove we were even at Inalco."

She pulled a paper from her purse and flipped it on the table. "This is the only record of us passing through the checkpoints, and they didn't register the car's license plate."

"And the other box?"

"Hitler's *Mein Kampf*, one of the first editions. Valuable because Hitler signed it. The world knows what's in it."

"And regrets they ignored it. I hope you're right," Sharon said, getting up to make more coffee. She busied herself with the coffeemaker, poured two cups, and returned to the table.

"Now let's concentrate on the real reason we're here. How's your arm?" Sharon asked.

The question triggered thoughts about the competition. She felt the pressure again, forgotten for a few days because of her trip to Bariloche. So much was riding on her performance. She carried not only the family's dreams but also its reputation. Her grandfather was cheated out of a medal, and her father almost died helping the Israeli's win one. Could she do it? It would be a grueling day of matches. She hoped the arm would hold up.

At this thought, she smiled to herself. She hadn't said *her* arm, rather *the* arm. It reminded her of opera singers that referred to their voice as *the* voice, and not *my* voice. She wondered what this impersonalization of a body part meant, treating it like an external piece of equipment rather than a part of you. Did boxers talk about *the* fists, or runners *the* legs? Maybe doing that removed the person from responsibility if they failed. It was an instrument failure and not personal. *The* legs gave out, *the* fists failed, or *the* voice cracked. She couldn't do that. If *the* arm failed, *she* failed.

Kirsten stretched *her* arm and flipped her wrist over and back in a fencing move. "I think it'll be fine. I've kept it clean, like the surgeon said, and my strength seems normal. The skin around the cut is tender and feels tight when I make a fist, but that's all. There's no redness or bleeding, so I'm good to go."

"The International Olympic Committee sent out a mass e-mail. The Olympic Village—they call it Athletes' Village—opens tomorrow. We can move in then," Sharon said.

"What's it like? Did they say?"

Sharon told her there were thirty-one buildings housing ten thousand athletes. She and Kirsten would share a bedroom in building 12, with the other Israeli athletes. A tram connected them to the track, field, and fencing in the Maracanã Stadium, which would also host the opening and closing ceremonies.

"Did you get the fencing schedule?" Kirsten asked, taking a deep breath and letting it out slowly. She had no idea who she was matched against.

Sharon nodded. "Your first bout's a week from today, against the Swedish fencer, Jenny Linder. Six elimination matches to pare sixty-four fencers down to one gold. Men's matches follow the next day."

Kirsten's heart raced, hearing that. Jenny Linder was fourth seed and a good fencer. Kirsten was glad she wouldn't face Monique in the opener.

She yawned and stretched. "The Jenny Linder news woke me up, but I'm still sleepy." She looked at the clock. "Stefan will be here in an hour for a run. We're doing ten kilometers, and when I get back, we can practice my footwork in the basement."

"Fine. I'll pack while you're jogging, and we'll move to the Village in the morning. They have a racquetball court that'll be the best conditioning for stamina and footwork. Does Stefan play racquetball?"

Kirsten gave Sharon a big grin. "I don't know." The thought tickled her as she considered all the time they would spend training and fencing together. She picked at a few crumbs left on her plate and reached for a banana. She was still hungry.

"This is serious?" Sharon asked.

"Very. I've never felt like this before."

"Happened pretty fast."

"Yes, but we've shared so much so quickly that it's like I've known him a long time," Kirsten said.

"What does he do?"

"Medical student in Paris."

"Family?"

"Parents divorced, and he lived with his mother growing up."

"What's his father do?"

"You're sounding like my parents."

"Well, somebody has to watch over you."

"I don't know what his father does. We didn't talk about him, and I don't think Stefan's seen him in a long time."

"What if—"

"Sharon, stop please," Kirsten said, holding up her hand. "This is like an inquisition, back and forth between lawyer and witness. I'm twenty-seven, for goodness sake."

"You are, but your parents left me to chaperone. I'm trying to do that." Then she looked at Kirsten with a widening smile.

"What are you hiding, Sharon? You look like you just swallowed the canary."

"I didn't tell you the most exciting news."

"Which is?" Kirsten asked.

"The male and female gold winners will face off against each other in a match the IOC is billing as the Super Bowl of Fencing. It's never been done before, but the IOC hopes it'll drum up interest and support for fencing. They felt it was the only combat sport in which a woman had a chance facing a man."

"Oh my God," Kirsten said. "What will we do if it comes to that?"

"Let's hope it does."

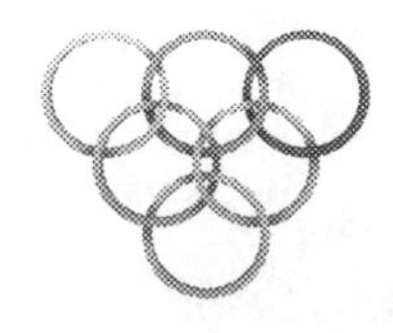

They jogged at a leisurely pace in the hills of Santa Teresa, just fast enough to generate a sweat, laughing and talking as they ran. The day was lovely—warm with the sun's rays, the heat from running, and their burgeoning love for each other. They tried jogging while holding hands but tripped and almost fell over a painter's easel planted in the middle of the sidewalk. Stefan caught her before she hit the ground. They stopped to catch their breaths.

"Let's have a drink," Kirsten said, pointing to the café with bright red and white tablecloths and climbing purple bougainvillea she and Sharon had stopped at days ago. They sat at a table overlooking artists painting on the street and ordered an ice tea and a beer.

"A beer so early in the morning?" Kirsten asked.

"Never too early for a cold beer on a hot day. Can you say Bariloche Blest Brewery?"

They both laughed. "It was a lovely dinner, wasn't it?" she asked.

"The best ever. Remember what we ate?" Stefan asked.

They tried but could recall only four courses. Kirsten looked around the café thinking she'd like a house like this, filled with bright colors and beautiful flowers. And, of course, Stefan. She reached across the table and took his hand. "Don't ever leave me."

"No chance," he said, leaning over to kiss her.

The waiter interrupted with their drinks.

"Will you still love me if I win gold and you don't?" Kirsten asked, sipping her tea.

"Ha!" Stefan said. "More likely the reverse. Will *you* still love *me*?"

"Maybe, if you're very nice and apologetic. And, of course, give me your gold medal to wear," she said, giggling.

"What if we end up in the Super Bowl against each other?" he said, his tone more serious.

"I haven't stopped thinking of that since Sharon told me. I hope it happens—and then again, I hope it doesn't."

"Me too," he said. After a sip, Stefan twisted the beer bottle around to read the label. It was from the Bariloche Blest Brewery. Carefully he peeled off the label, dried it on a napkin, and presented it to her.

"Is this in place of a rose that a girl's supposed to press in a book and keep forever as a memory of her first love?" she asked, smiling.

He stood from the table, picked off a small cluster of purple bougainvillea blossoms, and brought it back to her. "The best I can do under the circumstances."

She laughed. "I accept. For that, I *might* let you win, just to preserve the male ego."

"Yeah, right," he snorted. "No female ego?"

"Well, if I'm in the Super Bowl, I've already won gold, so I can let this one go," she said. "It's easier for a female to lose. I can say you won because you're bigger, stronger, and have a longer reach."

"Maybe you can let it go, but I can't. I love you but hate losing. We'll each have to go for the win."

"They said it'd be a platinum medal. Would look nice on a chain around my neck. I'd wear a dress with a low cut. Show a little cleavage with the medal. What color dress goes with platinum?"

"No need to worry. It'll be mine. Maybe I'll make it into a money clip. Or better yet, as the crown of our wedding cake."

Kirsten shook her head. "Not a good way to start a marriage."

The waiter came with the check. Stefan paid, and they stood.

"See that big building at the end of the block?" Kirsten asked, pointing.

"Yeah, so?"

"It's a museum with beautiful paintings," she said.

"You want to visit it?"

"No, just to beat you to it," Kirsten said, laughing as she ran into the street before Stefan had a chance to react. She had a ten-meter lead. He made up the distance, but Kirsten won. She danced about, in front of the house, hands high. "Yea for me," she shouted. "See, Stefan. *This* is the way to start a marriage." He stood there, a smile on his face, and nodded.

They continued on, finishing the morning's jog.

When they stopped running, he took her arm and planted a sweaty kiss on her lips. “Kirsten, I love you so much. How did it happen so fast?”

She shook her head. “I don’t know. It just did.”

They walked, cooling off and holding hands, breathing returning to normal. “When can we get married?” he asked.

“When we get home. It’ll have to be in Israel, okay?”

“Of course. My mom won’t have a problem with that.”

“First I’ll need to find a rabbi who’ll marry us. Some won’t perform a ceremony between a Jew and a Gentile.”

“Where will we live? Paris or Tel Aviv?”

“Good question. Maybe we should wait until you finish medical school?”

“No way. I’m not waiting a minute to marry you. As soon as we get home, done. I want to fall asleep every night and wake up every morning next to you.”

“Then I guess I’ll move to Paris for your last year, and we can decide where to go after that,” Kirsten said.

“Both France and Israel have superb hospitals, so I can practice medicine in either country.”

CHAPTER 29

STEFAN LET HIMSELF INTO HIS APARTMENT, still sweaty from his run with Kirsten. He looked forward to a long, hot shower. He had left the blinds drawn to keep the place cool, and the room was dark.

He turned on the light and gasped, "Holy Christ!"

A man was seated on the sofa, his head partially hidden by the table lamp. Stefan started for the door, but when the man didn't move, he stopped and took a closer look.

"Is it really you? It can't be. You scared the shit out of me. What are you doing here?"

The man remained seated, one hand resting on an ivory-topped cane propped next to his feet. "Sorry to shock you, Son. The building manager let me in after I told him I was your father. I wanted to surprise you."

Stefan stood in front of Max, hands on hips, studying his face. They did not shake hands. Was it really his father? He only had a newspaper picture to compare. A thousand questions whirred through his brain, each competing for an answer. Why did he leave? Where was he the past twenty years? What was he doing here now? *He must want something from me. It can't be money. What?*

"You did surprise me. It's only been—what—twenty years." Stefan reached around for a wooden kitchen chair, turned it backward, and set it a few feet from his father. He straddled the seat, the back of the chair a convenient though flimsy barrier. He didn't want to sit any closer than that to his father.

The man crossed his legs and leaned the cane against the sofa. "Maybe a little longer." He stared into his son's face. "You've matured nicely. Good-looking kid."

"Thanks."

"I've kept track of you, helped your mother pay your school expenses—I told her not to tell you—and watched your track achievements. I went to several races, though you didn't see me. Even when you turned to fencing, I went a few times."

"Why?" Stefan found that hard to believe. One of his last memories was of his father in a shouting match with his mother when Stefan was five or six, maybe seven. He was sitting on a chair in the kitchen, screaming for them to stop. His father had never hit his mother, but the big man towered over her, and when he leaned into her face, she was brought to her knees.

"Why, what?" Max asked.

"Why did you stay away so long, and why are you back?" Stefan asked, an edge to his voice.

The man nodded, acknowledging the fairness of the questions. "Your mother didn't want me around and e-mailed me only when she needed money, often attaching your latest picture. And I wasn't certain how you felt, that you might not want me around either, so I just watched from a distance."

Stefan was silent, considering. That was probably a bunch of bullshit. But his father did send money. That much was true.

"I sent her a picture once," Max said. "When the German government gave me a medal. It was five or six years ago. She ever show it to you?"

Stefan nodded. "That's how I recognized you, from that newspaper article." The German government had awarded Max the Order of Merit for entrepreneurial achievement in helping create a hundred thousand new jobs in the industrial sector. That Max had profited by over fifty million euros was not mentioned in the article. Max had bragged that fact to Stefan's mother.

"You ran track well. Reminded me of when I was your age. Too bad you didn't continue. But it seems like you're a pretty good fencer too."

"And now what's changed?" Stefan asked.

"How many times does a father have a chance to see his son compete for a medal in the Olympics? I couldn't miss this."

Stefan knew that was a bunch of garbage. The question in his mind was how to find out the real reason for his father's visit.

"That was your sole reason for flying ten thousand kilometers?" Stefan asked. "To see me fence?" Stefan shook his head. "I don't believe it."

"I did combine the trip with some business." The man shifted on the sofa. "I'm sorry your mother isn't here."

"She talked about coming, but sports isn't her thing, even the Olympics. Maybe if I were singing in an opera …"

Stefan remembered the fight was about going to some black-tie concert at the Deutsche Oper Berlin. His father had said he'd already contributed ten thousand euros to the damn opera house and that should have been enough to get out of going. He'd be damned if he was going to listen to Wagner's *Tannhäuser* for four or five hours, when he could be going to the Rennbahn Hoppegarten to bet on his favorite horses and drink beer with his good friends. Not some uppity intellectuals who couldn't make a euro if they tried.

Stefan recognized the name of the opera house and the racetrack but had to ask his teacher the next day what *Tannhäuser* was. He never forgot but had yet to see the opera.

Stefan and his mother had moved out shortly after that last battle.

"Another reason for me to come," he father continued. "An athlete ought to have family cheering him on."

"Thanks a whole lot. Now I'm sure to win gold."

His father ignored the sarcasm. "When do you compete?"

"I don't know. I just found out from Kirsten that the Athletes' Village opens tomorrow, so I'll plan to—"

"Who's Kirsten?"

Stefan smiled. His mood changed just saying her name. "A girl I met a few days ago. We've been sightseeing together and just got back from Patagonia."

The man nodded again. "Just the two of you?"

That triggered caution. Why so curious? Was this where his father was going? Stefan doubted the man gave a damn who he was with. Alert now, Stefan tried to read the old man's eyes but got nothing except—

"I don't remember you having blue eyes," Stefan said. "I thought they were brown in the picture you sent Mother."

Max brushed aside the query and repeated his. "Just the two of you?"

Stefan sat there wondering where this was going. Finally— "Why do you want to know?"

"Just curious about my son's life."

"Yes, just the two of us, but that's none of your business."

"Serious?"

"I'm going to marry her when the games are over," Stefan said in a tone that brooked no argument.

"That does sound serious—and pretty quick. Love at first sight. Have you proposed?"

Stefan was trying to remain civil. After all, it was his father, even if he'd been gone twenty years. But he was reaching the end of his patience. "This is really none of your business."

"Why are you so defensive, Stefan? Something to hide?" The man tapped his cane on the seatback of Stefan's chair. Stefan moved farther away, and the cane fell to the floor.

"Not in so many words, but we discussed marriage. When the Olympics are done, I'll formally ask her. I don't want to distract us from the games."

"Probably a good idea. What's her sport?"

"Fencing."

"She's from where?"

"Israel."

The old man sat silent and unmoving. His face darkened, a descending veil that blocked out the light from his eyes. They became tiny icy slits, and his lips pressed together in a mean line. He crossed his arms over his chest, setting his own barrier.

"You have a problem with that?" Stefan asked.

The man remained still and cold, sculpted in ice, staring unblinking at his son. Finally he said, "A Jew?"

"Yes, she was born in Israel."

"Jews are bad."

Stefan pushed his chair back a few inches more. "What're you talking about? Bad?"

"Just what I said. They're bad. All of them rotten."

"You've never even met her, and she's bad? That's irrational."

"I forbid you to see her."

Now it was Stefan's turn to narrow his eyes and thin his lips.

"You got to be kidding. You forbid me to see her? Who in hell are you to forbid me from doing anything? You drop into my life after twenty years and give me orders? No way, old man, no way." He shook his head.

"I'll stop supporting your education."

Stefan rose and stood towering over his father, glaring down at him. He gave a short laugh. "You can go to hell, for all I care. I'll get a loan or a part-time job. In fact, I'd *like* you to stop supporting my education. And get the hell out of my life for at least another twenty years." Stefan pointed to the door. "Starting right now. Get out. Now!"

His father didn't move from the sofa.

"I said, leave!"

"What's this girl's name?"

Stefan shook his head at the man. "None of your damn business."

"I already know her first name—Kirsten. It'll be easy to find out her last name."

"Then do your own dirty work. I'm sorry I told you as much as I have already. Out. Now. I mean it." He bent down to grab the man's elbow, but his father pulled his arm away.

"Hang on," his father said. "I'm going. Just one last question."

"Finish up. I want you the hell out of here."

"Did you kill old man Lobo? Or did she?" Max asked.

Stefan froze, and he felt the blood drain from his face. Now he was the ice statue, standing and staring at his father. Neither spoke, eyes fixed on each other.

Stefan sat down hard in the chair. Collapsed onto it, really. How could his father know about Lobo?

Moments later, after Stefan's color returned, he said, "So it *was* you in the car at the checkpoint. I couldn't be sure. You drove past quickly."

"I spoke with Lobo by phone early yesterday morning, and he seemed fine then. But when I got to his little cabin around three thirty yesterday afternoon, he was dead. Just sitting in his chair in front of that big, ornamental fireplace, cold dead. And the key to the Amber Room was missing from his key ring," Max said.

Stefan's eyebrows rose, and his eyes got big. He started to say something but couldn't find the words.

"Yes, that pretty little golden key was gone. Now, what do you think of that?" His father relaxed his arms, a smug look on his face.

Stefan couldn't move. He fought an impulse to look at where he had hidden the key and caught himself just in time.

"You know what else? Lobo's shirt was ripped, as if he had been in a fight. And the skin over his chest was bruised, like someone hit him, maybe broke a rib or two. Plus that awful cut on his forehead. What'd you use to bash in his brains? A fireplace poker? I'll bet if we looked, it would have his blood on it."

"I don't know what you're talking about," Stefan said without much conviction.

"Come now, Son, sure you do. The man's dead, killed by you or your girlfriend for that key. You know how much that Amber Room's worth? A billion euros—that's with a capital B. Fair amount of pocket change for a room nobody can find. But I suspect you already have. The German government is willing to pay that much to have the original reinstalled in the Charlottenberg Palace so they can thumb their noses at the Russians and their St. Petersburg's replica."

"How do you know about—" Stefan stopped abruptly. He knew he was on thin ice. He had been so certain only he and Kirsten knew. He wondered if Max knew the other secrets as well.

"Keep going. How do I know about the Amber Room? Maybe I should be asking you that question. How do *you* know about it? I can't imagine Lobo telling you, 'Hey, Stefan. Here's this room full of carved amber and jewels that Hitler imported from Germany. It's worth a whole bunch of money. Why don't you take this special key and have a look? If you like it, we can arrange to move it back to your place. You'll make a bundle of money.' Maybe you beat that out of him with the poker." Max frowned and pointed to the spot on his forehead where Lobo had hit the step when he fell.

Stefan sat frozen, his mind spinning. He didn't know how to respond. He ran his hands through his hair. Finally, "How do you know about the room?"

Stefan thought maybe Lobo wasn't dead after all when they left. No, impossible. He had no pulse, and there was no respiration or heartbeat. Lobo wasn't talking.

"You read the newspapers just as I do. Lots of interest in art masterpieces that disappeared during the war. Stolen by Göring and Bormann. One old guy in Munich had fourteen hundred paintings hidden in his apartment that his father 'acquired' in the 1930s and '40s. Worth hundreds of millions. Hollywood even made a movie about the stolen art. I got interested when I had to finance a new initiative of mine—very expensive—so I went to the Internet to see what else was still missing. And what do you know? I found the Amber Room."

"How's that connected to Lobo?" Stefan couldn't stop thinking that Lobo told him. Impossible. The man was dead. Absolutely dead.

"Lobo wasn't very bright, carrying a keychain with one amber key in the midst of all metal ones. It was so striking. I remembered it from a visit I made last year to tour Estancia Inalco."

"Why were you there?" Stefan asked.

"I travel to South America regularly," Max said, "usually Rio but Argentina also. Lots of business interests here. Last year I decided to visit

Hitler's house and met Lobo. I asked him about the key, but he gave me some ridiculous answer. It was easy to put two and two together after my Internet search."

So, in effect, Lobo *had* told him. His father had been smart enough to connect the dots. "Why do you need the money?" Stefan asked. "Mother said you were pretty wealthy. You made millions in a business deal."

"Some personal investments. Anyway, I called Lobo from Germany two weeks ago, and we agreed on a deal for the Amber Room. He wanted finally to leave Argentina, go sit on a beach in the French Riviera, and do nothing but watch the topless beauties. I told him I'd arrange it all.

"I went to meet him yesterday to complete the transaction, but the poor guy was dead—killed—brutally bludgeoned by my very own son and the girl he wants to marry. A Jew! And the golden key was gone."

Stefan's mind raced into high gear. How long had his father been in his apartment? Had he searched for the key? If he did, it wasn't likely he'd found it or he wouldn't be asking all these questions. No, not true. He could've found the key but didn't know where the Amber Room was.

The man sneered. "I can read your mind, Son. Yes, I did look before you came in, but I didn't have a chance for a thorough search. Your key is safe for the moment, wherever you've hidden it. I've not gone to the police because they'll complicate the whole deal and want a piece of the action. Maybe even prevent the Amber Room from leaving Argentina. But remember the Argentinean cops, many of whom I've known personally for years—"

"How do you know the cops?" Stefan asked. "You're bluffing about this whole thing." *Think, Stefan, think. How are you going to get out of this? He's not bluffing. He knows about Lobo, the room, and maybe the diary. Would he make a deal? Maybe for half the room? What am I thinking? I don't care about the money. I just want to win a medal, for Kirsten to win a medal, and to go home, marry her, and finish medical school. I don't want any part of this.*

"My naïve son. Business in South America thrives on bribes. Nothing happens without *soborno.* Anyway, my friends have more convincing ways to find things than I do. They'll cooperate with the local Rio police. I'd prefer to do this on my own, but if necessary—"

He stopped and looked at his son. "Anything you want to say?"

"I don't want anything to happen to Kirsten. You leave her alone."

"We'll see. You're hardly in the bargaining position, are you? In the meantime, I repeat what I said earlier. You are not to see this Kirsten woman ever again. I forbid it. If you do, I will go to the police and accuse you both of Lobo's murder. It may cost me the Amber Room, but I'm willing to take that chance to prevent a son of mine from marrying a Jew."

He stood slowly, pushing himself up by the sofa arm and reaching for the cane. He looked down at his son seated in his chair. "Remember, Stefan: unless you and your friend want to spend your Olympic days in a Brazilian jail instead of fencing—I've heard they're most unpleasant, and it would be weeks or months before all this got untangled—no contact with this Kirsten *at all*." He took out his wallet and extracted his business card. Without a word, he placed it on the table, turned, and left.

Stefan sat still, head in his hands, eyes closed. A pain grew deep in his gut, a vast emptiness. Eyes that had been brimming with happiness an hour ago were moist with despair.

The iPhone's ring jarred him from his daze. He knew it was Kirsten. They were supposed to meet for dinner, but he hadn't called because he didn't know what to say. He dreaded talking to her. How did you tell the girl you loved more than anything in the world that you couldn't see her anymore? That if you did, you both could go to jail?

Despite his father's warning, he had to give her a reason for canceling dinner—and possibly the rest of their lives. He couldn't tell her the truth. There was no way she'd be able to fence with that threat hanging over her head. He had to protect her. If he disobeyed his father, they could both end up in jail and blow the whole Olympics. The ringing stopped and then started again.

"Hi, Kirsten."

"Stefan, where were you? Didn't you hear the phone?"

"I did but—I misplaced the phone and had to search for it. Sorry."

"What's wrong?" she asked. "I hear it in your voice. Are you all right?"

"No, nothing's the matter, but something's come up, and I can't do dinner tonight."

"What do you mean, something's come up?"

"I just can't."

Stefan heard Kirsten exhale a loud breath. "Okay, then, tomorrow night," she said.

"No, not tomorrow, either. I'm so sorry, I just can't."

"Not more than an hour ago, I asked you to never leave me, and you said no chance of that ever happening. What's changed?"

"I think we should concentrate on the Olympics, and then when we leave South America, maybe we can get together again."

"You don't love me anymore," she said. He heard her begin to sob.

"Yes, I still care for you. It's just that—"

"Care for me? Care for me? What kind of … of feeling is that? Tell Monique I hope the two of you will be very happy together."

He heard her crying just before the phone went dead.

Tears ran down his cheeks, and he could no longer choke back the sobs. They started deep in his gut and doubled him over in pain. He collapsed on the rug and thought his life had just ended.

CHAPTER 30

KIRSTEN WAS STUNNED. WHAT HAD HAPPENED? He had left just an hour ago, saying how much he loved her, eager to get married. Monique? It had to be.

But he had said it was all over between them. How could she change his mind in an hour? Was she waiting for him in his apartment? Kirsten played out the scene in her head: Monique in a black see-through negligee with background lighting … her arms stretched out for Stefan … him walking toward her … carrying her into the bedroom.

In between the tears, she shook her head in disgust. *Stop it, Kirsten. Stop the damn crying and think logically. What could it be? It's not Monique.* Kirsten regretted her parting barb and debated calling him back. But if not Monique, then what?

Her sobbing brought Sharon running. She held Kirsten as her body shook. "What's the matter, baby? What is it? What's happened?"

"Stefan doesn't want to see me anymore. He said to forget him. Oh, Sharon, he told me he loved me, and I love him. What's happened?" She dissolved in Sharon's arms. Sharon held her until the crying stopped.

"Let's think logically," Sharon said, sitting them both down at the kitchen table. "Something extreme had to have triggered this."

"Yeah, extreme Monique," Kirsten said with a sneer.

"Do you really think so?" Sharon asked. "You know him better than I do, but I doubt that. He doesn't seem the type."

"No, I guess I honestly don't think so, but I can't come up with another explanation," Kirsten said.

"So, he's a bastard, like all the others, just playing around? Get into a girl's pants, and he's gone. Typical Frenchman? The chase, the conquest, and then the *ciao*?"

Kirsten shook her head. "No, Sharon, it's not that way. *He's* not that way. We love each other. I'm sure of it. Something's happened." She wiped her eyes with a dishcloth.

Kirsten stood and caught a glimpse of herself in the calendar mirror hanging on the wall. She looked closer. "My God, I'm a mess!" She snatched up a napkin, wet a corner, and dabbed at the smudged mascara lines under her eyes. She stiffened her back, plopped back down at the table, and sipped her coffee, now cold. "No, there's got to be another reason. Something's happened," she said. "But if it is Monique, she'd better watch out. I'm going to carve her heart out."

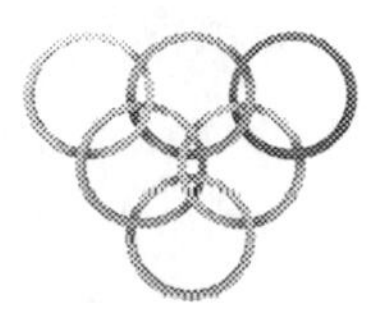

The next morning, Sharon and Kirsten moved to the Athletes' Village. The guard at the entrance stopped them for their passes. He scanned their badges electronically, and the gate opened when a green light in his scanner winked on. Their luggage was delivered after being x-rayed and sniffed by the dogs.

"Wear your badge at all times," the guard said. "People without proof are subject to arrest. And report any suspicious activity, unclaimed packages, and anybody using drugs."

The Village bustled with athletes, all wearing distinctive jackets from their countries of origin and an ID dangling from their necks. Since the '72 Munich games, a five-man security squad from the Mossad accompanied Israeli Olympians. Many other countries now provided similar protection. They blended in with the athletes, the only difference being telltale bulges beneath their jackets invisible to all but other bodyguards.

Sharon and Kirsten passed through a metal detector to enter building 12. Kirsten noticed an overhead security camera recording their arrival.

The second floor had twelve apartments, each barely big enough for twin beds and a tiny bathroom with a shower. But it was all sparkling yellow and white, and clean. Sharon was thrilled.

"You ought to call home," Sharon reminded Kirsten after they unpacked. "Your folks would like to know we're in the Village and preparing for the matches. Tell them how great this room is."

"Call them now?"

Sharon checked her watch. One o'clock. "It's 7:00 p.m. in Tel Aviv. Probably a good time to catch them. But remember—all communications will be screened. Be careful what you say."

Kirsten dialed. After several failed attempts, her mother answered.

"Hi, Mom."

"Kirsten, darling. How are you?" Dannie asked.

"We're both fine. We've moved into the Athletes' Village." She'd decided not to tell them about the bandido attack or Hitler's house. "I toured a bit. Went to Argentina to see Patagonia. Sharon stayed in Rio. I met this nice Frenchman and—"

"Is he Jewish?" Dannie asked.

"No, just another fencer. Maybe I'll see him again after the games end. Things are a little up in the air right now." She hesitated and changed the subject. "How's Dad?"

"He's okay," her mother said.

Her mother's response told her he was not. "Mom, tell me the truth. Your voice doesn't sound convincing."

"He had a slight fall."

"When?"

"Two days ago."

"What happened?"

"He had a dizzy spell, fell, and hit his head on the bathtub. There was a lot of bleeding, so I brought him to the hospital, and they sewed him up and kept him overnight. Seems okay now but still getting dizzy."

"What did the doctor say? Would you like me to come home? You know you two are more important than the Olympics."

"No, absolutely not. We want you to compete and win a medal. The doctor said he'll be fine."

"Okay, but let me know if Dad gets worse and if I can help. I love you both."

"We know, darling. We're okay. Just go out and do your best. *Tap, tap, tap.*"

"Thanks, I'm going for gold."

"All our love, baby."

"You have mine for Dad and for you. Keep in touch. Bye."

"What happened?" Sharon asked.

Kirsten told her. "Nothing I can do, but I feel guilty being here when they might need me at home."

"You know very well they'd want you here competing for gold more than anything else in the world," Sharon said. "Win a medal, and that'll be the biggest gift you can give them."

"You're right, I guess. Still—"

"No 'still' about it," Sharon said. "You need to focus on the games ahead. No Frenchman, no parents, no Hitler, no nothing except training for the first match. Jenny Linder in five days. She'll be tough, and so will the ones after her. Put everything else out of your mind."

"Okay," Kirsten said. "I need to focus. What do we work on this afternoon?"

"Stamina and footwork. We'll do blade technique tomorrow. I've got you scheduled for two hours of racquetball with the local pro. Best thing for practicing hand-eye coordination." She checked her watch. "We've got about an hour. Let's wrap your arm tight, grab a quick bite, then head to the court. You used to be good at racquetball. We'll see how well you handle this guy."

The pro was twenty years older than Kirsten but in fine shape and had years of racquetball savvy. Gray-haired and short with a potbelly, Luis moved with muscular grace. He controlled the court, standing dead center and effortlessly fielding her shots off the four walls for "kills" in one of the front corners. For the first few games, he could have kept her under ten points had he wanted, but he let her win a few volleys to keep up her spirits and level of competition. She lost the first game 21–12 and the second, 21–11.

By then, Kirsten was getting the hang of the court. Muscle memory revived, and she began to battle Luis for center position. She started returning his kill shots and had a string of her own. She lost the third game 21–16 and the fourth 21–19.

"You're toast," she told him before serving for the final game. "I want this one."

He waved his racquet at her, taking some deep breaths and wiping his sweaty brow with his shirttail. Almost two hours of racquetball was taking its toll, even on a well-conditioned athlete.

"Wanting and winning have the same first letter. That's all."

She playfully pushed him out of center court and prepared to serve. "True, but winning comes from wanting, and I *want* this one. *En garde*!"

Fifteen furious minutes later, the score was tied 20–20. Luis was dragging. Kirsten had the serve. She lined the ball down the right wall. Luis lunged but missed.

Twenty-one to twenty.

Her jubilation was short-lived.

"Need to win by two," Luis shouted, shaking his head.

"Damn," she muttered, flustered at forgetting the rule. She served another perfect shot, but Luis, courage beating out strength, got his racquet on the ball and killed Kirsten's return shot in the right front corner. His serve.

He hit the ball low in the far left corner of the front wall. It angled into the sidewall, boomeranged off the right wall, and died with hardly a bounce. He'd hit a perfect Z with reverse spin and caught her flat-footed.

Tied at twenty-one.

Luis, sensing victory, changed strategies. Instead of a hard, low serve, he lobbed an underhand shot that hit high on the left front wall and landed deep in the back left corner so perfectly close to the rear and side walls Kirsten's backhand hit the wall instead of the ball.

Twenty-two to twenty-one, Luis. He smiled at her, a battered pro still with some tricks. "Ready?"

She ran a finger across her brow to clear dripping sweat, wiped it on her shirt, and nodded.

He hit the same serve close to the wall, but she was ready. Not enough. Her return shot was weak, and he easily put it away.

Twenty-three to twenty-one, Luis.

"You fight like a champion, Kirsten," Luis said, shaking her hand while trying to catch his breath. "Never forget that. You're right about *wanting* to win. I was on my last legs, but I couldn't let an amateur beat me. I changed the rhythm of the game by changing my serve. That upset your momentum and stymied your rally. A good trick to remember."

"Thanks, Luis. I'll try. Super workout."

CHAPTER 31

"BECKER. THAT'S HER LAST NAME. BECKER. SHE'S Kirsten Becker."

"So?"

Max had demanded Stefan meet him at the Café Samba for coffee. Almost every corner in Rio had a café serving rich, dark, delicious coffee. Café Samba was far from Max's usual haunt that overlooked the beautiful Copacabana Beach. It was a secluded hangout for locals. Inside was dusky and damp, and it smelled like roasting coffee. No one bothered you. The coffee-stained tables were small, for two or squeeze-in four. Order your coffee, and you were good for as long as you wanted to stay. A high background noise blasted sambas from overhead speakers.

His father wasted no time before starting his rant.

"They were the worst of the Jews. Her father was Adam. We lived in the same building, went to the same school, and ran track on the same team."

"I know it's a small world," Stefan said, "but maybe you have the wrong family." Stefan thought it was a pretty far-fetched coincidence to be crossing paths ten thousand kilometers away and seventy years later. Becker was a pretty common last name.

"Not when you're talking about Olympics," Max said. "It's a small circle. Is her father's name Adam?"

"I don't know."

"Did he try out for the 1948 Olympics, and her grandfather ran in '36?"

Stefan thought back to their luncheon conversation at the Restaurante Aprazivel. It seemed ages ago.

"Yes," Stefan said.

"That's them," Max said. "No question."

"What made them the worst?" Stefan asked. "I don't understand." The conversation he had had with his father before Kirsten's name surfaced seemed to belong to another person.

"Just believe it. They were the worst."

"I can't *just believe it*. What did they do?"

"Everything."

Reasoning with the old man did not seem possible. "Be more specific. Did they steal from you? Shoot your dog? Dump your garbage in your hallway? What?"

"Never mind." His father flicked the argument away with the back of his hand. "You either believe or you don't. I don't need proof. Passion trumps reason."

Stefan shook his head. "Sorry, *you* may not need proof, but I do. Either show me or stop these raving accusations. Passion over reason is the *cause* of most of the world's problems." He wondered if his father was becoming senile. The man seemed beyond reason.

"Have you spoken with her?" Max asked.

"Just to break off our dinner date and—" Stefan took a deep breath.

"And what? I told you I don't want you to see her again. Or didn't I make that clear?" His father set down his coffee cup with a slam that almost broke the glass. The loud noise overcame the ambient noise level and drew looks from the table across the aisle.

"You did, and I told her that, in as many words," Stefan said.

"What does that mean 'in as many words'?" Max asked.

Stefan was as angry at his father as he'd ever been with anyone. But he was angrier with himself. The man had blackmailed him, and Stefan had yielded. He hated himself for being a coward and not standing up to his father to defend Kirsten. He would live with this guilt forever.

"Will you stop this, Father? I told you I wouldn't see her, and that should be enough."

"Be sure you don't. I hate that man, that family, and everything about them. No son of mine, whether you hide behind your mother's surname or use mine, is going to associate with them, never mind date the daughter. Clear?"

"Hide behind Pasteur?" Stefan ran his fingers through his hair, shaking his head. He couldn't believe what he was hearing. "You must be joking. I'm not hiding. I prefer that to Jaeger—for obvious reasons." Stefan stood and collected his things. "I've had enough. I'm leaving." He flipped a handful of reals on the table—he wasn't going to take anything from the man, even a coffee—and turned to go.

"You're not going anywhere until I say so. Sit down."

Stefan didn't move, his back to his father, and then began a determined walk to the exit.

"I said, turn around and sit down. Now!"

A waiter took a few steps toward Stefan, but Max waved him off with a headshake.

Stefan stopped short of the door and paused, deciding what to do. He thought his father was crazy enough he might turn them over to the police. He turned and walked back.

Stefan sat down but refused to make eye contact. He looked over Max's shoulder at the couple sitting at the next table. The elderly man and woman had suspended their conversation to listen. Max's rants were more interesting.

"Look at me, Stefan." Stefan didn't break his gaze. "I said look at me, damn it."

Stefan still stared over Max's shoulder, his mouth set in a firm line. Max started talking anyway. "You want facts? I'll tell you facts about the Beckers," he said. "They survived World War II." He said it with such a triumphant ring, as if he had found the reason to hate them; Stefan had to look at him.

"Thankfully, lots of Jews did. They escaped or were hidden by caring friends and neighbors," Stefan said in an even tone, his eyes back on his father's face.

"The Beckers were different. Everybody knew they were Jewish, and nothing bad happened to them."

"How did everybody know?" Stefan asked.

"Adam was circumcised," Max said, "and Dietrich, his father, must have been as well."

"Lots of non-Jews get circumcised. Besides, who would know except the family?"

"They were both athletes and took showers with teammates," Max said. "Everybody knew."

"Wasn't Adam's father an Olympian track star for Germany?" Stefan asked. Stefan remembered Kirsten had told him her grandfather had raced in the Olympics against Jesse Owens.

"He raced in the '36 Olympics, yes."

"Wouldn't that have protected him and his family until the end of the war?" Stefan said. "After that, they moved to Israel."

"The grandfather, Dietrich, committed suicide in 1936." Max sat back, a victorious smile on his face.

Stefan's eyebrows rose. "That's not what Kirsten told me."

"The family circulated the lie that he fell racing against Jesse Owens," Max said, "hit his head, and died. Actually, Dietrich couldn't take the pressure. He hung himself with the laces from his track shoes before his last race against Owens."

"How do you know this?" Stefan asked. He couldn't hide the surprise that showed on his face and crept into his voice.

"My father, Otto—your grandfather—was there." The rhyme Otto had taught Max as a child ran unbidden through his head, and he recited it, with a laugh, for his son.

"Adam, Adam has no father and isn't even worth the bother.
All the racers beat his stride, so his father committed suicide."

"That is one of the meanest and most sickening things I've heard in a long time." He felt his face grimace in disgust. "Why do you hate the Jews so much?" Stefan asked.

"Because they're bad."

Adam shook his head. Was there no way to impart logic in this discussion? "I asked you before, what did they do?"

"For one thing, they caused Germany to lose World War I. Hitler saved us, only to be overthrown by a Jewish conspiracy. He would have created the pure Aryan race for the new Germany."

Stefan had more explosive information than these tired arguments. What should he do with them, he wondered? He was still at his father's mercy, if the old man wanted to call the police. He had to tread carefully. He knew there was no chance he or Kirsten actually would be accused of murder—or was there? If they were jailed, they could kiss the Olympics good-bye. The red tape would take weeks to unravel.

"You think Hitler was a pure Aryan?" Stefan asked.

"Without a doubt," Max said. "If he were still alive, he would be leading us now. He was a god for the German people."

"What if he had offspring? Would they be leaders?"

"That's too incredible to even imagine. If they existed, of course one of them would be our leader," Max said. "We would all fall in line behind this new leader."

"Suppose he was Jewish?"

"Who, Hitler?" Max laughed. "You're like all the others with that crap. Hitler had his genealogy independently researched and verified when he was chancellor. It showed that accusation was garbage."

"Suppose there was proof?" Stefan said. "Not only that, suppose he had a Jewish son?" Stefan knew this was dangerous. He couldn't predict his father's reaction, but he couldn't let the old man rave and rant without objection. Stefan had folded once and was not about to again.

Max shifted in his seat and backhanded the thought. "Suppose, suppose, and suppose. You can suppose all you want. Play your 'what if this, and what if that.' The facts are he was a pure Aryan, celibate, and married only to the German people. Add to that, the man was a military genius." Max slapped the table with an open palm. The couple at the next table jumped in their seats.

Stefan watched his father's face turn red and his neck veins bulge. The old man was furious at the thought but trying not to show it. Stefan hoped his blood pressure was normal. He could be on the verge of a stroke. Stefan persisted.

"If I proved all that was bullshit, pure Nazi propaganda, fabrications spun by Goebbels, what would you say then?" he said, keeping his tone neutral.

Max shook his head. "I'd say you were crazy, because there's no way you can prove that."

"You're wrong, so wrong."

"How do you know about Hitler? How can you be that certain?" Max asked, leaning forward, elbows on the table, now an interested observer. "What crap stories have you read?"

"Like you said before, *just believe it.*"

"And you said before, 'Show me proof.' So, my son, show me proof of this blasphemy against the greatest man ever to grace this earth with his presence," Max said, his tone persuasive, pleasant. He sat back and rested a hand on the top of his cane.

Stefan was silent. His father's mood changes were rapid and unpredictable. His defense of an evil, mad man was infuriating. But Stefan couldn't tell him about the diary.

Max signaled the waiter for two more coffees. "And a chocotorta with two forks."

"What's that?" Stefan asked, suspicious.

"Relax, Son. It's just a chocolate cake. An Argentine specialty. Trust me—you'll love it."

Stefan's face had a bewildered look. The old man smiled. "Yes, I can be a nice person—sometimes. You can trust me."

"Trust you?" Stefan said. "Why? You disappeared from my life when I most needed a father, show up now all nice and cozy when I don't, and rave and rant defending the most despicable human being who ever lived.

You blackmailed me into doing something I will always be ashamed of and will live to regret, and now I should trust you?" Stefan shook his head. "No. Not even about the cake."

"I can't argue about the first part. Guilty as charged. But you'll learn that relationships between a husband and wife are complex, not always neat and tidy. Your mother didn't want me around, so I left. I'm sorry for what my leaving did to you, but she gave me no choice. I helped her every time she asked, mostly for you. Whether you realize it or not, you're here at these Olympics," he looked around, waving his hand over the panorama, "because of me."

Stefan regarded his father with a dubious look. He had paid for his education, Stefan conceded.

Max took a forkful of the chocotorta. "Hmm. Try it. Delicious." He pushed the plate toward Stefan and handed him a fork.

Stefan stared at his father a long moment, nodded just a bit, and took a bite. Despite not wanting to like it, the corners of his mouth turned up at the cake's sweetness. "I *can* trust you on this."

His father returned the smile. "But not about Hitler?"

"No. He was subhuman, preyed on young girls, and committed incest and murder. His whole life—the life you worship—was built on lies."

"Proof, my son. Where's the proof? Where do you get these fabrications?" The neck veins again bulged, and Max's face reddened.

Stefan flipped the same dismissive backhand his father used moments before. "I have it. Don't you worry. Definitive proof."

"I don't believe you."

Perhaps it was Max's insufferable certainty about Hitler. Maybe his civil tone. His patience. Perhaps it was a sense of financial obligation. Or a sense of power at being able to prove his father wrong. Or concern what his father might do if provoked further. Maybe it was less complex, like the sweet taste of the chocotorta. Or the sunny weather, the joy of being an Olympian.

Whatever it was, Stefan said, "We have Eva Braun's diary."

He realized his mistake as soon as he spoke. He put his hand over his mouth, as if trying to force the words back in. It was too late. The damage was done.

"We?" His father's tone altered, ominous. His face clouded.

"Not we," Stefan said quickly. "I."

Max saw right through him. "You speak German?"

"No."

"Read German?"

"No."

"Then let's stay with the 'we.' You and the Becker girl?"

"Her name is Kirsten."

"You and Kirsten?"

Stefan nodded.

"Which one of you has it?"

Stefan's moment of delay gave him away. "I do."

Max shook his head. "I don't believe you. Where did you get it? From Lobo? In the Amber Room?"

Stefan's nod was barely perceptible. "Did you read it there or take it with you?"

Again delay gave him away. "I took it."

"I don't believe you. More likely, the girl has it."

This time Stefan was more assertive. "I have it."

Max took another bite of the chocotorta and a sip of coffee. He looked out in the distance at the late-afternoon sun. The sun cast pinks and reds onto the water. His head was cocked to one side, brow furrowed. After several moments, his tone became harsh, threatening, as in the beginning of their conversation.

"I think you're lying. Ordinarily, I'd have the police on the way with sirens and lights to claim the diary. You'd both be charged with murder, robbery, and would be arrested. But I'm feeling softhearted and will give you both a chance. I want that diary, whoever has it. If you need to, you can see this woman one time to get it. Bring it to me, and maybe I'll leave her alone. I haven't decided yet. Depends on how you and I settle the score on the Amber Room."

Max checked his watch. "Opening Ceremony's tomorrow. I've got things to do, plans in the works. When do you compete?"

"What the hell do you care?" Stefan said.

"We've settled our differences," Max said. "Calm down. I'm trying to be civil. After all, you are my son."

"Not my choice."

"Wasn't your decision."

It was a standoff. They stared at each other from opposite sides of the table—opposite sides of their lives. Finally Stefan said, "Three days. After the women finish. We start in the morning with sixty-four fencers in an elimination contest. I should be practicing now."

Max said, "I did travel ten thousand kilometers in part to watch you fence. I'd like to see you win—the first Olympic medal for the Jaeger clan—and not be distracted by all this." He finished his coffee. "Okay, we'll put the diary and Amber Room on hold until after your matches. But then you deliver or else."

"Or else what?" Stefan asked.

"Don't push me, Stefan. Son or not, you'll not stand in my way. Don't forget a possible murder charge."

Stefan inhaled sharply. "There's this Super Bowl of Fencing between the male and female gold winners the day after the men's final. If Kirsten and I both win gold, we'll be fencing each other."

"I heard rumors about it. Just the two of you?"

Stefan nodded.

"Morning or afternoon?"

"Morning, I think."

"Okay, right after that, without fail." Max stood and grabbed his cane. "I'm done," he said. "Be here, and if you face off with that Jew, you'd better win." He started to walk away and turned back with a smile. He pointed the cane at the dessert.

"Finish the chocotorta. It's too good to waste."

CHAPTER 32

MARACANÃ, A SOCCER STADIUM BUILT IN 1950 and refurbished in 2014 for the World Soccer Cup, held almost one hundred thousand cheering fans from all over the world. The athletes dressed in Olympic uniforms assembled at the back of the stadium for the Opening Ceremonies. Each country's name marked a roped-off area for the teams to convene and prepare for their grand entrance. A drawn curtain secluded them from the spectators and the open arena.

As in the 2014 Sochi Winter Games, the Parade of Athletes would initiate the opening program rather than end it. Two and one half hours of entertainment would follow the athletes' introduction.

Israel had forty-four athletes competing in ten sports, evenly balanced between men and women. They had failed to win a medal in the 2012 London Summer Games, the first time since 1988, and had high hopes of redeeming themselves in Rio. Because Kirsten had the best chance of winning gold, they voted her to carry the Israeli flag.

Kirsten stood at the front of the group, talking with Sharon, the flagpole leaning against her hip and shoulder. She was fidgety, shifting from one foot to the other.

Sharon put a hand on her arm. "Calm down. This is nothing. All you have to do is lead the group, wave the Star of David, and follow that pretty Rio guide wearing the almost-nothing bathing suit. If you're nervous now, what will you be when you face Jenny Linder?"

"A total wreck, probably." She handed the flag to Sharon and poked her head through the curtain, looking for France.

"He's on the other side of the arena," Sharon said. "You can't see him from here. I already checked. His teammates picked him to carry their flag, like you, so they think he can win gold."

Kirsten pulled her head back inside the curtain and looked at Sharon.

Sharon said, "Yes, I know what you're thinking. You could end up facing him in the Super Bowl."

Kirsten groaned. "I thought it'd be exciting if we did. Right now I think it'd be awful."

"Nonsense." Sharon chuckled.

"What's funny?" Kirsten asked.

"You really want to know?"

Kirsten nodded.

"What a great opportunity to skewer the man who skewered you." Sharon burst out laughing.

Kirsten frowned, pushed her away, and took the flag back. "That's not funny. Not at all."

Sharon collected herself. "Sorry. Some day you'll see humor in it."

"Maybe, but not now. What're those five stages of grief? Whatever they are, I'm at the anger stage."

"Maybe so, but you've got to get though six consecutive elimination matches against very tough women before you have a chance to vent that anger. Stefan does as well, against the men. I'd say the chances of you two fighting it out in the Super Bowl are pretty remote."

The announcer interrupted their conversation, introducing the IOC chair, then the head of the local Rio organizing committee, and finally the president of Brazil. Mercifully, each gave brief introductory remarks.

"And now, ladies and gentlemen," the announcer said, "it is with the greatest pleasure and honor that Rio de Janeiro, host of the XXXI Summer Olympiad Games, presents the Parade of Athletes. We have more than ten thousand of the world's finest sportsmen and sportswomen who make the Olympics possible. As is custom, we'll start with the team from Greece where the Olympics began. A blind draw determined the order of almost two hundred countries that will follow Greece."

The spectacle unfolded as fireworks lit up the arena. The curtain parted, and Greece paraded its 105 athletes. They stayed bunched together, following their flag bearer, a muscular tae kwon do champion, who in turn followed a suntanned young Rio woman clad in a bikini holding a sign with the country's name. The crowd cheered, and the athletes waved and smiled. Many held cell phones, taking selfies and videoing the surroundings.

Sweden followed, then athletes from another twenty-two countries, accompanied by loud cheering. France drew the slot just ahead of Israel. Kirsten peeked through the curtain and watched Stefan walk by waving France's flag, smiling at the crowd. He wasn't more than ten feet away. Her heart jumped, and she suppressed an urge to call to him.

It was Israel's turn. Kirsten hoisted the flag and followed the girl holding the Israel sign into the arena.

As the Israeli athletes entered the arena, an elderly man in a back row waved his cane in the air. In response, five hundred spectators occupying an entire section of the Maracanã arena stood. They stripped off outer garments to reveal the Brownshirt uniforms of Nazi storm troopers. The men wore bright red armbands emblazoned with a white circle surrounding the black Nazi swastika. They waved flags with the same symbol. Together they rushed down the steps to the floor of the arena, pushing people out of their way. The sheer numbers overwhelmed the guards that tried to block them from the athletes. The guards could not use their firearms for fear of hitting innocents. Even pepper sprays or Tasers were useless against such numbers. Rio security was not ready for crowd control of this magnitude.

The horde elbowed, jostled, and rammed through all resistance. Their mission became clear as the Nazi tsunami surged to the floor toward the Israeli athletes. The first waves met solid resistance as the Israelis closed ranks and drove away the attackers. Big men formed a protective perimeter shielding the older coaches, trainers, and women herded to the center.

The Nazis began screaming, "*Juden, nach Hause*!"—Jews, go home!—and tried to break through the barrier.

However, these were not Munich Olympians caught sleeping. This was a young and healthy band of vibrant men and women from a generation that built a strong army and created a proud and thriving nation. They fought off the attackers.

One Nazi wearing a dirty hat low over his eyes spied an opening when heads were turned. He dropped to his knees and slipped inside the human barricade. Crabwise, he skulked toward Kirsten. When he got close, he grabbed for the Israeli flag. She yanked it away and pushed him back on his heels.

"*Puta suja!*" he yelled, scrambling to his feet. You dirty slut! "*Você se lembra de mim?*" Remember me? The bandido flipped open his knife blade and attacked.

Kirsten backed away and jabbed at him using the flag as her sword.

He batted it aside and came at her again. Before she could react, a Mossad agent, one of the five living with the athletes, jumped in front of her. The bandido was no match for a trained killer. A lightning fist to the stomach doubled him over, and a brutal karate chop to his neck sent him crashing to the ground. The agent stepped hard on his neck. The sound of breaking bone and the angular twist of his head signaled the bandido would never attack anyone again.

The clash shattered the group's continuity. Other Nazis, seeing one of their own felled so dramatically, poured in. Bruising behavior turned more violent as the fighting escalated. Israelis, even those in the protective center of the pack, began battling for their lives against the waves of Nazis.

The assailants unleashed expandable batons. They had telescoped these carbon steel clubs into short tubes and concealed them in their clothes, bypassing the porous security gates. With a shake, the tubes extended to lethal length and caliber. The Nazis began swinging them wildly. Israelis, even Mossad agents, fell under the blows. Nazis piled onto the bodies, striking with their clubs.

Kirsten, having survived one attack, stood her ground against another. This time it was a woman, and Kirsten was more than her equal. As the woman approached, someone from behind pinned Kirsten's arms in a powerful bear hug. She struggled to break free, but the Nazi was too strong, and he held her tight. His female counterpart advanced, smiling, steel club raised.

Kirsten heard the man scream, and she broke loose as he fell to the ground, holding his bleeding head in his hands.

It was Stefan. He had bashed the Nazi's head with his flagpole.

"How many times do I have to save you?" Stefan shouted over the bedlam, grinning despite the tumult. Before Kirsten could answer, the mass of surging Nazis separated them.

France's entire entourage of 350 athletes followed Stefan's lead. They came running to face the Nazis in hand-to-hand combat.

Athletes from other countries, triggered by France's response, joined the battle, and soon athletes from all over the world united in Israel's defense. They tore into the Nazis, ripped the steel batons from their hands, and beat them with their own weapons.

The Nazis were no match. Their bravery lasted only as long as did the odds. Those still standing broke rank and darted into the stands and up the stairs. They left downed colleagues where they lay, unconscious or moaning from wounds. The athletes pursued them, driving them from the Maracanã Stadium.

The old man in the back row silently stood and left, using his cane to push people out of his way.

The Olympians were jubilant as shouts of anger and fear turned to joyful outbursts. They surrounded the Israeli contingent, hugging them, lifting up the fallen, tending the wounded, and celebrating together their victory over the Nazi onslaught. They had banded together against a threat to one, perceived as a threat to all, and demonstrated the strength of the Olympic spirit.

As adrenaline levels subsided, and the wounded were cleared from the arena, the Olympians regrouped into their country teams and continued the Parade of Athletes. Proud before, athletes seemed even more so, locking arms and marching together, some even doing dance steps as they walked forward together. Stefan, pushed to the head of the French group, could only wave to Kirsten. Her heart jumped, and she waved back. *He saved me again*, she thought. *He must love me*. Or was he just tired of Monique?

The morning papers called it the "Rio Rescue" and compared it the Red Sea Rescue by Moses 3,500 years ago.

CHAPTER 33

KIRSTEN ROSE EARLY, DRESSED WITHOUT WAKING Sharon, and slipped outside. The air was cool and crisp, daylight an hour away. She was nervous and excited. Her day had finally arrived, the tumultuous events at the Opening Ceremony already fading into memory.

Except for seeing Stefan. She had hoped he'd call, and when he didn't, she almost called him. Sharon persuaded her not to. "If he wants to see you, he'll call," she said. "If he doesn't, forget him; he's not worth it." Kirsten fell asleep thinking about Stefan and then dreamt they had both won gold, but he refused to fence against her in the Super Bowl and conceded the match. She woke up crying. What could be going on? There was no other explanation. It had to be Monique.

Okay, enough, she told herself. Today was The Day.

She focused on the upcoming match against Jenny Linder. Ranked fourth in the fencing world, Jenny would be formidable. Kirsten had poured over videos of Linder's technique and thought she saw a weakness in Linder's pistol handgrip. But Linder would be just the first of five matches whittling the field from sixty-four to two. Kirsten was sure Monique would be one of those final two, and she was going to do everything she could to be the other one.

Since her racquetball exercise, she'd spent every waking minute practicing footwork and blade movements. Her strong arm and hand allowed her to use the French grip for épée fencing. Thumb on top, supported by her forefinger hooked beneath, and the other three fingers guiding alongside, her hand was well back from the bell guard. With that grip, she could hold the épée blade close to its end to increase her reach.

But the 770-gram steel blade was heavier than foil and sabre blades, and most women couldn't wield it easily.

"Kirsten, your French grip and long arms will be the killer," Sharon had told her. "Trust me. Compared to the pistol grip Linder uses, with your strength, you'll have longer reach, maneuverability, and speed. She's not strong enough for the French grip. Just remember—grasp it like you're holding a bird: tight enough so it can't escape but not so tight you crush it."

"Can't sleep?" Sharon startled her, coming from behind. "Me either."

Kirsten shook her head. "I can't focus. I'm trying to concentrate on Linder, but I keep thinking of Stefan."

"Control it. Turn it off. Think about all the people hoping and praying for you to win a medal. *Relying* on you to do that. Your parents, your grandparents—especially Dietrich, God rest his soul, and my husband, Levi, may he rest in peace. Think of them, not yourself. Win for them and forget Stefan. I've told you, mental preparation is the key to winning a fencing match, so take charge."

Kirsten ate a high-protein breakfast of salmon and eggs in the athletes' dining hall. Sharon had pancakes dripping with butter and syrup. "Bite?" she offered Kirsten.

Kirsten shook her head. "Not today." She pushed back from the table. "I'm done. Ready?"

Sharon downed the last drenched morsel, had a last sip of coffee, and stood. "Let's go."

They walked back to their room, and Sharon helped Kirsten pack her chest protector, jacket, and knickers. Kirsten tucked her glove inside her mask and, with her fencing shoes, stuffed it all into her gym bag. Bag slung over her shoulder, Kirsten walked with Sharon to the tram station and rode to Maracanã Stadium.

Once there, they followed signs to the fencing arena. Jenny Linder was already nearby, practicing with her coach. They greeted each other cordially and wished each other luck. Kirsten went to the locker room to suit up.

The Swedish fencer was not built for fencing. She was slightly taller than five feet, with short arms and a wasp waist. Her advantage was innate athleticism. Lightning speed and reflexive moves, as well as her small size, helped her elude sword thrusts. Kirsten noted in the videos that Linder often went for the shoe or leg of her opponent, probably because she was short. In épée fencing, a touch on any body part was a score.

"The trick here," Sharon stressed, "is when Linder bends for a toe touch, pull back quickly and use your long reach to score on Linder's bent back."

"Got it."

"And never make two thrusts when one will do. The second could elicit a response you don't want. Be quick, efficient, with as little risk to you as possible."

They assembled near the metal fencing strip called the *piste*, gladiators dressed all in white, save for the black facemask and ungloved nonfencing hand. White was a holdover from the preelectric days when an ink spot left by the weapon registered a score. Because cheaters soaked their uniforms in vinegar that dissolved the ink mark, modern scoring was done electronically; uniforms registered the touch when the weapon connected with the wired clothing.

Each contestant had her name on the back of her jacket, and country colors on her knickers. Sharon sat off to the side on the end Kirsten defended, and the Swedish coach at the other. The referee stood midway facing the strip, with two additional judges on each side.

Six pistes were distributed throughout the big hall to accommodate simultaneous matches. Seating surrounded the pistes, but there were few observers for this first round of sixty-four contestants, like the early matches at Wimbledon. Most fencers had some family members sitting together in their own cheering enclaves. Male fencers filled some of the seats. The final match for the woman's gold medal would be held all alone on the center raised piste later in the afternoon.

The fencers began the ritual observed before every match. Kirsten and Jenny met in the middle, each holding a mask with her nonfencing arm and the blunt ninety-centimeter épée weapon in the other. They touched each other's bell guard with their own épée to be sure it did not register a score. Then they saluted each other with raised épée tips, grips face-high, acknowledged the referee and audience, and donned masks. They retreated four meters apart to wait behind the en garde lines on the piste.

When they were positioned, the referee called out, "*En garde ... Prêt ... Allez!*" He brought his hands together prayer-like, signaling the start of the match.

Kirsten tensed, a wound spring poised to uncoil, and waited for Linder to approach. Kirsten's knees were slightly bent and body angled so her back shoulder turned away from Linder. Her right front foot was forward to lead the attack, with her back foot at a forty-five-degree angle and directly under her for stability. She gripped the épée firmly with her right hand, tip held slightly higher than the bell guard at chest height. Her front foot, right arm and shoulder, hip, and side were a continuous straight line, offering the narrowest hit zone possible. The épée formed the apex of this line. Her left hand and arm curled up behind her for balance.

From the start, Linder was the aggressor. She stamped her front foot several times, called an *appel*, as a distraction and advanced. She evaded touches and scored with swift lunges and flash attacks, taking the lead at three touches to one at the end of the first three-minute period. The audience applauded politely for these early points, but the crowd was thin, and it was too soon for real enthusiasm.

At the break, Kirsten removed her mask, wiped her brow, and gulped cold water from the bottle Sharon handed her.

"It's okay, Kirsten, just the first three minutes. Plenty of time left. She can't keep up her pace, so if you draw even during the next three minutes, you'll take her in the last three. Stand farther back from her so she has to stretch. Your longer reach will help you control her movements. That's what you want, weapon control."

Kirsten turned to step onto the piste. Sharon pulled her back and whispered in her ear. "One more thing. Watch your feet. She's going to go for them as she gets tired."

Linder didn't wait to get tired and immediately went for Kirsten's right leg with a flash attack. Kirsten retreated too slowly but managed to score a touch as well. Double hit.

Four to two, Linder.

Sharon's advice kicked in. Kirsten increased her distance from Linder. Linder missed on several attacks, and Kirsten scored a touch on Linder's chest. The feel of the capped épée tip hitting its target was reassuring.

Four to three, Linder.

The three minutes expired. Kirsten pushed up her mask, sweat pouring off her face. She wiped with a wet towel and gulped down slugs from a bottle of water.

"Here's the strategy for the last three minutes, Kirsten. She's watching your blade, not your eyes. Try this." Sharon whispered rapidly into Kirsten's ear.

Kirsten nodded. "Got it."

"Remember—*sentiment du fer.* Use that sixth sense. *Feel* her through her épée."

They returned to the piste, raised swords again before the final three minutes, and began. Linder immediately went for a toe touch, but Kirsten was ready. She pulled her foot away and scored on Linder's bent back.

Four to four.

Following Sharon's strategy, Kirsten initiated a fake attack with a blade thrust that drew a quick parry from Linder, deflecting the épée. Kirsten responded with a riposte that sparked a counter parry, followed by Kirsten's counter riposte. Then, in a flash, Kirsten lunged with a *balestra*, a short jump forward, and scored a touch on Linder's shoulder. Linder hadn't anticipated another riposte.

In an instant, Kirsten had changed the momentum of the match.

Five to four, Kirsten.

When Linder's coach started waving her arms frantically, Linder glanced at the clock. Thirty seconds left in the match. A loss meant she would go home. Her movements showed desperation and became erratic. Fatigue blunted her athleticism. Kirsten scored a chest touch, followed by double touches.

Seven to five, Kirsten.

Ten seconds to go, and Linder made a diving attack for Kirsten's shoe. Kirsten pulled her foot out of range and touched Linder's back as time ran out.

Final: eight to five, Kirsten.

Kirsten dropped her épée, fell to her knees, fists tight, elbows bent, and yelled, "Yes!" to the rafters overhead. She peeled off her mask, ran to Sharon, and lifted her off the floor in a wild dance. "Thank you, Sharon, thank you. We did it! We did it!" she shouted, hugging and kissing her. Then she jumped back onto the piste to shake hands with Linder and thank the referees, finally waving to the scattered onlookers. She scanned the audience for Stefan, but he was not there.

Sharon smiled at Kirsten's joy. Her heart was full. She said a silent, *Bless you, Levi. This win's for you. Help us win five more.*

CHAPTER 34

KIRSTEN SAT ON A WOODEN BENCH NEXT TO Sharon, legs splayed out in front of her, a cold, wet towel encircling her neck and another on her head. Her right arm sat in a bucket of ice water. She leaned back and sipped from a chilled bottle of Gatorade, eyes closed. She felt a little refreshed after changing her sweat-drenched chest protector, jacket, and knickers and taking a cooling sponge bath in the women's locker room. The high-energy protein bar helped also.

It had been a long day, with the climax yet to come. The five nine-minute matches were exhausting. Except for the semifinal, won by a single touch in the last ten seconds, her conquests had come by two or more touches in the final period, often in the last minute of the final period when she scored as her opponents fatigued.

But now she was tired. Her right arm felt like lead. She flexed her fingers in the cold water. They were starting to get numb, and she withdrew from the bucket. Sharon dried her arm and massaged the muscles.

Kirsten touched the stitches along her forearm. The sutures had held, with just some oozing in the last match. The muscle ached when she bent her wrist. She hoped her arm had one more match in it.

Shortly she would be facing Monique Cloutier, the number-one seed. More importantly, the one who'd stolen Stefan. Kirsten was out for blood. The thought galvanized her. All aches evaporated.

"Drink this," said Sharon, handing her a vitamin-enriched concoction she whipped up in a blender. The pink-colored smoothie held dietary supplements known only to her and her deceased husband. "You'll need all the energy you can get."

Kirsten nodded. "The only good thing is that Monique has to be as tired as I am. I'm going to tear her apart."

"Don't forget our planning, our strategy. Pace yourself and think ahead. Use that 'fencing surprise' gift you have. Remember: the perfect thrust is the one that scores—that's yours. And any thrust can be parried—that's hers."

The overhead speakers broadcast the start of the final match for the gold medal. The hall was already packed with fencing aficionados, and more poured in after hearing the announcement. The piste was raised in the center of the room, like center court at Wimbledon.

Kirsten gazed at the audience, and her eyes widened. She'd never fenced in front of such a large crowd before. They cheered as both fencers were introduced. The cheers seemed louder for Monique, Kirsten thought.

"Focus, Kirsten, focus," Sharon said. "Forget the audience and concentrate on Monique. Remember your *T*s."

The referee brought both women together on the piste. "Ladies and gentlemen," he announced to the audience. "This match is for the 2016 Olympic gold medal. We have Monique Clothier from France"—he pointed to Monique—"versus Kirsten Becker from Israel. Ladies, please shake hands, and then we shall begin."

Monique offered a limp handshake and smirked under her breath, "So sorry about Stefan." Kirsten was tempted to squeeze her knuckles as hard as she could. But she didn't. Épées raised, they formally acknowledged each other, then the referees, and then the audience, according to custom. They took their places behind the en garde lines.

The referee called out, "En garde … Prêt … Allez!" His hands prayed, and they started.

Kirsten forgot two of her three *T*s. Toughness remained, but tactic and technique seemed to evaporate. She was heedlessly aggressive, pushing Monique to her side of the strip with thrusts and lunges.

Monique's outstanding fencing skills were carrying the day. She'd parry, riposte, and score. After the first three-minute period, Monique was ahead four to one. Noise from the audience was deafening.

At the break, Sharon had one minute to reverse a match heading toward total disaster, a certain loss. "Kirsten, where's all the training gone? The hours spent preparing? The videos you've studied? You can't just go for her jugular. She's too smart for that. Frankly, you're lucky you're only down three. You're so angry, I think you've switched off your brain."

Kirsten was close to tears. "I hate her, Sharon. I want to slash her to pieces." Her body was shaking, and she rattled her épée in Monique's direction. "I wish this were a sabre so I could slash her with it."

"I suspect she'd be as good at sabre fencing as she is at épée, so I doubt you'd even get close. She's seeded number one for a reason."

Sharon glanced at the clock. Thirty seconds left before the second period started. "Pull yourself together and turn on your brain, for God's sake. Put your anger aside. It won't win for you. Remember—want is not the same as win. Change tactics. You've been the aggressor for this first period. Back off. Let her think you're tired and come to you. When she does, strike."

Kirsten wiped her forehead and took a last swig from the water bottle. "I'll try, Sharon. I want this so bad I can taste it."

But it wasn't working. With a three-point lead, Monique didn't need to be aggressive. She hung back, making Kirsten come to her. Then, with skillful épée maneuvers, she'd parry Kirsten's thrusts and eat up the clock. Intentionally or accidentally, Monique repeatedly bumped Kirsten's forearm during close-quarter fighting, and Kirsten cried out in pain. Sharon jumped up to call a medical timeout, but Kirsten waved her off.

The second period ended eight to five, Monique still ahead by three. Sharon had one minute left to change Kirsten's behavior.

"Kirsten, close your eyes."

"You're kidding."

"I'm not. Do as I ask."

Kirsten shut her eyes.

"Now, take three deep breaths. Good. Forget this is Monique. You're fencing Jane Doe, and you're way better than she is. Visualize your thrusts. Can you see them? You're easily getting past her parries."

A head nod.

"Can you anticipate Jane's next moves?"

"I think so."

"Sit here quietly and imagine the win. Go step-by-step to make your touches. Play it in your head, like a video. Go over what we've practiced. Stop going for the kill. Start fencing. Do what you're born to do."

The final three minutes started. Both fencers were wary. One minute passed, and no scores. They were two evenly matched opponents, like boxers in the last round of the World Heavyweight Championship, trading punch for punch. But one of them, behind on points, needed a knockout.

Less than two minutes stood between Monique and gold. Kirsten was starting to panic. For the first time in her career, she didn't think she could win, a fatal mistake for any athlete. Sharon's psychotherapy didn't stand a chance.

But something else did.

"C'mon, Kirsten, go for it. I know you can win!"

The male voice pierced her mask and bored its way into her brain.

Stefan!

From the corner of her eye, she saw him hurrying toward the first row of seats alongside the piste. Now he was standing just ten feet away, cheering her on, clapping and pumping his fist.

Monique heard it also and looked over. Huge blunder. Touch! Kirsten's lightning riposte scored on Monique's mask. Without it, she'd have lost an eye.

Eight to six, ninety seconds left.

Again Stefan yelled out encouragement, and again Monique seemed distracted, though this time her eyes remained fixed on Kirsten. Kirsten lunged with an upward circular épée thrust that surged into a flick to Monique's forward leg. Touch.

Eight to seven, Monique.

Fencing with renewed vigor, Kirsten again aggressively brought the match to Monique, pushing her to less than one meter from the end of the strip. Seeing an opening, Kirsten launched a *flèche*—a running attack—épée out front leading the way.

Monique, caught off guard, tried to parry the perfect thrust, lost her balance, and stepped off the side of the strip. The referee called, "Halt!" and penalized Monique with loss of a meter. That put her off the end of the strip, and he awarded Kirsten with a touch.

Eight to eight. Forty-five seconds left.

They fenced up and down the piste, each looking for an opening and not finding one. Épées slithered like steel snakes, clicking instead of hissing.

Fifteen seconds remained, and Kirsten saw Monique drop her blade a bit, apparent fatigue setting in. Kirsten attempted another flèche. She realized too late it had been a ruse. Monique easily parried the blade. As Kirsten's momentum carried her past, Monique turned, riposted, and touched Kirsten's back.

The light flashed, registering a score.

Nine to eight, Monique, with ten seconds left!

"No!" Sharon screamed, jumping from her seat. "Two motions, two motions! I want a video review!" If she was wrong, the match was lost.

The head referee stopped the clock and went to the video screen, accompanied by four other judges staring over his shoulder. The technician reversed the video and played it back.

"Again," said the referee, and the technician repeated the motion. After studying the video two more times, they conferred in a semicircle around the screen. Their discussion was animated, with loud voices, raised hands, and pointing fingers.

Finally, the head referee made his decision.

"Ms. Cloutier's touch is in two motions. The parry and initial riposte missed, and then she retried a second later. That second riposte represents an illegal touch and is voided. Put five seconds back on the clock. The score is tied at eight to eight. Resume your positions, and we will restart."

He gave them a moment and said, "En garde … Prêt … Allez."

Kirsten, still the aggressor, pushed Monique to the end of the strip with a *balestra*. Then she turned her body square to Monique, tempting her to lunge.

Five seconds left.

Monique hesitated, then took the bait. She charged. But her wrist and bell guard dipped the tiniest bit when she raised the épée tip.

Kirsten pivoted her shoulder away, backed up quickly, parried, and flicked her blade in a lightning move over Monique's oncoming bell guard. The movement demanded a wrist flip of great strength and dexterity and triggered excruciating pain up and down Kirsten's forearm.

But it was a touch—a fair touch.

Time expired, and the match was over. Kirsten won gold, Israel's first fencing medal ever, nine to eight.

Kirsten's screams were magnified by Sharon's, Stefan's, and the crowd.

The three joined a tight circle, hugging each other, jumping up and down, tears running down their cheeks. After a moment, Sharon dropped out, and Stefan seized Kirsten, lifted her off her feet, and twirled her around. He yelled, "I love you, my very own gold medalist," into her ear, but Kirsten could barely hear because the crowd was on its feet, applauding and shrieking.

An old man in the back of the hall scowled, his dark face a picture of anger. Half concealed by a post, he watched the celebrations through a pair of opera glasses and planned his next move. His hand trembled on the head of his cane as he stomped out.

CHAPTER 35

"I ALWAYS MAKE GOOD ON MY PROMISES," STEFAN said.

"The sunset is glorious," Kirsten answered, looking over the patio at downtown Rio as the setting sun cast shadowed colors of violet, pink, and russet.

They were sitting at the Restaurante Aprazivel in Santa Teresa, where they had lunched while planning the trip to Hitler's home.

"Too bad Monique isn't here to enjoy it." Kirsten put her fist to her mouth and bit down on a knuckle. "I shouldn't have said that."

Stefan laughed, took her hand from her mouth, and stroked the tooth marks her bite left. "I can't blame you. Her behavior after the match was unacceptable."

Monique had screeched at the referee that Kirsten's last touch hit her bell guard, not her wrist, and shouldn't be allowed. She demanded a video review, a reasonable request but not at the top of her lungs.

Upon review, the referee upheld the call, stood in the middle of the piste, and raised Kirsten's hand high for the entire assemblage. Using the overhead microphone, he announced, "Please join me in congratulating our first-place winner, Kirsten Becker, from Israel, who has won the gold medal for épée fencing at the 2016 Summer Games in Rio de Janeiro. This is the first fencing medal ever won by an Israeli Olympian. Kirsten will receive the medal at the awards ceremony shortly and will face the men's gold winner in the Super Bowl of Fencing the day after tomorrow. Monique Cloutier from France will be awarded silver."

The IOC had to mail Monique her medal. She boycotted the awards ceremony and left the Village immediately for the airport and the next flight home.

Kirsten asked no questions during dinner. Stefan waited until they finished and were sipping Brazilian coffee for dessert.

"I'm sorry for the last few days," he said.

Kirsten's eyes flooded.

"I love you, and that hasn't changed," he said. "Please remember that as I explain things I didn't want to tell you—*couldn't* tell you—before your matches." He pushed his coffee cup around, making nervous rings on the tabletop.

"How'd your folks react when you called them?" he asked.

"Ecstatic is the only word I can think of. They both screamed like we did. I pictured them jumping up and down, and I prayed my father wouldn't have a heart attack."

"He didn't, I hope," Stefan said, with a worried look.

"No, of course not. But it did come as a complete surprise. I didn't call them during the day, so they had no idea that I was still winning."

"They probably guessed, because you would've called them if you'd lost."

"True. Anyway, they went bonkers, with all the emotional stuff about my grandfather Dietrich and how much the medal would've meant to him and how much it means to my father."

Stefan reached for her hand and kissed each of the fingertips. "This is the hand I may face the day after tomorrow in the Super Bowl. Maybe I should bite off a finger." He put her pinky in his mouth.

She jerked her hand away.

He laughed. "Just joking."

She smiled. "You've stalled long enough. What's going on?"

He took a deep breath. "You remember that driver I thought I recognized at the checkpoint coming back from Estancia Inalco?"

She nodded.

"It was my father."

Her eyes opened wide.

"I hadn't seen him since I was six or seven, so I wasn't sure. He had sent my mother a picture taken a few years ago, and I recognized him from that. His name is Max Jaeger."

She felt the blood drain from her face, leaving her pale and lightheaded. Her mouth fell open, and she stared straight into Stefan's face, dazed, heart pounding.

"Kirsten, are you okay? You look like you've seen a ghost."

She didn't respond. Just kept staring at Stefan as if she was seeing him for the first time.

"Your father's name is Jaeger? That was your name?"

"Yes. My mother reclaimed her maiden name after the divorce, and I was raised as Pasteur. I told you this."

"And you're originally from Berlin. Right?" she said.

"Yes," Stefan said.

"How old is your father?"

"Late eighties," Stefan said.

"My father was born in 1930. He's eighty-six." Her breathing quickened, and she wiped her brow with a napkin.

"You told me he was elderly." Stefan looked around. "Actually here, when we had lunch last week. And that he almost competed in the '48 Olympics and that your grandfather ran against Jesse Owens in the '36 Olympics. He fell and died in the last race."

She shook her head. "That was a family lie. He committed suicide."

Stefan's look didn't change. "That's what my father said."

She ran fingers through her hair as if she could untangle and disperse memories as easily. Her hair became even more unruly, and red ringlets popped about.

She groped for words. "Our two fathers hate each other more than any other two people on earth. They're probably the two worst enemies in the world."

He studied her, waiting for more information.

"It's almost like the Montagues and the—what's the other family?"

"Capulets," he answered. "Why does your father hate mine?"

She sat there thinking what she could tell him. The suicide poem was on her lips and out before she could stop it.

"According to my father, your grandfather Otto made it up and taught it to your father, who broadcast it all over the school when they were little—not more than six or seven years old. Max bullied my father almost every day after that."

His brow furrowed, and he reached for her. "That's so awful. I'm sorry, Kirsten. My father recited it when we met yesterday."

"Wait, it gets worse." She told him about Max tying Adam nude to a chair after losing the German qualification slot for the '48 Olympics.

"My dad told me that story one evening after we returned from visiting the Holocaust museum in Jerusalem, Yad Vashem, so I would have a personal connection to German cruelty. Taunting my father with—I can barely say it—'Come see Becker's pecker.' Can you just imagine what was going through that poor boy's mind, tied to that chair, nude in front of all his schoolmates? Another reason for me to visit Hitler's house and spit on his German legacy."

"It's awful beyond words, Kirsten. But thank God, your family survived."

"They did. And as I grew older and read more about World War II, I questioned that more and more. It made no sense, especially once I knew Grandfather Dietrich committed suicide in 1936. My grandmother Gretchen always said it was the intercession of an athlete friend, a man named Lutz Long, who saved us. He was later killed in the war."

"I assume the suicide was public knowledge?"

"Not exactly. The Nazis kept it out of the newspapers. Goebbels did that. Certainly Hitler and the German officials at the Olympics knew about it."

"What do you know about your great-grandmother?"

She sipped her coffee and picked at crumbs left from dessert. She licked them off her fingertip. "I'm named after her. That's about it."

"How did that happen?" he asked.

"My grandmother suggested the name after I was born."

"Where did your great-grandmother live?"

"Some town in Austria, I'm pretty sure," Kirsten said. She had a faraway look.

There was a long silence as both took in this information. Finally Stefan said, "Are you thinking what I'm thinking?"

Her nod was barely perceptible. "Ever since I read Eva's diary, I haven't stopped thinking that. But I'm afraid to go there. It would be too incredible."

"It would be," Stefan said. "How could you prove it?"

"I don't know," she said, shaking her head. "Too implausible."

He took her hand. "I saved you twice. I'll do it again. I'm beginning to think it's my role in life."

"Am I in danger?"

"Could be." He sat back and rubbed his chin, thinking. "I wonder what my father would say if he suspected."

She shuddered, remembering the Opening Ceremony.

"What do you want to do?" he asked.

It was her turn to make nervous circles with her coffee cup. She looked over his shoulder at downtown Rio covered in the shadows of the setting sun. Her eyes glistened.

"What's wrong?" Stefan asked.

Kirsten didn't answer for a moment, and he asked again. She wiped a tear, brought her gaze back, and looked into his eyes.

"I have to ask this. I'm sorry, but after the last few days, I have to. Do you really love me? Can I trust you?"

He took her hands in his. "With your life … always."

"I'm frightened. I don't know what to do. I feel like I did in Lobo's cabin. You need to jump-start this car—or whatever it is you do."

He thought for a moment, then checked his watch. "It's getting late, but here's what I think we should do. We've got to do it quickly since I fence tomorrow at nine and need at least six hours of sleep."

He whispered even though they were the last diners in the restaurant. "Will you do it? Can you do it?"

Her head barely moved, and she squeezed his hand. "Yes, if you help me."

He made two phone calls. They left the restaurant and walked to the parking lot.

A black Volvo parked in the far corner of the lot followed, keeping one or two cars between them.

CHAPTER 36

STEFAN DROVE TO THE ATHLETES' VILLAGE AND parked. He and Kirsten slipped out and walked to building 12. They strolled arm in arm to her apartment. Kirsten knocked with a prearranged sequence and heard, "Kirsten, is that you?"

"Yes, Sharon. You can unlock." They walked in. "Everything okay?" Kirsten asked.

"Quiet as a graveyard," Sharon answered. Seeing Kirsten's face, Sharon said, "Sorry. Wrong metaphor. Quiet as a peaceful afternoon on the Copacabana Beach."

"Better. Keep practicing," Kirsten said with a wry smile. "Everything ready?"

Sharon nodded and handed her the packages. "Just like you asked."

"Thanks. I'll probably be late tonight," Kirsten said.

"Be as late as you want. Just come back in one piece."

"Not a problem." She put an arm around Stefan's waist. "Stefan's with me."

"You two good again?" Sharon asked, looking from one to the other.

Stefan answered by hugging Kirsten to him and kissing her on the lips. "I love her with my life," he said. Then he put his arm around Sharon and said, "*Tous pour un, un pour tous*—all for one, one for all."

They laughed.

"Do you have your gold medal?" Sharon asked.

"Too heavy to wear." Kirsten took it from her purse. "Put it someplace till I come back."

"Be sure you do," Sharon said.

Stefan and Kirsten walked to the car. As they drove off, the passenger in the Volvo got out and melted into the bushes. The driver stayed in the car, following several hundred yards behind them.

"How should we do this?" Kirsten asked after they'd driven a few minutes.

"How're your cramps?"

She looked at him quizzically. "Cramps? I don't have any cramps."

"I think you do. From dinner. We need to stop at the hospital first."

"Oh," she said. "*Those* cramps." She made a face and clutched her stomach. Groaning theatrically, she said, "They're pretty bad."

"I figured. We'll go to Hospital Copa D'or, then to the airport. Here are the directions from Google Maps."

Stefan drove cautiously, but aggressive enough at the intersections to look like a native.

"There's a sign for the hospital." She pointed, and he turned off the main road.

He parked in the small lot for hospital emergencies.

"Wait for me to open your door," he said.

When he did, she got out and stooped over, holding her stomach with one hand and the other to her mouth. A large handbag was slung over her shoulder. The black sedan, lights off, parked several rows away.

"Good job," Stefan said under his breath. "I'll prop you up, and we'll walk to the emergency department. Dr. Shemberg should be there waiting. You have the packages?"

She patted the bag. "We could ask him to take out my stitches while he checks my stomach."

"Good idea. Save a trip later."

Rubén Shemberg was waiting as they entered the hospital's emergency department. He directed them to a private room where acutely ill patients were evaluated, and closed the door.

He gave Kirsten a hug and shook Stefan's hand. "Congratulations, Kirsten. It must have been my superior surgical stitching that won the gold for you. Magic sutures."

"Without question, Doctor Shemberg. Thank you. Now that I'm done with them, you can have them back." She held out her arm.

He smiled. "Not reusable but a nice offer. You're sure you're finished with them?"

She nodded. "I have one more match the day after tomorrow." She smiled at Stefan and raised her eyebrows. "But I don't think I'll need them by then."

Shemberg paged a nurse. "Please get me a suture removal kit."

He placed Kirsten's arm on the surgical table, took the sterile kit from the nurse, and opened it. With gloves on, he used tweezers to hold one end of a suture, clipped the tie with a small, curved scissors, and gently tugged the black thread. It easily slipped from the skin.

"Reminds me of snipping off one of those plastic tags from a new dress," Kirsten said.

"Perhaps requiring a bit more skill but not much," Shemberg said with a laugh. When he was through, he sat back and admired his work. "A lovely piece of needlework. I could have sewn for Dior or Zegna," he said. He gave the remains of the suture kit to the nurse and dismissed her.

"But that's not why you're here, yes?" Shemberg asked.

"I have these cramps but not really," Kirsten said.

He scratched his head. "Please explain." He looked at Kirsten, but she nodded toward Stefan.

When Stefan finished, Shemberg sat back on the white metal stool and stroked his goatee. "How did you know I was Jewish?"

"We didn't but took a chance. Will you help us?" Kirsten asked.

He paused, weighing his decision. Finally, "Precisely what is it you want me to do?"

Stefan told him.

After another minute of deliberation, Shemberg said, "Kirsten, lie down, and I'll start an IV. It'll be just sugar water but will look convincing if anyone checks. After that, I'll need fifteen or twenty minutes and will return."

He secured the IV in Kirsten's arm, took the packages, and left.

After forty-five minutes, Kirsten asked, "Do you think we can trust him?"

"A bit late to ask," Stefan said.

"It is," Shemberg said, entering the room and answering the question, "but you can. It just took me longer than I thought. Here are your books."

He removed Kirsten's IV and placed a piece of gauze and tape over the puncture site. "I just need to complete your emergency record to show I removed your sutures and treated your abdominal cramps. Then you're free to go. Check back with me in a couple of days. I should have an answer by then."

"We are in your debt," said Stefan. "And perhaps the world will be."

"Who knows," said Shemberg. "It is what it is. The world's a funny place and often doesn't reward people for their contributions. Many Christians that helped save Jews in WWII were never recognized." He stroked his goatee. "My family was lucky. My grandparents fled Germany in 1935 and were welcomed to Argentina, along with many other Jewish families. They moved to Brazil, and my father went to school here in Rio to become a doctor. I followed his footsteps. I think he would be proud of the small role I may be playing here. I wish you safe passage with your plans." With that, he nodded at both of them, shook hands, turned, and left.

CHAPTER 37

IT WAS PAST ONE IN THE MORNING WHEN STEFAN dropped Kirsten off in front of building 12 in Athletes' Village. They'd completed what they'd set out to do and were exhausted.

"Will you be okay for your match tomorrow"—she checked her watch—"today?"

"I hope so. I can still get six or seven hours of sleep, eat a high-protein breakfast, and be ready."

"What time do you start?"

"Nine, so I should be okay."

He hesitated before reaching for her. "It's okay," she said, smiling, arms extended toward him. "I still love you. We're in this together." She leaned forward, and he enveloped her in his arms.

"I love you so. I know I told my father too much. But it won't happen again, I promise." They kissed. "Will you come watch?"

"Of course. Your father said you couldn't see me but not the reverse. I'll cheer you on from your first match in the morning to your gold in the afternoon. After all, if we're going to face off in the Super Bowl, I need to spy on the technique of the man I'm going to skewer."

Kirsten entered the lobby of building 12 and fumbled in her purse for her key. Without thinking, she turned the door handle to her apartment before inserting the key, and the door swung open. Her thoughts were about

Stefan, and she missed the first clue. That the lamplight in the room wasn't on was the second.

She gasped when she flipped on the overhead light. The room had been tossed, drawers pulled out and emptied, the bed stripped and mattress shredded. The closet was ransacked, and clothes were strewn on the floor. In the bathroom, the tank top to the toilet was fractured and on the floor, the medicine cabinet bare, and shower curtain ripped off its rod.

She sensed the presence of someone behind her before she felt the smelly handkerchief cover her nose and mouth. A muscular arm encircled her chest. She struggled a few moments, taking raspy breaths through the coarse material.

Then, nothing but darkness.

She woke in a pitch-black room, sitting upright in a tall chair, hands and feet bound, head throbbing. As she stirred, she heard Sharon beside her and saw she was tied up also.

"You okay?" Sharon asked. "It seemed like forever for you to wake up."

"Sharon! Thank God you're here. Where are we?" Kirsten twisted against the ropes. The chair tilted, and she almost tipped over.

"I don't know. I was asleep when a big goon jumped on top of me. He was waving a gun and wanted the Eva Braun diary. I told him I didn't have it, so he tied me up and ransacked the room. Then he put that nasty rag over my face—"

"I got the same thing."

"It must've been soaked in chloroform or something to put you to sleep. I woke up here."

"What happened to all that great security we heard about?" Kirsten asked.

"Frankly, I didn't anticipate much from the locals, but I expected our Mossad guys would've been around, like during the Opening Ceremony,"

Sharon said. “I hope they’re okay. This is starting to smell like the Munich Olympics.” She shivered and tried to hold back tears. “I’m really scared, Kirsten. What’s going to happen to us?” Kirsten heard panic in Sharon’s voice.

“I don’t know.” She was thinking about Stefan. Where was he? Did the same thing happen to him? Or was he free and coming to save her … again? “What time is it?” Kirsten asked.

“Probably morning or close to it,” Sharon said.

The door opened and flooded the room with light. Both women instinctively shut their eyes. They opened them to see an old man standing before them, leaning on a cane with an ivory handle.

A muscled young man stood beside him. He was a blond-haired giant wearing a white shirt, sleeves rolled to reveal a swastika tattooed on one bulging bicep and a dagger dripping blood on the other.

“Welcome to Hitler’s Great Hall,” the old man said, waving his hand around to take in the room. “I’m Max Jaeger. I know who you are.” He nodded first at one, then the other. “Sharon and Kirsten. I hope you don’t mind if I call you by your first names. I’d prefer you address me as Herr Jaeger, however. Just a little show of respect for our age and cultural differences. A habit left over from earlier, more genteel times. It is important to maintain a degree of refinement.”

He whispered to the blonde who walked quickly to the side of the room and brought back a tall wooden chair with a padded seat and back. Max sat down. “I get tired more easily than I used to,” he said. “It was a long night, following your escapades, Kirsten.”

Kirsten showed no response, but she was terrified. This was the German who bullied her father for years. She could only imagine what he would do to her. But she wasn’t going to give him the satisfaction of seeing her afraid, whatever the consequences. Her heart felt like a trip hammer in her chest, and she was breathing rapidly.

“I apologize for the way we’ve brought you here, but I really didn’t see another approach to this rather delicate situation.” He shrugged, hands extended and palms up, as if to say it wasn’t his fault. “I trust my colleague," he looked at the young man, "was reasonably pleasant and accommodating—under the present circumstances, that is."

Kirsten's eyes remained riveted on Max, welded to his face. She couldn't stop staring.

"Kirsten, you needn't look at me like that. I'm not so repulsive. I've not physically hurt you or your family. In fact, I knew your father quite well, from preschool to high school graduation. We interacted both in and out of school. I've not had any contact with him for almost seventy years—since about 1947, soon after the war. He's doing well, I trust?"

She spoke through clenched teeth. "He's doing fine. Better than you, I hope." Her response came out half snarl, half curse.

"Here I'm trying to be nice, and you attack me. Why? I tried to be kind to your father. He never wanted to be my friend, just to beat me in our races."

"You were kind to my father? What kind of garbage is that?"

"He survived the war, didn't he? I could've reported him to the authorities countless times, and I didn't. He's alive and well, with a family living in Israel because of me. Isn't that being kind?"

"Stop this bullshit, will you?" Kirsten said.

"Oh, my. The Jewish seductress has a mouth." He turned to the blond man. "We don't like to hear that from Jews, do we, Gordo?"

"No, Herr Jaeger, we don't. I will be happy to silence her if you wish." He raised a large fist. "Just give me the word."

Kirsten and Sharon both gasped. Kirsten's bravado faltered. But she was not going to give in.

"Eventually but not just yet. I need some information first." He held up the Braun diary. "I thought you were going to give this to my son so he could give it to me."

Kirsten inhaled sharply. *Control*, she thought. *Keep your cool. He will not see me afraid.* "Where did you find that?" She and Stefan had hidden the original in the spare wheel housing of Stefan's rental car.

"Weren't you going to give it to Stefan to give to me?"

"I was, but we planned to do it today, after he finished fencing and hopefully won the gold medal."

Max shook his head. "I think that's a lie. When I saw the two of you together yesterday, after you won gold—congratulations, by the way on your victory over the French woman; the last minute was quite exciting—I realized Stefan was just playing with me. He regretted telling me about the diary. I baited him as much as I could to get him to do that—and he was going to go back on his word. Was I right?" Max asked.

"It doesn't matter now, does it?" Kirsten said. "You've got the diary and all the information about your incestuous leader. We have no proof left for the world to see this Aryan mockery."

"How about the copy you had that doctor make at the hospital last night? The one you hid in the storage locker at the airport. What about it?"

"So you *did* follow us. Stefan thought you might."

"Of course, silly girl. What would you expect my men to do after they came up empty searching your room? I'm sorry you got sick though. Food at Aprazivel disagreed with you?"

"Yes, it did. I had terrible cramps and vomited several times. They gave me some medicine at the Hospital Copa D'or."

"I know. Stomach medicine, they told us. Or was that all planned to throw us off the trail? Even the IV medications they gave you? No matter. Anyway, I hope you're better now."

"Go to hell," Kirsten said. She would not give him an inch. To her, Max embodied the image of the cruel German.

"Now, see that?" He turned to Gordo. "I'm being solicitous, and she wishes to banish me to hell. That's what I mean about you Jews. Ungrateful curs, all of you. We Christians do so much for you. We even forgave you for killing Christ, and still you hate us." He pounded his cane on the floor. "You owe me your life, young woman, and you'd better treat me with respect."

"Or what?" Kirsten asked.

"I promise you'll not like the *or what.*" His voice was low, threatening.

Sharon spoke for the first time. Her voice quivered. "You're missing your son's fencing bouts. He started at nine o'clock. Don't you want to see him fence?"

"I do, Sharon, I do. But dealing with Miss Becker, daughter of the man with the you-know-what, takes precedence," Max said.

"I don't know what you're talking about," Sharon said.

"Kirsten never told you the story about Becker's pecker? Too bad. It was a fun event."

Kirsten lunged against her restraints, and her chair rocked. Gordo steadied it, and his touch made Kirsten shiver.

Max looked at her with bemusement. "I've gotten such joy through the years from that memory. I've got another little trick up my sleeve for Adam Becker that will be sure to provide good memories also. But more about that later."

Kirsten pursed her lips into a vicious flat line, her eyes flashing. "Don't you dare do anything to my father."

"What will you do?" Max asked.

"I promise you'll not like it."

"Oh, she's a quick study, Gordo," Max said. "We'll have to watch this one."

"If you're going to jabber on, at least untie our hands and legs. The rope's shutting off my circulation," Sharon said.

"Yes, ropes tend to do that. Especially around the neck."

"If you're trying to frighten us, you're doing a good job. What do you want? You've got the diary. What else?" Sharon asked.

"Certainly the key to the Amber Room, and where it's located."

"We don't have the key," Kirsten said.

"I assumed as much. My men searched your room thoroughly. In fact, Gordo's colleague, whom you met last night, Sharon, is searching Stefan's room right now. But it doesn't matter, as I have you. That will guarantee I get the amber key and the room's whereabouts."

Sharon looked around. "Where are we?"

Kirsten heard the pleading note in Sharon's voice. Maybe she was right. Better to be nice to this bastard? She thought of her father tied to that chair. No, she wouldn't do it.

"I told you earlier, but you weren't listening. Hitler's Great Hall, a special building I erected to honor our great departed leader."

Sharon glanced at Kirsten. "Does this special building have a bathroom? I have to pee."

"Hmm, Sharon. I hadn't planned on that. I don't have a woman to go with you." He thought a moment. "Tell you what. I'll have Gordo walk you to the ladies' room door and stand outside until you're done. Okay? And please remember—Kirsten will be here still tied up and waiting for your prompt return."

He turned to the muscleman. "Gordo, search them. Take their cell phones and turn them off."

"I did that when we captured them, Herr Jaeger."

"Excellent. Then go into the bathroom with Sharon. Make sure there's no backdoor and it's empty. Leave her and wait outside the bathroom."

"Yes, sir," Gordo said. He untied Sharon's hands and feet, grabbed her upper arm in a mammoth fist, and attempted to guide her away.

She pulled her arm loose. "Let me go, you big gorilla. I need to hold onto my crutches." He released his grip and Sharon hobbled away on her walking cast, leaning on her crutches.

"In these few minutes, Kirsten, let me explain my position. I'm sure you've read of honor killings in various Arab cultures of women who bring shame or dishonor to the family. You've humiliated my family name and me by associating—I don't want more intimate details than that—with my son. I cannot let that go unpunished. Contaminating the Aryan—"

"What kind of rock have you been living under, *Max*?" she asked.

He drew back, startled.

"The Nazi regime and hopes for world dominance are long gone. Hitler himself violated the myth of Aryan purity. That book you're holding explains it all. I don't think Eva ever expected her diary to be read by anyone outside the family, or she wouldn't have revealed all she does. She clearly says Hitler was part Jewish, from his grandfather. And even sired a Jewish son."

Kirsten saw Max's jaw muscles tense as he gritted his teeth. "You're lying."

She pushed harder, praying Sharon would take her time returning.

"Eva says Hitler told her his grandfather was a nineteen-year-old Jewish boy, Leopold Frankenberger. The Frankenbergers paid Hitler's grandfather to claim Alois as his son. Adolf, the man you worship, was actually a quarter Jewish."

Max riffled the pages of the diary. "Where does it say that?"

"Untie me, and I'll show you." She muttered *shit* under her breath as she saw Gordo returning with Sharon. Gordo sat Sharon down in the chair.

"Gordo, first tie Sharon back up, then untie Kirsten."

Sharon rubbed her wrist and pulled away from Gordo. "Wait, Herr Jaeger. Please let me stay free. We're locked in this building with no place to run, you've got this muscle-bound ape who could sit on us in a microsecond, and I promise to just sit here like a good lady. Leave me untied. The ropes hurt." She rubbed her wrists again. "Please."

Max pondered a moment and nodded.

"Thank you," Sharon said.

Kirsten reached for the diary and skimmed its pages. "Here it is, the second paragraph." She handed the opened book to Max, pointing to the page. "Do you want me to translate?"

"You do have a smart mouth," Max said.

As he read silently, his brow wrinkled, and the corners of his mouth turned down.

"This doesn't prove anything. It's just her word. Hearsay, lawyers would conclude."

She took the diary and showed him the page where Hitler confessed to having a Jewish son.

"Hearsay bullshit," he said.

"Now who has the foul mouth?"

Max glowered at her. Gordo moved closer with a raised hand. Max shook his head.

"Maybe hearsay, but as told to Eva by Hitler," Kirsten said. "People accept the Bible as the word of God, yet it was written hundreds if not thousands of years after events that happened. Eva wrote this the day he told her. You accept one and not the other?"

"You'd make a good lawyer," Max said.

"Your son told me the same thing."

"Your position is pointless because I don't believe this," he held up the diary, "or the Bible." He paused. "For argument's sake, let's say this entry is correct. So what?"

"That strikes a nail into your Nazi myths about Aryan supremacy."

"Not necessarily."

"Why not?" she asked.

"Hitler was pure in other ways."

"Like what?"

"He was married to the German people and devoted his entire adult life to them."

"Give me the diary." He handed it back to Kirsten. She found the pages about his incestuous romance with his niece, his intimacy with Eva, and the suicide attempts.

"Now what have you to say about your beloved leader?" He was silent. "And if you flip a few more pages, you'll see when they fled Germany to go to Argentina, Eva says this paragon of virtue was addicted to cocaine and amphetamines, and taking more than twenty medications daily, including testosterone injections when he wanted to have sex with Eva. She says his hands shook, probably from Parkinson's disease. Quite a specimen, this peerless leader of yours."

Max stood, rested on his cane, and said to Gordo, "Watch them. I need to stretch my legs a bit."

Supported by his cane, Max strolled the large, empty hall, touched the banners, straightened a picture or two, and gravitated to the side-by-side statues of Frederick the Great and Adolf Hitler. He stood in front of them, looking from one face to the other, examining similarities.

He noted the strong, prominent forehead of both, the piercing eyes, and thin lips slightly parted as if about to give an order. Frederick's nose was straight—certainly not Jewish—while Hitler's was broad and could've been.

Frederick had a more masculine, handsome face with strong, high cheekbones and hair curled at the back in the style of the times. Max had to admit Hitler's short mustache was bizarre. Hitler had trimmed it severely after he'd been gassed in World War I and almost died because his long, flowing mustache prevented the gas mask from making a proper seal. The mustard gas had left him temporarily blind.

"So, gentlemen," Max addressed the statues in a low voice, "what do you suggest I should do? You two have been the most successful rulers in German history. Frederick, you ruled as a Prussian king for over forty years, Adolf for only twelve, but both of you were undeviating in your loyalty to the German state. Maybe if we had a diary for you, Your Royal Highness," he addressed King Frederick, "we'd find skeletons in your closet also. But that wouldn't diminish your greatness, nor will it mine.

"I don't have your armies, but I do have legions of ordinary citizens ready to do battle with cell phones and social media, to proclaim Deutschland Über Alles and ensure Nazi dominance and Jewish suppression. We already made our presence here felt once and will do it again. I can't accomplish total domination if the truth about you, Herr führer, becomes known. Some skeletons continue to rattle their bones.

"Your womanizing I can handle. A virile leader needs female comfort and release. Your drugs also not a big problem, especially today. But Jewish blood is most difficult and damaging. How can I espouse anti-Semitism if our leader was Jewish, and especially if he sired a Jewish son? A Jewish lineage! Did you realize what you were doing when you conceived this child? Was that why you were so violently anti-Semitic? So you could hate a race of people to convince others you were not one of them?

"Anti-Semitism underlies our ability to dominate. We must focus on a cause to unite the people, to blame the Jews for everything. Islamic extremism succeeds because they do that so effectively, using jihads to push Israel into the sea. The press loves it and panders to them. The problem is modern Jews push back. That Iron Dome defense is pretty effective. Perhaps if the Jews were less successful, people wouldn't hate them as much. Much of the anger is jealousy. My God, ethnic groups slaughter people by the thousands all over the world with little condemnation. But not the Jews. Fortunately, they get nailed for any infraction, real or imagined."

Agitated, he paced around the statues, staring at them from every angle. He took out a handkerchief, wiped sweat from his own forehead, and then used it to brush a light patina of dust from the statues' faces.

"I suppose I could make the point that the führer had no control over who his grandparents were, or maybe that he experienced firsthand what Jews were like and that's what turned him against them. That might work but seems a bit weak. And won't explain the Jewish son. That is most damning.

"The only thing to do is to suppress this Jewish information totally. Burn the diary and the copy. Kill the women—but what about my son? He knows what's in it. Or the hospital person who copied it? Maybe that person read some of it, made an extra copy, or showed it to someone else. Where does it stop? Sadly, this isn't 1943 when we could make all those people disappear in the blink of an eye."

Shaking his head in bewilderment, he slowly walked back to the women, leaning heavily on his cane. He was tired.

The women were sitting in their chairs, talking softly to each other. Gordo stood nearby, a blond statue with arms crossed, alert to any threat to his master. Max sat down.

"Are there other copies of this diary?" He held up the original.

"No," Kirsten said a bit too quickly. She hoped if he thought there was no other copy, there'd be no need to hurt them, since it would only be their word against his without written proof.

Max beckoned to Gordo. "Perhaps a little persuasion"—he pointed to Sharon's neck—"will jar Kirsten's memory."

Gordo approached Sharon.

"You have the original and the only copy we made last night," Kirsten said. "I swear."

Gordo grabbed a handful of Sharon's hair, yanked her head back, and flipped out a knife. The blade glittered in the light. He placed the point against Sharon's throat and looked at Max for an order. Sharon was too petrified to move.

"Stop!" Kirsten yelled. "Stop, for God's sake! There is another copy. The hospital was to send it Federal Express this morning."

Max flicked his finger at Gordo. He removed the knife and let go of Sharon's hair. She rubbed her neck where a tiny drop of blood welled. Her eyes glistened, wide with fright, and her lips quivered, but no sound emerged.

Max checked his watch. Almost ten o'clock. "What time is pickup?"

"I don't know. They just said it goes out in the morning's mail," Kirsten said.

"Who said?" Max asked.

"A nurse or somebody last night."

"To whom is it addressed?"

Kirsten paused, silent.

Max nodded at Gordo. He took a step toward Sharon.

"My father," Kirsten said in a sob.

Max smiled. "I figured. Why didn't you FedEx the original?"

"We thought if we gave you the original and planted a copy, you'd stop," Kirsten said.

"Planted a copy?" Max asked.

"The one you found at the airport in case someone was following us."

"Stupid Jew. You've only made more trouble for everyone."

He walked out of hearing range and motioned Gordo over. "Tie them up again. Tight. Here's what we need to do."

CHAPTER 38

THE MATCH WAS GOING BADLY. KIRSTEN HADN'T shown, and Stefan couldn't concentrate. The fifth seed from Hungary was picking him apart with expert lunges and parries.

László Petschauer, six feet three inches tall, with long arms and impeccable technique, was totally focused on winning his match. His fluid grace revealed long practice hours and dedication. He made difficult moves look easy.

László had to win because Grandfather Attila's memory haunted him whenever he picked up a fencing weapon. Losing was not a consideration. Attila Petschauer had been a Hungarian sabre fencing hero, medalling in the 1928 and 1932 Summer Olympic Games. Initially granted a "document of exemption" from Nazi purges as an Olympic star—much like Dietrich Becker—Attila Petschauer had been arrested in 1943 and sent to a Nazi labor camp in the Ukrainian town of Davidovka. The camp commandant, whom Attila had beaten in an international fencing match in Germany the year before, murdered him by lashing him to a tree and hosing him with ice water "for Jewish purification." Attila froze to death during the winter night. László's recurrent dream was that he'd been at his grandfather's side, freed him, and together they'd killed the Nazis. In his mind, Attila rode each blade thrust.

After the first set, László Petschauer, fearlessly aggressive, led five to one.

Stefan's coach was angry. "Where's your head this morning? You'd better start concentrating, or you'll soon be on a plane to Paris."

Stefan kept glancing into the audience for Kirsten. A sudden movement at the back of the hall distracted him. Squinting into the distance, he failed to hear the referee call for the start of the second set. His coach had to push him forward onto the piste.

When Kirsten hadn't arrived by the beginning of the third set, Stefan knew something was wrong. With almost two minutes to go in the match, Petschauer reached fifteen points to Stefan's eight, winning the match.

Stefan ripped off his mask, shook Petschauer's hand, and bolted off the piste. He shoved his épée and mask into the coach's hands and strode from the arena, ignoring the coach's shouts to come back. Losing meant nothing compared with Kirsten's safety. His father was capable of evil things.

In the locker room, he changed into street clothes and dialed Kirsten's iPhone as he hurried to the tram station. No answer. When the tram hadn't arrived after five minutes, Stefan debated jogging to building 12, then thought better of it. When the tram arrived, he boarded, fidgeted during the short ride, and dialed again with no answer. He jumped out as soon as the doors opened and ran toward building 12. All seemed quiet.

He knocked at the apartment door but got no response. He tried the door handle; locked. Stefan debated calling the janitor for a key but decided the flimsy door would yield to a hard shoulder. He backed up several steps and hit the door with a crunch. It gave easily, and he crashed into the room. A quick look confirmed his fears.

He phoned Kirsten again, but still no answer. Aimlessly he wandered the apartment, collapsing into a chair. He shut his eyes and ran fingers through his hair. What to do? His mind was blank. Then he remembered.

He reached for his billfold. Buried deep in the wallet's side pocket to be forgotten was his father's business card. Stefan dialed the cell number. His father answered the first ring.

"Well, hello, my son. I was expecting your call. I heard your match didn't go too well."

"Never mind my match. Where are Kirsten and Sharon?"

"Safe and sound, not to worry. Sorry I couldn't be there to watch you fence."

"Stop this bullshit charade. Where are the women? What have you done to them?" Stefan stood and started pacing, his head whirling with possibilities. Where might they be? Could he find them? What should his next move be?

"Safe," his father said.

"What do you want?" Stefan asked.

"Come, come, Stefan. That should be obvious."

"What?"

"The amber key and the Amber Room. I've been told a thorough search of your room did not reveal the key, so I assume you have it on your person. Wise of you. Also, I want any diary copies you happened to take with you from the hospital."

"I have none."

"Just the one hidden at the airport and the FedEx copy?"

There was a long pause. "She told you?"

"Of course, after a bit of persuasion."

"Persuasion! What did you do to them? If you've hurt her, so help me, father or not—"

"Relax, Stefan, relax. They are fine—for now. What about other copies?" Max asked.

"We only had time to make two copies."

"You're sure?" Max asked.

"Yes." Stefan focused on noises in the background. "Put her on. I want to know she's safe."

"You can talk but briefly." He held the phone for Kirsten.

"Stefan, do whatever he asks," Kirsten sobbed. "He's vicious. He'll kill us. Hurry. We're at—"

Stefan heard the slap and Kirsten cry out.

"You son of a bitch! Leave her alone. Turn them free now," Stefan shouted into the phone. His knuckles were white, gripping the phone.

"Stefan, enough with this game. If you want these ladies to survive, I want you here, now, with the key."

"Where?"

"There's a small café called the Copa Café across the street from the Copacabana Beach on the Avenida Atlántica. Be there in thirty minutes. Someone will meet you." He hung up.

Stefan caught a cab to the café. He stood across the street watching patrons enter and exit for a full five minutes but saw no one who might be there to meet him. Finally, he sat at a front table near the street, refusing the waiter's request to order.

"Sorry you lost."

Stefan didn't see the man come up behind him. He sat down across from Stefan. He was Stefan's age, broad shouldered and muscular. His nose had probably been broken a few times.

"I heard that Hungarian fencer took you apart. You weren't really in the match."

"Were you there?"

He shook his head. "Working. A friend told me."

"Who're you?"

"Name's Gordo. Your father sent me to get you."

"To go where?"

"You'll find out. Ready?"

Stefan got up and walked toward the street.

Gordo grabbed his arm. "Where you going?"

"Get a cab."

"No, we can walk. Just follow me," Gordo said.

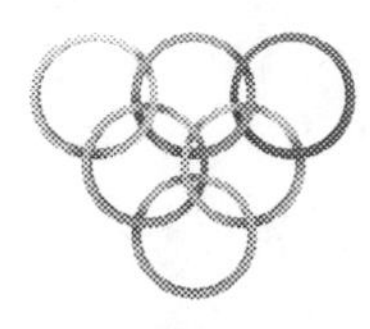

"Max, these ropes are too tight. I'm losing sensation in my fingertips," Kirsten said.

"I said before, ropes can do that."

"Especially around the neck. Yes, you told us."

"Your fingers are the least of your worries," Max said.

"What are my worries?" Kirsten asked, flexing her fingers.

"That you and your friend stay alive."

"You need us alive. You don't have the amber key, and you don't know where the room is. And you've got to deal with the diary and Hitler's heritage. For all you know, Hitler could have a dozen great-grandsons walking around in kippahs."

"Stefan has the key, and he or you will tell us where the room is. I'll destroy the diary and deny it ever existed. Without proof, all claims are bogus."

"What about the copy my father will get?"

"I have people meeting the FedEx plane at Ben Gurion Airport in Tel Aviv. If that fails, they'll visit your father. Maybe I'll go too. Good excuse for a reunion, don't you think, after so many years?"

"Don't you dare, you—you—"

"Words escape you, Kirsten? Maybe a rhyme will jar your brain? Shall I recite one?" He laughed.

She fought against her restraints. "You bastard. Untie me, and I'll give you a rhyme."

"Yes, I'm sure you'd like that. An athletic twenty-something against an eighty-seven-year-old. That's why I hire men like Gordo."

She looked around. "Where is he?"

"Meeting Stefan."

She knew they had to act now. Kirsten glanced at Sharon and nodded imperceptibly.

"I've got to pee again, Herr Jaeger," said Sharon.

"What's with you, Sharon? You can't have prostate problems."

"Just an old lady with a weak bladder. And too much excitement."

"You'll have to wait until Gordo gets back."

She shook her head. "I can't."

"Too risky, Sharon," Max said.

"What am I going to do to you?" Sharon said. "I'm almost as old as you and on crutches. You've got two good legs and a strong cane."

He sat still, studying her. Sharon shifted in the chair, crossed and uncrossed her legs. Her face grimaced. "Please, Herr Jaeger. I can't hold it much longer." She squeezed her legs tight. "I'm going to burst."

"Then burst," Max said. "Might be fun to see a Jew wet herself."

"Let her go, for God's sake!" Kirsten shouted. "Whatever happened to old-fashioned German Ritterlichkeit, Herr Jaeger? I thought you were a gentleman … something about refinement?"

He rose, stood in front of Sharon, and shook his cane in her face. "Try anything, and Kirsten will get this across her mouth, chivalry be damned. Understood?"

Sharon nodded. Max untied her, and she slipped off the chair, grabbed her crutches, and shuffled toward the bathroom. Kirsten pulled against her bonds. They wouldn't budge.

Max watched her struggle for several moments with a bemused look. Finally, he said, "Gordo ties a good knot, doesn't he? Perhaps a Gordian knot?" He laughed.

Over Max's shoulder, Kirsten saw Sharon spin around, and limp silently back toward them, finger to her lips. Kirsten had to keep Max distracted.

"He did, Max." She tugged again and grunted with dramatic effort. "Happy you have the daughter of your worst enemy tied in a chair? Kind of like you did to my father, only I have my clothes on?"

Max smiled. "Ah, yes, maybe we can change that—"

The crutch bounced off the back of his head with a resounding *thwack*. Max tottered from his chair and fell to the floor. Sharon hopped on one leg to Kirsten and fumbled with her ropes as Max groaned on the carpet. After a moment, he twitched and struggled to sit up.

"Hurry, Sharon. You only stunned him."

"Doing the best I can, Kirsten. These knots are tight." She ignored the arthritic pain and worked gnarled fingers on the rope. Finally Kirsten broke free.

Kirsten bent over Max and made sure he was breathing. She bound his hands and feet with her rope and tied the end to the chair. She retrieved Sharon's crutch, but the wood had splintered. "Good job," she said, smiling, holding the crutch for Sharon to see.

"Years of fencing will do that. Hand me his cane."

They went to the front door together, Sharon gripping the ivory handle with one hand and the wooden crutch with the other. Their uneven height made her list against Kirsten for stability.

Shuffling along, they reached the front of the room. Sharon put her hand on the doorknob. "I can't wait to get out of here."

"Stop," Kirsten said, placing her hand on Sharon's. She parted the curtain covering the window.

"That's what I was afraid of," Kirsten said. "Gordo and Stefan are coming up the walk."

"What should we do?" Sharon said, eyes wide.

Kirsten took her by the arm. "Stand behind the door. Give me Max's cane."

The key in the lock made a grinding noise, and the door swung open. Stefan entered first, followed by Gordo guiding him with a hand against his back.

Kirsten held the cane high over her shoulder and swung at Gordo's head. The ivory handle thumped with enough force to drive him to the floor. Blood trickled down his face as he shook his head and rubbed his scalp. He climbed to one knee, glassy-eyed, a hand braced against the wall for balance. Stefan pushed him down and kept a foot on Gordo's back.

"Thank God you're here. Your father's planning to destroy the diaries and us as well," Kirsten said. "Grab Sharon under one arm, I'll take the other."

"We can't leave him." Stefan nodded at Gordo, groaning and trying to push up. He moved sloth-like, still stunned.

Kirsten ran to where they had been sitting and grabbed the ropes that had bound Sharon. She hurried back and tied Gordo's hands and feet. Then they rushed out the door, supporting Sharon between them.

The weather had turned ugly, with dense black clouds overhead and a trickling rain building to a drenching downpour.

"He'll be after us in a minute," Stefan said. They hugged the building to keep dry.

Kirsten shook her head. "He'll have to untie himself, check on Max, and then untie him," she said, "so we've got a head start. Not much but some. We can't run carrying Sharon. Once we get to the street, we'll catch a cab."

"Good luck in this weather," he said.

They each took Sharon under one arm and half-ran to the street, swinging her between them. She bounced along on one leg, holding the walking cast high and out of puddles. The downpour intensified, and they were getting drenched. No cab in sight.

CHAPTER 39

"WHAT HAVE WE HERE?" ASKED A MAN AS HE opened the passenger door of a black SUV with tinted windows. He stepped out holding an umbrella. "Don't I know you?" It was Pepé from Bariloche. "Looks like you're having some trouble."

"Christ," Kirsten said, not certain what to make of the chance encounter. "Pepé, we've got to get out of here," she said. "They're bad people in there." Then she pulled back. "Are you one of them?"

He smiled and shook his head. "I just happen to have a car with a driver at your service." He walked over to help them with Sharon. "Can I drive you someplace special? How about the Israeli Consulate? Jump in before anyone sees us and we get drenched any more than we are."

The three piled into the backseat, Pepé in front with the driver, and they sped off.

"Okay Pepé," Kirsten said, "this is too crazy. You just show up in Bariloche, and now here. Who are you?"

Pepé spoke Portuguese to the driver, then fiddled with his face. He peeled off the beard, finger-combed his hair, and stripped off waxy layers of artificial skin. Wrinkles came away in his hand. He turned around and held up the facial strips for the backseat audience.

"I'm still Pepé but a slightly younger version. Your Mossad guys," he nodded at Sharon and Kirsten, "recruited me a year ago at the request of Jake Hertzog of the IDF. Mossad and IDF have been working together on this."

"Working together on what?" asked Kirsten.

"This," Pepé answered, gesturing at the building fading in the distance.

"You're not from Bariloche?" Kirsten asked.

"I actually did grow up there and did attend the Priebke school like I told you when we met in Bariloche. But I also spent several years in Israel, working with the Mossad."

"How did you know we were in there?" Kirsten asked.

"I didn't know about you two ladies. I've been following Stefan. I parked in front after he went inside with Gordo. That piece of shit is well known to us as Max Jaeger's enforcer."

"Wait a minute," said Stefan. "I'm all confused. Why were you following me?"

Pepé draped an arm over the backseat so he could talk more easily. "Let me start at the beginning."

Stefan nodded agreement.

"The Mossad's been tracking your father's company for years. He's a blatant Nazi supporter, donated big dollars in Argentina and Brazil for Nazi causes. In October 2009, just before the IOC selection committee met to choose a city to host these 2016 Olympics, the bank accounts of seven leading committee members grew by two hundred and fifty thousand euros each. That money was traced to your father."

"Why would he want the games here?"

"We suspected he was planning some sort of surprise. And since Munich in '72, we've been hyperalert at every Olympics, though I admit the shenanigans at the Opening Ceremony caught us flat-footed."

"How did you just happen to bump into us in Bariloche?" Kirsten asked.

"Of course it didn't just happen. Two things," he said, looking at Kirsten. "First, we'd been following Stefan because the Mossad had trouble infiltrating Max's company to find out what he was planning. We figured Max would make contact with his son. You happened to be with him."

"The second reason?" Stefan asked.

"We heard Max talk with Lobo and plan to visit."

"Phone tap?" Stefan asked.

Pepé nodded. "We got lucky."

"So you know about the Amber Room?"

"Only that it's there someplace, and Lobo had the key. I suppose you have it now," he said, looking at Stefan.

Stefan opened his mouth to speak and then closed it.

"You advised us not to visit Estancia Inalco," Kirsten said.

Pepé smiled. "I have three children and five grandchildren, Kirsten. Best way to get them to do something is tell them they shouldn't."

"Thanks a lot," said Kirsten, pouting.

"What we didn't plan was your busy night last night. Sorry about what happened to you two ladies. We had to make a choice and stuck with Stefan."

The SUV slowed, made a right turn into a driveway, and stopped in front of a building labeled Consulate General of the State of Israel. In the distance, the statue of Christ the Redeemer, the 125-foot art deco statue on the peak of Corcovado Mountain, cast its big shadow over the Star of David.

They all hustled out. Pepé flashed his pass at the guard, flipped him the car keys, and they entered the building. He led them to a door at the side of the entrance hall, placed his right forefinger in the lock, and the door sprang open. They walked into the Mossad war room.

Piles of papers, three containers of partially eaten lunches, bowls of fruit, and empty bottles of Coke and water littered a long, wooden table in the room's center. A bank of computer screens flanked one wall. Three technicians sat at desks typing while glued to the screens' responses. Two tables at the side tottered with thick volumes of black loose-leaf notebooks labeled *Summer Olympic Games,* each bearing a date from 1972 to 2012. One wall held an outsized, detailed map of Rio de Janeiro tacked onto a corkboard, alongside another one of San Carlos de Bariloche.

Pepé cleared a space at the center table for them to sit.

With a groan, Sharon propped her foot cast on a chair. "Tough life when you're old," she said to no one in particular, rubbing her leg. "This thing's throbbing like a drum."

People sporting IDF and Mossad badges hanging from their necks scurried about, checking papers, computer screens, and whispering to each other.

Pepé waved a hand around to take in the room.

"As you can see, we're on hyperalert. We're live 24-7 with the IDF and Mossad in Jerusalem, trading and integrating information—stuff we pick up with what they decipher. We still don't know what your father's planning, Stefan, but it's something big. We're seeing increased media traffic among the Nazis, so it involves a lot of people. It'll either happen during your Super Bowl fencing match tomorrow, Kirsten, or the Closing Ceremony two days later. Both will be big draws, though the closing will be much bigger."

"Lots of people coming?" Stefan asked.

"If the numbers from Bariloche are any indication, thousands of Nazis are here already and thousands more en route. Maybe not like the Hajj to Mecca—that drew two million pilgrims two years ago—but several hundred thousand."

"How can you be sure?" Stefan asked.

Pepé shrugged. "Not totally sure but lots of clues. Airlines in South America for the past month have been offering group package deals to Rio at less than half price. Your father's company has been subsidizing them. Same for buses and hotel rooms. Airport and bus stations have been flooded with arrivals. Hotels are all booked solid. Your father's set up a tent city in a thirty-acre park just outside town for the overflow. Capacity's a hundred thousand. Probably more if people share tents. Complete with food and water, blankets, and toilets. About everything you could need."

"With that many coming, he can't be planning a bomb or something like that at the Maracanã Stadium. He'd blow up his own people," Kirsten said.

"True, applying Western logic and values," Pepé said. "But remember—Hamas didn't care about their own people being killed. They got more public support in their fight with Israel when their women and children were blown up."

"Kill your own, and the world cries for you," Stefan said.

"In some places. We've not excluded a bomb or bombs or other violent acts. We've got sniffer dogs and bomb surveillance experts from Israel just in case. It could also be a large peaceful uprising, just showing huge numbers of Nazis, saber rattling of things to come," Pepé said.

"I'm fencing épée, not sabre." When they all turned to her without laughing, Kirsten made a face and said self-consciously, "Sorry. Trying to lighten the mood."

Pepé nodded and continued. "Far as we know, Max is unaware of our interest in him. He obviously doesn't know you're here at the consulate."

"You could have him arrested for kidnapping. Maybe even attempted murder," Sharon said, touching the fresh scab at her throat.

"We could, but that would blow our cover, and probably any hope to find out what he's planning or who the other leaders are. We—that is, Hertzog in Jerusalem, the Mossad brain trust here, and I—think if we put you two back into commission and act normal, we'll have a better chance to discover their plot."

"Wouldn't Max expect us to go to the police?" Kirsten asked.

"No, for two reasons," Stefan said. "First, he threatened to tell the police we killed Lobo and have us arrested. Second, it would screw up your match tomorrow. If he's got something planned, he wouldn't want it spoiled by you not fencing."

"Speaking of which, do I know who I'll be facing?" Kirsten asked.

They looked at each other and shrugged until one of the technicians turned around. "Yes, men's finals just came in. Some Hungarian named Petschauer. László Petschauer has just won men's gold. Blew away most of the field. Stefan should know him."

Stefan grimaced. "He beat the stuffing out of me in the first match this morning."

"He's that good?" Kirsten asked.

"Superb technique. Long arms. Quick moves," Stefan said.

"Wonderful. Just what I need now. Why am I here and not practicing?" Kirsten asked.

"A little matter of saving your life," Pepé answered with a smile. "That's over now, so you can go back to routine. That's precisely what we want. Routine. We'll have you covered, but I doubt Max will try anything now. It's too close to his big finale."

"And that will be—?" Kirsten asked.

"Precisely. A question mark for now," said Pepé.

"When you find out, would you mind letting me know?" Kirsten asked. "Be sure to protect my papa. I may have lineage at stake."

"That bitch. She sideswiped me with her crutch. I knew I shouldn't have let her go to the bathroom." Max stood on wobbly legs, leaning against Gordo. Gingerly he fingered the welt on the back of his head.

"Sorry, Herr Jaeger," Gordo said, also rubbing his head. "Somebody nailed me too."

"You checked thoroughly outside? No place to hide?"

"No, sir. They must have caught a cab. It's pouring down rain, and I looked all over, especially under cover where they might be out of the rain. They're gone. What do you want me to do?"

Jaeger sat down hard on the chair. His face was pale and sweaty. "I don't feel so good, Gordo. A little dizzy. Give me a minute to think."

"Can I bring you something? Water, maybe?"

"Yes, and a wet cloth. And an ice pack for my head."

"Right away, sir." Gordo walked to the kitchen at the back of the main hall and returned with Max's requests.

Max wiped his face, put the cloth around his neck, and sipped slowly from the water bottle. He held the ice pack on his head. After a few minutes, his color began to return. "Gordo, we need to go ahead with our plans as scheduled."

"What about the ladies and your son, Herr Jaeger?"

The old man thought a moment. "Leave them alone for now. They're not going anyplace, what with the Super Bowl of Fencing tomorrow. Stefan knows what'll happen if he calls the police. The big issue is the diary they FedExed to Israel and what'll happen if—more likely when—that becomes public."

"We can have people in Jerusalem meet the plane or the FedEx truck. Or go to their home and retrieve it."

Max shook his head. "Too late for that, Gordo. Kirsten's bound to tell her parents, and that will tip off the local police. They'll be waiting. We'll just have to deal with the publicity when it happens. I'll claim the diary's a forgery. After all, I have the original. We'll say it's Israeli propaganda, even more believable because the press release would come from Jerusalem. What we do here will overshadow it."

"Yes, Herr Jaeger. What do you want me to do now?"

"Everything's set for tomorrow?"

"It should be. I'll check one more time."

"Tomorrow's our penultimate celebration."

Gordo looked at Max with a question on his face.

"Don't know what that means?"

"No, Herr Jaeger. I'm sorry, but I don't."

"Next to the last in a series. I'm sure you've heard the famous quote by King Louis XV, '*Après moi le déluge*.' After me the deluge. He was the penultimate French king. After him, the deluge came, and King Louis XVI was executed. After tomorrow comes my deluge of retribution. You are my Louis XV, Gordo."

"I understand. Thank you, Herr Jaeger."

Max retreated to his office off the lobby. The room was not much larger than a big closet, but—in contrast to the space Frederick the Great and Adolf Hitler required to start a war—Max had enough for a desk and a computer. All he needed. The message sent on Facebook, LinkedIn, and Twitter was simple:

"*Jetzt ist die Zeit*." The time is now.

CHAPTER 40

THAT CALL TO JIHAD—A STRUGGLE NOT IN THE way of Allah but in the way of Hitler—spawned the beginnings of the Nazi Fourth Reich. Hitler's efforts, begun seventy-one years earlier in San Carlos de Bariloche, were finally paying off. Fanatical believers walked, boarded cars, buses, boats, trains, and planes to make the pilgrimage—not to Mecca but to Rio de Janeiro and the Games of the XXXI Olympiad.

Nazi jihadi poured into the city. They intermingled with the locals, flooded hotels, restaurants, and shopping malls. Some moved in with residential families, cramming a dozen people into space for two or three. Others packed the pousadas until they ballooned to bursting.

The overflow bused to Tent City, claimed their piece of turf, and set up camp. The spirit was jovial, the meeting of like minds embarking on a new adventure. Like a festive tailgate party before the big football game, they set up grills beneath umbrellas and unpacked coolers filled with cold Brahma beer, so refreshing on a hot day. They donned Olympic jerseys, though the games were just an excuse for most. Enterprising businessmen transformed tents into mini restaurants and sold grilled skewers of barbecued rabbit, beef, and chicken. Nazi flags fluttered from tent poles in the afternoon breeze. The veneer of happiness masked the layer of violence floating beneath the surface.

The IOC scheduled the Super Bowl of Fencing in the main arena, with no other games scheduled at that time. The piste, just a narrow strip two meters wide and fourteen long, was lost in the center of the vast Maracanã Stadium. Six television cameras focused on the runway from every angle and displayed images on ten giant screens scattered throughout the arena. The match, televised live around the world, anticipated viewing second only to the World Cup FIFA Soccer Finals from Rio two years before when more than seven hundred million watched Germany beat Argentina.

The next morning, Tent City emptied, and spectators began piling into the stadium an hour before the scheduled eleven o'clock start. The hall vibrated with shouted conversations and shuffling feet. Air conditioners couldn't keep pace, and the air was heavy, clinging.

Pedestrian progress slowed because of intense security. Rio organizers, educated on crowd control by the Mossad and IDF, vowed not to be surprised again. Israel had sent a core of twenty-five safety experts, along with security scanning equipment used at the Ben Gurion International Airport. All personal articles were x-rayed, inspected by hand, and swabbed for explosives. Metal coolers were forbidden. The lines grew long, and the happy atmosphere began to wilt in the heat.

Kirsten paced the ladies' locker room floor, dressed and ready to go. She was surprised at herself. She thought gold medal would have been sufficient. It wasn't. She wanted platinum.

"You're driving me nutty, Kirsten. Can you stop for a few minutes and just sit?"

"I'm too wound up. I'm going to explode if this thing doesn't start soon." Kirsten bounced up and down on her toes, shadow fencing, and resumed walking.

"Pacing isn't going to hurry Rio officials. They start when they want, regardless of schedules. So cool your jets."

"It's past eleven."

"Sit," said Sharon. "You're driving me bonkers!"

Kirsten sighed and plunked down onto a wooden bench. Her legs kept bouncing, knees churning the air.

"Can you run the video of László Petschauer again? I've got his moves memorized, but once more won't hurt."

Sharon flipped the remote, and Petschauer's first match against Stefan popped up on the screen. "Poor Stefan," Kirsten said. "László really took him apart."

"Stefan said he was so preoccupied worrying about you, he wasn't thinking about the match," Sharon said.

Kirsten flipped fast forward. "Maybe, but László beat them all pretty good. None of his matches were even close. Not like mine."

"Don't be getting all psyched out about him. He's just another fencer, maybe taller than you and with a slightly longer reach, but you're as technically skilled, just as fast, and smarter."

"How's that?"

"You just are. It's in your genes. You have the *feel*."

"And Petschauer doesn't have the feel or good genes? C'mon, Sharon. His grandfather was the sabre champion of Hungary and an Olympic medalist."

"Your grandfather was an Olympian—albeit a runner—and your father was almost an Olympian. You were practically born with an épée in your hands, so it's in your blood too."

Kirsten shook her head. "Not the same."

"Maybe not, but as I've told you, it's all a head game. You can beat him, but you've got to believe in yourself. Believe you can do it."

Kirsten stood and bowed to Sharon. "I believe, oh mighty oracle. I believe."

Sharon smiled. "Speaking of genes, have you talked with your parents?"

"Yesterday and early this morning."

"They okay?"

"As nervous as I am. They said Keshet Broadcasting is airing the match live on channel two. They've installed huge TV screens in every park throughout Jerusalem and Tel Aviv. Everybody's outside watching and partying."

"They say anything about the diary?"

"Later, Sharon. I don't want to think about that now."

"Okay, but—"

A warning buzzer interrupted Sharon's response. "Ready?" she asked.

"I'm so ready."

"Remember it's just a game. Do your best, that's all. You've already won gold. Nobody could ask for more."

"But they are, Sharon, they are. My whole country wants more. It's not just a game anymore."

The stands were full. Almost one hundred thousand cheering spectators stood and applauded as Kirsten walked into the stadium from the ladies' locker room, and László Petschauer from the men's. Banners unfurled saying *Killer Kirsten!*, while others had *Leaping László!* Their images were fifteen feet tall on huge TV screens.

Kirsten strode to her end of the piste platform. Chairs were set for her and Sharon, with a small plastic cooler holding bottled water and Gatorade, and a pile of fresh towels on a small table. She looked around at the audience and waved, triggering a roar from the crowd.

"Oh, my," she said, taking it all in. "I feel so insignificant."

"Nonsense," Sharon said, shielding her eyes against the glare of the lights and gazing into the stands. "You're the reason so many have come. Look at all the women in the audience. They want to see the so-called weaker sex beat the stronger one. I can see headlines tomorrow: *Estrogen Triumphs Testosterone*. Or maybe, *Venus Vanquishes Mars*."

"Ha. And the men are cramming in to see me lose."

"Of course. No way someone wearing a dress can win the Super Bowl of Fencing."

"Good thing I'm wearing pants."

Kirsten looked at the other end of the piste where Petschauer was limbering up. *He's good,* she thought. *Pants certainly will prevail. But his or mine?*

Stefan pushed his way through the crowd. "Sorry I'm late. I had to take care of a few things."

Sharon looked at her watch. "Like what?" she asked, frowning.

Stefan smiled. "Things." He turned to Kirsten. "Ready?"

"As I'll ever be," Kirsten said.

"Why the defeatist tone?"

Kirsten nodded at Petschauer standing at the other end of the piste. "He looks tough."

"So are you. I could've beaten him—I *should've* beaten him."

"But?"

He held her shoulders, drew her toward him, and kissed her forehead. "My heart took my head elsewhere."

"And now?"

"Right here with my Super Bowl heroine." He drew her closer to whisper in her ear. "I love you, and, win or lose, you're the best fencer in these Olympics, and the best fencer Israel's ever seen. Don't forget that." Then, more softly, "You could beat me, but I'll never admit it in public."

The loudspeaker interrupted as the IOC chairman began the program. "Ladies and gentlemen. As you all know, this is a first for the Olympic games: a face-off between a man and a woman athlete. Women have competed in the Olympics since 1900, four years after the modern games began in Athens, but they've never fought against a man. Although we have women's boxing and weight lifting, wrestling, and tae kwon do, because of the obvious physical differences, none of them allow for mano a mano between sexes. Since the IOC is committed to sex equality in all sports, we concluded that fencing offered the best opportunity for intersex combat—outside of marriage, that is."

The crowd erupted. Couples turned to each other, laughing, fists raised in fighting poses. A few threw soft punches.

The chairman continued. "That brings us to the present bout. We have two formidable opponents, each gold winners and each coming from Olympian families. László Petschauer's grandfather, Attila, was an Olympic fencer, and Kirsten Becker's grandfather, Dietrich, an Olympic track star. I cannot think of a better matchup for our first Super Bowl of Fencing. Please welcome, on my right, Kirsten Becker, and on my left, László Petschauer."

Kirsten walked to the center of the piste. László met her halfway. She saw he was taller than she, with a broad chest, long arms, and a thick neck. Swarthy, with several days of black stubble on a square jaw, his dark, brooding eyes appraised her with a haughty smile. He could've played D'Artagnan in *The Three Musketeers* or been in an ad, shirtless, for King Solomon men's cologne, with a half-naked woman draped over his back.

Kirsten shook her head, angry with herself for such thoughts. *Fencing, Kirsten*, she scolded. *Focus on fencing, not his looks.*

They shook hands in the center of the piste, a gesture that raised eyebrows among the experts. It was an unorthodox beginning of a match.

The IOC chairman stood between them, grasped each by a hand, and raised them to the audience, repeating the wave to all four quadrants of the stadium. Stomping feet, clapping, and shouting greeted his theatrics. He handed the microphone to the chief fencing referee.

The referee was formally dressed in a navy blue blazer issued by the IOC with the Olympic seal on the left breast pocket, gray slacks, white shirt, and Olympic tie. He spoke into the microphone, reviewing the rules.

"While this is the first Super Bowl of Fencing," he concluded, "it will be held like any other fencing match, with the usual three three-minute bouts. The only difference will be two minutes rest between each bout, rather than one. Are you both ready?"

Nods.

"Then let's begin the first ever Olympic Super Bowl of Fencing!" He held onto each of the last five words, seeming to savor their taste on his tongue before releasing them to the audience.

Kirsten and László retreated to the ends of the piste, conferred with their coaches, sipped water, and, épée armed, returned to the center of the piste.

The referee spoke into the microphone. "We shall now begin the Olympic Super Bowl of Fencing. May the best man—or woman—win.

"En garde … Prêt …"

Blaring music interrupted and suppressed the *Allez*.

CHAPTER 41

"THE HORST WESSEL SONG" BURST FROM OVERHEAD amplifiers. Music rocked the stadium. TV screens blazed with the Nazi swastika, then showed a chorus of Nazi youths in the Berlin cathedral singing "Horst Wessel," and finally highlighted an old video of Hitler reviewing thousands of troops in the Potsdamer Platz.

Kirsten and László stood motionless, blades hanging at their sides. They removed their facemasks and looked around the stadium, bewildered. From the back of the audience, a group of fifty men materialized, ten rows deep and five across, marching toward them. SA storm troopers goose-stepped in time to the song, brown shirts crisp, pants creased, and shined boots striking the floor as one and reverberating throughout the stadium. Men in the front row and at the sides of the procession streamed Nazi banners and raised Nazi flags high overhead. Right arms stretched to the heavens in the Nazi salute.

TV cameras focused on a blond-haired giant, blue eyes sparkling, leading the group. He strode out front, high-stepping like a drum major, brandishing a towering sword in the air that he pumped to the cadence of the music. The shiny steel caught the overhead lights, sparkling rainbows of color into the seats.

Kirsten stared at the TV screen. Gordo!

Gordo's left chest blazed with buffed WWII medals. Thick gold braids bordering a red armband with a black Nazi swastika in the middle of a white circle identified his rank as Reichsleiter, national leader. The armband circled his huge right bicep. Though the music drowned out his voice, his thick lips synced to the words of "The Horst Wessel Song."

Kirsten and László turned to the referee, who shrugged. "I don't know what in hell's going on. Go back to your seats and wait. We'll start when this has played out." He hurried off, cell phone at his ear, talking rapidly and pointing.

They both paused, not knowing what to do. Kirsten watched László's face, trying to read his expression. His eyes were slits, lips seared in a grim line, and nostrils dilated. His breathing increased, and beads of sweat broke out on his forehead as his chest heaved. He looked from the TV screen to the approaching storm troopers and back to the screen. Abruptly he turned without speaking and walked stiff-legged to his coach, trancelike.

Kirsten rushed to Sharon and Stefan. "It's Gordo," she said, pointing her épée at the storm troopers. "What's going on?"

"'The Horst Wessel Song,'" Stefan answered.

"The what?"

"Horst Wessel was a Nazi Storm Trooper killed by his prostitute's boyfriend. He'd written a poem glorifying the storm troopers that became the official song for the Nazi Party. Sing it publicly in Germany now, and you go to jail."

Kirsten looked around, still puzzled. She gestured toward the TV screens.

"They hijacked the broadcasting booth," Stefan said.

"Where are our guys?" she asked. "This garbage is being broadcast all over Israel!"

Stefan shrugged.

"What do we do now?" Sharon asked. "Where are the cops? This is creepy."

"As long as they're peaceful, I guess we do nothing," Stefan said. "I have no idea why the police aren't reacting." He thought for a moment. "My father. I bet he got to them."

"I'm frightened," Kirsten said. "These guys," she nodded at the approaching storm troopers, "are scary." She stared at Gordo, wondering if he knew who hit him in the head and if he was here for revenge. She looked around for protection but spotted only two Israelis hurrying toward her. She could only hope the rest of Israeli security was somewhere close.

"Stay loose, Kirsten," Sharon ordered, focused on fencing. "Our guys must be here somewhere."

Kirsten jogged in place, trying to keep her muscles warm and flexible. She put on a jacket, stretched, and jabbed her épée at an imaginary target. She glanced at László to see if he was doing the same.

He wasn't. He stood at his end of the piste, dark eyes staring at the advancing storm troopers. He arched the épée in front of him with one hand on the grip and the other on the covered tip, the blade curved almost to breaking. Once, twice, three times he repeated the maneuver, each time letting the épée recoil to its natural shape.

Kirsten saw his face was transformed by a look reflecting another time, another place. Later, when questioned by the police, she could only describe it as otherworldly, menacing.

Suddenly, László ripped the protective rubber plug from the end of his épée. He picked up his fencing mask and started to put it on. Just before he brought it over his face, he looked from it to the Reichsleiter and threw the mask aside with disdain. Then he charged.

Gordo saw him coming and smiled in anticipation. He turned to his troops and ordered, "Halt. Stay here. Do not interfere. I will deal with this personally." He rushed toward László, slicing the air with his sword.

They met on the piste. Seventy-one years after the end of World War II, the first Olympic Super Bowl of Fencing beamed live to TV stations throughout the world became transformed into a life-and-death battle between a Nazi Reichsleiter and a Hungarian Jew.

Fédération Internationale d'Escrime Rules of Fencing did not regulate this battle. Gordo slashed chaotically—no fencing technique, just brute strength. László parried and danced out of the way. Like a boxer fighting a slugger, he jabbed his épée to keep the blond giant at bay. But the slugger brushed aside the lightweight weapon, like the annoyed swatting of a fly. Even so, pinpricks of blood appeared on the Reichsleiter's neck and trickled down his jacket where the épée tip pierced his skin. Still he attacked, the hacking sword making whooshing sounds amplified by the TV microphones.

Despite their command, the storm troopers edged nearer the piste, crowding the fighting pair, perhaps to see better or, more likely, to attack László if their leader became seriously wounded.

As they moved closer, surrounding the piste, another group of men wedged in. All wore yellow Stars of David pinned to their chests, the badge Nazis mandated Jews wear to humiliate and distinguish them from Aryans.

Kirsten recognized men of the IDF and Mossad, as well as Israeli Olympians. Stefan *had* been busy. They insinuated themselves between the storm troopers. They looked marchers in the face, stared into their eyes, and shook their heads: *No, don't even think about interfering,* the expressions said. *Get out of here. Now, while you still can.* They patted bulging jackets and pants pockets, wordlessly warning what would happen if the Nazis didn't obey. Without a word spoken, they dispersed the group, following them to be sure they left peacefully.

A collective gasp rose from the audience when Gordo landed a cutting blow to László's left side. He fell to the ground, gushing blood. The Reichsleiter was over him in an instant, moving in for the kill, sword held in both hands high overhead. At the last instant, László dodged the killing blow, rolling sideways as the blade fell. It found only empty air and thumped off the piste. László regained his feet but held his bleeding side with one hand. Blood oozed through his fingers.

The remaining Israelis pushed forward, preparing to intervene. László shook them off.

Gordo pressed the fight, driving László backward off the piste onto the stadium floor. László's bleeding increased, slowing his movements as blood loss began to take its toll. Still, he parried killing blow after blow, trying to find an opening in the giant's maelstrom of sword thrusts.

As Gordo charged, his foot slipped in László's blood, pooled on the smooth wooden floor. The giant grounded his sword tip a moment to steady himself.

With a lightning thrust, László drove his épée deep into the Reichsleiter's neck, straight through his Adam's apple. The force of the blade severed the spinal column behind, instantly rendering Gordo quadriplegic. Muscles disconnected from their command center became flaccid, paralyzed. The big man crashed to the floor.

Ambulance crews had been ordered to the stadium at the start of "The Horst Wessel Song." They were courtside immediately.

Medics inserted a breathing tube in Gordo and staunched László's pulsing artery. They loaded both fighters into the same ambulance and whisked them to the hospital amid blaring sirens and flashing red lights.

"Hatikvah," the Israeli national anthem, replaced "The Horst Wessel Song" and boomed throughout the stadium.

An elderly gentleman at the back of the audience rose slowly and wobbled against a young man on his right. He regained stability by leaning on a wooden cane, turned, and left.

CHAPTER 42

"KIRSTEN, I'M SO SORRY FOR YOU. ARE YOU okay?" her father, Adam, asked, his voice tremulous over the phone. He had called after the fight ended, as Sharon and Kirsten trammed back to Athletes' Village. Stefan left for his apartment, and they planned to meet later.

"I'm fine, Dad. Not to worry. I was not involved at all. Just a bystander."

"Yes, we saw it on TV in the Orchid Park Plaza. They had a big screen set up, back near the pine trees. Most of Tel Aviv was outside watching. Pretty dramatic for the first Olympic Super Bowl. Revived ugly memories for many Jews."

"I'm sure it did. Sorry I couldn't bring home the trophy."

"What you've accomplished is amazing. A gold medal in your first Olympics! Mom and I couldn't be prouder. Or Grandfather Dietrich, God rest his soul. He would've loved watching his granddaughter take home Olympic gold. Pretty awesome."

"I feel sorry for László Petschauer. He's so talented. He might've won," Kirsten said.

"You would've beaten him."

"Maybe."

"How're they doing?" Adam asked. "Wasn't very pretty at the end."

"Petschauer went to surgery. The surgeon who sewed up my arm operated on him. The word we got was that his spleen was slashed and was removed, along with a rib. But he's going to be okay. Could even fence again after he recovers."

"The Nazi?" her father asked.

"Paralyzed from the neck down. Once he's medically stable, they plan to airlift him to Israel for stem cell injections. If he survives, I guess he'll face charges."

"Incredible, isn't it? A Nazi traveling to Israel to seek help from Jews," Adam said. "I never thought I'd live to see that happen."

"Equally incredible is that we're going to give it," Kirsten answered. "Hitler must be rolling over in his grave."

"I hope so, wherever that grave is. What do you do now? When are you coming home?" Adam asked.

"We have an open day tomorrow, and I'm just going to relax with Stefan. The past few days have been a bit stressful. Closing ceremonies are two days after tomorrow. Since I'm the only Israeli to win gold, I get to carry the flag again."

"How'd the others do?"

"Two bronze, one in gymnastics and one in weight lifting. Better than 2012 but lots of room for improvement," Kirsten said. "We don't invest enough time and money training world-class athletes."

"Tell me," Adam said. "Nothing's changed. Lots of priorities competing for support."

Both fell silent. Kirsten wanted to ask about the diary but was concerned about its effect on her father. Finally she spoke.

"I assume you got my package?"

"I did. What am I supposed to do with it?" he asked.

"You saw what it was?"

"Gave me chills. Mom too. Authentic?"

"Far as I can tell."

"How'd you get it?"

"Long story, but Stefan and I found the original when we visited Hitler's home in Bariloche. I sent you a copy."

"Thanks a bunch," Adam said. "And the original?"

This is what she was afraid of. But she had to let him know in case he was in danger.

"Are you sitting down?"

"Do I need to?"

"Yes."

Pause. "Okay, I'm sitting," Adam said.

"Max Jaeger has it."

A much longer pause. "Dad, you still there?"

Kirsten couldn't make out the garbled response.

"Dad, I didn't get that." Silence. "Dad, are you okay?"

After a few moments, Kirsten's mother, Dannie, came on the line. "Hi, darling. What'd you say to upset Dad?"

"Is he okay?"

"He will be. He got dizzy, and I made him lie down."

Kirsten told her about the diary.

"No wonder. I think I am also."

"Don't go, Mom. Just listen." Kirsten summarized the last few days.

"How frightening. I've never met him, but from what your father's told me, Max hasn't changed. If anything, he's worse. I think you should come home immediately."

"I can't, Mom. The Mossad guys want Stefan and me to act natural. They think Max's got something big planned for the closing ceremony, and they're trying to find out so they can stop him. If we bolt, he'll be spooked, and they won't be able to uncover it."

"Not worth risking your life."

"Actually, it may be, if it saves lots of others."

"What's Sharon think of all this?"

Kirsten looked at Sharon sitting next to her on the tram and winked. "She's a real trouper. She remembers 1972. We'll be okay. They're watching out for us."

"Who're they?"

"Our guys. A Mossad agent now follows us wherever we go." She looked at the young man sitting opposite them and smiled.

Dannie's voice was hesitant. "Okay, but be careful. I don't want anything to happen to my Olympic star."

"Not to worry, Mom. I'll personally bring you my gold medal in a couple of days. Meanwhile, it's probably best to keep silent about the diary. Max's got a long reach, and the less said right now the better. If anything changes, I'll let you know."

"Mum's the word until you get home. In fact, I think I'll put it in our safe deposit box at the bank."

"Good idea." Sharon poked her. They had reached the end of their ride. "Gotta go, Mom. Love you. Tell Dad I hope he's feeling better. See you soon."

"Stay safe. Love you too."

"Are they okay?" Sharon asked as they were leaving the tram.

"My father flipped out when I mentioned Max Jaeger. I knew he would. Except for that, they seem fine. They watched the fight from Orchid Park Plaza."

"Lovely setting, right on the water. Wish we were there."

"You sound like my mother. We'll be home soon enough."

They pushed open the door to their apartment. All had been restored to order, courtesy of the Mossad crime scene guys who'd been there to collect evidence.

"We should hire them for cleaning service," Sharon joked.

"Doubt they do windows."

"Or toilets."

"Maybe they do. Could be DNA there," Kirsten said.

"Speaking of which, any results yet?"

"Still waiting," Kirsten said. "Dr. Shemberg said we'd know by today, tomorrow latest."

"Anxious?"

"Are you kidding? This could be the biggest thing since … since … since I don't know when," Kirsten said.

"What'll you do if it's true?"

"I've asked myself that very question a hundred—no, a thousand times since we found the diary. I still don't know the answer."

CHAPTER 43

MAX JAEGER SAT ALONE AT A CORNER TABLE IN the bar of the Belmond Copacabana Palace Hotel and ordered a second Glenlivet, neat. Though lunch had not yet arrived, he wasn't about to wait for food. His jangled nerves needed—no, *demanded* alcohol. Now.

Stupid Gordo. If only he hadn't slipped, Petschauer would be dead, and that would've been the end of it. No way was a Jew—*any* Jew, man or woman—going to win the first Olympic Super Bowl of Fencing. It cost Max five hundred thousand euros in payoffs to set it up. Gordo had goaded Petschauer as planned, though it took the Hungarian a while to react.

With Petschauer dead, the Closing Ceremony would have been a quiet affair, a parade of Nazi strength touting the birth of the Fourth Reich for the entire world to see. Max had bribed enough people to know it would have been pleasant, peaceful, lots of flag waving, and muscle flexing by tens of thousands of Nazi loyalists marching together in uniform, broadcast live on Olympic TV stations to countries across the globe. A rallying cry to join the jihad against Jews and other inferior races. Gordo's foot slip changed everything.

After his third scotch, Max called Carlos to pick him up. He wasn't as confident in Gordo's assistant, but Max was too unsteady to walk.

He returned to his office and booted up his computer. He smiled when he heard the chimes. He'd made his decision.

"*Beginnen Sie Kristallnacht*," he typed into Facebook, LinkedIn, and Twitter. Begin Kristallnacht. Then he went to take a nap.

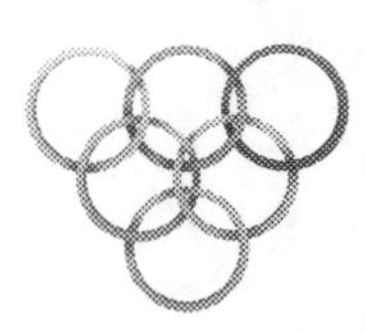

Kristallnacht, the Night of the Broken Glass, struck Jews living in Germany and its annexed territories the evening of November 9, 1938, and continued into the early morning hours of November 10. The Nazis said it was because Herschel Grynszpan, a seventeen-year-old Polish Jew, shot and killed Ernest von Rath, a minor German embassy official, to avenge his parents' unjustified expulsion from Germany. In fact, it was Hitler's excuse to begin the onslaught of the Holocaust.

Storm troopers and Gestapo men plundered and destroyed hundreds of synagogues, thousands of Jewish homes and businesses. Throughout the night, they raped, killed, and imprisoned thirty thousand innocent Jews, sending them to concentration camps like Dachau and Buchenwald. By sunrise, shards of shattered glass littered the streets and sidewalks all over Germany. Concerned that non-Jewish insurance companies would be liable for property losses, the German government decreed the Jews themselves were to blame for the pogrom. The government fined them one billion Reichsmarks ($400,000 USD in 1938 dollars) to pay the cost of repairs.

Jews had inhabited Brazil since the 1500s, prospering under a constitution that mandated religious freedom. The Jewish population had grown to 110,000, tenth in the world, with more than 30,000 living in Rio, even though it was predominantly a Catholic city.

The Rio riots began at sunset. Men dressed as storm troopers and Gestapo, armed with clubs, knives, and guns, roamed in hundreds of groups of four or five, attacking Jewish properties. All thirty synagogues and thousands of businesses and homes were fair game.

Rio's main synagogue, Grande Templo Israelita, became ground zero.

The sacred building sat on peaceful Rue Tenente Possolo in downtown Rio. A cluster of men gathered in front. They talked in whispers and devised a plan.

Moments later, a grapefruit-sized rock soared out of the tranquil sky. It shattered the priceless stained-glass front window, which depicted Abraham offering his son Isaac as a sacrifice before God. Blue, gold, green, and red glass splinters scattered in the evening breeze and carpeted the green grass, shimmering in the moonlight like discarded party baubles. A Molotov cocktail followed, and flames engulfed the old building. Fire engines, racing to extinguish the blaze, slammed on their brakes and whipped a rapid U-turn when bullets strafed their windshields.

Congregants sprinted to save the seven Torahs, four hundred prayer books, and three silver menorahs smuggled from war-torn Germany three-quarters of a century before. Hot, burning cinders drove them away. A wall of flames trapped the rabbi and ten parishioners praying in the sanctuary. They perished in the inferno. Two were cousins, descendants of a family that had escaped the Nazis during WWII.

Rioters danced outside on the street for hours, playing music until flickering flames faltered in early morning.

Three other synagogues, Sinagoga Kehilat Yaacov of Copacabana, Sinagoga Maimonides, and Sinagoga Kehilat Moriah, were burned to the ground while ten others escaped total destruction but suffered heavy damage.

The small groups grew to mob size and roamed downtown Rio, darting about like a flock of birds, swirling first this way and then that, trailing a leader shouting orders into a megaphone.

Clusters of men assimilated, broke apart, and reunited a block later, bent on more destruction.

Stores with obvious Jewish signs, like a kosher delicatessen, or with a Jewish-sounding name like Goldberg and Sons, were immediate targets. Rocks shattered windows, bombs blew doors off hinges, and owners protecting their property were attacked and bludgeoned, lucky to escape with their lives.

Looting was contagious. Jewelry and liquor stores were prime goals and didn't need a Jewish name. General department and appliance stores followed, and soon, most large retail stores were vandalized, regardless of ownership. The streets were filled with people carrying TV sets or lugging washing machines.

Hundreds of Nazis became thousands, and thousands became tens of thousands. They carried blazing torches as the violence escalated. They blocked traffic, overturned police cars, and set them on fire. The pungent smell of burning rubber filled the night air.

Police in riot gear rolled out emergency response units, but they were no match for the numbers of demonstrators that overran barricades and checkpoints. From a command post, police dispensed an arsenal of rubber bullets, water cannons, pepper spray, and tear gas to street patrols to break up the groups. Even where they weren't outnumbered, police merely looked on, turning their backs on violence committed by Nazi friends. Max's bribes had been well distributed.

The chairman of the IOC convened an emergency meeting at ten at night with his committee members. "What can we do?" he asked. "We must protect our athletes, and we have the Closing Ceremony in two days. The Rio police are in way over their heads."

No one had answers. An invasion force bigger than they could handle was capturing the city.

Responsibility spiraled upward along predictable lines. The chief of police, his men outnumbered and outmaneuvered, punted to the Rio mayor. The mayor met with his political leaders who threw up their hands. At one in the morning, they called the president of the Federative Republic of Brazil, who called in the Forças Armadas Brasileiras, IPA, the Brazilian Armed Forces. He was told most were deployed on offshore maneuvers or could not be mobilized in time to help. That bribe alone to the four top generals had cost Max five million euros, a million and a quarter to each. The president finally decided, "Jews were the cause of this. Let them end it. Get Israeli security to help."

Rioting continued through the night but was confined to downtown Rio.

As Tent City inhabitants were about to be bused to private neighborhoods to begin ransacking Jewish homes, dawn broke, and with the emerging light came a sliver of sanity, as if illuminating the dark recesses of the city exposed the same in people's minds.

"*Für jetzt genug*," Max messaged. Enough for now. "We'll resume tomorrow."

CHAPTER 44

THE NEXT MORNING, KIRSTEN SAT IN THE WAR room of the consulate general of the State of Israel. She had received multiple death threats during the night, and Pepé had spirited her, Sharon, and Stefan away from Athletes' Village. They sat together around the large table in the center of the room. The techs, backs turned, were busy typing at their screens, assessing the night's damage.

"They destroyed so much Jewish property," Pepé said. "It was reliving Berlin during the war. Anti-Semitism never stops."

"It's always just beneath the surface. Only takes a nudge," Sharon said.

Pepé stood, conferred with one of the techs, returned, and sat down. "Kirsten, are you ready to come clean with us?" he asked.

She bolted upright. "Meaning what?"

"You know what I mean. Let's quit playing games."

She shook her head. "No, you tell me."

He walked to the tech's computer screen, typed a command, and pulled up a page of text. "The last time you were here, you said something at 4:42 p.m. that piqued my interest."

"And that was?" she asked.

He read from the screen. "You said 'When you find out, would you mind letting me know? I've got lineage at stake.' What did you mean by that?"

Kirsten looked first at Stefan, then at Sharon. She rose from her seat. "You taped our conversation?"

He smiled. "Routine practice in this room. That way, there's no ambiguity about who said what and when. What did you mean?"

She was silent, unsure how to answer, and sat down.

"While you're deciding, let me tell you about some sleuthing we've been doing. What do you know about the woman you're named for, your great-grandmother?"

Kirsten shook her head. "Not much. She lived in Austria. Gave birth to my grandfather, Dietrich, in 1906. He was training for the '36 Olympics when she died. He buried her in the cemetery in her hometown. That's about it."

"And your great-grandfather, what do you know about him?"

"Nothing. I assumed she got pregnant in a one-night stand, and whoever he was dropped out of the picture. Why do you want to know?"

"We're in the middle of riots threatening Rio. The entire city could go up in flames tonight, and I think you might be able to help." He nodded to an assistant who brought over a small package wrapped in brown paper. He set it on the table.

"I hope you don't mind, but I retrieved this from Dr. Shemberg."

She grabbed the package, turned it over, and saw it had been opened. "You're damned right I mind. This is none of your business."

"Kirsten, I hate to use that worn-out line about national security," Pepé said, "but that's what's involved here. You can either tell me everything you know and help stop these Nazi riots, or stay silent and watch thousands of Jewish homes burn tonight. That's what's going to happen. And if it starts here, it may spread to Europe and around the world."

"What makes you think that?"

"At 2:00 a.m. this morning, the Nazis broke into the headquarters of the Jewish Federation of Rio de Janeiro on Copacabana Avenue. Before they torched it, they stole computers with the home addresses of all the prominent Jewish families in Rio. Each had made a donation to the Federation in 2015, and their names and addresses were stored in a database. We think the Nazis will go door-by-door tonight, looting and burning—and maybe raping, kidnapping, or killing—Jewish families. Rio authorities don't have the manpower to stop them." He left unsaid what they all knew. Well-placed bribes had crippled the response.

"Fly in Israel Defense Forces or your Mossad buddies. Maybe get help from the United States. They can't be that far away," Kirsten said.

Pepé spread his hands, palms up. "I wish it were that easy. First, the logistics make it impossible to fly in the number of troops we'd need on such short notice. We're talking many thousands. Second, and most important, Rio authorities won't let us. On the one hand, they're telling us to solve the problem they say we created, and on the other hand, they won't let us fly in reinforcements. 'Would look bad to the world if we can't handle our own domestic problem,' they're saying."

"This is unbelievable," Stefan said. "No country would tolerate a Nazi takeover."

"Unbelievable or not, that's what's happening," Pepé said. "This isn't France or Germany. Remember—the Nazi Party is legal in Argentina and tolerated here."

"Don't they have a national guard or armed forces or something?" Stefan asked.

"They do but not available," Pepé said.

Kirsten toyed with the cardboard package. "What do you want from me?"

"Open the package, and we'll talk."

She opened it. Eva Braun's hairbrush, Adolf Hitler's mustache comb, and a cellophane envelope with a lock of her own hair sat inside. At the bottom of the box lay an unopened letter addressed to her, sealed and marked confidential.

"I didn't open that," Pepé said, pointing to the letter.

"Thanks a bunch," Kirsten said.

"Before you open it," Pepé said, "let me tell you what else we've found out about your great-grandmother."

Kirsten set the box aside.

Pepé glanced at pages of notes in front of him. "She came from a working-class Jewish family and was a waitress or a barmaid at the Bummerlhaus in Steyr, Austria. Steyr is an old industrial city—more than a thousand years old—in northern Austria. In the middle of the town is the Bummerlhaus, a gothic building dating back to the fifteenth century. It served as an inn."

Pepé paced in front of the table, excitement in his voice, notes discarded.

"Your great-grandmother was around twenty when she worked there, got pregnant, and gave birth to your grandfather in 1906. After she had Dietrich, she worked at the Bummerlhaus a few months, then stopped and lived off a pension or something until she died in 1936 at about age fifty. She's buried in the Jewish Cemetery in Steyr. Her gravestone—very large and beautifully carved, by the way—lists her name, Kirsten Becker, date of birth and death, that's all. Your great-grandfather's name, however, is lost to history."

"There must be town records. Someplace, even back then, had to record births and deaths," Sharon said.

He stopped pacing a moment. "Yes, the Steyr Town Hall. Allied bombs totally demolished it during the war, and all records burned."

"Then all you've established is that great-grandmother Kirsten was Jewish, had no husband, and the father's identity is unknown."

He shrugged. "Basically, that's true."

"I knew all that," Kirsten said.

He nodded. "If you were so certain, why did you ask Dr. Shemberg to send hair samples from Hitler's comb and Eva's brush for a genetic analysis, along with a sample of your own?"

She stared at him. "You tell me."

Pepé hesitated and then leaned on the table across from Kirsten, supported by his palms, his face inches from hers.

"Because you thought your grandfather Dietrich might be Hitler's son; your father, Adam, his grandson; and you, Hitler's great-granddaughter."

Everyone stared at Kirsten.

After a moment, Pepé continued. "I think Adolf Hitler, a teenager at the time, was your great-grandmother Kirsten's one-night stand at the Bummerlhaus, just as Hitler told Eva, and as she wrote in her diary."

"You've seen her diary?" Kirsten asked, surprised.

"Your father's been very cooperative."

"He didn't tell me."

Pepé nodded. "He didn't have time to tell you. The diary's all hearsay, anyway. Fascinating reading, but the real proof is in that unopened envelope, which I assume is an analysis of the genes from the hair samples you gave Dr. Shemberg." Pepé picked up the envelope and dropped it on the table in front of Kirsten.

The room fell deathly quiet. No one moved. Even breathing seemed suspended. The techs stopped typing and turned around. Every eye focused on Kirsten. She felt paralyzed, only her eyes darting from Sharon to Stefan and back again.

Kirsten's fingers inched toward the envelope. Her forefinger and thumb made contact, barely touching, as if the envelope was hot and could burn. She held it to the light but couldn't see through it. She closed her eyes for a moment, and her lips moved silently, perhaps in prayer. Then she slipped her forefinger beneath the flap and peeled back the seal. The paper yielded with a soft tearing sound magnified as the only noise in the room. Slowly she extracted several pages filled with lines of genetic symbols. The last page was a letter from Dr. Shemberg explaining the results.

As she read, her face turned ashen, and the paper shook uncontrollably in her hand. She tried to take a sip of coffee, but her cup wobbled so much, she couldn't bring it to her mouth. She looked at Sharon, then at Stefan. Her mouth opened, but no sound emerged. The cup crashed to the floor as Kirsten fainted.

She woke to Stefan holding smelling salts under her nose. She shook her head and sneezed. She rubbed her nose and tried to sit up on the floor, but Stefan gently pushed her back down.

"Wait a minute or two to get your bearings."

She pushed his hand away. "I've got my bearings. Let me up. I feel ridiculous down here." She stood, but her rubbery knees failed, and she collapsed again. Stefan caught her and helped her to a chair. He elevated her legs on a footstool until color seeped back into her face. The entire room was looking at her.

"Well, that was interesting," she said, wiping her pale, sweaty face with a wet washcloth Pepé handed her. "I've never fainted before." She managed a wry smile. "I don't recommend it."

"Can we get you anything?" Pepé asked. "Water or more coffee? You didn't like the last cup." They all laughed as he pointed to the dark wet stain in the rug.

"Thanks, but I'm fine now. Stupid reaction, like some southern belle in *Gone with the Wind*. Sorry, everybody." She looked at the carpet. "Send me the cleaning bill."

Kirsten stood, wobbled a bit, kept her balance, and walked to the center table.

She picked up Hitler's comb, stared at it a moment, and said, "Hello, Great-Grandfather, you lying, murderous, malevolent son of a bitch. I can't believe you're a part of my family." She put the comb down and held up Eva's hairbrush. "I guess you're my step-great-grandmother, if there's any such thing."

"That explains why your great-grandmother had support while raising Dietrich," Pepé said. "And her big headstone."

"Even more than that," Kirsten said. "It explains why my grandfather had total backing for three years to train for the Berlin Olympics. Hitler was hoping his son would win a medal. And why the government sustained my grandmother and my father after Grandfather's suicide. I always thought it was because of Lutz Long," she continued, "but it must've been Hitler. He's why they survived the war."

"Hitler saving Jews while trying to eradicate the entire population?" Stefan said in disbelief.

"They were family," Sharon said sarcastically.

Kirsten picked up the paper from Shemberg and continued to read. "There's more. While the genetic analysis clearly makes him my great-grandfather, it also says that all three of us—Hitler, Eva, and I—have something, a genetic marker, on our DNA called the haplogroup N1b1, which is, the letter reads, 'strongly associated with Ashkenazi Jews from central and Eastern Europe.' It looks like we all have Jewish blood."

"I'm sure that'll make the Nazis very happy," Stefan said.

CHAPTER 45

PEPÉ CHECKED HIS WATCH. "IT'S NOON. WE CAN grab some lunch—send out for sandwiches—while we strategize how to exploit Kirsten's lineage. In my opinion, she must be presented as the new leader of the Nazi movement. That's the only way to head off the rioting once the sun sets."

"Good luck with that," Stefan said, frowning.

"I know," Pepé said, looking at Stefan. "Your father's not going to take this lying down."

"That's an understatement," said Stefan. "The old man will throw a fit."

Pepé shrugged. "If you or anybody else has other suggestions, speak up. I'm open to new ideas."

No one said anything.

"We do have some good news," Pepé said. "The government has given us permission to use national TV, and the president himself may speak. All the stations are covering the Olympics, so we'll get the exposure we need."

"What in the world are you talking about?" Kirsten asked. "What exposure?"

"For you," Pepé said.

"Are you saying you want me to be on TV?"

"How else will we get the word out?" Pepé said.

"What word," Kirsten replied, still disoriented from the fall and not paying attention.

"The truth," Pepé said. "You are the rightful heir to the title as the legitimate leader of the Nazi Party."

Dizzy and now coping with a horrendous headache, Kirsten heard Pepé's words, but her mind was elsewhere. Stunned, she was fixated on the letter and Dr. Shemberg's diagnosis that "... the genetic analysis clearly makes Hitler ..." *My great-grandfather? That murderous, malignant son of a bitch is actually part of my family. I'm part of his ...* She buried her face in her hands.

"Kirsten?" Pepé said, leaning in. "Are you okay? Did you hear what I said? You must go on national TV and tell them."

"That I'm related to the most reviled person on earth?" Kirsten answered. "On national TV?"

"I'm open to other suggestions," Pepé again said. "I know the facts are hard to deal with, but I don't see any other option."

Kirsten stared vacantly ahead, still disoriented.

"I just can't believe what I'm hearing," Kirsten said. "Even if I agree to do this Nazi thing, I've never been on TV before."

"Your match was on TV," Stefan said.

She shook her head. "That's not what I meant. I mean, just talking, not fencing. I've never done that."

"Nervous?" Pepé asked.

"Yes."

He brushed it aside. "No need. We'll write out your talk in the next several hours, and then you can read the script from the teleprompters. No big deal."

"You make it sound too easy."

"It is. Trust me."

"Trust you? Ha. Trusting you is what got us into this mess in the first place."

Pepé chuckled. "I told you *not* to visit Estancia Inalco," he said. "I can't help it if you didn't take my advice."

"Right," she said, pushing back from the table. She stood, tottered a moment, and then caught her balance. "Pepé, I need some time to process. This is all happening too fast."

He started to interrupt, but she silenced him, hand up, palm forward.

"Don't misunderstand me. I realize the seriousness of the situation, and what could happen tonight is horrific. But what you're asking—" Kirsten looked around the room, all eyes again focused on her.

"It's not just being on TV," she said. "That doesn't thrill me, but I suppose I can handle it. But you're asking me to step forward as the heir and rightful leader of the most diabolical organization the world has ever known—even compared to Muslim extremists. Beheadings are subhuman, but the scope of the Nazi atrocities during the Holocaust was on a scale unprecedented in human history. The death camps, the unimaginable cruelty and depravity, the gassing with Zyklon B, the crematoria—" She shuddered, head pounding. "Nazi barbarism never stopped and puts ISIS to shame." She looked to Stefan.

He put his arms around her and hugged. She smiled, seemed to gain strength, and continued.

"How can I have anything to do with them?" she cried. "Even today saying the N-word makes me want to spit, brush my teeth, and gargle with an antiseptic. Pure filth. How can I shake the memories and feelings I had when I visited Auschwitz and Estancia Inalco?"

Stefan squeezed her gently. "Yes, I know, Kirsten. But remember how you told me being at those places was also a triumph for you, defying Hitler and what he stood for, trampling his grave. You said it was a victory for humanity. Imagine how he'd feel knowing a Jew—a woman, even—was leading his precious Nazi Party. You didn't walk through his house, but this would be your ultimate victory."

She gave him a weak smile.

Stefan continued. "You asked me then to feel what you're feeling, the intensity of it. I do now. Kirsten, you're the only hope to prevent a certain massacre tonight."

"Why should they listen to me?" Kirsten asked.

"Lineage is crucial," Pepé said. "We've researched that. Most Nazis, especially the younger ones, consider Hitler godlike, like Muslims venerate Muhammad. A direct descendent will inherit Hitler's title, his throne, and his influence. They'll listen. Besides, you're our only hope."

No one spoke.

Pepé extended his arms, palms up, and shrugged. “Like I said, I’m open to other suggestions.”

As before, no one had any.

CHAPTER 46

THREE HOURS LATER, THE CAMERAS OF REDE Globo, the second largest commercial TV network in the world, TV Brasil, and Nacional Brasil zoomed in on the president of the Federative Republic of Brazil. Alberte Hernandez sat behind a polished wooden desk in his presidential office, flanked by the national flag of Brazil on his right and that of Israel on his left. A banner with the five interlocking Olympic rings hung on the wall behind. Teleprompters positioned off each front corner of the desk were barely visible.

Dark-featured, Hernandez had a short gray beard and mustache and comb-over gray hair. Always conscious of looking presidential, he wore a navy blue suit, white shirt, and a solid maroon tie. A tiny replica of the Brazilian national flag, a blue disc with a starry sky, sat in a lapel buttonhole. To avoid appearing too removed from his subjects, an inexpensive Timex with a leather band replaced his Rolex President Day Date gold wristwatch.

"Ladies and gentlemen," he began in a somber tone, speaking Portuguese. A translator in a booth off-camera repeated in English. "Thank you for letting me speak to you this afternoon. I know it is an interruption of your normal daily activities. But we need to talk." He pushed back from the desk a bit and tried to look more relaxed. The interrupted sleep and strain of last night's events showed in the lines around his eyes and the set of his mouth.

"Regardless of the cause," he began, "the riots we experienced are unprecedented in the history of Brazil. Our constitution since 1824 recognizes and protects religious freedom as one of the basic principles governing our lives. The constitution does not distinguish between faiths; all are treated equally in our country.

"For members of the Nazi Party to inflict such barbaric behavior on our Jewish population cannot be tolerated. This is not 1938 Germany. I never thought I'd see Kristallnacht reenacted in the country we love and live in, perpetrated on innocent and peaceful neighbors and friends. My fellow citizens, how *could* you participate? Why *would* you participate? What is the sense of brutality for the sake of brutality? Of hurting people because they are different or don't believe as you do? How could you think they are inferior to some artificial, mad Aryan world of your own creation? How could you destroy property for the fun of it? As you found out, destruction spreads and impacts non-Jews as well.

"Our government has known for some time that a German named Max Jaeger has been supporting a resurgence of the Nazi Party in South America, mainly Argentina and here in Brazil. We have tolerated his actions as long as they were peaceful. And if you want to believe in a Fourth Reich, that's fine, as long as it does not encroach the rights and properties of others. Cross that line, you break the law, and that will not be tolerated.

"The perpetrators who did that last night will be found and punished. We will hunt down all of them.

"You need to reconsider who your leader is—or should be. Maybe Max Jaeger is not the one you should follow."

Hernandez paused and tried to smile into the camera.

"I want to introduce to you a woman named Kirsten Becker." He turned to look at Kirsten sitting beside him. The cameras widened their angle to include her in the shot.

"Some of you may recognize Kirsten as the winner of the Olympic gold medal for women's fencing several days ago. You also might know she is from Israel, and is, naturally, Jewish. There is some interesting precedent for this. In the 1936 Olympics in Berlin, a Jewish woman named Helene Mayer won a silver medal fencing for Germany. A German national, Mayer had been living in America when Hitler invited her—a Jew—back to fence for Germany in the Olympics. Being Jewish was not a problem when he wanted to win an Olympic medal."

He paused and smiled at Kirsten. "What you don't know about Kirsten Becker is what I will now tell you."

He again stopped and looked deadeye into the camera. The view tightened, and every line on his face was visible. He held up the letter from Shemberg and waved the paper in front of the cameras.

"Kirsten Becker is the great-granddaughter of Adolf Hitler." He waited a moment, allowing time for his words to sink in.

"Many of you will not believe me, but the genetic proof is right here in my hand. It is incontrovertible, established by two independent genetic laboratories, one in Rio and the other in São Paulo, and verified by professors of genetics in both cities." He read from the paper. "Professor Gabriel Calvalcanti at the University of São Paulo and Professor Matheus Ferreira at the Federal University of Rio de Janeiro have staked their reputations on this."

Kirsten struggled to focus on the words Hernandez was saying and how she would respond.

Hernandez went on. "The genetic experts have also concluded that Hitler himself had Jewish blood running through his veins. That fact, too, is irrefutably authenticated by these experts through DNA analysis." He waved the paper again.

"Every time you brutalize Jews because they are Jewish, you are brutalizing the memory of your hero, the founder of the Nazi Party, Adolf Hitler. Think about that the next time you contemplate burning your Jewish neighbor's house, business, or synagogue. You are doing it to him too."

He stopped and stared into the cameras, letting his passion cool a little. "I hope you all will consider my words carefully. End this insanity. The future of Brazil is at stake. Do not jeopardize it and your own future. I will now ask Kirsten Becker to speak to you."

The TV cameras turned to Kirsten. She was wearing a simple white blouse and the blue skirt she had on when Pepé picked her up early this morning. She wore no jewelry and had to borrow lipstick from Sharon.

Kirsten sat silent a moment, staring into the camera lenses, trying to compose herself. Her throat was dry, and her heart was racing. Could she do this? Leader of the Nazi Party? Should she? Would that be a betrayal of all she believed as a Jew? But how could she not help save Jewish families from an onslaught tonight?

Someone off-camera pointed at her. She was now live.

CHAPTER 47

"HELLO," KIRSTEN BEGAN IN ENGLISH, VOICE tremulous. The translator switched to Portuguese as the cameras zoomed in. Kirsten focused her eyes on the teleprompter and tried to appear natural while reading the printed lines.

"As you heard from President Hernandez, my name is Kirsten Becker. I came to Brazil for no other reason than to fence in the Olympics. If someone had told me I was related to the most contemptible, depraved man who ever walked on this planet, I would not have believed him. I had no inkling whatsoever about Hitler being a relative and only stumbled into this role after a friend and I visited Hitler's house, Estancia Inalco, in Bariloche, Argentina."

She told viewers about her visit and the events since. The teleprompter kept pace with her; when she sped or slowed, the typed lines did as well—until the teleprompter screeched, and the screen went blank. The man behind the controls shrugged, arms in the air, and then bent over the machine with a screwdriver.

She panicked. *What should I do*? She ran fingers through her hair, twirling a wayward curl, trying to think, stalling a moment. From somewhere, words spoken more than two thousand years ago came to her, reassured and calmed her, and she knew exactly what she had to do.

"A famous rabbi named Hillel once said, '*If I am not for myself, who is for me? And being for my own self, what am I? And if not now, when?*'"

Repeating the words made her feel like Hillel was talking to her—or through her. "So, I have to help, now, in any way I can, and try to make you realize what you are doing and the horrible consequences of your actions.

"All this is as new to me as it is to you. I didn't ask for the role. In truth, I would have refused, except for what Max Jaeger has planned for tonight. Over the years, the Jewish people have learned that when an enemy says he plans to destroy us, believe him and unite to fight him. I must try to prevent a second night of Kristallnacht." She stopped, sipped from a water glass, and took a deep breath.

"I didn't ask to become the leader of the Nazi Party. Certainly, as a Jew, that would be inconceivable. But as a direct descendent of Hitler, that may be my role, like it or not. If it is to be, then I implore you, I ask you, and as your new leader I *order* you: go back to your homes, to your families and jobs, to the meaningful things in your lives. If you want to be a Nazi, I can't stop you, but create a new order, not one that perpetuates the hate my great-grandfather started, founded on the false belief that anyone is a superior race. Superior to what? To whom? How could my great-grandfather advocate being superior to Jews when he was one? It makes no sense. Stop the bloodshed. Stop the destruction. Stop the anti-Semitism."

The teleprompter coughed into life, then died again, but she was on a roll and didn't need it. Her university religious studies helped.

"Why single out the Jews, anyway? If you want to better the world, why not focus on countries and governments that kill their own people, torture and imprison dissenters, oppress women, and commit unspeakable atrocities and crimes against humanity? Why focus on Jews who have created a democratic nation in the Middle East based on values similar to your own, with social equality for men and women, freedom of press and speech, an independent judiciary, and the rule of law? Redirecting your energies at oppressive regimes could be a new goal for all of you. I would be proud to help lead that kind of humane effort.

"But," she paused for emphasis, "and there's a big *but*. The name, Nazi, and Third Reich, or even Fourth Reich, are abhorrent to Jews and many Gentiles alike. The names strike terror and revulsion into our hearts, though it's been almost seventy-five years since the concentration camps and the atrocities. The jackboots, the uniforms, even for our younger generation that did not personally experience the horrors, are repugnant and need to be changed. So, the first challenge would be to rename our effort, to call it something that focuses on humanity and not depravity, and to choose a life style that reflects our goals. Those of you with creative minds, come up with a new name, a new set of core values, and a new look."

She hesitated and was about to continue when a sudden noise to her left caught her attention. She glanced over, saw nothing, and returned to the TV cameras.

"Look at me," she said, staring directly into the camera lens. "I am no different than you. I have the same eyes, ears, and mouth," she said, touching her face, "to see, hear, and speak, the same as you. I want the same things you do, a loving family, a productive life, to be healthy, to raise and educate my children, and to live in peace. Can't we work together to make that happen? I hope so." Her eyes misted over, and she wiped a tear trickling down her cheek.

"That's all I have to say. Go home and do good. May you all prosper and turn an unacceptable Fourth Reich movement into an initiative benefitting all humankind, not destroying it. Build, don't demolish. Thank you." Kirsten swiveled to shake hands with the president when the door to the office flew open and a figure burst into the room.

CHAPTER 48

"HOW DARE YOU! HOW *DARE* YOU!" MAX SCREAMED at Kirsten, barging into the president's office and pounding the desk top with his cane. Hernandez shoved his chair back in alarm. An aide hustled the president out of the office. The TV cameras swiveled to catch the action.

Max stood in front of her, his face contorted in anger. He spit his words at her. "Who do you think you are, passing yourself off as the führer's great-granddaughter? Proclaiming yourself the leader of—of *my* organization? How darc you? Are you insane, or just incredibly stupid to think I would let this happen?"

Two security guards entered the office, hands raised over their heads, followed by Carlos holding a gun at their backs. "Sit down on the floor over there," he ordered, nodding to the corner furthest from his boss. "Don't move and don't make a sound." He followed them, and when they were on the floor, he leaned back against the wall near them, gun at his side.

"If I order my legions to attack Jewish homes, they will do so as loyal members of the party. Obedience is sacred. Nothing you can say or do will prevent—"

Stefan pushed his way into the office. He, Sharon, and Pepé were waiting outside for the end of the broadcast when Max and Carlos, gun drawn, overpowered the guards and charged in. Pepé remained in the foyer a moment longer than the others. He moved to a corner, turned his back, and spoke softly into his iPhone.

"What in hell are you doing?" Stefan shouted, and ran toward Max. Carlos blocked him. Stefan tried to push past and got a gun butt to his chest that sent him spinning into a chair.

"You sound like a senile old man raving and ranting about the past," Stefan said, rubbing his chest and pointing at his father. "You and Hitler and your Nazi buddies killed millions. That's done. Over. You're dethroned, old man. As President Hernandez and Kirsten said, this is time for a new party."

Max turned to his son, a sneer on his face. "Old man, certainly, but hardly senile. What if I told them about you and this … this woman murdering Lobo in Bariloche? Or about the Amber Room you've got hidden? What then?"

Stefan rolled his eyes. "I'd say you were crazy, hallucinating, maybe smoking something. Or senile. I don't know what in hell you're talking about. Neither does Kirsten." He dared a quick look at her.

She nodded as the cameras spun from Stefan to Max to her.

"Lies," Max shouted. "All lies." He turned to the cameras. "All you people out there, listen to me. *I* am your leader, not this …" He looked at Kirsten and shook his finger at her. "This piece of Jewish trash from Israel. *I* supported our Nazi movement in South America and built it to what it is. *I* constructed our building as a monument to our führer. *I* have—" He stopped suddenly, short of breath. Panting, he put a hand over his chest. Beads of sweat dotted his forehead, and he leaned heavily on his cane.

Stefan saw the signs. Worried, he moved toward his father. Carlos blocked him again.

"You talk about lineage," Max said between breaths. "I go back almost to the very origins of our party. My father, Otto—your grandfather," he said, pointing at Stefan, "was a favorite of Hitler who chose him to race in the Berlin Olympics."

"That's garbage, Max, and you know it." It was Kirsten's turn to shout. "My grandfather Dietrich was Hitler's son. Hitler supported him for three years of training to race in those Olympics."

"Ah yes, the one who 'tripped and hit his head,' poor man. That was the family lie, wasn't it?" Max retorted, pounding his cane. "To hide your grandfather's suicide because he was weak and couldn't handle the stress of losing."

"Isn't that what history books say Hitler did?" Kirsten said. "Committed suicide by poisoning Eva Braun and shooting himself because he couldn't cope with losing World War II?"

Max allowed a tight smile and shook his cane at her. "I said once you'd be a good lawyer." He then frowned and flipped the back of his hand at her. "But don't presume to compare your grandfather with the führer, even in suicide." He paused. "Besides, those history books are wrong. Hitler didn't commit suicide. You visited his house."

Max paused a fraction of a second. "Maybe your grandfather didn't either."

Kirsten gasped. "What are you talking about?"

"Nothing." He turned away, shaking his head. "A slip of the tongue. Stefan's right. Maybe I'm getting senile."

"The Reichsleiter slipped, not you," Kirsten said. "What did you mean?"

He stopped, his eyes studying her. "You want to know? I'll tell you what I mean. That snivelly Jew grandfather of yours didn't have the courage to commit suicide. He should have, considering how poorly he performed, but he didn't."

"But he left a note."

"Stupid woman. Anybody can leave a note. You *really* want to know what happened?"

Kirsten nodded.

"My father killed him. Otto hung him by his racing shoelaces—after making him scribble a farewell at the bottom of Himmler's letter."

Kirsten was stunned, speechless. She needed a moment to recover. Then she asked, "But why?"

"Because my father was the first alternate to race if Dietrich got sick. Father wanted to win a medal for the führer, and he knew he could run faster than Dietrich. My father raced well, but that black guy still beat him."

Kirsten sat motionless, staring at Max. "How do you know this?"

"My father told me. Suicide was a good alibi all these years. But when you try to compare suicide of a lowly Jew with even rumors of our führer's suicide—I can't let that go unchallenged. Completely unacceptable."

No one moved. The cameras panned from one person to the other, uncertain where the next action would be.

Kirsten broke the spell. "Thank you, Max. If viewers weren't convinced before, they should be now. Ladies and gentlemen, I ask you," she said, turning to the cameras. "Do you want a leader proud of a murder his father committed and got away with? Obviously, the millions of other murders the Nazis committed during the war make this one an insignificant speck. But this one was personal, very personal, fueled by jealousy and revenge, and long before the war began."

"Why, you Jewish bitch, twisting things around," Max roared, raising his cane to strike her.

Before he could, Stefan barreled into his father, his face distorted in anger. They went down in a tangle of arms and legs. Carlos jumped forward, gun raised.

"Hold it right there, Carlos," Pepé shouted, flanked by two Mossad agents, each holding a TAR-21 assault rifle aimed at Carlos. "Move a muscle and you're a dead man."

Carlos stopped.

"Drop your gun and get down on your knees, hands behind your back," Pepé commanded. Carlos eyed the guns trained at him and obeyed. The Mossad men cuffed him and dragged him from the office.

The cameras panned to Stefan and Max on the floor. Stefan was kneeling alongside his father, performing CPR. Stefan's face was contorted, a mixture of anger and remorse. He thrust his hands against Max's chest, pushing down on his heart, trying to revive it, mumbling, "C'mon, live, you bastard. Live, Father."

Max was nonresponsive. With each passing minute, the cyanosis deepened around his lips, spread to his face, became dull gray, then almost black.

After several minutes, Stefan shook his head, stood, and looked down at his father's dead body. Kirsten took his hand.

"Death is sad, some more than others. But this one—I don't know," he said, eyes searching Kirsten's face. "I'm mixed up, in knots. I hardly knew him, and what I knew, I didn't like, and now I hate. But he was my father."

"I love you," Kirsten said, hugging him.

"And I love you too," Stefan replied, "and want to marry you and have babies with you."

"We will," she said.

"But what will our children be like? You carry Hitler's genes," Stefan said, shaking his head, "and I carry his. We could have monsters."

"Or leaders who will change the world for the good?" she said.

CHAPTER 49

THE PARADE OF ATHLETES THROUGH THE Maracanã Stadium ended, and the final entertaining routines by Brazilian performers were over. Only thanks from the IOC chairman remained.

"Ladies and gentlemen, we draw to a close these XXXI Summer Olympiad Games in Rio de Janeiro. I would like to thank you all for attending, the athletes for competing, and in particular, our women's fencing gold medalist, Kirsten Becker from Israel. She played a big role in these games, bigger than any of you will know. The Olympics and all of Rio are very indebted to her.

"She asked me for a favor, one which I will gladly perform and which should have been done years ago. I would like to formally recognize the eleven Israeli athletes brutally killed in the 1972 Olympics held in Munich. Terrorists captured and murdered these brave men in cold blood. We will honor them now in a moment of silence, all flags at half-mast, and we will do the same at the beginning of every summer Olympics henceforth. We vow to do everything in our power to prevent such an episode in the future. From this time forward, the Olympics will include a moment of recognition for all our fallen athletes. It is the right thing to do for these outstanding men and women who have given their lives for their sport."

He bowed his head, as did attendees in the stands. Sharon held back her sobs, but wet tears fell onto her sweater. She hugged Kirsten and whispered in her ear, "Thank you, dearest Kirsten. I thank you, and so does my Levi."

The IOC chairman continued. "I now declare these Olympic games to be over. I hope to see you in Tokyo, Japan, for the XXXII 2020 Summer Olympic Games. In the meantime, be peaceful, do good works, and God bless you all."

"Will you marry me?" Stefan asked Kirsten that night at the Restaurante Aprazivel, over a shrimp dish of *bobó de camarão*."

She took a bite. "Hmm, good. We had this the last time we were here."

"We did. A lifetime ago," he said.

"It was."

"Well?" he asked.

"Will you fence with me?" she asked.

"Of course," he said.

"Let me win?"

"Won't need to. You're better than I am."

"When?"

"Whenever you want to fence."

"No, silly," Kirsten said. "I mean when do you want to get married?"

"Now."

"Here or home?"

"You decide."

"Here," she said. "How about in two days? Gives us a chance to fly my folks in, and your mother."

"Okay. Where?"

"I know a beautiful room of carved amber and glittering jewels that would be perfect. Lots of people would enjoy seeing it after so many years."

"Not too far from here?" he asked, grinning.

"A little, but plenty of plane flights every day."

"Probably have to buy a pass from some guy named Jorge at the tourist bureau in Bariloche," he said.

"Got enough money?" she asked.

He nodded. “One hundred and fifty US dollars, unless he’s raised his rates again.”

“It was $175 last time.”

“Yeah, but that included twenty-five dollars for directions. I don’t need them anymore.”

“Okay, then. Done,” Kirsten said, leaning across the table for a kiss.

CHAPTER 50

"YOU WERE SPECTACULAR," HER FATHER SHOUTED over the phone, as if he needed a loud voice to carry from Tel Aviv. "The whole scene in the president's office was on national TV. We were frightened when Max came at you, but your new friend—what's his name, Stefan?—was quite the hero."

Kirsten laughed and motioned for Stefan to sit beside her. They were all back in the war room at the Israeli consulate for final good-byes, gathered around the center table, now bare. She angled the phone against her ear so Stefan could listen.

"Yes, he's done that a few times. Saving me is his role in life." She smiled at Stefan, and he kissed her cheek.

"Tell him he's doing a good job protecting the girl I love," Adam said.

"He loves me too. You can tell him yourself." She handed the phone to Stefan.

Stefan kissed her lightly on the lips as he took the phone.

"Hello …" Stefan hesitated, unsure how to address Adam. "Hello, Mr. Becker. It's nice to meet you, even over the phone."

"Hello, Stefan. And please, it's Adam. But any guy saving my daughter can call me Papa."

"Then Papa it is. It's been a real pleasure saving her. We've had some interesting times."

"Sounds like it. Be sure and bring her back in one piece."

"I promise."

"Dannie and I look forward to meeting you."

"Me too … Papa."

Kirsten took back the phone. “We want to talk to you about that. How’re you feeling?”

“Great, why?” her father asked.

“Strong enough to fly here?”

“We agreed I shouldn’t make the trip for the Olympics, but now you want me to travel to Rio?” Adam asked.

“How about for your only daughter’s wedding?” Kirsten said, eyes smiling.

Adam said, “Am I hearing what I think I’m hearing? For that, of course! Wait, let me get Mama.”

There was a moment of silence until Dannie got on the phone, bubbling. “You’re getting married? My Kirsten’s getting married? So quick? Tell me everything.”

Twenty minutes later, Dannie said, “Of course we’re coming. Papa’s been doing really well, and I’m sure he can make the trip. Wait, he’s grabbing the phone from me.”

Adam was back on. “Like Mama said, we’re coming. And maybe a second wedding at the Wailing Wall when you come home? What do you think?”

Kirsten looked at Stefan. He nodded.

“A wonderful idea, Papa. We’ll do it.”

“We’re so proud of you winning the gold medal, and now a wedding too. And, by the way, I want to compliment you on your Academy Award performance before Max attacked. You should win an Oscar. Max looked so old, didn’t he? It’s not surprising he died.”

Kirsten’s pushed back a red ringlet. “Wait, wait. You’re talking too fast for me. Thanks for the compliments. Yes, Max did look old. And, no, I guess it wasn’t surprising the strain killed him. But what Academy Award performance? What are you talking about?”

“About being Hitler’s great-granddaughter.”

Kirsten’s face blanched, and her brow furrowed. “Wait. I still don’t know what you’re talking about.” She looked at Stefan, his face next to hers, listening on the phone. He shrugged.

"I may be his grandson—we're waiting on my genetic analysis—but regardless, you cannot be his great-granddaughter. Didn't Pepé tell you?"

"Papa, I don't have the foggiest idea what you're talking about." She took the phone, pushed back from the table, and began pacing. Her eyes flitted about, unfocused. She tried to swallow, but her throat was dry. "Tell me what? Please explain."

"I told Pepé all of it when we talked."

"Papa, what? *What* did you explain to Pepé?" Exasperation showed on her face and in her voice.

She mouthed to Pepé, "What is he talking about?"

Pepé sat stone-faced.

"Wait, let me put Mama back on. It's difficult for me to talk about," Adam said.

Several moments later, Kirsten said, "Mama, this is killing me. For God's sake, what is it? What's going on?"

"I understand, Kirsten," Dannie said. "But slow down, and I'll tell you. It's difficult. We should have told you before."

"*Told me what*?" Kirsten shouted into the phone, heart pounding.

"I had trouble conceiving, darling, after your Papa and I got married. He was older, and there was something wrong with his sperm—because of his age, the doctors said. And we desperately wanted a baby, so we used a sperm bank. All we know is that the donor was young, Jewish, educated, and from a good Jerusalem family. We were told he was handsome and had red hair."

Kirsten didn't hear any more. She dropped the phone as waves of dizziness hit her. This time, Stefan was at her side, grabbed her in a bear hug, and eased her back into her chair.

"I'm okay," Kirsten said, pushing against Stefan a moment later. "Not like last time. But these spells are getting to be a nuisance."

He picked up the phone and handed it to her.

"Mama, are you still there?" Kirsten asked. "I dropped the phone."

"I'm here. Are you all right?" Dannie asked.

"Fine, just shocked—and I guess relieved."

"Nothing's changed," Dannie said. "You know we couldn't love you any more than we do, that—"

"It's okay, Mama, I know all that. Not to worry. Nothing's changed ... but everything has."

"I understand, darling. We love you and can't wait to see you."

Kirsten stared hard at Pepé. She was now anxious to get off the phone and confront him. "Me too, Mama. We'll be in touch later today about the plane flights. See you soon. Give my love to Papa. Bye."

Kirsten hadn't taken her eyes off Pepé. She leaned across the table and shook her finger at him. "You better start talking and better make it good. You have humiliated me in front of ... in front of the entire world!"

Pepé shrugged, unruffled. "I had no choice. You were the only one who could stop the riots, but only if you were Hitler's great-granddaughter. When your father told me about the sperm donor, I had to make a decision, and with Dr. Shemberg's help, I did what I did. There was no way I could let any of you know, because you couldn't have carried it out as convincingly as you did."

"What did Shemberg do?" Stefan asked.

Pepé glanced at him but returned his gaze to Kirsten. "The Mossad has a lot of talent at its disposal. With Shemberg's help, we falsified your genetic results in a way that even convinced the genetic professors in São Paulo and Rio."

"And my father. What about him?" Kirsten asked.

"Of course he had no inkling of any relationship to Hitler," Pepé said. "That only surfaced with Braun's diary. Your dad wanted absolute proof, so he sent off his own genetic sample after we spoke to a lab in Jerusalem. He should have results in a day or two."

Kirsten shook her head, as if trying to clear cobwebs. "I couldn't believe what happened before, and now this. It's too much."

"At least you'll know the lineage ends with your father, and you have nothing to worry about," Pepé said.

"Yeah, right. Nothing to worry about. Only that I'm the leader of some sort of a group of thousands of people, and I'm not really who they think I am." She stood and started pacing.

"True, but consider the lives you've saved, the families protected, and property preserved. Wasn't it worth it?" Pepé said.

She stopped in front of Pepé, hands on her hips, and looked down at him. "Of course it was, but that's not the point any longer, is it? Now I have to live the lie. I thought our family was done with lies."

THE END

AFTERWORD

I have relied on various source documents for the facts in this story, including the following:

Cooper, Harry. *Hitler in Argentina. The documented truth of Hitler's escape from Berlin*. Sharkhunters, International, 1984, 2006, 2014.

Görtemaker, Heike B. *Eva Braun. Life with Hitler.* New York: Alfred A. Knopf, 2011.

Klein, Aaron J. *Striking Back: The 1972 Munich Olympics Massacre.* New York: Random House, 2005.

Large, David Clay. *Nazi Games. The Olympics of 1936.* New York: W.W. Norton and Company, 2007.

Rosenbaum, Ron. *Explaining Hitler.* New York: Random House, 1998.

Scott-Clark, Catherine, and Adrian Levy. *The Amber Room.* New York: Walker Publishing, 2004.

Shirer, William L. *The Rise and Fall of the Third Reich.* New York: Simon and Schuster, 1959, 1960, 1987, 1988, 1990, 2011.

Speer, Albert. *Inside the Third Reich. Memoirs.* New York: Simon and Schuster Paperbacks, 1970.

Taylor, Paul. *Jews and the Olympic Games: The Clash Between Sports and Politics—With a Complete Review of Jewish Medalists.* Eastbourne, UK: Sussex Academic Press, 2004.

Williams, Gerard, and Simon Dunstan. *Grey Wolf: The Escape of Adolf Hitler.* New York: Sterling, 2011.

This is an historical fiction novel. Since I couldn't use real people in fictitious ways, I had to rename some important people and invent new characters. I also had to bend the truth sometimes to fit the story line. The names of the Israeli athletes killed in Munich are accurate except for Andrei Spitzer. I used their real names because they are heroes and the world needs to know them. The fictitious Levi Frankel is Andrei Spitzer, also a hero. It was Andrei who the terrorists made answer questions on the balcony, and clubbed in the back of the head when his answer wasn't what they wanted. His widow, Ankiee Spitzer, along with Elana Romano, led the fight against the German government to uncover exactly what had happened to their husbands and the others in Munich, and who lived through the horror of the event. Ankiee also fought the IOC to recognize the murdered athletes and is reported to have had the repartee with the IOC chairman, saying, "My husband's hands were tied, not yours." I had to change Andrei's and Ankiee's names because Sharon Frankel features prominently in the novel after Munich as Kirsten's companion and coach, which is fictitious. A part of Sharon's story leading up to Munich is based on the life of Ankiee Spitzer. I hope she will forgive me for any inaccuracies. I tried to tell the story of the massacre accurately, except for Adam's role, which is fictitious. Gobbles is fictitious, though most of his inept actions were based on facts.

Naturally, events surrounding the 2016 Olympics are fictitious. This novel was written in 2014 and 2015. The recognition by the IOC of the

Munich athletes is what Ankiee Spitzer has been fighting for and what I hope will happen in the future.

Attila Petschauer was real, his life story captured in the brilliant movie *Sunshine*, starring Ralph Fiennes. Attila was also a hero. Grandson László is fictitious.

The Beckers and Jaegers and Stefan Pasteur are fictitious, as is Lobo. Lutz Long and Jesse Owens are real, essentially as portrayed, except for interactions with Dietrich. The order of Jesse Owens's Olympic events was changed to fit the story.

The information about Adolf Hitler and Eva Braun was gleaned from several sources, cited. The Eva Braun diary is fictitious, though her first meeting with Hitler, the incestuous relationship Hitler had with Geli, Geli's suicide, and Eva's attempted suicide come from published sources. The Amber Room is real but was lost during WWII, perhaps destroyed by Allied bombing, never to be seen again, despite the search by many investigators. A replica exists in Russia.

Any other similarities to people, events, or names are purely coincidental.